GUY ADAMS

THE WORLD HOUSE
Restoration

**ANGRY
ROBOT**

ANGRY ROBOT

A member of the Osprey Group
Midland House, West Way
Botley, Oxford
OX2 0PH
UK

www.angryrobotbooks.com
Woo-wooooooo

An Angry Robot paperback original 2011
1

A catalogue record for this book is available
from the British Library.

ISBN 978-0-85766-117-3
EBook ISBN 978-0-85766-119-7

Set in Meridien by THL Design.

Printed in the UK by CPI Mackays, Chatham, ME5 8TD.

RESTORATION

PROLOGUE

Florida is a conflicted state. Outside the cities it's a mess of swamp broken up by Styrofoam tourist Meccas. Places so colourful and false the buildings look like they have e-numbers. Once you step away from the Interstate – which curls, like the large intestine, between these theme park fabrications – there's little to see. In 1976 considerably less. Back then the insects counted as night-life.

Hughie Bones sat on his front porch and struggled not to die of apathy. One day he would solidify in that chair; suffocated by the swamp and his own lack of imagination. Property developers would find him years later when they came to bulldoze his house in the name of the tourist dollar. Just another awkward nigger getting in the way of beautification.

Hughie worked for a letting firm over in Kissimmee. His boss the sort of asshole that thought a wallet full of cash compensated for having the personality of sun-baked roadkill. Perhaps it did, he never seemed short of friends. The company paid Hughie just enough for his days emptying septic tanks that he could afford to spend his nights living in one. His free time filled with nothing but sitcom reruns and beer. Which would have been almost tolerable were the beer not warm. Six months ago, the cooler had lost all its confidence. Now, it puffed the occasional spurt of cool air inside itself before settling into a neurotic buzz, its motor grinding its teeth like a special needs child. Hughie hated that fucking cooler and kept promising himself a trip to a remote section of swamp, just him and that rebellious piece of shit, maybe a baseball bat or a length of chain. He'd show Mr Electrolux a thing or two.

But tonight was too hot for swinging a weapon, however much the white goods might be asking for it. Hughie just sat on the porch and dared the mosquitoes to bite him. This they duly did, a fact that Hughie took as a victory despite the itching. "Can't get enough of the Bones," he muttered, basking in the edibility of his blood. Sitting in the fug of another man's shit all day long gave you a musk that only insects and dogs took a shine to.

On the radio, Waylon Jennings and Willie Nelson were extolling the virtues of a goodhearted woman. Hughie couldn't comment from experience but they sang with such conviction he was sure they were right. Ever since high school, women had been something imagined rather than physically experienced. Hughie's lovers had glossy paper skins. Briefly, Hughie considered paying a visit to one of his staple-breasted honeys but the night was too hot and even the effort of masturbation seemed too steep a mountain to climb. Instead, he rolled himself a smoke and lost himself in the late-night radio tunes. The swamp sang along.

Then the air in front of his porch suddenly filled with noise and whizzing metal. The trees split in a shower of shed leaves. The earth erupted in fist-sized divots, splattering against the front of Hughie's home with a drumroll. Hughie rolled off his chair, as much in surprise as from the impact of mud and vegetation. His first thought was a grenade. Vietnam had been pretty uneventful for Hughie but he'd seen enough combat to think the worst of a loud noise.

It wasn't a grenade.

Hughie's eyes were tightly closed. Had he been watching, he would have seen an old-fashioned steam train cut its way through the detritus and come to a halt in a diagonal line across his backyard. The train smoked like an earth-struck comet, white plumes rising from its glistening iron body. Hughie, aware only that he wasn't as dead as he had expected to be, opened his eyes and stared at the foreign object on his land. There is a limit to what one can say about seeing an antique locomotive appear out of nowhere and Hughie summed it up with a whispered "motherfucker..." as he rolled onto his ass and tried to make the damn thing disappear by staring at it. It refused, despite his best efforts.

There was a solid crack of metal against metal as one of the passenger carriage doors opened. A small man, wearing a raincoat and hat stepped down. He looked like a Brit in an old movie comedy: a bank manager caught up in a stately farce of manners, a man to be viewed in black and white. The man lifted his hat and straightened his thinning hair beneath it before trapping it back under respectable brown felt. He reached into the carriage behind him and pulled out the body of a man. He lifted him by the belt as if he weighed no more than a small briefcase. He marched up to Hughie's veranda, dropping the body casually to the boards and raising his hat in greeting.

"Good evening," he said, the train's engine screeching into life again behind him as it prepared to leave, "what a splendid little world you appear to have here. Mind if I play with it a little?"

Hughie wasn't even listening. After the initial shock his brain had fallen back on self-preservation. He ran into the house to dig out his shotgun. He'd bought the thing a couple of years ago after spotting an alligator working his way through his trash. That kind of thing sharpened a man's need for more firearms in his life. The 'gator had been a small one, four or five feet all in, but Hughie had been so convinced that the walking suitcase would tell his big friends about the rich pickings to be found that he'd slept uneasy for weeks. He'd even kept the gun on the bed for awhile, as if it were likely one of the bastards would creep under his bedlinen, wake him up with one of those flatulent smiles they had before taking him for a roll in the swamp. He'd never seen another gator since. The gun gathered dust next to that useless goddamned cooler. No more. He grabbed it, and swung both barrels to cover the door, through which he could see that impossible train surging past to stations new. A train, he thought to himself, *a fucking train*. He cracked the shotgun open, just to make sure it was loaded (safety be damned, if you bought a gun to protect yourself you didn't leave the thing lying empty). The train was gone, the screeching of its whistle and the pounding of its piston engine vanished leaving a Florida night scared into temporary silence. A moment passed. Somewhere in the swamp a toad croaked. Probably telling its toad friends all about the fucking train, Hughie thought, bet they'll think he's drunk.

"Nice gun," the man whispered in his ear.

Hughie squeezed both triggers, blowing a jagged crescent out of the side of his front door. It looked like a rhino had just stepped outside taking some of his wall with it.

"Twitchy on the trigger though, eh?" the man said, pulling the gun from Hughie as if he'd been barely holding it – as opposed to gripping it with white knuckles as had actually been the case. "Let me take it away before you get hurt." With a gentle smile, the man swung the butt of the shotgun towards Hughie's face. He didn't do it hard, it was a methodical move that popped Hughie's nose with precision. Hughie shouted, a spray of blood splattering his faded linoleum. It didn't spoil the look of the room. "See?" said the man, "dangerous things, guns."

The man pulled out a chair at Hughie's small, Formica-topped kitchen table and sat down. He rested the gun against his leg, took off his glasses and cleaned them on his woollen vest. "Humid here," he said, as if the pair of them were making small talk at a boring party. "Reminds me of a greenhouse I used to own."

Hughie was still fretting about his nose, cradling it in one hand while staring at the funny little man that had so casually invaded his life.

"*Oo tha fugger oo*?" he grunted, taken aback by how incomprehensible he sounded.

"Who the fuck am I?" the little man replied, "Well now, that's a good question." He put his glasses back on and gave Hughie a smile. "What say we find out?"

ONE
All Change

1.

The train now arriving at platform 3.149 to the power of 4 is delusional, passengers are advised they board it at their own risk.

Train stations are broken places. Echo chambers crammed with the bewildered and lost. They exist only to be departed from as quickly as possible. Crowds gather beneath the information boards like starving animals at a trough. They are angry, or impatient, or lonely, or panicked. That emotion bounces off the cold tiles and iron arches, filling every inch of the place. The act of sitting in this atmosphere is akin to lying in bed after an argument, all weighty silence and an urge to scream. Train stations are ghastly.

"This place is amazing!" said Miles, which goes to show what a hard time he's had of late. "I wonder if the coffee shops will serve us."

"We have more important things to think about than lattes," said Ashe.

"Lattes *and* pastries?"

Ashe ignored him, crouching down to check on the unconscious bodies of Tom, Alan and Sophie.

"Should you be doing that?" asked Miles as Ashe pressed his fingers to Alan's neck. "Two versions of the same person touching... I've seen movies, won't the world explode or something?"

A savage crack heralded another section of roof tumbling to the floor.

"Don't tempt fate," said Penelope, looking around at the devastation.

Perhaps the most accurate part of the illusory St. Pancras was the way the crowds carried on their business despite the chaos. Glass shattered, cracks appeared in the concourse, bricks crumbled in torrents of dust. Nobody batted an eyelid. They could only be the ghosts of Londoners.

"She's saying something," said Ashe, picking up Sophie in his arms.

Carruthers leaned in, pressing his ear to the girl's lips. "Build not break, build not break... she just keeps repeating herself, poor thing."

"We should get somewhere a bit safer." Penelope suggested. "While we decide what to do."

"How about a coffee shop?" Miles asked.

"I'm not sure anywhere is safe at this juncture," said Carruthers. "But I agree we should take stock."

"And eat a cinnamon swirl," Miles added, "to help us focus."

"You're obsessed," Penelope smiled.

"About lots of things, can't deny it."

"We need to get away from the glass roof," Ashe mumbled, "and if it shuts him up..." He marched towards a nearby crêperie.

Miles and Carruthers stared at the bodies of Alan and Tom, one portly, one skeletal. "Toss you for it?" suggested Miles.

"Allow me," Penelope grabbed Tom under the arms and scooted him off towards the cafe.

"You get his legs," said Carruthers with a smile.

"Fine," Miles agreed, "you get his pies."

Stepping through the door of the cafe, Ashe glanced up at the roof. "Should provide a little more cover," he said, "keep away from the front window though, no point substituting one hail of glass for another."

"Yes boss," Penelope muttered, pushing past him and dragging Tom over to the far corner, "we know you have our best interests at heart after all."

Ashe didn't rise to the bait, he was far too concerned with Sophie, brushing the hair out of her eyes and whispering reassurance. It seemed bizarre to Penelope, the mental image she held of Ashe as a young man was completely scotched by this aging version. Before proven otherwise she had always seen Chester as gentle but cold. This man was filled with emotion and so utterly in control of himself that – even in his dotage – he screamed alpha male the minute he walked into a room. She wondered for a moment what it was that had changed him but then realised they were living it.

"I've been thinking," said Miles as he and Carruthers carried Alan inside.

"About time you started," Ashe mumbled.

"If we're dealing with time travel then the key to stabilising this place isn't so much in act as intention."

"What do you mean?" asked Penelope.

"We need to agree, and stick to, our plan to get everything back on track. That first step alone should buy us time."

"Explain," said Ashe, attentive to him for once.

"You need to go back in time and ensure the box travels its pre-ordained path, yes?"

"It seems we have little choice."

14

"Then you'll do it?"

"Like I said… there's not a lot of options."

From outside the cafe there was another crack as the roof continued to give way. A large triangle of glass dropped towards the floor and then froze, at midpoint, hovering in the air.

"That's it!" Miles shouted. "It works."

"I don't follow…" admitted Carruthers.

"You have to think about time in the right way," Miles explained. "Ashe has committed to ensuring our recent history stays on track. At this point he will either succeed or he won't. It's all up in the air. If he succeeds the damage ceases, if he fails it will complete itself."

He stepped out of the cafe and looked around, the others following. "We're living alongside Schrödinger's cat."

"Has he gone mad do you think?" Carruthers asked.

"No," Ashe replied, "it's a thought experiment devised in the 1930's. On a quantum level, everything is governed by probability and it is only in the recording – the observation – of events that probabilities resolve into certainties."

Carruthers glanced at Penelope. "Seems to me they've both lost it now."

"A man takes a cat," Ashe continued, "and places it in a sealed box alongside a Geiger counter, a small amount of radioactive material and a flask of poison."

"What on earth would someone do that for?" Penelope asked, "Did he have a pathological hatred of cats?"

"The cat is unimportant," said Miles.

"Not to the cat, one imagines." Penelope replied.

"It's purely hypothetical!" said Ashe, "he didn't do it for real… The point is this: the radioactive substance is tiny, chosen for its equal probability to decay or not over a given time period. In that period – say an hour – it will either trigger the Geiger counter or it won't. If it does then the counter trips a system that will shatter the flask of poison killing the cat. If it doesn't... well, then it won't. After that hour has elapsed the probability of the cat being alive is equal to the probability of it being dead."

"So the cat is both alive and dead." Miles continued, "the only way of resolving the probability waveforms is by opening the box and observing one way or the other."

"That's silly," said Penelope.

"According to Schrödinger, so was Quantum theory, that was his point." Miles replied.

"Forgive me," said Carruthers, "but I'm completely at a loss as to how this is relevant."

"I will go back in time with the box," explained Ashe, "and the probability of my succeeding or not is in balance, the outcome unknown. The house is therefore in a state of stasis until the probability is resolved one way or the other."

"Exactly," said Miles, "so can we have a latte now?"

They settled around one of the larger tables.

There was a frantic hammering from the direction of the coffee machine as Miles tried to make it bleed hot beverages.

"What's happening?" Alan shouted, snapping awake. He thrashed around in panic and sent a couple of chairs careering across the floor. "Sophie?"

Ashe was straight to his feet. "She's okay," he insisted, grabbing Alan and trying to restrain him. "You're safe, calm down."

"Not altogether sure I agree with anything he's said to him so far," Carruthers whispered to Penelope.

"Where is she?" Alan shouted. He jumped to his feet and over to where Ashe had laid Sophie across a sofa.

"What happened?" Alan asked, checking Sophie's pulse and pupils. He held his face close to hers. "'Build not break?'" he repeated, "What's that mean honey?"

"She's connected to the house," Ashe explained, "she's part of the place now, her thoughts are helping to keep it together."

"And that's a good thing?" Alan asked looking around. "Who are you all? Last thing I remember…"

"You heard a voice on the other side of a door, asking for help," said Ashe, "you opened it. The man who stepped out was more than he seemed. He's to blame for the current situation."

"Him and that bastard Chester," said Tom, having also woken up. "Let's not forget that little shit."

There was an awkward silence at that, broken by Miles as he shuffled over with a tray of coffees. "Oh," he said, "don't tell me I have to wrestle another two mugs out of the bloody thing."

For a while there was nothing but chaos. Contrary opinions, heated voices, fear and distrust. This can have surprised nobody, however frustrating. Everyone sat at the table, now that the chaos had been put on hold temporarily, had a head full and ready to boil over.

Tom – by nature a man given to going with the flow, most especially if it was Vermouth that was flowing – was the hardest to quell. It's hard to think reasonably when the cold, dead face of a woman you loved is hovering in your mind's eye like the after-shadow of a lightbulb. Tom could think of nothing else.

No. That wasn't altogether true. He could think how it would feel to neck a scotch on the rocks, or a Martini so cold it coated the glass in condensation. He could think about that pretty fucking well. Tom didn't like to drink, he *needed* to drink. He had crossed the fine line between hobby and addiction long ago and that was a line that was only easily crossed in one direction.

Penelope was also suffering. Though she would never admit as much. The sight of Alan and Ashe together was enough to break her resilience. She accepted they may not share the attitudes (or perhaps perversions would be a better word) of their younger counterpart but that didn't shake the fear and disgust she felt when looking at them. Carruthers had made a point of pulling her and Miles to one side as soon as he was able, insisting that no good would come from making the relation between Chester and the other two clear to Tom (or Alan for that matter, after all they could only assume he was in the dark as to his identity). She had agreed to this, things could only be worsened by Tom exacting revenge. Though, if she was honest, the idea was attractive to her. When she looked at Alan she was struck by the smell of leather upholstery and the taste of blood in her mouth. It was an association that would take some time to fade.

Penelope was wrong to assume Alan hadn't recognised Chester as his younger self. After all, memory loss or no, he knew his own face well enough. Back in the "real" world – a place that seemed absurdly distant given that he had only been gone from it a handful of days – he had been convinced that the block on his memory hid a past that was unconscionable to the man he had become. Given the accusations Tom had made it would seem his instincts had been right. As to what he should do about it… well, that was a different matter entirely. If there was one thing that could save him from Chester – and however hard his subconscious preached otherwise Chester would always be a separate person – it was Sophie. He looked at her while the others argued about their plans. It was clear to him that she was beyond his reach, muttering the same phrase over and over again. "Build not break". But he *would* reach her, somehow...

Ashe knew this devotion of course, after all it was what had brought him back to the House in the first place, determined to rescue Sophie from the position his younger self had inadvertently placed her in. He had been too late for that, circumstances – or perhaps the unbeatable forces of cause and effect – had insisted she play her part as she always had. He had his own part to play now and if these damned fools would stop their bickering maybe he could get on with it.

In the end it was Carruthers who managed to bring order. "This is getting us nowhere," he announced, and with that everyone had to agree. "We need to work together, make our plans and then act on them. All of this..." he struggled to think of a polite word, "...bickering should be beyond us."

"Agreed," said Ashe, thankful that at least one of the others seemed as driven toward action as himself.

"Let's try and gather what we know," said Carruthers, "I'm sure I'm not the only one still baffled by our circumstances."

"It's certainly beyond me," agreed Penelope.

"It's beyond any sane mind, my dear," Carruthers assured her, "which is why our first step must be to lay it all out and try to gain perspective on the situation."

Everyone else was quiet now, happy to give Carruthers the floor. For all their anger or impatience not one of them truly understood what had become of them.

"Very well," Carruthers continued, "let us first deal with the House."

"You can hear the capital a mile off," said Miles. "No ordinary house this..."

"Indeed not," agreed Carruthers, "from what I understand from Ashe and that hateful fellow who just abandoned us here, this building exists through the power of thought."

"It's imagination that fuels it," clarified Ashe, "though it's a mistake to think that makes it any less real."

"A mistake none of us could make given the threats to our safety we have all endured," agreed Carruthers. "It exists outside of what we know of reality – which I begin to suspect is very little – an almost infinite labyrinth of dangers that has grown strong through its attachment to our world."

"It started as a small prison," said Ashe, "supposedly unreachable, existing in a pocket reality of its own. It was built by…" here he struggled to think of a word to describe the architects of the House.

"Aliens?" suggested Miles, always happy to lean toward the fantastical.

"I don't know that they come from outer space," Ashe replied, then shook his head, "I don't know where they come from…"

"And, for now," Carruthers chipped in, "we will have to accept that it doesn't matter. Whoever they are their abilities are far beyond our own, able to fashion a solid reality from nothing more tangible than thought."

"This is bullshit," Tom whined, *Twilight Zone* stuff."

"It's fact," countered Ashe, "however hard to swallow."

"Indeed," agreed Carruthers. "As I've said countless times: there is no limit to what mankind does not understand, but when faced with inarguable evidence he can do little but accept it."

"'When you've eliminated the impossible'," said Miles, "'whatever remains, however improbable, must be the truth'." The others stared at him. "Sherlock Holmes," he admitted.

"That's the first reference from you I'm actually familiar with," admitted Carruthers with a brief smile. "So," he continued. "Through its link to mankind – using the focal point of the library – the prison fed off our worst nightmares, taking every imagined scenario and letting it flourish here."

"Meanwhile," said Ashe, "the prisoner was making plans of his own."

"We need to give him a name," suggested Miles, "we can't just keep calling him 'the prisoner'."

"Does it really matter?" asked Carruthers, determined not to let the conversation become too distracted.

"Just makes things easier," said Miles, "give him a name and he becomes more real, not so much of an abstract."

"Well…" Carruthers scratched at his moustache, "what do you suggest?"

Miles foundered, having not really thought the situation through.

"It's hardly a priority," said Ashe, fixing the young man with an angry stare.

"Just a thought."

"Well, never mind for now," said Carruthers, glad they could move on. "The prisoner – whatever he might be called – constructed a box that would act as a gateway from our world to this. A box that we all discovered and then travelled through."

"At a point when our lives were in danger," Alan clarified – the box was, after all, something he had dedicated years of research to. "Danger acts as a trigger, otherwise anyone that touched it would have ended up here. It's passed through many hands in its time."

"Agreed," said Ashe, placing the box on the table, "it acts as a filter, a way of limiting how many people made the journey here."

"We know that others have arrived here of course," said Carruthers. "I've seen a handful of other people during my time here."

"There are lots of others," agreed Alan, thinking of the tribe he had encountered in the greenhouse, not to mention the crew of the *Intrepid*. "Most just don't survive for long."

"Just the really lucky ones like us," said Penelope, not without a degree of sarcasm.

"We *are* the important ones," said Ashe, "we're the few who are all connected to the events that led to his escape."

"As arrogant as that sounds it is certainly true," Carruthers agreed, "no doubt many other poor souls have stories to tell about their time here but it's we who unwittingly let him out."

"Speak for yourself," said Tom. "I had nothing to do with it."

Carruthers floundered at this, still not willing to explain that Tom had played his part, keeping Chester alive so that one day – as Alan Arthur – he would be the man to open the door. "Well, yes," he said in the end, "I'll agree your involvement was somewhat tangential."

"Up until now," suggested Ashe, only too happy to move the subject on. "Who knows how important a part you'll play in what's to come?"

"Indeed," said Carruthers, "we are facing a blank slate, let us hope we have the strength to make something worthwhile of that."

"So…" said Miles, "where do we go from here?"

"We could just leave," said Penelope, knowing that it wasn't that simple but feeling it had to be said.

"We could," said Ashe, "though to *what* is the question."

"According to the prisoner," said Carruthers, "this

House is permanently linked to our world, tethered to every mind on the planet."

"And if the House falls so do we," added Miles.

"Not that the future looks all that bright with the prisoner wandering around anyway," reminded Penelope.

"And that's the other point," insisted Carruthers, "we are faced with two potentially catastrophic outcomes. In order to avoid them we have to both preserve the House and also recapture the prisoner."

"Jesus…" Tom muttered, "listen to yourself, as if we stand the least chance."

"We have to hope that we do," Carruthers replied, "we know that his powers are limited for now, his incarceration saw to that."

"But he'll be getting stronger all the time," warned Ashe.

"So we need to move quickly," Carruthers agreed, "we know where he's going and, thanks to the rather daunting method of transport we've been left with we can follow him."

"Oh," said Tom, "that's alright then. For a moment I thought you were out of your minds."

"The death of your friends lies at his door," said Carruthers, aware he was manipulating the man and not liking himself much for it, "just as much as it does anyone else. Chester was manipulated by him the minute he arrived here, their death was a part of the prisoner's plan. I would have thought you would relish the opportunity to see him pay for that."

"That's unfair," said Penelope, only too aware of what Carruthers was doing.

"No," Tom answered, that sick feeling that wracked him whenever he pictured Elise with a bullet hole in her head fading for a moment. "He has a point. And he took Chester with him."

"This isn't just about revenge," Penelope insisted, sickened by the direction the conversation had taken.

"No," agreed Carruthers, "it's far more important than that. But if it takes something personal for Tom to see that…"

Tom stared at him. "Don't mistake common sense for apathy, man," he said, "I know the consequences of what we're looking at here."

"Of course you do," said Carruthers, "as do we all. So… we need to split up and start *facing* those consequences. Ashe has to take the box and ensure that we all receive it so that the timeline of the House can be assured."

"And I'll do that on my own."

There was a momentary outcry at that. "Don't be so bloody pigheaded!" Miles insisted, "This is far too important for you to go playing Clint Eastwood."

Ashe looked to Tom, ignoring the arguing. "How did you get the box?"

Tom stared at him, seeing a momentary flash of an old man in a fedora raising a gun at he and Elise through rain-streaked glass. It had been such a brief glimpse – and his attention had been on the gun in Ashe's hand, not his face. Now the penny dropped. "It was you!" He shot to his feet, making to grab at Ashe. "You gave Elise the damn thing, if it weren't for you she would never have even been here."

Alan, sat between the two of them, jumped to his feet to hold Tom back, Miles grabbing him from behind.

"That's the point," said Ashe, "like it or not that's what I have to do."

"He's right Tom," said Penelope, hoping that, of all of them, she might be able to get through to him, "we have to make sure that we keep history on track."

"That's the last goddamned thing we want!" Tom

shouted, though he stopped fighting against Alan and Miles. "If he does nothing then Elise would be safe. Pablo too…"

"No," Carruthers insisted, "if only that were true. They would still be lost, alongside everyone else on the planet."

"You think I relish the idea?" asked Ashe, "Every bit of me is sickened by the thought… but the consequences of doing nothing are even worse."

"Shit." Tom dropped his head into his hands, "This is so fucked up."

"Damn right," agreed Ashe. "Be thankful you're not the poor bastard who'll have to go through with it."

Tom waved Ashe away, he knew the man was right but that didn't mean he wanted to discuss it.

"The point still stands," said Carruthers, "you shouldn't go alone."

"I know what I'm doing," said Ashe, "or at least I will do once I get everyone's story as to how they came into contact with the box. On my own I'll be quicker, besides…" he turned to Tom again, "was I on my own when you saw me." Tom nodded. "There you go," said Ashe. "I'm sticking to what we know should happen. Besides, you'll need all the manpower you can get if you're going after the prisoner, that's where the numbers will be needed and don't think otherwise."

On this, Carruthers had to conceded Ashe's point. "Very well," he said eventually. "But it's not just the prisoner, someone will have to stay here too."

"Why?" asked Miles. "What good will that do?"

"May I remind you of the poor state of our young friend?" said Carruthers pointing towards Sophie. "Do you really think she could leave?"

"I'm staying with her," said Alan. "I'm not leaving her side for a minute."

"That's commendable," said Carruthers, "but I thought perhaps Penelope…"

"I could see this coming," she said, "let's make sure the silly little girl doesn't get in the way. She'd better look after the child, that's what women are for after all."

"Dear Lord!" cried Carruthers, his anger surprising everyone, "Does *everything* have to be about emancipation? I thought you were the ideal choice because I trusted you, and if you think staying here, with all the House's dangers is the gentle option then may I remind you of what we've been through for the last few days?"

"I just…" Penelope was utterly taken aback, she had never seen Carruthers lose his temper. "I thought…"

"With all due respect you thought *wrong*. We need someone to stay here and safeguard the most important member of our group. I wanted that person to be someone who had proved time and again that they were extremely capable of facing almost anything life chose to throw at them."

"I'll do it!" said Penelope, still flustered. "I'm sorry."

Carruthers took a deep breath and winked at Miles. "Thank you my dear, do forgive my outburst."

Cunning old sod, Miles thought, but said nothing.

"I'm still staying," said Alan, "whether I'm trustworthy enough for you or not."

Carruthers kept the charm flowing: "Please don't think I have any lack of faith in you," he insisted. "In truth it needs two people to do the job, it would hardly be fair to leave one person to safeguard Sophie on their own, not when we know what this horrid building can throw at one."

"That's sorted then," said Miles, "leaving you, me and Tom to go chasing after the prisoner."

"Yes," Carruthers smiled, "exciting isn't it?"

"You are one mixed-up old dude," muttered Tom.

"No doubt," Carruthers agreed, not having the first idea what Tom was saying. "One final point: might I suggest we all take advantage of the temporary reprieve from danger we seem to have found in order to gather our strength? As we intend to travel to the precise time and location we need using those infernal trains out there, a twenty-four hour reprieve to get our breath back can do no harm."

"I don't see the point in hanging around," said Ashe, impatient to be getting on with things.

"You, perhaps most of all, would benefit from the time," insisted Carruthers. "You need to plan your trip, gather what supplies you may need…"

"There's a hell of a shopping centre," said Miles, "they've even got a bookshop."

"I was thinking more of food and clothing," Carruthers replied. "But, more than anything else, we need rest. We don't stand a chance of succeeding unless we allow ourselves the opportunity to build up our reserves."

"Okay," Ashe agreed, "I'll go along with that."

"I'm in no rush," said Miles. "As much as certain death appeals I can wait a day or so."

Tom shrugged. "Fine by me too. You reckon this place has a bar?"

2.

The group naturally broke apart. As is the way after something big has been discussed they all craved minutiae, the reassuring nonsense of finding lunch or a change of clothes.

Ashe moved over to Alan once the place had cleared. "We need to talk," he said.

Alan had an idea that he wasn't going to like whatever Ashe had to say. "I don't want to leave Sophie on her own."

"Then bring her," Ashe replied, "we need privacy."

They walked out of the cafe, Sophie in Alan's arms. Ashe walked quickly, not wanting the others to see the three of them and start asking questions. "This'll do," he said, nodding towards a clothes shop whose window display hid the inside from view.

Once inside, Alan rested Sophie down on a table display of sweaters, figuring it would be as comfortable as anywhere else. Ashe was twitchy, keeping his eyes on the front door and pacing around the rotating racks of clothing.

"You know who I am?" he asked.

Alan felt his stomach churn. Of course he knew... but he still hadn't the first idea how to feel about it, let alone discuss it.

"It's okay," said Ashe, "you only have to worry about the past – about who we used to be – I'm batting for the right team."

"It's just..." Alan found he didn't even have the words, "it's hard to get the head around."

"It gets worse," Ashe admitted, "but we have to discuss it nonetheless. There's stuff that the others don't know... haven't asked. And for the most part I'm grateful for that but I need you to be on the same page."

"But isn't it bad to know your own future? Another paradox..."

"You and I are beyond paradox, let's face it. You – we – were born in 1915, vanished into the House at the age of eighteen only to end up back in the real world, no older, found on a roadside in 1976. That's forty three years later..."

"I don't really remember."

"I know. You then end up back here, aged fifty-two…"

"Fifty."

"Fifty *two*… all people knew was your name, not surprising they got your age out by a couple of years is it?"

"I…" Alan waved his hands in the air, this was too much to get his head around, far too much.

For Alan Arthur life had begun on a roadside. He had been born covered in dust and grass stains, then weaned in a hospital room, plied with hot drinks and sympathy. In his pockets there had been nothing but a short note – handwritten – that said "I'm Alan Arthur, please help me…" And they'd tried – after running the name through a bunch of police checks, naturally, nobody had been willing to take that note on face value, including Alan.

The nurses and doctors had flitted around him, drawn by curiosity as much as the urge to help. Who the hell was he? How did he come to be just lying there? Of course their first assumption had been drink or drugs and they were quick to run blood tests. By the time the results came through though it told them nothing they hadn't already guessed, after a few minutes talking to him you could tell he wasn't high; confused, yes… borderline delirious, but not caught on the tail-end of a bender.

But beyond that… nobody knew what the hell to do with him. There seemed nothing wrong with him physically – beyond the odd bruise at least, certainly nothing that could account for his condition – and that was all they were set up to deal with.

One particular nurse had taken only five minutes to pronounce – out of earshot of the patient – "That guy's shrink food." And she had been right. Once the police had run their identity checks he had been dumped into the hands of the Florida Department of Health and Rehabilitative Services.

But even the shrinks didn't really know what to do with him. He was a mystery with no clues and that swiftly becomes irritating rather than intriguing. His state-assigned psychotherapist was a chain-smoking stick of a man named Whilcott who had been in the business of therapy long enough to hate most people on principle. "Humans suck," he frequently announced. Particularly when sat on his usual stool at Frankie's trying to scrub his brain clean with rum and coke after a long day of psyche-digging. Not that he wasn't good at what he did, he could turn a broken mind into a healthier one sure enough, you didn't have to love cows in order to make burgers.

In all fairness, the kid didn't bother Whilcott as much as his usual clients, he was a blank slate and there was much to be said for that. Their meetings were devoid of the usual sexual outpourings and childhood hangups. But then, they were devoid of pretty much anything... The kid would just stare at the walls of Whilcott's office, not unwilling to learn but unable, and it wasn't long before Whilcott had to admit there was little that could be done for him. Amnesia just didn't tend to work the way it seemed to have done on Alan Arthur – whatever the movies might lead you to believe – it was usually partial and temporary. To be faced with someone so completely empty... there was just nothing to latch on to, nothing to build from.

In the end he did the only thing he could: marked him down as a minor – nobody really knew how old he was but the red tape was certainly easier if he was legally underage – and farmed him out for care.

Alan Arthur became a child of the state, left with little choice but to get on with his new life.

Something he managed to do, rather well, for thirty-four years. Then things got a little more complicated…

"I know it's a lot to deal with," Ashe said, "of course I do, but you need to pull yourself together. None of it really matters anyway, it's who you are in here," he tapped at his temple, "that's all."

"But that's the point," Alan replied, "I'm not sure I know who I am…"

"Bullshit," said Ashe, "you're Alan Arthur, a history professor and decent man. You've spent the last thirty-four years of your life proving as much. Not to mention the extra twenty three years of hard work that'll put you in my shoes."

"And you want to tell me what happens in those twenty-three years?"

"Not all of it, just a little…" Ashe glanced once more at the door, they were getting to the hub of it now and, more than ever, this was something he didn't want the others hearing. "Think of this… at some point you must leave here so that you can age into me."

Alan could grasp that, of course he could. "Yeah…"

"And yet we know that something that just escaped from here that could ensure there isn't that future to grow old into."

"A paradox again?"

"No…" Ashe shook his head, "that's the thing. I left here – as you – knowing what had been set loose, knowing what had to be done to fix it. The question is, what sort of world did I leave here to live in?"

Alan could see the contradictions now. His future self had come back here hoping to change the past, a past in which he should have been unable to have existed anyway… "What happens?"

Ashe told him.

"I might have guessed you'd end up here," said Penelope as she found Miles sat behind one of the bookshelves in Foyles.

"I just wanted a little time to get my head around things," he admitted.

"I don't want to interrupt."

Miles smiled. "Sit down. A mind like mine needs interruption… I'll only get all maudlin otherwise."

Penelope dropped down next to him, scanning the spines of the books in front of them. "Makes me think of the library," she said.

"I was thinking the same thing," Miles admitted, "wondering what memories I lost exactly."

"Not as many as some," Penelope replied.

"No," said Miles. There was a pause then, as both of them turned their thoughts to Chester and the man – men – he had become. "I think he's okay," Miles said eventually.

"I hope you're right."

"It all comes down to nature or nurture doesn't it?"

"Excuse me?"

"What makes a man? Is someone born a monster or do they become one through the things that happen to them, the way their parents treat them…"

"Chester's parents were certainly monstrous," admitted Penelope.

"There you go. Wiped clean – utterly clean – he was given the chance to become someone new."

"I hope you're right," Penelope thought back to the De Soto. As she thought about it she saw Chester's face changing, swelling up and becoming Alan, then thinning back out, wrinkling and becoming Ashe. "Reformed or not, I can't say I relish spending any time in his company."

"Perhaps I'd better stay here to make sure you're safe, eh?"

Penelope took Miles' hand. "Nothing to do with not wanting to face up to that thing we set free, of course."

"Actually," Miles sat forward, "I mean it, it can't be safe to leave you here alone with him."

"It's not safe anywhere, Miles, let's be honest. I'll be fine. Besides, at least I'll have all this to entertain me," she gestured at the bookshelves.

Miles opened the novel he'd been flicking through. "Blank pages," he said, "the illusion only stretches so far. There's a lovely lingerie shop around the corner though, I'll help you try things on if you like?"

She slapped him playfully. "You're getting altogether more sure of yourself."

"I'll be dead within twenty-four hours if Carruthers has his way, no time to be bashful."

"Don't talk like that," she said, "I don't want to hear it."

Miles shrugged. "Sorry, I was trying to make light of it."

"Don't, you're being brave to even consider chasing after him, that's not something you should just dismiss."

"Honestly? It's not even bravery... more like momentum. If I think too hard about any of this then I reckon I'll just crumble. But, go with the flow. Don't question any of it too deeply... well, then I can just about get on with it."

She turned and kissed him, gently but with intent, the sort of kiss that is the beginning of a journey rather than the end of one.

"What was that for?" he asked, before kicking himself for asking anything.

"It was because I don't believe you, brave man," she replied and kissed him again.

Miles suddenly felt incredibly shy. Eager but also fearful. He leaned back as she climbed over to sit on his lap, squeezing his waist with her knees.

"I didn't think you'd…" he began to say but Penelope put her hand on his mouth.

"Don't talk yourself out of this," she said, "not one word."

So he didn't.

4.

Carruthers bumped into Alan as he was carrying Sophie back to the coffee shop.

"Have you seen Ashe?" he asked, holding up his notebook. "Thought it might be a good idea to swap some historical notes, just to make sure we all know where we're going."

"You need to be in Florida, Kissimmee Highway 192, just a few kilometres short of where it meets I-4," said Alan, "I was found there on the morning of March 23rd, 1976."

"Oh," Carruthers replied, somewhat thrown.

"Ashe just told me." Alan admitted, "If I'm honest I didn't know. I wasn't really processing at the time, I didn't take note of my surroundings until I got to the hospital."

"Understandable of course, you must have been in a highly confused state."

"I was borderline comatose by all accounts."

"So, Ashe told you…"

"I was always fully aware of my connection to him and Chester, though I appreciated you not bringing it up in front of Tom."

"Oh, well… nothing to be gained really…"

"I appreciate your trust too," Alan continued. "I promise I'll do my best to look after both Penelope and Sophie."

"I'm sure she'll say the same about you," Carruthers chuckled. "Frightfully boisterous that one."

Alan nodded and then made to walk away before something occurred to him. "A weird thing…"

"We need more of those."

"The place where I was found… it can't be more than a stone's throw from where I bought the box."

"You bought it?"

"I'd been hunting for it for years, after reading about you in a magazine…"

"Really?" Carruthers struggled to restrain his pleasure, maybe later he'd ask the fellow whether he had a spare copy.

"Of course, subconsciously I knew about the box, but I only realise that now. At the time it was a hobby… Anyway, I met the guy selling it at a tourist place called Home Town, pretty much right on top of where I'd turned up all those years before."

"An extraordinary coincidence,"

"Hmm… I don't think you believe in those any more than I do."

"No, perhaps not."

Alan shrugged. "Probably won't help, wasn't even built in '76." He carried on towards the coffee shop.

5.

Night-time in the station and the crowds had washed away, leaving only the driftwood of those who had missed their final connection. Homeless bundles of well-travelled blankets and stained woollens were curled on metal benches like musky caterpillars.

Ashe sat beneath an advert for high-speed euro-connections. He had spent the day gathering notes on the box's journey. Sketching out a timeline taking in Tibet, the journey of the *Intrepid*, Spain and New York. He had a hard enough time keeping track of his own journey through the years let alone that of the box. Still, taken one at a time, he should be fine. If he could figure out how to use the trains that was.

He cradled Sophie in his arms, having lifted her from her coffee shop sofa so he could talk to her without the others hanging on his every word. He sat her down on the seat next to him. She didn't like people hugging her so he tried to give her space.

"Sophie honey?" he whispered, self-conscious despite the fact that the few people around him weren't real. "Sorry... 'not honey, plain, no butter or jam or marmalade or Marmite or honey or anything, *plain*.'"

"Plain," she said, her litany of 'build not break' pausing briefly, "setting number four."

"That's right," Ashe replied, immeasurably pleased at this tiny sign of life, "don't want it too burned do we? We want that toast *perfect*."

Sophie didn't reply, just returned to repeating "build not break" as before.

"Build not break," Ashe agreed, "that's the thing. I need your help with that, Sophie. Need your help really bad." Sophie made no sign of having heard him, he continued anyway. "You see I need to do some travelling, all over the world, forward and back in time. Now that should be impossible but nothing's impossible here is it sweetheart? If it can be imagined it can be done. Look at this place... this wonderful place you made. I can get on any one of these trains and find myself anywhere – or when – in the world. That's amazing, you're so damn clever, Sophie. Thing is, I need to be able to come back, you see? Not just leave here but come back again. I could use the box I guess but there's no knowing where I'll arrive is there? Jungles or libraries? Oceans or cellars? I need to come back here so I can jump on another train and go somewhere else again. Alan's got a lot of travelling to do... he needs to be quick, too. Make sure everything's alright again. Get us all home safe. You think that's something you might be able to help me with?"

He sat down in front of her, his knees popping as he crossed his legs. He tried to make eye contact but her gaze was empty. He didn't have the first idea if any of this meant a damned thing to her. He looked around, watching an old woman, the worse for drink, tug her blanket tight around her and make her way along the polished floor as if ice-skating in slow motion.

"What do you think?" he asked Sophie. "If I can leave I must be able to come back, right? I mean that makes sense doesn't it? Trains always go in both directions don't they? A to B and back to A. That's how it works isn't it?"

"Build not break, build not break."

"Because it will break," Ashe insisted, feeling a twinge of guilt for playing on her fear, "if I don't do this. If I can't go everywhere I need to it will break completely..."

"Build not break, build not break."

"So we really need to make this work, between the two of us. You need to talk to the house and build a way into all of this that will let me come back. Can you do that?"

"Build not break, buy a ticket, build not break."

"What?" Ashe wasn't sure if he'd heard her right. "Did you say 'buy a ticket?'"

"Build not break, build not break, can't travel without one, not allowed, build not break."

Ashe stood up, looking around. A few feet away, one of the electronic information pillars fizzed and sparked.

It was about seven feet tall, all brushed steel and touch-screens. The sort of object that Ashe always suspected was designed to make life as complex for the user as possible. He walked up to it, slightly wary of its flickering screen. He was still only too aware that things in this house rarely had the visitor's best interests at heart. Further along the arcade another of the information posts was mirroring the behaviour of the one in front of him. The St. Pancras logo dispersed in a snowstorm of pixels to be replaced by the head and shoulders of a man. He appeared in his late forties, a miserable expression crumpled beneath an old-fashioned train conductor's peaked cap.

"Yes?" the man said. The screen flickered as if disturbed by his impatient tone.

"Er…" Ashe looked over his shoulder to check on Sophie. She was still sat where he had left her, quietly mumbling to herself.

"Well?" the man on the screen insisted. "I've better things to do than sit here waiting for you to make your mind up about where you want to go."

"Where I want to go?"

"Yes, where you want to go… this is a train station isn't it? Usually people have a fixed idea of where they want to get to."

"I need to go to lots of places…"

"Philosophically interesting but still no use to me. I need a specific destination."

Ashe thought about the timeline of the box. The first stop needed to be Carruthers in Tibet. "Tibet, 1904."

"Tibet, 1904 he says…" the man snapped. "Precision!"

Ashe pulled out the notes he'd made. "The Dhuru Monastery, 20 miles or so south of the Nepalese border. I need to be there on the third of March."

"Time?"

38

"Doesn't matter, it's a flying visit."

The man stared at him for a second, sighed, and then his eyes rolled up to reveal their whites as he mumbled to himself. "Dhuru Monastery, arriving, 16.58, March third." He reasserted himself and stared at Ashe. "How long do you need for your visit?"

"Not long, a few hours..."

"'A few'… how helpful."

Ashe growled slightly, losing his patience with the man's rudeness.

The screen flickered violently, like a TV suffering from storm interference. "Wait!" the inspector barked.

With a fizz of electrics, a hand emerged from the screen holding a pair of train tickets. "Return tickets to Dhuru monastery, 3rd of March 1904. Arriving 16.58 leaving seven hours later at two minutes to midnight. Don't lose them," the man insisted, as if speaking to a particularly dense child.

"How do I find the train on the way back?" Ashe asked.

The man smiled in a particularly unpleasant manner. "It will find *you*," he said. The screen fizzed once more and he was gone, replaced by the station logo.

6.

The champagne bar was a better class of joint than Tom was used to but if there was a dress code in place the phantom staff didn't enforce it. He made his way behind the ridiculously long bar, grabbed a glass and wondered what to fill it with.

"When in Rome," he said to himself, grabbing a bottle of champagne. He couldn't pretend to know the difference between labels but wasn't fussed.

When you went about it seriously, drink was a vehicle and a battered Ford got you to your destination just as surely as a beamer. He sat down on one of the barside swivel chairs and began to unwrap the foil from the bottle's neck.

"The longest champagne bar in Europe, apparently."

He glanced up at Elise, who had appeared on the stool next to him. He wasn't altogether surprised to see her, he was a man comfortable with delusions. "So I read on the sign coming in." He cast the foil aside and begin uncoiling the wire cap.

"Seems a strange ambition to me," said Elise. "Not the nicest or best-stocked, the *longest*."

"You know what Brits are like," Tom replied, popping the cork carefully – only racing drivers and children were stupid enough to spray good champagne everywhere, "always trying to be the best at something."

"They'd say the same about us."

"I guess." Tom poured champagne slowly into his tumbler, trying not to let it flow over the brim.

"Champagne in a hi-ball, damn but you've got class."

"I'm thirsty, would have taken a tankard if they'd had one."

"Or just a couple of straws?"

"Now there's a thought."

He took a mouthful of his drink and grimaced. "Like fizzy water. Pretend champagne."

"Bar sure is long though."

"This is true." Tom got up and walked around the bar to see what else he could find.

"It'll all be the same you know," said Elise, pulling a cigarette from the pocket of her raincoat. "Light?"

He stared at her for a moment, tempted to ignore her. But he could never ignore Elise, even if she was only a figment of his imagination. He pulled out his Zippo and lit her illusory cigarette before resuming his hunt for a drink that might hit the spot.

"Ever the optimist?" she asked, and damn if he couldn't smell the smoke of her cigarette as she exhaled over the bar.

"Just being thorough," he replied, opening a bottle of pink champagne with a lot less care than he had the first bottle. The cork popped, ricocheting off the concealed lighting and he dipped his mouth to the overflowing froth as if it were a water fountain. "This place is made by people that just don't have enough imagination," he decided.

"If you'd dreamed it people could have got high just by licking the bar," Elise noted. "The goddamned mints would have had an alcoholic content."

"Damn right, that's what a bar's there for after all. I'm a functionalist."

"A man who thirsts."

Tom looked at Elise over the neck of the champagne bottle, analysing her face for a clue as to where she was going with this, the last thing he needed right now – particularly from a ghost – was a dressing down for his alcoholism. "Yes," he admitted, saying no more in case it encouraged her in some way.

"Those thirsts aren't getting quenched are they honey?" said Elise. "You think that might have consequences as time rolls on?"

"I guess I'll crave more, nothing I can't handle."

"You sure?" Elise gave him a gentle smile. "Honey, you can dress it up however you want to but a man that gets through two bottles of vodka a day – without even trying – is an alcoholic, you do know that don't you?"

This was the conversation Tom didn't want to have, certainly not with Elise – and in the back of his head a small part of him despaired that he was already thinking of this figment as the real thing.

"I'm not being judgmental honey," she said, stubbing out her cigarette. "We all have our problems, our addictions and hangups. I'm dead… now *that's* a cross to bear, I can tell you." She tugged at a couple of wisps of her red hair. "And still suffering from split ends… My point was that unless you get yourself a proper drink or some kind of medication you're heading for a downturn, baby."

"I'll be okay." Tom reached for a cigarette himself, all the easier to lie behind.

"You're talking to dead people, babe," said Elise, "I don't think 'okay' ever really covers that."

7.

Build not break. Build not break. Build not break.

It is very quiet here, Sophie thinks. Very quiet is good. But then she is inside her own head and if you can't like it there then where can you?

This is not always true. Many people do not like it inside their own heads. That is because their heads are untidy places. It is where they hide everything that they do not want to see. Sophie is not like that. As soon as things get untidy inside her head she takes the time to tidy it. She sits and she hums. She empties herself of all the untidy things. She makes sure that everything else is stored neatly – like her toys in her bedroom, ordered alphabetically on her shelves. Once she has done this then her head is a good place to be. At the moment the tidying is taking a long time. This is because she has a house in her head. This is bad. But she is making things tidy so soon it will be good. Soon.

Sometimes she becomes aware of things that are happening outside her own head. They are distant. Like when her father used to listen to the radio in the garage. She would hear those voices – he liked his radio loud – but she would not be able to hear the words because she was not in the garage with them. They would be shapes not words. Up and down shapes. Happy or angry shapes. Singing shapes or talking shapes. She grew to like those shapes. They meant her father was close-by. They meant her father was happy. Sometimes he would add his own shapes to them, singing along or telling the footballers what to do. The footballers were silly, they always needed him to tell them what to do. They would have been lost without him.

The shapes of the people on the outside of her head where like that. Sometimes she could tell when it was Alan who was talking. Or the Other Alan, the Older Alan. To have two Alans was very strange. To begin with she had wondered if everybody everywhere was Alan but some of the shapes were lady shapes and so that couldn't be right. Then she remembered that everything in this House was strange and so decided that two Alans was good. If only there were three. Three was good.

But mostly she didn't hear the outside shapes. She had enough to deal with inside her own head and that meant that she didn't have time for anything else.

Besides, sometimes there were sound shapes inside her own head. She thought they were from the House. Houses did not speak. This was a fact. There were a lot of things Houses Did Not Do. She started to make a list:

1. Houses do not speak.
2. Houses do not walk.
3. Houses do not eat.
4. Houses do not...

There were lots of things Houses Did Not Do and she grew bored before she'd even begun. Besides, if somebody had asked her to make a list of things Houses Did Not Do before she had come here she would have definitely put things like…

1. Houses do not have jungles in their greenhouse.
2. Houses do not have seas in their bathroom.
3. Houses do not change shape.

…on the list. And so her list would have been wrong. You had to be careful of lists. They kept changing unless you were very, *very* careful about what you put on them.

So maybe the House *was* talking to her. Maybe this was one of those things that Houses Should Not Be Able To Do But Apparently Can.

Sophie couldn't understand what it was saying. She thought that perhaps this was because the sounds were not really words. When she had been younger she had talked to a dog she met outside the Post Office. Her mother had wanted stamps (the stamps that make letters go not the stamps that hurt) so she had been queuing to buy some. This had made Sophie Very Bored so she had gone to stand outside and talk to the dog. This had been frustrating. Not because the dog couldn't talk. Lots of things could not talk and they didn't make Sophie angry. It was because the dog could nearly talk but not quite. It had inclined its head to listen to her words and then made its barking noise as a reply. But Sophie could not understand what the barking noise meant. The dog had been trying to talk to her. She just couldn't understand what it was saying. That was what made Sophie frustrated. When her mother had been given her stamps she came outside and laughed at Sophie. This made Sophie cross. But not as cross as when her mother had said that dogs couldn't talk. Sophie knew that was one of those things that grown-ups tell Sophie because they cannot explain the truth. Like how babies happen. Of course dogs could talk. Humans just couldn't understand them. She later decided that might be because dogs spoke French. Her father had to go to France a lot with his work and he could never understand what they said to him when he was there. Just the same.

But the House wasn't speaking French. Sophie couldn't know this for sure but thought it was true anyway. She thought the House was talking in a way that nobody had ever talked before. It was the language of bricks and monsters. If she listened really hard maybe she might be able to learn it.

Bits of the House were falling apart. This was something she not only knew but also felt. She knew she shouldn't be able to feel the House but she did. This was because the House was part of her now. She tried not to think about that too much as if she did it would make her Very Scared. Instead she just thought about how she could make things tidy. Make things better. Everything In Its Right Place.

Build not break. Build not break. Build not break.

INTERLUDE
The Door

Martin first noticed the door after remembering to eat something.

Meals, like most of life's habits, were something that happened sporadically these days. When Jo had shared the flat with him he had lived a more regulated existence. They slept common hours and showered and breakfasted in step, believing the importance of staring at one another wearily over steaming coffee the only true way to start a day. Once that was done he would write at his desk while she clocked up unpleasant hours of piss-stains and tears at the nursing home where she worked. The nights were theirs to share – in principle at least – for food, for conversation, for each other's company. He would tell her how his work was going, what had sold and for how much; she would pluck black humour from a world that possessed little – better that than wallow in the depressing truth of what lay in everybody's future. Hers was a job that required mental editing, otherwise you wouldn't last a week at it.

With single existence had come a more fluid manner of getting through the day. He woke naturally, grazed on coffee and cigarettes until his imagination took over and work began. He would write until the churning of his stomach or a stumble in creativity forced a break. With belly or inspiration refilled he would continue until the problems reoccurred. Sometimes, if the words were too productive to be ignored, then nothing could tear his fingers from the keyboard. Not hunger, thirst or the attentions of a girl who loved him. Ultimately, while his body forgave him such ill manners, she did not and that was why he now lived alone.

He stood there in the doorway of his office staring at the door that now filled a previously blank stretch of plaster and brick. The impossibility of it had him half-determined to believe the door had always been there. He walked past it and into the kitchen, set to rummaging through microwaveable food in the freezer while trying to remember what might lie on the other side. The truth of course was nothing. He lived twelve floors up and the door was in an external wall. Panic sent him back into the hall.

There was no comfortable solution. Doors did not just appear in walls, nor did people forget those that had always existed. Accepting these two viewpoints – and how could he not? – left him with little room for negotiation.

He took a closer look at the door. The peeling paint-work was fragile and cracked – a cream psoriasis that exposed baby-sick green flesh beneath. That also marked it as different from the others in the flat. All of the doors were cheap pine, stained dark when he and Jo had first taken over the tenancy. Flecks of varnish still marked the bedroom carpet where the plastic sheeting had come awry, just one of the many stains that haunted that room in Jo's absence. A faded brown ring from an overfull coffee mug mocked the bedside table like the after-effect of a joke shop telescope; a tapering black line stretched across the wall from where the metal bed frame had scratched the paint during the move; crisp droplets of blood sat on the rug from a nosebleed. This was a home of dirt ghosts.

He was reluctant to touch the door but the urge to know that it was solid and real was strong. He gently brushed the surface, scattering a puff of foreign paint chips.

Having no idea what to do, he postponed the problem by grabbing his coat and leaving the flat. Outside, the city was an alien darkness, safe paths lit by the scattered glow of grafittied lampposts and shop signs. He felt lonelier than ever. He had nobody to call on or to run to. When they had first moved here he had felt no need to make friendships; now that she was gone he found he had no idea how to. Singularity was a virus and became more debilitating with time.

To be out and in the air was still a relief. He felt surrounded by space, despite the towering tenements and office blocks. The sound of a train rattling its way across ancient track a few streets away reminded him there was a world beyond the city... if only he could find the reason to visit it.

Eventually, sick of directionless walking, he sat at a bus stop and smoked a cigarette.

Time to go home.

The door was still there but he avoided looking at it and went to bed. Perhaps sleep would steal it from the wall and he could wake to clean white plaster and the flat he knew. Despite lying awake for hours – attempting to not think about the door with such fervour it kept him awake – he eventually lost consciousness and any dreams he had were so loose that the morning sun knocked them away when it woke him hours later.

He lay there a while, taking comfort in the fact that if the door was unobserved it could be argued not to exist. Eventually curiosity got the better of him and he crawled out of bed and into the hall.

It was still there.

At that point even the flimsiest of hopes and arguments were gone and he sank to his haunches and cried for a while; he really couldn't think of anything else to do.

Eventually, feeling more drained than he had before falling asleep, he walked into the kitchen and made himself a cup of coffee. While it cooled he smoked a cigarette. What else was there to do but to hold on to as much of his normal routine as possible?

He dressed and examined the door again. He tried the handle, giving a yelp of surprise as static electricity bit into his palm. He shoved it with his foot to see if there was any give in it. The door didn't move in the frame, it remained as resolute as if it were painted on the brick. He touched it again and whipped his hand away instantly, startled by how desperately cold the wood felt, like frozen logs waiting the axe and an open fire. He placed his fingertips to the wood again; this time it was warm. Finishing his coffee he fetched a tea towel to protect him from the static discharge and tried the handle again. It swung the quarter circle on its bolt but wouldn't open. What was the point of a door if you couldn't step through it?

He went into the lounge, just to get away from it, sat down and lit another cigarette. What to do? What to think?

He grabbed his coat and went out again, having grown uncomfortable in his flat with the door there.

After walking in circles, much as he had done the night before, he settled in a coffee shop and drank cappuccino and noise. Half the coffee grew cold as he stared at the walls, trying (and failing) to come up with a single rational course of action. He could think of no-body to call: Jo, even if he had decided to try and talk to her about it, had left no forwarding number. If he did call someone, what would he say? This was hardly a problem that could be solved by conversation.

He went home.

He hadn't bothered to hope the door would be gone and it didn't disappoint him. Having decided that there was nothing he could do, he walked straight past it and into the lounge. He turned on the computer and went online, Googling ludicrously for "door appearing", "magic door", "impossible door". It didn't help.

When the knock came he ran to the front door of his flat with an urge to cry or laugh – it was too brief a sen-sation to decide which: he was so glad of the idea of company. He opened the door to find the corridor out-side empty. As he was stood there the knocking came again and, as the penny dropped, he ran out and down the stairs, finally giving in to a terror that felt almost liberating after the confusion of inaction.

Standing in the street outside he looked up at his flat and found he was crying again. A few passers-by gave him space as tears turned to shouting and he began to run up and down the street in wild panic.

It was some time later when he found his thoughts clearing. He was sat in a rough area of park that the council had planted between the urban concrete, no doubt convinced that a little spurt of nature would be an inspiration to the poor bastards that lived there. His hands were bleeding on the palms but he had no memory of the injury. A couple of bits of grit popped out as he picked at the raw skin. He must have fallen somewhere.

He got to his feet, rubbing at the dirty seat of his trousers, and walked out onto the street. He wasn't entirely sure where he was but if he kept walking he was confident he'd see something familiar.

It took him a couple of hours to find his way home, by which time he had become so disgusted at the idea of staring at the door that another thought had occurred to him. Stepping out of the lift he walked through his flat and into the kitchen. He pulled open the cupboard beneath the sink and dragged out his toolbox. When they had first moved in he had decided that he would end up doing lots of jobs around the flat. He had bought and filled this cheap plastic box with anything he thought a toolbox should contain. Of course it had sat there since, unopened and unused as the urge had passed almost as quickly as the money spent. He took the hammer and a broad-ended chisel (which still had the price label on it) and marched back to the door. Placing the cutting edge of the chisel against where he imagined the door's lock casing must be, he took a deep breath and began to swing. The hammer chimed against the fat metal end of the chisel and he gritted his teeth, lusting for the sound of splitting wood. It didn't come. After a few minutes he stopped hammering, dropped to his haunches and searched for sign of his work. Some of the paint had fallen away but he had done that much with his fingers. Face pressed tight against the wood, he poked at the gap with his fingernail. There was nothing, not a mark.

Something whispered on the other side of the door. He heard no words but it was enough to send him running into his bedroom, slamming the door behind him and sitting in the far corner.

Night fell. He didn't move. The bedroom grew darker and his frantic imagination set to work when he least wished it to. He saw things that weren't there in the shadows thrown across his bedroom wall from the lampposts. The telegraph wires stretched, hanging the misshapen lump of a windowsill ornament by the throat; clouds grew faces that grinned at this desperate man beneath them; a dinner suit hanging by a hook on the door fattened with a dead man's flesh.

At some point he slept. He woke several times to noises from the hallway. First it was the sound of a woman talking, then a pounding that he took to be something trying to get into his flat from wherever lay on the other side. As a fragile dawn fell through the traffic-smeared glass of his windows he even heard music. Old and crackly, ghost Jazz of the sort trapped on brittle 78's. As the tinny echoes of a horn section long dead permeated the flat he found himself biting his lip with discomfort even as he subconsciously tapped a foot to the rhythm.

Eventually it grew light and, emboldened by the possibility of sun and the real world, he pulled himself to his feet. He had to lean on the bed as pins and needles rioted in his legs. Once he could move, he tip-toed to his bedroom door and slowly opened it. The door in the hall was as it always was and there was no way of telling if the welcome mat of paint dust that lay across the carpet was the result of his chiselling or the pounding he had heard in the night.

He ran from his bedroom and out of the front door. He had things to buy.

The large hardware store presented DIY. as a gleeful pastime. Cardboard cut-outs of cheerful men and women brandished their power tools and immaculate aprons, a world away from sweating hard work. He steered an unreliable trolley up and down the aisles. Young couples idled in front of rows of paint, selecting colours to make a place their own. Middle-aged men weighed up saws and hammers, making a pretence at expertise that everyone – not least their wives – could see for the sham it was. An elderly lady positioned herself on a display toilet, taking in the luxuriousness of its thick wooden seat as she stroked the cool enamel of the bath displayed next to her. "Who wouldn't be happy with this?" she muttered to nobody in particular and settled back to imagine such decadent bowel-emptying.

He queued up at the wood counter. The constant whine of the band-saw and bored staff banter made him feel sleepy. Men in tatty padded shirts loitered, feeling the grain of wood with their callused thumbs and consulting arcane biro scribbles in their notebooks. He waited and did his best to seem invisible.

Outside, having paid on a credit card that had given up despairing of its owner, he waited at the taxi rank with his laden trolley, only now aware of the impracticality of his shop. Eventually a driver took pity on him, scratching at rough stubble cultivated during long night shifts and helping load the wood and tools into the back of his people carrier.

Back at the flat he tipped the taxi driver for helping him get his purchases into the lift. On the twelfth floor he dropped one of the stout planks across the sliding doors to hold them in place as he ferried the rest into his flat. He piled the planks in front of the door in his hall and unpacked the electric drill. He glanced vaguely at the instructions but was too impatient for the job in hand to give them much attention. He slit the sealing tape on a pack of large masonry drill bits with his thumbnail and selected the largest. He spun the drill head, watching it open its mouth like a fat grub and dropped the bit into its jaw.

He began to drill, a foot or so away from the door frame, spitting the pinkish-brown plaster dust that blew into his mouth onto the carpet at his feet. He measured the holes, drilled the wood to match and began to build his barricade.

It took him three hours. The things on the other side of the door mumbled to him occasionally as he worked. He did his best to ignore them, drowning them out with the sound of the drill as it bore into the wall or drove thick screws into splitting, plastic-filled wounds. He stood back to inspect his work. The door was now invisible beneath thick slabs of unpainted wood. To think that, the day before, he had been so eager to crack the door open, to see what might lie on the other side. Whatever was in the impossible room adjoined to his flat he couldn't begin to imagine or deal with it – that was the only thing about this he had become sure of, far better to seal it in.

He decided he would eat something, a celebration of his counter-attack against whatever was trying to invade his home. He microwaved a pasta dish and sat in his lounge puffing at the sickly cheese sauce with lips still coated with sawdust. When the voices from the hall got too loud to ignore he turned some music on and blanked them out with chirpy drum beats and guitar chords. He found himself growing drowsy in his chair, his head nodding as indigestion hissed in his guts.

In his sleep he heard the sound of the band-saw from the hardware store. Flashing metal teeth gnashed at wood in a spray of sawdust.

He found himself at the barricade. The noise of the saw was the drone of a blanket of flies that coated the wooden planks. Pressed against them he felt them roll and pop under his fingers and cheeks. They tasted of copper on his tongue. Their buzz was loud enough to be felt as much as heard but he didn't flinch as they squeezed their juice on him, as they rooted through his hair laying their eggs, as they scurried across the wet ice rink of his eyeballs.

He was sat in the corner of the hall, unsure as to whether he had been dreaming. The flies were gone – he could still taste metal at the back of his throat but that could as easily be the lingering of imagination as the blood of insects. He could hear the sound of something being dragged across dusty concrete. Then a humming noise, a vibration that made his fillings ache. The swing music returned, Glen Miller riding the Chattanooga Choo Choo.

As he watched, one of the fat silver screws spiralled out from the wood and fell onto the carpet. It was followed by another. And again. The first plank fell.

He stayed quite still. He had neither the energy nor inclination to run. The door would always be there when he returned.

The screws from the second plank worked themselves free, metal woodworms glinting in the 60 watt light of his hallway. The second plank fell on top of the first.

What was the point of a door if you couldn't step through it, he had wondered a day ago. What indeed?

The third plank began to spit out its screws, one by one.

The woman was talking again though he couldn't tell what she was saying. However loud her voice grew, there was no distinction to the words; it was as if they were muffled, by a gripped hand perhaps, or a firmly pressed pillow.

The fourth plank fell.

He thought about Jo, wondered what she would have made of this. She had always been more practical than he, a man prone to losing himself in his own mind. Would she have even seen it?

The fifth joined the others in a pile.

As the sixth plank fell, the woman stopped talking and was replaced by the castanet chatter of what may have been a sewing machine. Thrusting needles and spinning cogs.

The seventh, and last, plank fell to the floor and for a moment there was silence.

Then the door opened.

TWO
Seven (and a Half) Hours in Tibet

1.

The silence was so absolute it was brittle as bone china. The snow glowed with an inherited luminescence too bright for unshielded eyes. A small amount of wind moved with grace and reverence along the sides of the mountain, delicately brushing the snow into smoky plumes. There are places on Earth that hold such serenity, such purity, that the mere act of walking in them feels a sacrilege. This was one of those places and, in truth, it wasn't patient to intruders. Its peaks were so lofty, it's air so thin, the fresh snow so treacherous, that it was a lucky man that survived in it for long.

The train arrived with a roar of brakes, bursting from mid-air and grinding through the snow. It came to a stop at an angle and its doors opened with the hiss of hydraulics. Ashe clambered over the snow drift caused by the train's passage, cursing to himself as the sound of an automated announcement echoed from the carriage behind him.

"We regret to announce that, due to the presence of leaves on the track, this, the 16.58 service to Dhuru Monastery will be unable to stop at its destination. Passengers are advised to alight here and make their own arrangements. Virgin Rail is unable to be held accountable for any passengers dying of exposure as it falls outside our insurance remit. Please contact our representative on your return for full details."

Ashe toppled down the far side of the snow bank, roaring an anatomical suggestion that any rail company would struggle to fulfil. He got to his feet, tugging his overcoat around him, and shuffled away from the train. He had been sensible enough to shoplift some extra clothing from the station's branch of *Fat Face*. His usual coat now accessorised by a fur hat and woollen scarf that he had considered frankly ridiculous when looking in the dressing room mirror but a godsend now. The extra pair of jumpers he was wearing made him ungainly as he tried to run a good distance away before the time the train departed.

The doors hissed closed and the train punched its way out of this time zone and on to destinations equally improbable. Ashe watched it go, then continued to shuffle down the mountain. As he waddled through the snow he became aware of a rumbling from further up the peak, the passage of the train having shaken the snow loose.

"I suppose death by avalanche is also not covered by insurance." He struggled to move quicker as a fat wave of snow rolled towards him.

The incline dropped sharply ahead, the land cutting back in on itself in a row of exposed rock. Ashe lowered himself over, dropping to a covered ledge as the snow shot past him in a waterfall of dust. He shuffled further along the ledge to an opening in the rock. Stumbling inside he was grateful for the padding of his extra layers as he lost his footing and fell a few feet into the centre of the cave.

"Hello," someone said, holding a lantern aloft to illumine a narrow, bearded face. "Was that bloody racket your doing?"

Ashe looked at the stranger, he was middle-aged, layered with thick tweed and wool. Propped next to him was an old-fashioned rifle (not old-fashioned here, Ashe reminded himself, everything had a chance to be new again when you were time travelling). Ashe got to his knees and slipped his hands in his coat pockets, ensuring his revolver was still to hand. Looping his finger through the trigger guard he kept the gun out of sight until he knew he'd need it.

"Sorry," he replied, "problem with my transport."

"Transport?" the man scoffed. "Your feet are the only transport you can rely on up here."

"You may be right." Ashe decided to change the subject, he had no intention of trying to explain his circumstances to this man. "Mark Spencer," he said, extending the hand not gripping his revolver. The man stared at the gesture for a moment, either deciding whether he was willing to let the matter of Ashe's transport drop or wondering what sort of man wore gloves knitted in pink herringbone. Eventually he shook it, his Victorian breeding getting the better of his concerns.

"Nigel Walsingham, good to meet someone with whom I share a language at least."

"Likewise." Ashe was relieved – if surprised – to hear the man's name, it would appear that he might get this conversation under control at last. "Forgive me, but are you Walsingham, the botanist?"

"One and the same." Walsingham's gruff manner thawed slightly. "Here on behalf of the British Society taking samples of medicinal herbs. I'm sorry but if we've met…"

"We haven't, but we have a friend in common, Roger Carruthers?"

At the mention of Carruthers' name all animosity vanished from Walsingham. "My dear fellow! I've known Carruthers for years, a pleasure to make your acquaintance!" Walsingham shook Ashe's hand again, this time with a genuine vigour. "What are the odds on two such souls meeting in such circumstances?"

What indeed? Ashe thought. He was wondering how bizarre it was that his train should go out of its way to avoid his original destination and drop him here, mere feet away from the man he was after. Was Sophie helping them somehow?

"My being here isn't a complete coincidence," Ashe admitted. "In fact I'm engaged in business on Carruthers' behalf."

"Really?" Walsingham replied. "I had no idea he had interests in Tibet."

Neither does he, thought Ashe, not yet anyway.

2.

His discussion with Carruthers before leaving for the past had been unsurprisingly detailed. After all, if there was one thing Carruthers enjoyed it was discussing himself.

"Walsingham's a fine chap," Carruthers had said, "as far as any man that can get excited over moss can be described as such. His heart's in the right place though he can kill a dinner party stone dead with his interminable waffle about flora. It was him that told me about the box."

Which had marked Walsingham out as the man Ashe needed to meet.

"He wrote to me," Carruthers had continued, "claiming to have met a man by the name of Mark Spencer. Apparently this fellow had traced the artifact to a Buddhist temple in one of the corners of Tibet less marked by the British interest."

"By which you mean invasion force?"

"Well, yes, I suppose so, though I will say that that was never the intention of many of the men involved. We were just eager to see what the hitherto unexplored country could offer. I suppose many indecencies have been committed in the name of curiosity. Anyway, I had no knowledge of the gentleman mentioned which made the matter all the more intriguing. Walsingham had me endorsed by his fellows at the British Museum and I made my way out there as fast as a boat could carry me."

"Well," Ashe had noted, "at least one mystery is now solved for you."

"Really?"

"The identity of this unknown acquaintance." Ashe held up the box. "It must have been me."

"Hmm." Carruthers had nodded. "Rum business time travel."

3.

"Once the snow has settled a little," said Walsingham, "I'll lead you down to the monastery and introduce you to the rest of my party. At the very least we can make sure you have a bed and some warm provisions. The monks bend over backwards to ensure we're comfortable. Though I can't say I take to the tea much, oily stuff, like drinking paraffin. They swear it's good for you."

"Are they not opposed to your presence then?" asked Ashe.

"Opposed? Oh, being Westerners you mean? No, the Abbot's a friendly sort, head in the clouds of course, but the perfect host. The soldiers we've encountered on our travels have been a bit more trigger happy but everyone's accommodating enough for the most part, Younghusband was sensible enough to release most of his Tibetan prisoners once our interests here were endorsed by the Dalai Lama so everyone's on the same side."

"We'll see how long it lasts," Ashe replied, only too aware that it wouldn't. Time travel turned one into such a know-it-all.

"Our military companion shares your doubt," said Walsingham. "Major Kilworth, he's somewhat uneasy about the whole affair."

"I thought there was nothing a military man liked more than occupation."

"He was stationed in India for years and, unlike many of his fellows, came to sympathise with the locals."

"A military man who has lost his taste for colonisation... I bet that attitude has helped his career no end."

Walsingham smiled. "He's stuck nursemaiding a botanist and his party, make of that what you will."

"What's the purpose of the expedition?" asked Ashe.

"We're exploring the pharmacological value of the Tibetan medicine. These chaps swear by their brews and the medical profession is always eager to add new munitions to its armoury. I'm the botanist of course, and Lawrence Rhodes is the chemist. We also have Doctor Andrew Haywood with us, though I must confess it's not always a pleasure. The man's a wreck... cold sweats and delusions when he's at his worst."

"Sounds helpful."

"Claims it's altitude sickness but there's a suspicion that he has a taste for his own medicine cabinet."

"I'm surprised you put up with him."

"Can't really send him home can we? He was the measure of civility on our voyage but since taking residency here he grows from bad to worse. It's a damned mess... my wife has been under the weather recently but she refuses to let him anywhere near her. Can't say I blame her."

"You've brought your wife with you?" Ashe found the idea startling given the politics of the time.

"Oh she's a bright spark, my Helen, wouldn't dream of waiting dutifully behind for my return. Besides, she has always taken an interest in my work, her knowledge would put many lesser botanists to shame."

"Taught her all you know."

"I suppose I have," Walsingham smiled. "Besides, it makes these long expeditions all the more palatable to have her by my side. A marriage withers in isolation don't you think?"

"Indeed I do," admitted Ashe, though he couldn't lay claim to any personal experience. There was an air of nervousness to Walsingham when he discussed his wife that Ashe found curious. For all his sentimental words, there was discomfort there. His "bright spark" was not the source of pleasure he made her out to be.

"I think we can risk moving now," Walsingham said, poking his head out of the cave. "The light will be gone soon and the last thing we want is to be stuck out here in the dark." He pulled his pack on and tightened his scarf around his face. "Do you have no equipment?" he asked, his voice muffled by the thick wool.

I didn't think I'd need any for such a brief trip, thought Ashe, I certainly never intended to go trekking over mountains. "I'm travelling light," he said. "Left the main party just over the last ridge." He hoped

Walsingham didn't question him further. Next time he should prepare a cover story.

"A proper Sherpa, eh?" Walsingham replied, heading out into the open air.

They made their way out onto the narrow ledge, Walsingham leading the way. "The journey is a short one," Walsingham continued, "you should be fine. I have rope if we come unstuck *en route*."

The ledge widened out a few yards from the cave and the going was as easy as Walsingham promised. Ashe couldn't help but be reminded of his recent trek within the house, where he, Carruthers, Miles and Penelope had travelled up the side of a mountain rising – in typically preposterous fashion – within the walls of one of the sitting rooms. Then they had been lucky enough to have a staircase to follow and regular pitstops within furnished caves.

"It should only take us half an hour or so," shouted Walsingham. "Once we get around the next bend you'll see the monastery. I make it a point never to travel too far from the base on my own, once you get further afield the climb is far too dangerous to be attempted without roped support."

"No need to make your wife a widow in the name of botany," Ashe replied.

"Indeed not."

After a few minutes the landscape below revealed itself. Further down, in the shelter of a narrow valley, a building pulled its stone walls around itself as if for warmth. Banners fluttered on parapets, shivering from exposure. A bell sounded, ringing around the central courtyard and calling the monks that lived there to prayer. Prayer was good, Ashe thought, bodies huddled in the fug of incense fires as they chanted. Even if nobody was listening it took the chill off.

"Sounds like evening prayer's started," he said to Walsingham.

"They never stop," Walsingham replied. "A more devout band cannot be imagined."

"I suppose there's not much else to do up here," said Ashe.

"Hello," said Walsingham, "who's this?"

Ahead of them, no more than a silhouette in the dimming light, a figure was making its way towards them from the monastery gates.

"Nigel," a voice shouted as the figure drew closer, "is that you?"

"Sounds like Helen," Walsingham said. "What is she playing at coming out here?" He pulled his scarf away from his mouth, the better to project his voice. "Helen?" he called. He began to trot faster down the mountainside, clearly concerned as to what had brought his wife out into the cold.

"Nigel," Helen sighed with palpable relief once they were face to face, "I came out to fetch you, something terrible's happened to Rhodes."

"What is it?" Walsingham asked. "Some sort of accident?"

Helen shook her head. "I wish." She struggled for a moment, as if uncertain how to express the news. Eventually she took the no-frills approach: "Someone's murdered him."

4.

Ashe felt a sinking feeling in his stomach, his simple plans were clearly about to complicate themselves.

"Who's this?" Helen asked, looking at Ashe with undisguised suspicion.

"What?" Walsingham was still trying to assimilate the news that one of his party was dead. "Oh... Mark Spencer, a colleague of Roger's, we met a little way up the mountain."

"Really?" Helen replied. "How bizarre."

"I'm actually here on Roger's behalf," Ashe explained. "I have an artifact that may be of interest to him."

"We'll hear all about it later," she replied. "We have more important matters on hand for now."

"Of course," Ashe nodded. "May I suggest we keep moving; you can explain everything once we're in the comfort of the monastery."

"Spencer's right," agreed Walsingham, taking Helen's arm and leading her back the way she had come. "I can't believe the major let you out here on your own as it is."

"He could hardly claim I would be safer at the monastery," she replied, "and our good doctor's suffering from one of his 'blue funks' again."

"Dear Lord, the man's a liability." Walsingham was in shock, stumbling along in a twitchy state that wasn't due to the cold. "I can't believe it," he said, his voice quiet, almost lost beneath the increasing volume of the monk's chanting. "Rhodes dead... but, darling, you must be overreacting... it can hardly be murder." He was asserting a sense of calming logic. "There must be an alternative explanation."

"We found him in the stables with an ice pick in the back of his head," Helen countered. "He didn't end up like that by losing his footing."

She was a cold hearted creature, Ashe thought. There seemed to be little sense of sadness at the death of one of her colleagues, more an irritation that her life had been cluttered up by the fact.

They reached the entrance to the monastery, a tall set of wooden doors fixed into the stone wall. It made

Ashe think of a Medieval castle, barricaded to repel invaders. Helen yanked at the cord of an iron bell, its chime bouncing between the walls of the valley as if the noise were a creature gleeful to be let loose. After a few moments the door opened, a slender monk stepping to one side to let them enter. He bowed as they filed past, his pointed hat looming towards their faces. He gave the ground a double tap with the base of the long pole he carried, a fighting stick, Ashe assumed.

"Thank you," said Walsingham, giving a rather self-conscious bow in return.

The door opened into a central courtyard. Ashe turned slowly, getting the lay of the land. A pair of monks worked their way around the perimeter, lighting heavy sconces in preparation for the night ahead. There was the thick smell of manure coming from what Ashe took to be the stables, a small, two-level outbuilding to the left of the courtyard. "That was where the body was found?" he asked, pointing.

"Yes," Helen answered, "though we've taken him upstairs."

"Our accommodation is directly above," Walsingham explained, "what it lacks in pleasant odour it makes up for in warmth."

"Not sure you should have moved the body," Ashe commented.

"Oh really?" Helen retorted. "And who are you to have an opinion one way or the other?"

"Helen!" Walsingham snapped. "That is no way to address our guest."

"Forgive me Nigel," she replied, "but I would hope you understand that the notion of a stranger appearing on the mountainside at the same time one of our party meets his end is a source of great concern for me. It seems somewhat coincidental don't you think? I mean, what are the odds of you bumping into the gentleman up there? This is a sparsely inhabited valley in Tibet not Oxford Street."

"I understand your concern," Ashe admitted, thinking quickly before he lost all sense of credence amongst the party. "My appearance here at the same time as your own was completely intentional. As I partly explained to your husband I came here with the interests of Roger Carruthers at heart. I've been researching the history of an artifact that would interest him. I traced it here and, learning that your party were also in residence, it made sense to coincide my visit with yours. I left my main party up the mountain there, planning to drop in for an hour or two before rejoining them. Roger assured me that I would be made welcome."

"And so you are," Walsingham insisted.

"It is a wonder to me that Roger didn't see fit to warn us of your impending arrival," Helen noted, though it was clear that – whether through deference to her husband's feelings or her own – she was willing to let go of some of her hostility. "That would have avoided any misunderstandings, would it not?"

"I left some time after your own departure so unfortunately…"

"It is of no matter," insisted Walsingham, losing his patience. "Can we please deal with the business in hand? I want to know what happened to Rhodes."

Helen gave him an irked glance – it was clear to Ashe that this was a partnership she was in control of, however much that may be against the period's norms, and she didn't like being snapped at. "Forgive me if I thought we were discussing just that."

Walsingham didn't rise to the comment, following his wife up a creaking wooden staircase to a heavy Dutch door. She yanked on the handle, grunting as it held fast in its frame. "It's locked. The major no doubt."

"He's only concerned with our safety, dear, that is, after all, his job."

Ashe expected Helen to make the obvious comment that, seeing as one of them had died, the major wasn't doing his job very well. If the comment occurred to her, she kept it to herself, hammering on the door and waiting in silence to be let in.

After a few moments there was the solid crack of a bolt being drawn. It was slammed into place with military precision so that nobody could be in doubt that the door had been well and truly opened.

The major's face appeared within the revealed slice of candlelight. "Oh, Walsingham, it's you." He stepped back to allow them room to enter.

"And you are?" he asked Ashe, his eyes narrowing over a Roman nose that had sneezed salt and pepper curls over the lower half of his face.

"Mark Spencer," Walsingham said perhaps determined not to let Ashe's relationship with Major Kilworth get off on the same wrong foot as it had with his wife. "He is a colleague of Roger Carruthers and is here under his recommendation."

"You've picked a bad time to join us," the major said to Ashe, "as you have no doubt heard."

"Indeed."

"Where is he?" Walsingham asked.

"Through there," the major answered, nodding towards a door in the corner, "Helen has donated her accommodation for the time being."

"Better that than have a corpse in the middle of the room," she said. Now that Ashe could see her clearly he was less struck by her coldness. There was a vacuousness to her gaze as she picked at the wool of her scarf as if trying to remove invisible insects from its weave. She was in shock and not half as strong as she had been trying to suggest. Easier to deal with her dismissive comments than a tearful breakdown, Ashe supposed.

"Has the doctor examined him?" asked Walsingham.

The major gave a pointed look at them and shook his head. "Our medical expert is suffering from another bout of his 'altitude sickness'," the skepticism in his voice couldn't have been clearer. "'Physician heal thyself', eh? He's sleeping it off in his bedroll."

"Much use the blasted man is," Walsingham said. "He's more of a hindrance than a help."

"Can I take a look at the body?" asked Ashe.

They looked at him, Walsingham hopeful, the others still wary.

"Do you have medical experience, sir?" Helen asked.

"I have experience with violent death," Ashe admitted, and there was a good deal of truth to that.

"I'm not sure I find that reassuring," she replied though was clearly not concerned enough to argue further.

"There can be no harm in it," offered the major, "though the issue lies not so much with the departed Rhodes as ensuring the rest of us don't end up sharing his condition."

"The two aren't mutually exclusive," said Ashe, opening the door to the small side-room where the body lay.

"Allow me," said Walsingham, pushing ahead with a lit lantern. He hung it from an iron hook in the centre of the ceiling where it swung gently, throwing black, syrupy shadows across the walls. The ice pick was still in place, the shadow of its elevated handle turning the corpse into a sundial, telling the time against the straw covered floor.

"Whose is the pick?" asked Ashe.

"Mine," the major admitted, "though it scarcely means much, the equipment is all stored together in a bridle room just off the stables."

"So anyone could grab it?" Ashe clarified.

"Precisely."

"But why would they?" Ashe asked, squatting over the body.

"I'm sorry?"

"Motive," Ashe replied, squinting at Rhodes' face. He was a handsome chap, early thirties, with that look of the gentleman adventurer much favoured by Hollywood period movies.

"As much as I hate to say it," the major replied, "surely that's obvious?"

"Really?" Ashe looked up at him, trying to read his facial expressions in the dim light.

"One of the locals has issue with our presence."

"Issue enough to sneak up behind one of you and put several inches of steel in his head? I find that hard to imagine."

Walsingham crouched next to him. "Rhodes was often somewhat… expressive about his feelings towards the locals."

"He was a racist."

There was an awkward pause as the major glanced at Walsingham and his wife. "Not sure I know the term," he admitted. "He had no great love for foreigners if that's what you're driving at?"

Ashe shook his head, he'd forgotten how modern a word – or indeed concept – racism was.

"You make it sound like he was permanently abusing the monks," Helen commented. "That's hardly the case."

"Well, no…" the major admitted, "but he could be somewhat insensitive."

Only Victorians could see insensitivity as a crime worthy of murder, Ashe thought.

"It still seems slender motive to me," Ashe said, "but then it's none of my business."

He stood up, a little angry with himself for being drawn into the matter. If these people were picking one another off – certainly he didn't believe for a minute an over-sensitive Buddhist was behind the murder – then it was no business of his. Unless… a worrying thought occurred to him: what if the murderer attacked Walsingham next? If the man was dead he could hardly contact Carruthers and play out his role in the historical scheme of things. For all Ashe knew, it was only through his own involvement that the murderer was exposed and Walsingham preserved from harm. Or, of course, the opposite could be true and Ashe was putting all their lives at risk by involving himself.

Time travel was a pain in the ass.

"Without wishing to fall out with my husband again," said Helen, "we only have your word that this is no business of yours. For all we know you could have murdered him yourself."

"Before popping up the hill to introduce myself to your husband?"

"Well… yes."

"True, I suppose I could have. Equally your husband could have killed the man before returning to his researches and establishing an alibi."

"I say!" Walsingham was somewhat put out to find himself put in the frame.

"Just making a point, I'm not saying I think you did it for one moment – and I know for a fact that I had nothing to do with it – but, yes, if we are to be thorough about this we're potential suspects as much as anyone else."

"Have you told the Abbot?" Walsingham asked Kilworth.

"That rather presupposes he doesn't already know," his wife muttered.

"I thought it best to keep the situation to ourselves for the moment," said the major, "until we decided how to respond to it."

"That sounds like fighting talk," Ashe commented.

"Fighting talk?" the major raised an eyebrow at Ashe. "You have a most peculiar turn of phrase, sir."

"Spent a lot of time in distant climes," Ashe admitted. "You pick up the vernacular."

"More distant than Tibet?" Helen joked.

Ashe chose to say nothing. Just looking at Rhodes' dead body. "It's a cowardly injury," he commented finally.

"Cowardly?" the major pulled a *moue*, though the lustre of his beard did its best to spare anyone's feelings by concealing it. "Is not all murder cowardly?"

"You misunderstand," Ashe explained. "I wasn't making a moral point, I was making a practical one. The murder was committed from behind, with little fear of reprisal – you simply don't fight back after someone's put a pick in the back of your skull. Also, the assailant was intent on murder – you don't accidentally kill someone from behind with an ice pick. This wasn't a scuffle gone wrong."

"Yes 'Holmes'," Helen mocked.

Walsingham gave her an irritated glance. "Fair points, neither of which discount the possibility that it was one of the monks, surely?"

"True. One thing though: do all of the monks carry those fighting poles that the man at the gate had?"

"Many of them," the major admitted.

"Then it would be ludicrous to put that down in order to pick up an ice pick wouldn't it? A stout blow to the base of the skull with one of those would have just the same outcome."

"Perhaps we should see the abbot," admitted Walsingham. "I shall ask Kusang to arrange an audience."

"Kusang?" asked Ashe.

"Our interpreter and go-between, provided by the Museum," Walsingham explained. "A surly fellow but we'd be lost without him."

"Nobody else speaks Tibetan?"

"No." answered Helen.

"Then let's talk to Kusang."

5.

Kusang was found sitting in the shadows of the courtyard, wrapped in several animal skins and the reek of whisky. "If you are going to start killing one another," he said, "I am safer out here I think."

"What do you know about that?" asked Walsingham.

"I hear your Major shouting about it," the interpreter said. "An Englishman is not stealthy."

"We wish to consult with the abbot," Walsingham explained, not wanting to be drawn on the deficits of his military officer. "Can you request an audience?"

"I can request, but I will not blame him if he refuses. For all he knows one of you may stab him the minute you enter his quarters."

Walsingham was becoming tired of the insinuation that his party were a bloodthirsty liability to the rest of the monastery's safety. "He need fear nothing from us."

Kusang offered a smirk that turned into a gently alcoholic belch. "Give me five minutes," he said and shuffled off into the main building.

"I'm guessing he's not a Buddhist," said Ashe after he'd gone.

"What makes you think that?" asked Walsingham.

"Buddhists don't drink," Ashe replied.

"Oh... Kusang does little else. I'd fall off a mountain

as soon as look at it with the amount he consumes but he always seems steady as a rock."

"Some people can take more than others," Ashe commented, shivering against the cold wind that had started to build.

The courtyard was dark but for the flaming torches, all remnants of daylight having vanished in the time that they had been in the stables. Whereas the weather had been gentle during their climb down the mountain it was taking a turn for the worse now. Thick flakes of snow were beginning to fall, spinning in the meagre orange light as they tumbled towards the cobbled ground. Ashe hoped that it wouldn't keep him from his train.

"The weather's getting bad," he said to Walsingham.

"It often does at night," the botanist agreed. "We'll be safely under cover though, no need to worry."

No need to worry? Ashe thought there were several reasons but saw nothing constructive in outlining them.

Kusang reappeared at the main door to the monastery, gave a little bow and beckoned them over. "His holiness will see you now," he announced pompously.

"Time for you to meet the abbot," said Walsingham.

"Should I be worried?"

Walsingham smiled. "He's charm itself. At least I'm assuming so, it's difficult to tell as Kusang always translates. He certainly smiles a lot."

They entered the monastery, the warmth of the fires enveloping them as surely as the clouds of incense. There was the smell of cooking, something beaten up by heavy spices and set to boil. Even though the chanting had ceased there was a heaviness to the air that made Ashe feel self-conscious as he followed Kusang and Walsingham along the corridor. There was an atmosphere to places of worship, he had always found, a weighty expectancy as if the very air was waiting to ignite. He wasn't a religious man but walking through places like this made him feel like he might be missing out on something.

They entered the main meeting hall, where recent prayers still dripped from the stone walls. The abbot was sat in his throne at the end of the room, old bones folded within purple robes that looked heavy enough to crush them. He bowed his wrinkled forehead toward them, his smile so wide it looked likely to split his face. Kusang bowed, with Walsingham and Ashe following suit. The old abbot called a greeting, his voice so thin and high pitched Ashe was hard-pressed to define a single consonant. Kusang clearly had a better trained ear as he replied, gesturing over his shoulder to the two westerners. The abbot crowed once more prompting Kusang to turn to Ashe. "His holiness bids you welcome to Dhuru," he explained.

"Tell him I am grateful of his hospitality," Ashe replied. The interpreter nodded and gabbled a few words to the abbot who bowed toward Ashe.

"Have you told the abbot what has happened?" Walsingham asked.

Kusang nodded. "Naturally."

Walsingham was frustrated at the manner in which he was forced to communicate with the abbot. Kusang controlled the flow of conversation completely and was only too happy to illustrate the fact.

"Well then," Walsingham continued, trying not to let his irritation show to the abbot, "would you like to ask him his thoughts on the matter?"

Kusang smiled, turned to the abbot and rattled off a few Tibetan phrases. The old man nodded a couple of times and then seemed to sink inside his gown, retreating into his silk shelter to think. After a few moments he began to speak, Kusang talking over him once the abbot had a head start, translating to Ashe and Walsingham.

"Dhuru is a place of peace and contemplation," he said. Kusang's voice was toneless, the words meant nothing to him, he was just their vehicle. "It is not intended for those outside our faith, and yet it is due to our faith that we took you in. We believe in treating others with respect and consideration. Even now, I am between two ideals, to offer you protection or to banish you for the safety of my brothers."

"It seems you are not willing to consider the possibility that the culprit was one of your monks." Walsingham interrupted.

Kusang stared at him, blatant disgust in his eyes. He was not a man who felt the need to hide his feelings. He knew how much Walsingham needed him. After holding Walsingham's eye contact for a moment, he turned over his shoulder and talked to the abbot. The abbot inclined his head as if to let the words in more easily, giving a slight nod once he understood. There was silence for a moment and then he replied.

"No, the abbot isn't willing to consider that possibility," Kusang said. "If there is violence within the corridors of Dhuru then you have brought it with you."

"As long as he's being completely reasonable…" Walsingham sighed. "This is clearly a waste of time. We're to be labelled the aggressors regardless of evidence."

"The abbot understands why you may wish to look to strangers to explain things – the bird always looks outside its own nest for danger – but sooner or later he fears you may have to accept the threat that comes from within."

Dear God, thought Ashe, the man was turning into a cliché… this was a waste of everyone's time. "I think you're right," he said to Walsingham, "this meeting's pointless."

"With your holiness' permission," Walsingham said, "it is clear that we have little to discuss until more evidence can be unearthed."

Kusang passed this on and the abbot nodded, waving a small hand graciously towards the main doors.

"Our audience is clearly at an end," said Ashe, bowing towards the abbot and marching out of the room, Walsingham directly behind him. They walked quickly, only too happy to leave Kusang behind, having had more than enough of the man's company.

6.

In the courtyard the wind was howling now, utterly unrestrained and out to do some damage. Ashe glanced at his watch before realising that such a modern timepiece was likely to raise eyebrows if seen by the others. He tugged his cuff back over it. Five and a half hours left before his return train. Not long. But then he hadn't these complications. There was a lesson to be learned here: he should never assume that these visits would be simple, there was no accounting for the problems of others.

Back in the stables the smell of food was wrestling with the scent of the horses. A large iron pot was bubbling in the corner of the room. Helen listlessly stirred at its contents while the major polished his rifle.

"He cleans the damn thing more often than himself," Walsingham muttered as he and Ashe entered. "The man's obsessed."

"Let's hope we don't end up being glad of the fact before the night's out," Ashe replied.

"Let me guess," said Helen, looking up from her cooking, "the abbot wishes no part of it?"

"You are, as ever, correct my dear," Walsingham sighed. "He refuses to consider for one moment that the attacker is one of his brethren."

Helen shrugged, she had expected nothing else. "He was never going to take any responsibility, we are here under sufferance. I dare say they will be quick to evict us now."

Walsingham nodded. "He did hint as much."

"One can hardly blame them," said the major, leaning his gleaming rifle against the wall behind him. "We've forced our way into their country after all."

"Don't fret over your sensibilities, Major," Helen replied, "and do try to remember whose side you're on."

The major bristled. "You will never need to remind me of that madam."

"Pleased to hear it."

A ruckus from one of the adjoining rooms stopped their conversation descending further. A shambolic-looking man appeared in the doorway, his face as grey and pallid as a victim of drowning.

"Ah, Haywood," said Walsingham, "how good of you to join us."

"Most intolerable," the man whispered. "Never known sickness like it… forgive me."

"I am inclined to do no such thing!" Walsingham shouted, relieved to have a source for his anger that was undeniable. "Your constant lack of coherence – or, for that matter, consciousness – is becoming a major liability to this party."

Haywood held up his hands in a gesture of surrender, wincing at the volume of Walsingham's words. "I don't disagree," he replied. "Perhaps it would be better for me to leave."

"We're in Tibet, man!" Walsingham replied. "You don't get to just 'leave' it's a three day trek to the next

British encampment… given that you seem incapable of so much as staying upright for a few hours you'll forgive me if I assume the effort to be beyond you!"

Haywood said nothing to that. He opened his mouth, tried to think of something constructive and then, with no thoughts forthcoming, closed it again. He sat down near the cooking stove – wanting some of its warmth for himself Ashe assumed, certainly he looked like he had need of it. Then he thought of something to say though the reluctance with which he said it weighed on Ashe; there was something in his tone that didn't gel with the impression he had been given of the man.

"Perhaps it would be for the best were Rhodes to take over as physician," he said. "He has some of the training and none of the shortcomings."

It wasn't the fact that Haywood was denying knowledge of Rhodes' death that stuck with Ashe – if Haywood had anything to do with that then it was a simple enough ruse to deflect blame – rather the reluctance he showed to offload his responsibility. That seemed wrong, Ashe couldn't say for sure why, but it did.

"He has one distinct shortcoming," Helen replied. "He's dead."

And now Ashe paid even closer attention to Haywood's response. He couldn't lay claim to sharp deductive skills. True, he had spent much of his life trying to solve the mystery of the box but that was different, that was *research*, and the two were really not alike. Research was cold, the sifting of minutiae, the retention of facts. Trying to deduce the identity of a murderer? That was something else again, that was about reading people and empathising with motive. Still, Ashe had lived long enough that he liked to think he could tell a liar when he saw one. He had been a college professor and if there was one body of people who knew how to lie it was students.

"Dead?" Haywood said, his face drawing paler still. "How can he be?"

And there Ashe settled upon his decision. Whatever the truth behind Haywood's frequent bouts of "illness" he was no murderer, Ashe was sure of it. "How can he be?" Haywood had asked, a question rooted in shock not logic. He hadn't asked "what happened?" just that single brain-fart: 'how can he be?' That was the sound of a man who couldn't process what he had just been told.

"I can assure you he is," said Walsingham, some of his anger lifted, you could only stay angry at a rag doll for so long, they just didn't give you the responses needed to stoke the fires, "and in circumstances that jeopardise this expedition beyond even your unreliability."

"He was murdered," said the major. "Icepick to the back of the head." He clapped his hands as if this statement really needed extra impact. "The prevailing assumption being that one of our Tibetan friends decided that they'd had enough of him."

"That may be your assumption," said Walsingham, "but we have no evidence to back it up."

"He's dead," said the major, coldly and as if reciting a list of tactical maneuvers, "and I think I speak for all of us when I say that it wasn't at our hands. We would have no reason for killing one of our own team. It stands to reason that it was one of the Tibetans. I'd place money on Kusang were it down to me…"

"You're our military bodyguard," said Helen. "If it's not down to you then who is it down to?"

"I merely meant," the major gestured towards Walsingham, "well… as leader of the expedition."

"Typical military man," Helen sighed, "always looking for someone higher up the chain of command when it comes to making the difficult decisions."

"Do be quiet, Helen," snapped Walsingham, "we're all in shock but your attitude is not helping. We need to be working together not taking pot shots at one another."

She stared at him, whipping the food with her wooden spoon, wondering if she should continue the argument. Ashe wouldn't have been in the least surprised to see her hurl the cooking pot at her husband, she was angry enough, he could see it in her eyes. She looked away, not with acquiescence, she was still too angry for that, but a resentful understanding that more arguments would get her nowhere.

"Thank you," Walsingham said to her. "Now I suggest that we barricade ourselves in here for the rest of the night. Tomorrow we may have to accept that the only way forward is for us to leave... I don't intend to place any more lives in danger."

Ashe had seen it coming but it didn't help his mood. Everything he had been prepared for – the easy mission of handing the box to Walsingham in the knowledge that he in turn would pass it to Carruthers – was falling apart. If the expedition left tomorrow then how would he ensure the chain of events that would lead to Carruthers arriving at the house? He wracked his brains for alternatives and came up short. It was only as he watched the major bolt the external door that he realised he had a problem even closer to hand: if they were all sealed in for the night then how exactly was he to slip away and catch his train?

He was a damned idiot... so much to play for – and the rest of them back at the House didn't know the half of it – and here he was, stumbling at the very first hurdle. This was becoming too complex, too fast...

7.

Dinner was served in silence, nobody knew what to say and small talk was beyond them. As Ashe ate the lukewarm broth he realised it was the first proper food he'd eaten for some time. His stomach groaned appreciatively and it was all he could do not to ditch the spoon and pour the contents of the bowl straight into his mouth. Certainly such table manners wouldn't help his already precarious standing with the rest of the expedition. It was fine. They should be suspicious. It didn't help him any but he couldn't blame them for it.

First things first. He needed to talk to Walsingham, get the box in his hands and on its way towards its first prisoner. He didn't really want to discuss it in front of everyone else, though he accepted he might have to. Half an hour after dinner, however he had his chance.

"A cigar I think," announced Walsingham. "After that excellent meal of yours dear, I can think of nothing better."

"Well I certainly can," she replied. "Our accommodation is confined and foul smelling enough without the stench of those damned cigars of yours."

Walsingham sighed. "Then I shall go outside."

"I don't think that's a good idea," said the major, "not on your own at least."

"Oh for goodness sake!" Walsingham exclaimed. "Is a man not allowed to enjoy a simple cigar?"

"I'll join you," said Ashe. "If it makes the major relax."

"I'm not sure it should," Helen replied, still not willing to extend her trust.

"You can open the shutters and watch through the window, dear," said Walsingham with a sarcastic smile. "If you fear for my safety so much." He pulled on his heavy coat and held his arm out to Ashe. "Come sir! Let us see if we can find greater civility outside shall we?"

Ashe stepped out of the door, smiling slightly as he heard the major bolt it closed again behind them. They walked along the balcony a little way where a slight gap in the wooden window shutters allowed a sliver of light to help them see.

"I must apologise," said Walsingham pulling a pair of cigars out of a large metal case and offering one to Ashe. Ashe couldn't remember the last time he had smoked but thought it might be best to take it, if only to put Walsingham more at ease. "You are not seeing us at our best."

Not seeing my wife at her best is what he means to say, thought Ashe. The thought triggered something in his memory.

"Your wife hasn't been well," he replied, watching Walsingham cut the end of his cigar with a pocket knife.

"Indeed not," said Walsingham, rather relieved that Ashe had given him a good excuse for her mood. "One worries about her in fact." He passed Ashe the knife. "For the last few weeks she has suffered from bouts of nausea. She brushes it off but I know her well enough and can see she suffers."

Ashe cut the end off his own cigar, rather roughly and handed the knife back. "How long has it been going on?"

"Oh, a week or so, not long," Walsingham lit a match and offered it in his cupped hands to Ashe. Ashe poked the end of his cigar at the flame and inhaled cautiously. The smoke hit the back of his throat and he couldn't help but cough.

"You alright old chap?" Walsingham asked, a slight smile on his face.

"Been a while," Ashe replied, holding up his cigar.

Walsingham nodded graciously, lighting his own cigar and dropping the spent match over the balcony where it whipped away in the wind that circled the courtyard below them.

Ashe smoked carefully, ensuring that he didn't inhale. He was silent for a moment, thinking about Helen Walsingham and the "illness" that seemed to be affecting her of late.

"I've tried to convince Helen to let Haywood take a look at her," Walsingham continued, "but she won't have it. I understand of course, the man's an ass. But it seems pointless to put oneself through unnecessary suffering when it may be easily dealt with by some preparation or another." He looked at Ashe, lowering his voice. "She woke me up the other day, poor thing was quite violently sick."

Could Walsingham be so naïve as to not have a good idea what was causing his wife's nausea? Ashe thought it was possible – the era being what it was – but more than that, morning sickness would likely not occur to the man if it seemed utterly impossible to the man that his wife could be pregnant. And Ashe imagined it had been a long time since Walsingham and Helen had been close enough to cause that condition...

Or maybe he was simply getting carried away with his own suspicions. Enough of Walsingham's problems, Ashe decided, he had enough of his own.

"I'm sure it will pass," he said. "Perhaps it's something as simple as the change in food."

"Perhaps," agreed Walsingham and the disappointment in his voice when he said it changed Ashe's view of the man entirely. *He knows*, he thought, knows damn well what's causing his wife to throw up every morning. Just hasn't got the balls to come out and say it. Wants somebody else to suggest it. Ashe didn't know how to feel about that, didn't know whether to sympathise with the man or despair of his weakness. Was it love for her that held him back? Or fear? He was as much a prisoner in his own damned marriage as Ashe had been in that House. But Walsingham had made his own chains. So many do. Ashe smoked his cigar... not his problem. Time for the box.

"I need you to do something for me," he told Walsingham. "For Carruthers too." He knew mentioning that name would give the notion extra weight. He was right.

"I'd do anything for Roger," Walsingham replied, a false smile choking back the fears about his wife, "he knows that."

"I'm sure he does," said Ashe, "and I know it may seem bizarre that I can't do it myself but..." but what? "...I have to rejoin the rest of my party very soon and we're heading into..." God this was bullshit, could Walsingham not see that he was lying? "...rather treacherous territory. We will likely be gone some time, in fact if things go badly, I may not be back at all."

"What on earth are you up to?" Walsingham asked, curiosity piqued.

Ashe tapped at his nose. "Need to know, I'm afraid, government business. You know how it is."

Walsingham didn't. The most exciting thing he got up to was cataloguing new species of fern. Nonetheless he nodded, one didn't like to admit to ignorance. "Oh, well, ask no questions... you can be assured I can be relied on in matters of discretion."

"I have no doubt." Ashe reached into his pocket and pulled out the box. "I need to ensure that Carruthers gets this."

"I'll gladly take it to him on my return."

"No, sorry but he must come here and fetch it for himself."

"Come here? Well that hardly makes good sense, surely?"

An idea struck Ashe. "Try and open it."

Walsingham did so, Ashe momentarily concerned that the bluff would blow up in his face.

"Won't open," Walsingham said, "iced shut is it?"

"No. Carruthers will know how to open it but he must be here to do so. I know it seems bizarre and I'm asking you to take a great deal on trust but it really is important."

Walsingham stared at the box, turning it in the meagre light offered by the second-hand glow of the lamps coming through the window behind them. "What is that?" he asked, noting the writing on the box's surface, "Chinese?"

"Khitan," Ashe replied, "a related dialect but much, much older."

"Not heard of it," Walsingham admitted. He shrugged and placed the box in his pocket. "As I said, anything for Carruthers. Though I suspect we shall be leaving the monastery come the morning, I'll be damned if I'm leaving the country just yet. Far too much to discover, eh?"

Was that good enough? Carruthers had come here, to this very monastery… Ashe was at a loss as to how he could convince Walsingham to risk the lives of his party further by hanging around on his behalf. He'd screwed this up from beginning to end. He should have prepared much more…

"Right," Walsingham said, slapping his hands together, "I don't know about you but I've had quite enough of this cold. Shall we call our cigars done and return to the warm?"

Ashe had barely smoked his and was happy to leave it that way. "Fine by me."

Walsingham reached for the door to open it before remembering that the major had locked them out. "Damned paranoid..."

He lifted his hand to knock on the wood when the explosive report of a rifle went off from the other side.

"Haywood!" they heard Helen shout. "No!" She screamed just before another gunshot reverberated around the enclosed walls of their cabin.

"Helen!" Walsingham shouted, yanking pointlessly at the door.

"The window," Ashe said, dashing back to where they had been smoking. "Your knife," he shouted to Walsingham, "quickly!"

Walsingham ran along the balcony, scrabbling for it in his pocket. Ashe watched in absolute disbelief as the box tumbled from Walsingham's coat – the man's hands diving hectically into each pocket as he tried to remember where he had put the knife. It bounced off the wooden planks of the balcony and tumbled into the darkness of the courtyard below.

"Here!" Walsingham shouted having found the knife. He held it out to Ashe, utterly oblivious as to what had just happened. For a moment Ashe just stared and then Helen screamed once more and the terror on Walsingham's face – made all the more horrible for the scant slit of light he could glimpse it in – pushed him on. He would have to hope the box was easily found once they had dealt with... well, with whatever the hell was going on in the cabin.

He shoved the knife blade into the gap between the shutters, sliding it up and down to find the catch on the other side. It was basic enough, a length of wood that held the shutters in place running across the gap between the two doors, hinged on one end. Once found he flipped it up with the knife and shoved the shutters inward with the butt of his hand. "Back!" he shouted at Walsingham, kicking out at him so as to stop him shoving his face in the window and having it blown off by whoever was wielding the rifle inside. Nobody fired. Ashe tried to think what he knew about old firearms, which wasn't much. Didn't old rifles have to be reloaded after each shot? He pictured old Westerns he'd seen... Audie Murphy ejecting the spent casing and sliding another shell in place. Not that whoever was inside hadn't had time to reload...

"Helen?" Walsingham wasn't hanging back, whatever the risk he needed to make sure his wife was okay. Well, thought Ashe, that explains that one anyway, he loves her sure enough.

"I'm alright," she called back, "it's Haywood, he's..."

"Shut your mouth!" Haywood screamed.

Ashe – deciding that if anyone was going to get shot through the window they would have done by now – joined Walsingham.

Inside, Helen was huddled in the far corner of the room. Haywood was pointing the rifle at her. Of the major there was no sign... wait... on the floor a semicircle of blood was reaching out from beneath the window. Great, looked like they'd found the major.

Haywood was constantly on the move, his body shaking as he paced back and forth, the rifle's aim never leaving Helen's head. It seemed he had little interest in Ashe or Walsingham.

"Haywood!" Walsingham shouted. "If you hurt her..."

Ashe grabbed Walsingham and put his hand to the man's mouth.

"I'll handle this," he whispered.

He tried to keep his voice steady, to sound calming

rather than confrontational. "It's alright Haywood," he said, "everything's fine now. We can sort it all out."

"The bastard's going to shoot my bloody wife!" Walsingham argued.

Ashe shot him a look that shut him up. "I know what I'm doing," he said. *Yeah sure*, a little voice piped up in his head, because you've seen *all* the best movies. He turned back to the window. "Let us take over from here," he said. "Let us get this all squared away."

"You have no idea," said Haywood, "this bitch…"

"Is pregnant," said Ashe, "she has a baby. You would have noticed if you weren't so ill, wouldn't you?"

Out of the corner of his eye he saw Walsingham's face crumple. There, it was out in the open now, much good it'll do him.

"Pregnant?" Haywood said, the rifle twitching slightly as a fraction of uncertainty crept in. "You're pregnant?"

Helen looked at Ashe and, even in these extreme circumstances, her anger at him was profound.

"Yes," she said finally, turning her attention back to Haywood.

He stared at her, blinking repeatedly, trying to focus. Whatever drug was coursing through his system it was really doing a number on him. "Pregnant?" it was no more than a whisper… he just couldn't process this new information. Ashe thought they might just stand a chance if they could keep him on the back foot. Not let him reclaim the upper hand.

"Yes, she's pregnant so you need to be really careful now, as her doctor, you need to make sure the baby stays safe. As her doctor it's your duty isn't it Haywood?"

"Her doctor."

"That's it. Her doctor. Your duty."

"Stays safe."

"Yes."

"Not dead?" There was a tinge of hysteria creeping back into the voice.

"No."

"Dead like Rhodes?" The voice creeping ever higher. Shit... he was losing him. Haywood wobbled on his feet, a tremor working its way through his body.

"Haywood!" The voice was the major's... it sounded like he was shouting through treacle.

No! Not now! Ashe thought.

The major reared up in front of the window as he forced himself to his feet and stumbled towards Haywood.

If anything, Haywood's face grew calmer in response to the rather lame attack. It put him back on the defensive and he knew how to handle that.

"Get back!" Ashe said, tugging Walsingham to one side as Haywood pulled the trigger and put a shell straight into the major's face. A light spray of blood and the lumpen, scrambled egg of brain matter came through the window, glinting slightly as it caught the moonlight.

Now! Ashe thought, *while he reloads!*

He pulled his revolver from his pocket and tried to get an aim through the window. Helen had got to her feet – maybe making a break for the door – and was in the way. He pushed himself through the window, old muscles demanding to know what he thought he was doing. As he hit the floor on the other side he heard the sound of a shell clicking into place and realised he'd been an idiot... started to believe those movies for a minute there, he thought, stupid old man. He rolled onto his back, his left arm throbbing from where he had dropped his weight on it. Hope it's not broken... not that it'll matter in a second...

"Sorry," he said, dropping the gun and holding his hands out in as deferential manner as he could.

Haywood was pointing the rifle between Ashe and Helen, his pupils bloated black bullet-holes swamping the irises. He didn't fire but that was as lucky as Ashe was going to get. He glanced at the body of the major, his head now no more than a fur collar of that salt and pepper beard.

"Need to think," Haywood said, edging to the door, shaky on his feet but not letting the rifle lose its aim. He pulled back the bolt and stood out of the way. "Come in," he called to Walsingham, who needed no further encouragement.

"Helen," he said as entered, "are you alright?"

"Just marvellous thank you darling," she replied.

"Need to think," Haywood repeated. He used the rifle to gesture Helen over to the door. "Outside."

This is not good, Ashe thought, in a moment this whole situation was going to become untenable. "You don't want to go out there, Haywood," he said, shifting on the floor and grimacing as he placed a flat palm in Kilworth's still warm blood.

"Need to think," the doctor said again, his mind spasming now, stuck on a single track and seeming unable to veer from it. He gestured with the rifle again.

Helen grabbed her coat and walked out of the door.

"Don't, Helen!" Walsingham begged.

"If you have an alternative I'd be glad to hear it," she said, tugging on her coat as she walked.

Haywood shifted sideways to the door, keeping the rifle moving, switching back and forth between Walsingham, Ashe and Helen's retreating back.

"Need to think," he said, one more time, "don't follow."

Yeah right, thought Ashe, like that's going to happen.

Haywood vanished through the door and they listened to his steps descend the wooden stairs.

"What are we to do?" Walsingham asked, close to tears. He wasn't cut out for this sort of thing, Ashe realised. He was a man of display cases and samples, quiet dinner parties and lecture tours. Well, he was going to have to learn… He grabbed the revolver from where it was beginning to stick in the major's blood and moved to the door. He looked out, could just see Haywood and Helen crossing towards the main gate. He didn't trust his aim. If he missed then Haywood would have all the time he needed to shoot Helen. He was only likely to get one chance at this so he'd better be damn sure it was the right one.

"We follow them," he said to Walsingham, "what else can we do?"

8.

Helen Walsingham stumbled ahead of Haywood, screwing her face against the cold wind as she stepped off the wooden steps and into the thin coating of snow in the courtyard. Behind her Haywood showed none of the same signs of discomfort – madness was the warmest outfit of all. "Keep walking," he said, "go to the gate."

She shuffled forward, her toes suddenly colliding with something on the floor. In the light of the torches she could see it was a small wooden box, the one Spencer had handed to her husband – for certainly she had been watching, eye pressed against the crack in the shutter, she hadn't intended to let them out of her sight for any longer than she needed to. If it's so important, she thought, then it can come with me. She stooped and grabbed it, moving as quickly as she could so as not to antagonise Haywood.

"What was that?" he asked, not quite delusional enough to have missed it.

"Dropped something," she replied, saying no more and walking quickly towards the gate and the monk that stood guard against it.

"Help me?" she asked quietly. Whether the wind was too loud for him to hear or he just didn't understand she couldn't be sure.

"Don't talk to him," Haywood insisted, having jogged up behind her, the barrel of the rifle pressing into the small of her back. "We want to leave," he shouted at the monk. Again the Tibetan made no response. Haywood pointed at the gate. "Open it!"

Still no response. Helen suspected the monk knew only too well what Haywood wanted but was disinclined to give it to him.

Glancing over his shoulder, only too aware even in his drugged state that they would be followed soon enough, Haywood lost his patience. With a yell he swung the rifle's butt at the monk's head, clubbing him to the floor. "Open it!" he screamed at Helen, pointing the gun at her once more.

She did as she was told, straining as she pulled the heavy bolt to one side and pushed at the gate. Haywood surged forward, the barrel of the rifle nearly cutting her cheek as he came alongside her and threw his own weight against the door. It swung open and he kicked out at her, forcing her outside.

"We'll freeze to death out there!" she insisted. You before me though, she thought, there's that slim chance.

"Need to think!" Haywood roared, raising the rifle as if he meant to shoot her here and now, no more deliberation.

She turned on her heels and moved out onto the mountainside, moving as quickly as her legs could manage.

9.

Ashe took the time to pull on his warm clothing and insisted that Walsingham did the same. "We're no use to her if we're crippled by exposure," he insisted. "If he wanted to shoot her he'd have done it already, we just have to hope she doesn't do anything to antagonise him."

"This is my wife we're talking about," Walsingham moaned, pulling on his coat and gloves despite his protestations. "She does little else but antagonise people."

"I think you'll find most people can be polite when at the end of a gun," Ashe replied, tugging his hat over his head and ushering Walsingham out of the door.

They moved quickly down the steps, Ashe scanning the ground beneath the balcony, hoping for sign of the box. There was none. Kusang walked towards them. "Your friend just clubbed one of the monks down," he said, "and took the woman out there. It would be better I think were they not to come back."

"Hang around," said Ashe, "one of them probably won't."

They moved to the open gate, Ashe sticking his head around the opening to make sure they weren't going to march right into fire from Haywood's rifle.

"The minute I get a clear shot," he said to Walsingham, "I'll take it. This needn't end badly for anyone but Haywood." Still, at the back of his head, none of it sat right. Haywood was high, that was clear enough, but Ashe had convinced himself that the man was no murderer. Not that he should trust his instincts on that… as he had to keep reminding himself, he was an ex-college professor, not Columbo. But he did know something about murderers didn't he? After all, didn't he used to be one? You still are… he thought, remembering the feel of discharging his pistol at Whitstable, that raving lunatic who had been so determined to slit Sophie's throat. Oh yes, it seemed he knew a lot about murder once you really got down to it.

"Just kill him," Walsingham begged, his tears turning to a rime of ice around his squinting eyelids. "The first chance you get…"

Ashe nodded – after all what else could he do? – and they marched out into the snow.

10.

Walsingham had a heavy electric flashlight which he shone sporadically into the dark, checking on the footprints left by his wife and Haywood. Ashe found the device frustrating rather than helpful, it could only be used in short bursts, the bulb and old batteries needing constant rest periods between. He thought they were probably better off using the light of the moon and told Walsingham so.

"All you're doing is signalling to him," he said, "letting him know where we are."

Walsingham nodded, poking the device back into his coat and trudging behind Ashe in silence.

It wasn't as if their quarry was that far ahead, reasoned Ashe, they could be almost on top of them for all he knew. The wind stole away any noise but its own, if Haywood was still screaming then it was lost to them.

The ground undulated in the incline leading away from the monastery, Ashe always afraid that they would stride over one of the peaks of snow only to come face to face with the crazy doctor and his rifle. He held his gun with the safety off, his finger looped out of the trigger guard so that he didn't risk stumbling and blowing his own foot off.

"There!" said Walsingham, pointing towards a mound in the distance. Ashe saw the silhouettes for himself. One was sat down, the other pacing... Ashe could guess who was who.

"Okay," he shouted in Walsingham's ear. "We need to play this carefully." He looked at the terrain leading up to the next mound, they would be visible as they descended into the next dip but hopefully hidden from view by the gradient as they climbed the other side. "We need to take the next drop quickly," he shouted, "if we can just get to the lowest point without being seen we'll have surprise on our side."

Walsingham nodded, though Ashe was only too aware that, with his wife now in view, he was barely listening. He had only one thought in mind and Ashe could sympathise with that blinkered attitude only too well. For Walsingham, life was all about Helen, to Ashe it was Sophie. They weren't so different.

Ashe waited until it appeared that Haywood had his back to them before grabbing Walsingham's arm and yanking them both over the summit of the mound. This was the worst moment, the point when the two of them would be just as visible against the moonlight as Haywood and Helen. He moved as fast as he could in the thick snow, not running so much as flinging them down the side of the slope, great flurries of snow kicking up all around them. He tightened his grip on the revolver, not taking his eyes off Haywood for a second as they barrelled into the dip. Walsingham lost his footing, stumbling forward into a roll and pulling Ashe after him. Ashe let himself go, better that than lose momentum, he reckoned. The pair of them tumbled like a pair of kids through the drift, gathering snow to them as they went.

They hit the lowest point and Ashe was only too grateful for the thickness of snow as his body had taken enough knocks already. Gesturing for Walsingham to keep low, they began to climb the far side, moving in a half crawl as they ascended the slope.

As they got closer the sound of Haywood's shouting began to descend towards them, the wind changing direction and carrying it to them rather than stealing it away. There wasn't much sense in the words – was there much sense in any of this? – but the fever pitch that Haywood had been building towards back at the stables had well and truly hit its crescendo.

Slowly they approached the peak, Haywood and Helen now only feet away. Ashe tried to catch a breath, determined to enter this moment as calm and focused as possible. He was about to take another life, the knowledge of that tightening his muscles more than even this damned cold could manage. Was this the way of things now? Was this the role he was trapped into playing, the man on the business end of death time and again? It seemed so.

Walsingham, mistaking Ashe's pause for uncertainty – and maybe he was right – charged over the mound, running towards Haywood with that stupid flashlight in his hand, held aloft like a club. Ashe had little time to react, raising his gun even as Walsingham blocked his clear aim. Somebody else is about to die… Ashe thought, a stupid husband driven lunatic by his obsession for a cold and probably unfaithful wife. Haywood raised the rifle, Helen, shaking from the cold, got to her feet. Here it is, Ashe thought, here comes the gunfire…

But Haywood didn't shoot Walsingham, he pulled the trigger sure enough but his aim was still on Helen. What came next was beyond Ashe's comprehension for a moment – but only a moment – he had got better at understanding the impossible these days. Helen vanished, just as the rifle fired. She had tumbled backwards, aware as Ashe had been that the moment had come for a trigger to be pulled. Then she was gone, a great cloud of snow erupting around her that settled to nothing. No, not nothing... even in that meagre light, Ashe caught a glimpse of the box. A dark shape against the white, a tiny glint of the moonlight on its hinges. Then Walsingham was on Haywood, the roar that erupted from him as unlikely a sound for the mild botanist as a barking horse. He brought the flashlight down, and even over the roar of the wind Ashe heard the crack of bone and wood as it met Haywood's skull. The doctor tumbled back, his mad eyes bulging further still. Walsingham hammered them back into their sockets, pounding and pounding with the flashlight, no more able to stop his attack than a bullet can change its course.

Ashe cleared the summit and grabbed at Walsingham, dropping his – miraculously unfired – revolver into the snow so that he could loop his arms under Walsingham's. He felt a muscle in his stupid old back pop as Walsingham raged against him, determined to continue his assault on the man who had threatened his wife. There was nothing more to be achieved in that regard, it didn't take more than moonlight to tell that. Haywood's forehead was caved in, his mouth slack, eyes white. Walsingham had done what his rage had demanded. Now it was all just fire with nothing to burn.

"He's dead!" Ashe screamed into Walsingham's ear. "Quit it! He's dead!"

Eventually Walsingham did, falling back against Ashe, the pair of them on their backs in the snow. The splintered and bloody flashlight was still fixed to Walsingham's hand. Ashe imagined he would have an effort letting go.

"He shot her." Walsingham moaned eventually. "After everything... he shot her."

No he didn't, Ashe thought, at least I don't think so. The box did its job just in time. Though you may wish she had taken the bullet later.

"I killed him," Walsingham said, his voice so quiet that Ashe could barely hear it even though the man's head was right next to his.

"I know," Ashe replied.

"Not Haywood," Walsingham replied. "Rhodes. I killed him."

Ashe sighed, finding that once it was said he had somehow known that too.

"Shouldn't have been fornicating with my wife." Walsingham said.

He said nothing more.

11.

Eventually, Ashe pulled himself out from underneath Walsingham and walked over to where Helen had vanished. He checked the snow for blood as best he could, it seemed there was none. "Vanished in time," he said to himself, picking up the box and putting it back into his coat pocket. He moved over to Walsingham, who was now utterly lost to himself, staring up into the falling snow as blindly as Haywood only a few feet away.

"Come on," said Ashe, slapping his face until he saw a sign of life. "Helen's not dead." Yet anyway...

"Not dead?" Walsingham asked, his voice still thin and dreamy.

"No, so get on your feet and follow me."

Ashe began the march back down the mountainside. He didn't check to see if Walsingham followed, once he'd got through to him he knew the man had little choice. He would follow Ashe to ends of the Earth if that's what it took to find his wife. It disgusted Ashe, though mostly because he disgusted himself.

"Where is she?" Walsingham asked, skittering along next to him. "Where has she gone."

"You'll see," said Ashe and would say nothing more.

12.

Ashe half wondered if they would be refused entry to the monastery but, for once, Kusang's willingness to talk seemed to have acted in their favour. "Did you kill him?" the Tibetan asked as they appeared at the gate. "That crazy man of yours... did you kill him?"

"Yeah," said Ashe, "we killed him. No more talking now. Tomorrow... we'll talk all you like tomorrow."

For once Kusang didn't argue, whether it was the look in Ashe's eyes or just the relief that there was blood on the mountainside that wasn't his, Ashe neither knew nor cared. He walked up the stairs to the room above the stables, Walsingham trotting along behind him.

Inside their accommodation, Ashe went straight to Haywood's food bowl, picked it up and sniffed it. There was a bitter smell there, sure as hell wasn't the meat. "Poisoned," Ashe said. "No more a drug addict than he was a murderer..." then he saw the dead body of the major and, for a moment, changed his mind.

But no, the major's death was no more the fault of Haywood than an abused dog could be blamed for biting its owner.

"Poisoned!" he shouted at Walsingham, who was now shaking by the front door. "You?"

"I don't know what you mean…"

Ashe shook his head, flinging the bowl against the wall. No, not Walsingham, he would never endanger his wife. "Close the door," he told him, "tight. I don't want that bastard Kusang eavesdropping and neither do you."

No, Walsingham wouldn't have poisoned Haywood. To do that would risk endangering all of them – *had* endangered all of them – so that must have been Helen. So scared of the doctor in the party recognising her condition that she spiked his goddamned food. "Stupid bitch!" Ashe hissed, kicking at the wall.

He was close to snapping, couldn't believe the mess he'd wandered into. Petty, selfish, obsessive, hateful… the only two members of the party he might have had time for were dead due to the sickening attitudes of the rest of them.

"Where is she?" asked Walsingham.

Ashe charged at him, holding him up against the wall, his old arms only too up for the job now they had anger to fuel them. "Where you'll never find her unless you do exactly as I say," he spat, "understand me? Because you've fucked everything. Your wife most of all." He let go of him, Walsingham's face crumpling as he began to cry.

"Don't snivel," Ashe said, pulling the box from his pocket before thinking to glance at his watch. Just over twenty minutes left until his train… it would seem a lifetime if he was to spend it with Walsingham. "This box," he said, "is more dangerous than you could know." He rattled it in Walsingham's face. "It took your wife and only I can get her back."

Walsingham was predictably glassy-eyed at this. "But it's just…"

"It's not 'just' anything." Ashe pushed his face closer to Walsingham's. "Same deal as before, I need you to get Carruthers here – and no mention of any of this…"

Walsingham was shaking his head. Of course he was, whatever he told people about tonight it would have precious little to do with the truth.

"You get Carruthers here and you put this box in his hands… he'll be safe, Helen will be safe…" Oh how easily the lies come these days… "but only if you do it exactly as I tell you. Do you understand?"

"Of course," Walsingham took the box, "and your masters? You know, the government…"

Ashe had forgotten all about that little lie. He was a government man wasn't he? Occupied on weighty matters of state. "They will be suitably grateful that no mention of what you've done will leak out."

"And Helen will be safe?"

Oh one more, what the hell? Once you've started what use is stopping. "Safe and delivered back to you. But one mistake…"

"I won't make any mistakes."

"Better not, because if you do then not only will you be named as the murderer of Rhodes, Haywood and Kilworth but we'll make sure everyone knows you killed your wife too."

Walsingham's face crumpled then and the rest of him wasn't far behind. He slumped to the floor in tears, clutching the box. "I love her," he said, "that's all."

"Yeah," Ashe sighed, "tell it to the dead."

He drew back the bolt and walked outside. Kusang

was predictably close, Ashe beckoned him over. "Haywood killed all of them," he told him, in a voice loud enough for Walsingham to still hear. "He brained Rhodes, shot Kilworth and Helen and very nearly saw to us too."

"The bodies?"

Ashe shook his head. "Leave them. There's nothing of worth to bury."

He walked down the steps, across the courtyard and out the front gate. Nothing could have made him look back.

13.

"It will find you," the Controller had said after handing Ashe the tickets. Ashe didn't doubt it, the House had miracles to spare. It couldn't come soon enough for his liking. Not just to get him out of the cold but also the whole mess he had left behind. He had known that these trips would end up bringing the worst out in him, how could they not? He was now the ultimate pragmatist, he would do whatever needed to be done, all in the name of that damned box. It made him want to retch.

Once he had got far enough away from the monastery, the landscape hiding it from view. He stopped walking and checked his watch.

"Come on then damn you," he called into the wind, kicking at the snow to keep his legs moving.

It burst out of the air as if tearing the night in half. Great waves of ice sprayed out from either side, like the curved wings of a bird in a child's drawing. Ashe couldn't bring himself to feel the least impressed, waiting for it to stop then climbing aboard and settling into an empty carriage. As the engine built up steam to pull out he lifted his gun out of his pocket and dumped it on the seat next to him. It was sticky with Major Kilworth's blood.

"Not even fired but still painted in death," Ashe whispered as the train shot away back towards the House.

14.

The warmer months brought a small thaw to the valley in which Dhuru lay. It also brought soldiers.

Roger Carruthers – the renowned explorer, essayist and gourmand – was nervous in the mixed company but the mystery of what lay ahead made him tolerate it. The English were no longer so welcome in Tibet, if there had ever been a time when they truly were. The Tibetan soldiers that approached from one side of the valley – just as he and his party approached from the other – might mean conflict. Not that he was a stranger to such unsteady political situations – in his travels he had seen three civil wars, an invasion and a slave's revolt – but the idea that the day might end in crossfire was both fearful and irritating. He hoped Nigel was alright. The tone of his letter had been brusque to say the least, not to mention enigmatic to the point of blatant obfuscation. Not like old Nigel, he had thought, not like old Nigel at all.

As his party approached the monastery, Carruthers could see Nigel Walsingham appear at the main gate. "An eager welcome," he murmured to one of the soldiers that accompanied him, a fresh-faced fellow from Portsmouth that Carruthers had taken a liking to. The boy had the restless feet of an explorer in him, Carruthers had decided, and he had put it on himself to encourage the chap to wander as soon as the opportunity arose.

"Probably scared of the opposition, sir," the soldier replied, nodding towards the Tibetan soldiers who were now only a few yards away from the monastery themselves.

"Roger!" Walsingham shouted, "thank goodness! I've been going spare waiting for you to arrive."

"Well, rest easy now old chap," Carruthers replied, "though we may have a somewhat awkward clash of opinion with the locals forthcoming."

"Never mind that," Walsingham snapped, shoving a small wooden box into Carruthers' hands.

"What's this old chap?" Carruthers asked. "Not sure it's quite the time or place for…"

A gunshot rang out and the soldiers around him snapped their rifles to their shoulders just as the Tibetans, mere feet away did the same.

"Who fired?" shouted Carruthers. "Damn it! Who fired?"

It was too late to worry about the finer details of that, as one of the Tibetans, no doubt convinced that the English meant to shoot them down, fired his rifle.

One shot can almost be tolerated, when two have fired it will always bring more… both sides took their aim and pulled their triggers. Carruthers shouting in the middle of it, dropping to the ground where he appeared to vanish as if he had dived into water, not solid, Tibetan earth.

A little way up the mountain, Ashe – who had fired the first shot – watched Walsingham run back towards Dhuru Monastery, hands above his head, screaming impartiality all the way. Ashe pointed the barrel of his revolver at him, wondering if it might not be better if he just…

He put the gun away, quickly and with disgust. This is not who I am, he thought as he walked back into the mountains to catch his train.

THREE
Where People go to Die (1)

1.

Miles ran along the platform, Carruthers striding along-side. Tom ambled behind. "Come on!" Miles shouted, "Or the bloody thing will leave without us."

"And that would be a real bummer," Tom mumbled.

Ghost passengers darted around them, performing that elaborate commuter dance designed to gain a few inches on your fellow passenger. Miles reached the tail-end of the train. A large sticker on the window announced that it was first class.

"Why not?" Miles said. "May as well grab every inch of illusory luxury we can."

"One would never travel another way," Carruthers assured him with a smile.

They climbed through the open door, Miles strolling along the aisle until he found an empty table. Carruthers wedged his pack on the baggage shelf and sat down with a contented sigh. Tom followed a few seconds later, slumping into the corner.

"I can see you're going to be great company," mumbled

Miles. Tom pulled out a packet of cigarettes.

"Are those real?" Miles asked, changing his mind about Tom's value instantly.

Tom shook one into his mouth. "No, you're dreaming them."

"I mean: did they come from the real world?" Miles explained. "You didn't find them here?"

Tom shook his head, scooting the pack across the table to Miles with a flick of his fingers. Miles pulled out a slightly crooked cigarette with all the reverence of a holy relic, sniffing it and stroking it back into shape.

"You going to smoke it or fuck it?" Tom asked. He lit his own cigarette and held his flickering Zippo out to Miles.

"You have no idea how much I've been craving one since I got here," Miles explained. "I am a man of addictions."

Tom didn't reply to that, was too concerned he'd wind up on the subject of drink. He wasn't in the mood for a heart to heart. Wasn't in the mood for much more than climbing under the table and seeing if he could will himself out of existence. He offered the pack to Carruthers.

"No thank you," the explorer said. "An evening cigar is the limit of my tobacco needs."

"You don't know what you're missing," Miles enthused, huffing a cloud of smoke into the face of a phantom ticket inspector.

"Oh to be so easily pleased," Carruthers commented with a smile.

Tom stretched out on the double seat, letting his legs jut into the aisle.

"Listen," said Miles, feeling that they should build a relationship with the man, "if you want to talk about…"

"I don't."

"Okay, but, you know, if you did…"

"I don't."

"Fine."

Carruthers raised his eyebrow at Miles but wouldn't be drawn into the attempts at conversation. There was a loaded moment of silence, the sort that can reduce a guilty man to tears and confession. Try as he might, Miles couldn't bear it for long.

"So what do you do for a living?"

"Play piano."

"Oh! Cool... like in a band or something?"

"A bar."

"Right, and that keeps you in the essentials does it?"

"The essentials come free with the job, kind of why it suits me."

"Right." Miles felt like an irate driver, stuck behind the wheel of a car with a flat battery. There was just no way of getting this conversation turning over. "I was in antiques." Tom gave a disinterested nod.

Miles decided to give up, Tom would either open up or he wouldn't. Carruthers had removed his battered journal from the hip pocket of his jacket and was contentedly making notes.

"What are you writing about?" Miles asked.

Carruthers smiled. He might have known that Miles would shift his attention to him.

"I am chronicling our trip," he said. "One never knows, on my return to the correct time and place there may be a book in it."

"Weird book," said Miles. "I'd read it."

He smoked the rest of his cigarette and watched the ghostly passengers fill the seats around them. A translucent woman fought to cram a holdall in the overhead rack, Miles stood up, meaning to help before remembering how pointless it would be. A pair of business men occupied the table across from them, dropping their briefcases onto the spare seats to dissuade anyone else from sitting down. Miles watched an elderly lady shuffle her way along the aisle. A small terrier in her arms matched her fur hat. She looked around at the empty seats, eyeing her fellow passengers with the sort of open disapproval ladies of a certain age reserve for absolutely everyone else in the world. She marched over to their table and sat directly on his lap.

"For fuck's sake," Miles moaned, shifting around inside the ethereal woman. Her little terrier stared at him and began to bark. "Little shit…" Miles involuntarily lashed out as the dog made to nip him on the nose. "The thing's not even real, how come it can see me?"

"Or sense you." Carruthers added, scribbling an excited note in the margin of his notebook.

"I'll put that pencil *in* you in a minute," Miles snapped, irritated. The dog continued to bark, the noise muted, one step removed from their reality, but loud enough to be annoying. The rest of the passengers clearly thought so too as, one by one, they began to complain. The elderly lady scrunched up her face and basked in her unpopularity. After a few moments – perhaps realising her position was untenable – she stood up and marched out of the carriage, the dog straining over her shoulder to continue barking at Miles.

"So," said Tom, removing another cigarette from the pack, "you're good with animals then?"

"Normally," Miles replied, "it's just illusory ones that don't like me."

"Fascinating isn't it?" asked Carruthers. "They're clearly not quite as illusory as we had imagined!"

"Fascinating." Tom choked off his lopsided curls inside a large flat cap he'd found at the station, yanking the brim down over his eyes. "I reckon I'll think about it quietly to myself." He slouched back, getting as comfortable as it was possible to be – which wasn't very – and sucked on his cigarette.

"Don't worry," said Carruthers, "from our experience the journey is unlikely to be long."

"Cool."

Carruthers looked baffled for a moment and then nodded. "Splendid, two travelling companions who speak an almost alien language to me, what fun we'll have."

Tom's lips curled into a smile around the tip of his cigarette. "Just chill daddy-o, everything's copacetic. You'll get the skinny on my jive talk after we've been groovin' a little."

"I can speak upwards of six languages," Carruthers sighed, "including classical Greek and Latin…"

"Oolcay orfay ouyay anmay," Tom chuckled.

Carruthers threw his hands in the air. "I give up!"

"Ytray otnay otay ebay ootay uchmay ofway anway assholeway." Miles said to Tom, not to be outdone in Pig Latin.

Tom gave another smile. "I'll try."

"Have you both gone completely mad?" Carruthers asked. "Am I suffering from some unfortunate mental condition that has rendered all speech utterly incomprehensible?"

"You should be so lucky," said Miles as the train began to slow down. The darkness outside the windows fell away revealing an old-fashioned street outside. It was night and the lights of one of the nearby buildings did their best to beat away the shadows with flashes of green and red.

"Rosie O'Grady's Goodtime Emporium," Carruthers read, looking at the sign. "Please tell me that's not what it sounds like."

"I doubt it somehow," Miles replied, lifting Carruthers

bag down for him, "they don't tend to be quite as brazen in their advertising."

"In America," Carruthers replied, "one never knows."

They clambered off the train, concerned to discover it had come to a halt in the middle of the street. "I do hope nobody's watching…" said Carruthers, gesturing for the other two to be quick.

"If they are then Rosie's not doing her job," Tom replied.

"It's just a bar," said Miles, walking towards it.

"No such thing as 'just' a bar in my opinion," said Tom. "Let's wet our whistles shall we?"

"Shouldn't we figure out where we are first?" asked Carruthers

"Church Street," said Tom. "Read the signs, explorer boy."

He dashed inside, Miles and Carruthers having little choice but to follow.

2.

Inside the place was done out in a predictably retro style. Miles found himself thinking of New Orleans Riverboats and clean-suited cowboys.

"Well," said Carruthers, "America hasn't changed much."

"It's retro," Miles explained, "designed to look older than it is."

"Then it seems I'm not the only one with misgivings about your brave new future."

Tom made a beeline for the bar, so enthusiastically in fact that he nearly knocked a man over who was on his way out.

"Sorry, man," he said, grabbing the guy and steadying him on his feet. "Got a thirst on me that could kill a camel, y'know?"

"No harm," the man said, a short and round fellow who looked like he might do something in real estate. Tom thought he had the sort of fawn suit and thick moustache that just screamed "realtor".

"Buy you a drink?" asked Tom. "Just to show there's no misgivings."

"No need, honestly," the man replied, "I have a bitch of a day tomorrow, stayed too late as it is."

"What do you do?" Tom asked.

"I'm in property," the man said. Tom grinned, he still had his eye. "Ted Loomis… of Loomis Rentals?" he had the expectant air of a man who thinks he's a much bigger fish than he really is. "Say, let me give you a card."

"That would be cool," Tom said, beckoning Miles and Carruthers over.

"God damn it," Loomis whined, rifling through his pockets, "some son of a bitch has had my wallet."

"No!" said Tom, his face a perfect mask of disgust. He started looking around. "Did you see anyone suspicious?" he introduced Miles and Carruthers. "Hey guys, some bastard's just helped themselves to this guy's wallet. My friends," he said to Loomis, "Roger Carruthers, the explorer? And Miles Caulfield, one of the biggest antiques dealers in Europe. We're here on a bit of business. This is Ted Loomis," he said to Miles and Carruthers, "of Loomis Rentals no less."

"My condolences on your property, good sir," said Carruthers, "if we can assist in catching the rogue then consider us at your service."

"Kind of you fellers but whoever took it's likely long gone."

"Yeah," said Miles, "not going to hang around here is he?"

"Look," Tom insisted, "let me get you that drink. Just

a quick measure of something to take the edge off. I'd feel bad letting you just wander off."

Loomis was certainly a man who liked a drink. Besides, you didn't meet two well-connected Brits every day, there might even be a bit of business in it. The chatty guy didn't look like much, tatty suit and flat cap, and that hair hadn't seen a pair of scissors for a summer or two. Still, these bohemian sorts were often loaded. Probably an artist or something, one of those weird bastards who threw paint at a wall and called it a masterpiece. "Hell with it," he said, "I'll have a whisky and soda if you insist, just a small one though."

"Great!" said Tom. "You guys grab a table and I'll get us watered."

"Erm… I'll have a beer," said Miles, "you know, in case you were wondering." He wandered off towards an empty table, Loomis following behind.

"I don't suppose they might have a sherry?" asked Carruthers

"No, I don't suppose they might. Have a man's drink for Christ's sake."

"Ah… well, might as well go native I suppose."

"When in Rome…"

"Mind the lions, yes… I shall try one of those Harvey Wallbangers if I may. That sounds masculine enough."

Tom rolled his eyes. "Harvey Wallbanger it is. Now go and find out whereabouts we need to head to."

"Beg pardon?"

"Why do you think I was making friends with the guy? He's local… find out whereabouts it is that Chester turns up."

"You're sharper than I had given you credit," Carruthers smiled. "Rest assured I shall not underestimate you again."

"Cool… I think."

"I take it you have enough money to cover the bill?"

Tom pulled Ted Loomis' wallet from his trouser pocket and smiled appreciatively at the thick wad of notes inside. "More than enough," he said. "Take a seat, I'll bring 'em over."

3.

It took Tom a little while to arrive with the drinks. He had been slightly, though not *hugely*, delayed by the triple bourbon he had necked at the bar – just to give him a little step up the ladder as it were – that and the fact that he wanted to transfer Loomis' money and cards into his own wallet. No need to take too many risks, after all. He dropped the now empty wallet into the open purse of a loud-mouthed creature whose appetite for the cocktail menu seemed matched only by her lust for the barmen who tirelessly poured them for her.

By the time he arrived at the table Loomis had regained his confidence and was regaling Miles and Carruthers with thrilling adventures in the world of real estate. They both looked about thrilled enough to kill him.

"Oh hey!" Loomis said. "Here he is, the man with the provisions."

"Damn right," said Tom, placing the drinks on the table, "here's to hairs on your chest."

Carruthers raised an eyebrow at that but was used to the conversation enough by now not to take it too literally. "Our new friend here has been telling us about a construction project he's involved in that may be of interest," he told Tom.

"Home Town," said Loomis. "It'll be the biggest draw around these parts, may God strike me down if I tell a lie."

Tom wished he believed enough in God to hope for just that. Experience told him that a truthful realtor was a rare breed.

"Sounds interesting," Tom heard himself say; that bourbon must be working its magic already, he thought.

"It's a cross between a mall and a theme park," Loomis explained, "all themed around fifties America, you know, lots of Chrome and jukeboxes... few Chevys parked here and there."

And we're discussing this because...? Tom wondered.

"I brokered the deal myself," Loomis continued, "had that patch of land along Highway 192 for a couple of years now, just waiting for the right buyer. It's just shy of the interstate, perfect accessibility."

A small bell began to ring at the back of Tom's speedily mellowing head. He glanced at Miles who gave a slight nod. Well, okay... now Tom was more interested. It seemed they might have found their location. Small world... Tom thought. Who would credit that they'd be dropped off at the right place and time to meet this guy? Little did he know that, many miles – and years – away Ashe had been having similar thoughts. The House seemed to be placing them just where they needed to be. He attacked his drink, wondering why it was still being so rude as to not be on the inside of his body. Oops, looked like he'd finished that one...

"We should think of ordering some food," suggested Miles, noticing the speed with which Tom was drinking.

"Or some more drinks?" Tom countered. Nobody else had put a serious dent into theirs. Though Carruthers was clearly enjoying his "masculine" Harvey Wallbanger.

"Most refreshing," he said after taking a mouthful.

"Say, what is it you guys are up to here anyway?" said Loomis, determined to suss out whether there was any business to be had.

"We're meeting up with a friend of ours," Miles said.

"And looking into sites for a new antiques outlet," added Tom, knowing how to keep a man like Loomis on the hook.

"Well, hell…" Loomis said, with a grin so wide you might think he was trying to eat his own moustache off. "You should come over and take a look at the Home Town construction, we've some prime units left."

"Maybe we should at that," agreed Tom.

"Definitely," Loomis reached for his jacket, "let me give you a card… oh shit it…" he remembered he'd lost his wallet. "I can give you my number if one of you guys has a pen?"

Carruthers pulled his pencil and notebook out of his rucksack. "By all means," he said, opening the book at a blank page and offering it to Loomis.

Loomis wrote down his number, adding his name underneath with the sort of flourish that befitted a rock star rather than a beige-suited hawker of bricks and mortar. "You just give me a call in the morning," he said. "And I'll get you guys over. Damn sure you won't regret it."

He drained his drink and got to his feet. "Look forward to hearing from you!"

"We'll give you a call first thing," Tom said. "Before you go, don't suppose you know a hotel around here?"

"Hell yeah, there's the Plaza just round the corner, give 'em my name and they'll treat you special, use the place for a lot of business."

Tom wondered if that was the sort of business that had secretaries sitting awkwardly in their office chair for the rest of the afternoon.

"Great, we'll be sure to do that."

Loomis offered another of those huge, *grotesque*, smiles and made his way out of the bar.

"Well," said Miles, "he's lovely. Our new best friend."

"More drinks!" said Tom.

Carruthers drained his Harvey Wallbanger. "More drinks and food," he said. "Then we can see about this hotel our 'new best friend' has suggested."

"Night's young," grinned Tom, dashing to the bar.

4.

In the end it was Carruthers that forced them to leave, his enjoyment of the cocktails having been over and above his ability to process them. They had seen their way through a round of burgers – with Carruthers insisting on eating his with a knife and fork naturally – followed by several more rounds of drinks. Miles, having stuck to beer, survived the intake. Tom was born to deal with it, Carruthers on the other hand... They had to drag him out of there before he caused problems they could well do with out. After five minutes climbing through the decorative plants, begging the band to shut up and then talking to a black guy in a "curious dialect I picked up while cruising along the Zambezi" they decided it was leave or end up throwing punches. Neither Miles nor Tom fancied their odds on the latter so leave they did.

They got a cab to drop them at the hotel. A towering construction that offered the sort of faux opulence that only *slightly* rich people can afford. The sort of class that rubs off if you lean on it too hard, all glitter and plastic flowers. They didn't care, it was a step up from their recent accommodation. Tom introduced them to the old guy behind reception as "clients of Ted Loomis" offering him Ted's card to run a tab. "That Ted, he sure knows how to look after a guy," he whispered, "I've never known such a big spender!"

The receptionist – tired and wanting nothing more from the rest of his shift than a few chapters of the Ira Levin novel he had on the boil – just nodded and took an imprint of the card. He knew Loomis well enough not to give two shits whether these drunken assholes broke the man's card in two. He handed them a key each and wished them a good night in the neutral tone employed by night shift receptionists everywhere. The sort of tone that says "get the hell to your rooms and stop bothering me, I'm pulling minimum wage and my give-a-fuck threshold is way too low tonight". Tom had no problem with that, took the keys and wished the guy well.

He and Miles bundled Carruthers into the elevator, ignoring his mumbled "because even the stairs that move are too much like hard work for some". They rode up to the tenth floor, the ping of the elevator bringing another drunken pronouncement from the explorer: "Tea is served!" he bellowed before promptly falling onto the hallway carpet and beginning to snore.

"I'll let you put the old man to bed," said Tom with a smile after helping Miles drag him as far as his room.

"Too kind," Miles replied, opening the door and rolling Carruthers inside.

Tom let himself into his own room, slung his jacket on a chair by the window and loaded a small selection of mini bar miniatures into his hat. He didn't bother with a glass, no need to stand on ceremony after all, just kicked off his shoes and lay down to quench the thirst that never died. For a short while he listened to the ruckus coming from the adjoining room as Miles tried to roll Carruthers into the bed. Eventually all fell quiet and Tom, lost in his own thoughts, realised he'd drained all his little bottles. Briefly he considered calling the old guy on reception to have more brought up but by then reaching for the phone was beyond him. He managed to knock the lights off and closed his eyes. He was asleep in moments.

A few hours later he was woken by the sensation of someone getting into bed with him. "Elise?" he asked.

"Go to sleep Tom," she replied.

He did so, crying all the way.

5.

Ted Loomis stumbled out into the gentle heat of the night. His anger at having his wallet stolen somewhat tempered by the glistening promise of cash on the horizon. He wasn't altogether sold on the three weirdos he'd met. But then he never could get his head around Brits – in his head they all wore bowler hats and had butlers, he was not a man that had travelled – so he put his reservations down to that. What the hell, either they would be a little gift from the Patron Saint of Realtors or they would wind up a waste of his time. Business as usual. He'd know for sure once he got them on site, Ted Loomis was a man who prided himself on being able to hear the first leathery creaks of a wallet opening or the death knell clang of it staying shut altogether. Tomorrow would tell.

He fished his car keys out of his pocket and let himself into the tan Oldsmobile that served as his home from home during days at the Home Town site. "Goddamn thing's bigger than my wife's ass," his golfing partner, Davey Lyons, had been heard to say, "and that's too big by a country mile." *So's your goddamned mouth*, Loomis frequently thought, but never said. Lyons had several of the Orlando councillors so deep in his pocket they tickled his balls. A man like that was just about as useful as you got. Which meant you laughed at his jokes, however lousy they were.

Loomis relaxed back into the Oldsmobile's easy-chair of a driving seat. He wanted to get home, shower and crash out on some clean sheets. He supposed he ought to call the bank first, get his cards struck out... Son of a bitch has probably already maxed them out, he thought... let the insurance deal with that shit, that's what it's there for. He was about to turn the ignition when someone tapped on his window. For a minute he wished he'd popped a couple of breath mints before getting in the car, last thing he needed was for some eager-beaver Trooper to catch the whiff of scotch on his breath and start getting clever. He'd lost enough money tonight without adding a fine. Then the man outside stooped down and Loomis caught a look at his face.

"Bones?" he asked, before realising he'd have to wind the window down if he expected to be heard. "What the fuck are you doing here?" he asked once the window was open.

"He's with me," said a small white guy appearing alongside him. "We fancied a chat."

He reached in and punched Loomis to the side of the head. Loomis went out instantly, headbutting the luxuriantly padded steering wheel of his precious car.

6.

Hughie Bones had no idea how best to respond to the presence of this new housemate. For certainly, that's how the stranger presented himself. He didn't make any demands – beyond a compulsive need to work his way through the local pizza takeout menu at least –

just sat in Hughie's front room, watching the TV and staring into space.

"What do you want?" Hughie had asked him one day.

"What does everyone want?" the man had replied, a cat's cradle of melted cheese strings hanging from his mouth as he worked his way through a fat slice of Meatball Madness with Extra Onions, "I want entertainment, amusement, distraction."

This seemed no kind of answer to Hughie and he said so.

"I just want to stretch my limbs a little," the stranger insisted, "I've been out of things for a while…"

"You've been inside?" Hughie asked. Though he'd never served time himself it was at least a concept he could relate to, as far as this guy was concerned that was rare.

"Yes," the stranger answered, "and now I'm free, so just relax and let me enjoy the fact will you?"

Hughie had little choice in the matter so did the only sane thing and left the man to it.

In the few days that his house had been invaded, Hughie's view of reality had been forever skewed. The worst wasn't the man's constant presence in his house – and it hadn't taken long for Hughie to use the word "man" loosely in the case of his visitor – rather the presence in his mind. To begin with he had dismissed the notion that the guy was taking a stroll around his thoughts as casually as he did the swamps. After a while he could deny it no more. He heard the man's voice, heard him comment on the things he found rattling around in Hughie's brain like discarded postcards of days gone by. He was like a tourist, cooing in interest at each new detail.

When Hughie slept, the sensation was worse. Often he would dream of his visitor, looking through his life like an enthusiastic desk clerk rummaging through a filing cabinet. He would wake even more tired than before he'd gone to sleep.

The final moment of proof had come the first time Hughie had tried to escape. Let him keep the goddamn house, he had thought… no great loss. He had run into the swamp, meaning to cut over to the Interstate and thumb his way as far from the invader as possible. He had been gone no more than five minutes by the time the stranger's voice began chuckling inside his head. "Where are you going, Hughie?" he had asked. "Don't you know it's rude for a host to abandon his guests?"

Hughie had thought himself quite mad, shouting at the flies that encircled him out there in the humid swamp. Crashing through the undergrowth with no concern about the creatures that might take a fancy to a piece of strolling T-Bone. "Go away!" he had screamed, opening up the skin of his knuckles as he punched the twisted trunk of a cypress tree.

Soon, robbed of all sense of direction through his panic and the sound of the man in his head, he had dropped, exhausted, into the undergrowth. After a few minutes he had walked home, legs moving almost independently of his own mind, nothing but a marionette brought back and laid down in the toy box for future games.

The second time had been much more cautious. Only too aware of his visitor's abilities – however impossible they might be – he had snuck out of the window in the middle of the night, like a teenager creeping away from his folks when he wanted to party. He had hopeful thoughts of a limited range to the man's powers, a zone around his old shack that, once breached, would see him away scot-free. He had no intention of risking the depths of the swamp this time, not in the dark. He made his way along the track that led from his home to the narrow access road that allowed the few houses around here to drive up to the Interstate and into civilisation. The ground was dry and it was easy going once his eyes got used to the lack of light. His head was mercifully silent as he approached the edge of his property. The visitor had been watching the television – wasn't he always? He had seen the second-hand flicker of a news station through the window as he had crept past. It was as if the guy had never seen the TV before, obsessed with everything it offered, from *Fox News* to *I Love Lucy* reruns. He was welcome to it, Hughie hoped it rotted his damned brain right out of his ears.

Just as he was about to cross onto the access road a light-headedness surged up from his shoulders, as if he'd stood up too fast. He fought to keep standing but failed miserably, toppling into the grass by the side of the track. What the hell was that? he wondered, his body fizzing with pins and needles and utterly uninterested in responding to his attempts to move.

"You really like to push your luck, don't you Hughie?" the stranger asked, floating into vision just above him. "You try a man's patience."

Hughie tried to reply but his mouth was as slack and useless as his legs.

"I've made no attempt to hurt you," the stranger continued, "beyond that little love-tap when we first met, anyway. Haven't I been a polite house guest?"

Oh yeah, thought Hughie, real polite. Made yourself right at home, in my house and my head.

"As if either were precious," the stranger replied. "Last chance, Hughie, do as your're told or I'm done with you. I'll leave you here to think about that." He walked out of Hughie's field of vision. "I'll make sure you're not lonely."

Hughie had a few minutes to wonder what that might mean until he felt the weight of something creeping along his leg and onto his chest. It was too dark to see clearly but the gentle rattle of the Diamondback told him all he needed to know. The first was joined by another and another, all curling their way around his limbs, hovering near the warm air-vent of his mouth, running their tongues over his clenched teeth. He had stayed like that until dawn, the first light ushering the snakes home to their inherited holes or onto rocks where they could bask in the heat. Eventually his legs twitched back into use again and he stumbled, aching and scared, back to his house.

The stranger was sat on his veranda, that slack-mouthed companion of his propped up on the swing seat next to him. Hughie had no idea what was wrong with this guy, he had all the life of a coma victim. "So," the stranger said, "what's your answer?"

"You know what it is," said Hughie, "I may not be much but I'm sure as hell not stupid. I won't try and leave again."

"Good man," the stranger replied, "now why not get a bit of shut eye? Looks like you didn't get a wink last night."

Hughie didn't grace that with a reply, though if the stranger was as at home in his thoughts as he suspected then he would hear Hughie's opinion of him clear enough. He pushed his front door open (having repaired the hole in his wall caused by the shotgun the door stuck like a bitch these days) and went straight to his room.

The stranger had been speaking the truth about his lack of interest in killing Hughie. In fact the stranger only lied if it amused him, he had no other cause to. Lies are a defensive strategy and he was impervious enough to harm not to need them. He had threatened this reality on leaving the House – had in fact been clear about the jeopardy it was already in – but he had no intention of tearing it apart just yet. What would be the point? As he had explained to Hughie, his only real interest was entertainment and there was a limit to how entertaining this world would be if he snuffed it out of existence. This was not to say that he had no intention of roughing it up a little. He did and would. But it should survive his attentions well enough for as long as it continued to amuse.

Hughie was also useful. He wasn't far from the truth when he had pictured the stranger rifling through his thoughts as if his head were a filing cabinet. It had only been a few years since the stranger had last walked this planet but they had been busy years. He found himself utterly enthralled by the things he saw in Hughie's mind. Not just the events that the man defined as major (the wars, the space missions, the assassinations) but also the trivia... He adored the television, he loved the pointless enthusiasm of it, its brightly-coloured shallowness, its lack of attention span. It would seem that mankind had taken one more step along the evolutionary ladder... it had made a number of scientific breakthroughs, advanced its thinking just that fraction... then promptly sat down and demanded to be entertained. To hell with advancement, mankind said, show me some cool shit and take me out of myself for awhile. Mankind had become just like him! He couldn't help but love them a little for that...

He looked across at Chester, little more than a dull flicker of consciousness surrounded by meat. "There's hope for you lot yet!" the stranger said, poking Chester's pallid cheeks.

Hughie had slept for awhile but the phone woke him just as he had begun to sink into worthwhile, deep sleep.

"Bones," he murmured, trying to rub his face awake.

"You're not fucking dead then?" Ted Loomis, his employer, shouted down the receiver. "I felt sure you must be, given that you hadn't showed up for work for two days."

Shit… This Hughie did not need.

"I've been real ill, Mr Loomis," he said, his voice sounding rough enough to convince, "tell the truth just now's the first time I've really woken up."

"Ill?" Loomis asked, damned if he was going to believe a word of it.

"Yes sir, sorry sir I should have called but it just kind of hit and I've been off my feet for…"

"Damn right you should have called!" Loomis shouted, "I run a respected business here, one that relies on people knowing that if they ask me to do something that something gets done. How do you think it looks when I get a phone call telling me that my staff haven't showed up?"

"Awful, Mr Loomis," Hughie said, omitting to suggest that perhaps Loomis could go and suck his own shit for a few days, he sure had the capacity for it. He needed his job and if that meant leaving things unsaid then that was just the way it would have to be.

"So what do you intend to do about it?" Loomis asked. Loomis liked it when his staff hanged themselves, he was happy to provide the rope, hell yes, but he much preferred it when they tied the knots themselves.

"I'll make up the time tomorrow, sir," Hughie promised. "I'll just pull a couple of double shifts until I'm caught up."

"Well now," Loomis' voice softened a touch, "just mind you do. I'd hate to have to replace you and that's a fact."

Sure it is, thought Hughie, you'd never find another nigger dumb enough to put up with your shit.

"That won't be necessary sir," Hughie said. "It'll all get cleared by the end of the week."

"Then we'll say no more about it." Loomis hung up, apparently determined to be true to his word.

"Motherfucker," Hughie whispered.

"Problem?" the stranger asked, loitering in Hughie's doorway.

"My boss," Hughie replied, "wondering where I've been."

"What did you tell him?"

"Said I was sick,"

"He believe you?"

"What the fuck do you care?"

The stranger shrugged. "Couldn't care less, you're quite right."

"I need my job," Hughie said.

The stranger shrugged again.

"Seriously, if I don't turn up tomorrow then Loomis will fire me, then I'm fucked."

The stranger wondered what business any of this was of his. He checked in Hughie's head about this "Loomis" he had mentioned and then drew up short. How interesting, he thought, there are patterns at work here...

"Tell me about the Home Town project," he said.

8.

Hughie hadn't known what to expect after the stranger had made it clear that they were going to go and talk to Loomis. It was the first time the guy had wanted to leave the house and that was good enough for him. He would be lying if he hadn't hoped there might be an opportunity to lose his new tenant somewhere along the line – though that had soon turned out to be a fruitless hope, he had dragged him around like a dog on a leash the whole time they were out. "Just look at all this," the man had said, taking in the sky-line of Orlando like a tourist, "how you've come on in just a few years."

"I'll take you to Disney World tomorrow," Hughie said, "you'll cream your pants."

The stranger looked at him askance, inclining his head like a bird on a telegraph wire listening to the hum of long distance calls. Hughie felt the tickle of the stranger's fingers inside his head, flipping through those mental folders one by one. The stranger chuckled.

"Maybe I would," he said.

Hughie didn't ask how the man had known where to find Loomis, didn't want to know. He wouldn't have understood the answer anyway so what was the point?

They watched his boss come strolling out of that new bar, the sound of Dixieland and the murmur of drunken happiness rolling behind him like the train of a wedding dress.

"That's his car," Hughie said, nodding towards the behemoth sat beside the sidewalk. "Damn thing's more comfortable than my house."

Loomis climbed behind the wheel and the stranger pushed Hughie forward. "Go and speak to him."

"And say what?"

The stranger dismissed the question with an irritated flick of his hands. "Doesn't matter."

Hughie walked forward, not having the first idea of

how this clusterfuck was likely to pan out, knowing only that it would. Things were coming to a head, the bizarre events of the last few days bubbling over. Things wouldn't be the same after tonight, that was for sure. He wasn't stupid enough to think he could do a thing about it one way or the other. *Hughie Bones*, he thought, *just another of life's passengers, here for the ride*. He tapped on Loomis' window.

His employer lurched in his seat, startled and afraid, just for a moment. Then he saw Hughie's face and, slowly, began to relax.

"Bones?" he saw him mouth before, irritated, he pressed the electric switch for the window and let some of the night in. "What the fuck are you doing here?"

Good question, Bones thought, before that phrase ran through his mind again: *just here for the ride. Some of us are always just sitting shotgun.*

"He's with me," the stranger said. "We fancied a chat."

Then he hit him, and just as he had done when he had popped Hughie's nose with the butt of his gun, the move appeared gentle and controlled. It was just as potent too, Loomis went out like someone had just pulled his plug, slumping in a dead weight over the wheel.

"Oh Jesus," Hughie whined. That was it, as predicted, no going back now…

"Shut up and drive," said the stranger. "Mr Loomis and I will keep each other company on the back seat."

Hughie did as he was asked, things were too far gone now to sweat the small stuff. He drove the car back out of the city, glancing at the rear-view mirror when Loomis woke up with an agonised moan.

"Shush," the stranger said. Hughie was unable to take his eyes off the mirror as the man pushed his index finger against the corner of Loomis' mouth and ran it across the man's lips. The lips came together like zippered fabric, the teeth vanishing beneath a perfect sheet of skin.

"Oh fuck..." Hughie whispered, snapping his eyes back to the road and wishing like hell that he hadn't seen that.

"Keep your eyes on the road, Hughie," the stranger said. "Safety first." Loomis was panicking... muffled noises puffing that smooth expanse of skin out in a fat bubble. "Shush now," the stranger whispered in the man's ear – though not quiet enough that Hughie couldn't hear, Christ how he wished otherwise – "or I'll seal those piggy little nostrils of yours too and you can suffocate, or split open your face with the pressure... whichever comes first."

Loomis kept quiet all the way back.

9.

Hughie parked the Olds out front of his house. He didn't like leaving it there... felt as if it was a flashing neon sign that would shout to any passers-by that Hughie was complicit in Loomis' abduction. But then he didn't get any passers-by, and he *was* complicit... complicit to the fucking hilt.

The stranger dragged Loomis into the house but Hughie had no intention of watching what came next. He grabbed one of those damned warm beers and sat outside, trying not to look at the slack face of Chester, still propped up in the corner of his veranda.

"Here's to not ending up like you," Hughie said, tipping the neck of the beer bottle towards the comatose man before draining half of it.

Carruthers woke to a pain behind the eyes that brought to mind his recent experience in the House library. Unfortunately the effects of Mr Wallbanger and his deceptively refreshing drink didn't have the same effect on his memory as the bookworms had. In fact he could remember the night before only too well. He would have been happier were it not so.

"You're a fool Roger Carruthers," he murmured, rubbing at his numb face.

He shuffled into the en suite bathroom and sat on the edge of the bath to decipher the controls. The taps were linked to a pipe that fuelled some form of shower contraption. Carruthers had heard of such things but never used one. He stared, bleary eyed, at the diagram on the side of the bath, turned on the taps and then yanked the handle that alleged to control the shower. A burst of cold water landed on his head making him roar in surprise. It was not the most noble of mornings. Once he had managed to control the temperature he stripped off and climbed in, standing under the jet of hot water and sighing as it attempted to beat away the brittle edges of his hangover. After a few minutes of woolgathering, he found the wrapped bar of soap and began using it. By the time he had finished he was willing to allow the future some merit. Showers were good, he could get quite fond of them in fact.

He towelled himself off and shuffled back into the bedroom. Being more aware of his surroundings than before his shower, he spotted a note propped up on the top of one of those viewing boxes they seemed to love so much in this century.

Morning! it said, *you will no doubt be feeling as rough as a donkey's arse.* Typical Miles, always concerned with rumps. *I'm in the room next door (704). Come and knock when you're awake and we'll have some breakfast.*

Breakfast. Carruthers wasn't convinced that he could survive such a thing.

He pulled on his clothes and went to the next room. Miles opened his door with a smile that made Carruthers' eyes hurt.

"Morning!" Miles said, in a voice too loud to be tolerable.

"Yes it is," Carruthers replied, "though I would be grateful were you not to be so enthusiastic about it."

Miles grinned again, but lowered his voice in sympathy. "Heavy night wasn't it?"

"It was a living hell, I am sure I shall never restore my reputation for as long as I live."

"Rubbish," Miles replied, "we've all ended up dancing with the decorative plants in our time."

"Speak for yourself," Carruthers' memory was clearly not as intact as he had believed, he had quite forgotten about the dancing. Though now Miles mentioned it an image flashed through his head of him trying to climb a rubber plant "to see if the giant was home". Dear Lord… how could he ever hold his head high again? "You mentioned breakfast?"

"Indeed I did, hang on," Miles dashed back into his room to turn his viewing box off and then returned to Carruthers in the corridor. "Let's see if Tom's up shall we?"

"Hmm… I fear that man is a bad influence."

"He certainly has a thirst on him," Miles agreed, knocking on Tom's door.

11.

Tom woke to a wet pillow and a mouthful of that old familiar, drunk musk. Just like old times, he thought, rubbing at the unruly pile of curly hair that had no doubt stiffened into a fat quotation mark after sleeping on it. Remembering the sensation of being visited in the night he reached out and patted the far side of the bed. It was empty of course. No doubt it always had been.

There was a knocking at his door. This seemed deeply unreasonable to Tom, in the way that such things always are to those that have only just awoken. He lay there for a moment hoping it would have the common decency not to happen again. It didn't. Three chirpy knocks followed by Miles' voice: "You there Tom? We were going to grab some breakfast."

Dear Christ... did the man have no mercy?

"Be down in a few minutes," Tom replied, hoping the pillow didn't smother the words too much. "Just finish dying first."

"Righto," Miles replied, in that insufferably cheerful tone reserved by those without hangovers for talking to those with them.

Tom listened to their footsteps move away, then the distant ping of the elevator as it arrived to ferry them to the restaurant. He breathed a sigh of relief. He wasn't quite ready for company yet. He rolled slowly out of his bed and stared at his face in the mirror. It was not the most reassuring sight to wake up to. Tom scowled but that only made his reflection look worse so he got up and moved out of the mirror's range. He felt an empty miniature bottle pop beneath his heel as he plodded towards the bathroom. And that's why the professional drunk goes to bed with his shoes on, he thought. Unzipping his fly he took the long, long piss of the morning after. The sort of marathon evacuation that usually sees you resting your head against the wall and taking a nap halfway through. Once done he shuffled back out, catching another glimpse of himself in the bathroom mirror. He looked like the ghost of a man who had been struck by lightning. He beat at his rebellious hair, though knew it was pointless. Best plan was just to wedge it under his cap and move on. After the act of finding and then fixing his hat on his head forced him to take a sit down in order to get his breath back he turned his thoughts to breakfast. Maybe it wasn't such a bad idea after all… apparently the human body responded well to food. Turned it into energy or something… what the hell, Tom would try anything once.

12.

The restaurant was beige and gold, entering it was like walking into an old-fashioned handbag. The overload to his senses was so high that Miles felt full even before he'd visited the breakfast buffet. In the corner a TV blared that morning's news in such an over-enthusiastic manner you'd think war had been declared. The current item was a piece of filler, a kooky old lady from Massachusetts had glimpsed the face of Jesus in her morning pancakes. The reporter was enthusing over this as if it may very well be the second coming, the camera offering a maple-syrup drizzled messiah from all angles.

"This place is making my head ache," Carruthers complained.

"No, the amount of vodka you drank last night is doing that… you need to eat and drink as much as you can, it's the only thing that will fix you."

"Like Alice switching from one magical potion to the next… I am quite aware how to restore my health thank you."

"Really?" Miles smiled. "Given how you went at it last night I got the impression you'd never drunk before in your life."

"I'm just not used to your noxious, future brews."

"Then get used to our dazzling future bacon and hash browns, they can cure anything."

"I shall endeavour to do so."

They piled their plates high and returned to their table.

"Get you some coffee?" asked a waitress who clearly needed some herself, she certainly seemed in danger of falling asleep.

"I suppose tea's out of the question?" Carruthers asked.

She looked at him as if he'd just asked for a glass of duck urine. "I'm sure we can rustle some up for you," she replied, though her lack of conviction was pronounced.

"Coffee's fine," said Miles, "lots of it. Some orange juice too if you have it."

"You're in the Orange State, sir, I'm sure we can find some somewhere." She smiled, just. Miles felt like applauding her effort, it clearly hadn't been easy. He settled for a polite nod and went back to attacking his eggs.

"She was charming," Carruthers said after she'd gone. "Nice to see you can still manage customer service in your enlightened age."

"We excel at it, now eat your bacon."

They ate in silence, grazing on their breakfast and washing it down with all the coffee they could consume. Tom appeared, following the routine they had laid down, piling his plate with scrambled eggs and bacon rashers.

Once they were done, stuffed full and well on their way towards a more productive state of mind, Carruthers brought out his notebook. Tom made a crack at that – he wasn't one for organisation – but it was light-hearted, today was going to be a good day, he'd decided.

"So," said Carruthers "we know that Chester will be discovered tomorrow, walking up Highway 192 – very lyrical name by the way. We can't precisely mark the place where he was dumped…"

"Can't mark it all in fact," Tom said. He shrugged as the other two looked at him. "What? I'm just being honest here. The guy's walking along the hard shoulder for how long? I mean he could have been dumped miles away."

"True," Carruthers admitted, "but it's all we have to go on."

"That's the problem with this whole fool's errand," Tom said.

In the corner the TV flickered. It had left Christ the Breakfast Redeemer alone and jumped to the weather – which, a surprise to nobody, was due to be hot and sunny round their way. The oiled and tanned fellow – who appeared no less animalistic than a baby orangutan rammed in a suit – was guffawing about all the great sunshine that was headed their way when the screen pixellated and fuzzed, the negative ghost of a man's face appearing through the snow. Nobody noticed.

"There's this place that Loomis was building," said Miles, "hell of a coincidence that don't you think? Right where we're thinking of looking and he just comes out with it?"

The screen returned to the apelike weatherman who was now hurling cartoon suns in the air. Perhaps he too had seen the face of Christ in his breakfast.

"But coincidence is all it is," insisted Tom. "We may as well check our horoscopes and plan the day that way."

The static swamped the screen again, that vague out-line of a face, struggling to be born.

"I'm not sure I believe in coincidence either," Carruthers admitted, "but we do know that there are forces at work here that…"

"Have no fucking interest in real estate, you can bet your ass on that!" Tom shouted. The waitress gave him a dirty look but he ignored her.

The sound on the TV cut out and that did draw attention, they had all got used to its incessant chirpiness in the background and its absence was as distracting as a shout across the room.

"TV's on the fritz," Tom muttered. "Some hotel this is."

The face on the screen solidified, just for a second, it was the Grumpy Controller, his mood not in the least improved by the effort he was having to expend in his attempts to communicate. "Home Town!" he shouted and with an awesome popping noise the glass screen exploded outwards, making the waitress scream and showering them all in thick glass fragments.

As the moment passed, all of them staring at the smouldering box in the corner, Miles drained his coffee cup and got to his feet.

"Max Headroom says we follow Loomis and that's good enough for me."

13.

Hughie listened to the night orchestra. In Florida the nights were when the animals woke up and gave a shit. Maybe they just liked to avoid the tourists. The frogs were calling back and forth, the cicadas running their crappy moped engine of a song, the hoot and caw of the night birds, rolling their beady little eyes over the black undergrowth for something to rip and tear. Hughie listened to it all. It sure beat the noises coming from inside his own house. Those noises had started out as conversation, somewhere along the line they had grown wet as the stranger gave up talking nicely and started playing hard. Hughie didn't want to listen to those noises. Not because he feared for Loomis – God help him he had been far beyond the point of safe return the minute he had lowered that car window. Not because he felt guilt at what was happening, as much as it pained him to admit it, Hughie just didn't have space in his pounding heart for sympathy right now. Hughie didn't want to hear those noises because he couldn't shake the conviction that one day soon he'd be making some just like it. That was the cold, selfish truth of it and while Hughie wasn't proud, he had known himself far too long to deny the truth. So he listened to the animals and wished he could be out there with them.

After a couple of hours the stranger stepped out onto the veranda next to him. He held a pair of beers in his glistening hands and he handed one to Hughie. Hughie took it, dared do nothing else. He tried not to think about how sticky it felt where the stranger had held it. He was glad he never had fixed that outside light, darkness could be a blessing.

"Thought you might want another," the stranger explained, tipping his own beer to his lips and taking a long draught.

Hughie drank too, startled by how ice-cold the beer was.

"I fixed the refrigerator," the stranger explained. "Warm beer's no good to anyone."

A rogue thought popped into Hughie's head and he spoke it, better that than talk about Loomis. "First time I've seen you drink anything."

"I don't make a habit of it," the stranger admitted. "Like food, I consume it for the hell of it, for the dirty thrill."

Hughie couldn't quite view food and drink in those terms and his confusion was pronounced enough for the stranger to pick up on it.

"I'm not human, Hughie, you've always known that."

Yes, Hughie supposed he always had. "Yeah," he admitted, washing the solitary word back down with another mouthful of beer.

"You can ask me, Hughie," the stranger said, and even in the dark Hughie knew he was grinning from ear to ear. "Go on, ask me."

"What are you?"

"You ever play with ants when you were a kid Hughie?" the stranger replied, rather than answer the question. "Maybe hold a glass bottle up in the sun and watch them burn in the heat of the rays?"

"No," and it was true, Hughie had never taken pleasure in destroying something else. When he was a kid he'd got guilty just swatting flies. He just didn't have the strength of self to go beating up on something else, as much as he might have been tempted from time to time.

The stranger chuckled. "Good for you, your God probably loves you for it."

"Don't believe in God," Hughie replied.

"You do now!" the stranger laughed, spitting a thin jet of beer onto the wood between his feet. "OK…" he said once he'd got his laughter under control, "so you never tortured ants, good for you… spoils my analogy but we can run with it anyway. What does the ant think? When the heat starts eating into his shiny little carapace, turning his miniature guts into stew?"

"I don't know…" Hughie shrugged, "it don't think nothing… it just burns."

"It can't understand, the scale is too big. It can't crook its head over its singed shoulder and think 'that damned kid burned me' it has no concept of the kid or the bottle, can barely even discern them with its tiny little eyes... they are utterly beyond it."

"Yeah."

The stranger nodded and drained his beer. "I'm the kid with the bottle, Hughie." He threw his own empty bottle into the undergrowth and turned to go back inside. "Now come and help me clean up this shit."

Hughie did as he was told. However many principles a man may have, he does what he needs to in order to keep on breathing.

They had gathered the meat and bones of what had once been Ted Loomis in a bed sheet – Hughie's only bed sheet now he came to think about it – and lifted them out to the swamp. Hughie, thinking about how the stranger had carried Loomis into the house in the first place, not even breaking a sweat, couldn't help but ask as the corpse splashed and began to sink in the gloomy water: "Why d'you get me to do this? You could have managed on your own."

The stranger patted him on his back, leaving a red hand print that would glare at Hughie a couple of hours later when he caught sight of it in the bathroom mirror. "Of course I could have managed," he said, "but I wanted you to do it."

"Holding up your bottle in the light of the sun."

The stranger laughed at that. "You've got it Hughie, you've got it."

They walked back towards the house. Now Hughie had started asking the questions he figured he might as well go for broke and ask the one that hung in his mind most often. "You going to kill me?"

The stranger shrugged. "Maybe, I doubt it though... can't see the fun in it."

"Why do you keep me around then?"

"Because sometimes things only mean something when you have an audience," the stranger admitted. "That and the fact that you're useful as a resource. You taught me all you know!"

There was one question left and Hughie couldn't leave it hanging there: "What are you going to do?"

"What, now? Watch TV for a bit probably... I like TV."

"No, you know what I mean, what are you going to do in the end? What's your plan?"

The stranger took a deep breath, enjoying the feel of it in the silly meat and gristle of his chest. "To be honest Hughie I just don't know, I guess the only honest answer is: whatever I like."

14.

The stranger was being as truthful as ever. When he had left his prison he had always imagined he would just go back to his old lifestyle, wallow in the flesh of these creatures and play for a while – that kid with the bottle that he had alluded to – but the more he thought about it the more he guessed that wouldn't be the case. It wasn't boredom, though that would come soon enough, it always had. It was just an itch... a leaning towards something bigger. There was an element of fear there, an emotion that was still incredibly new to him, a feeling only just learned, knocked into him when his own kind had come back to this reality and put him in his place. Would they return? Would they know that he had slipped out of their cage and was on the loose? Would they even care? He didn't know. But he feared the answers just the same. He had an idea that the next time they came calling they may not settle for imprisonment. They didn't have his patience, his love of games. No, he thought they'd likely just wipe him out of existence entirely, a tiresome little aberration that was too much trouble for his own good.

So what to do?

Home Town intrigued him. Intrigued him because it was a mystery and there had been precious few of those in his existence. It was a place layered in coincidence. It was where he was supposed to abandon Chester – and he would, in his own good time, he had an idea that he might have a game or two to offer Chester yet. It was also where the kid would grow up and set his hands on the box again. A coincidence. The stranger didn't believe in coincidences. He believed in patterns. Was this a pattern? Barely... with only two events linked to it... but maybe... He would go take a look, get a feel for the place himself. Then he would see how he felt. Then he would begin to make plans.

15.

Hughie had mopped the floor of his kitchen where the stranger had carried out his interrogation. No, not an interrogation, the stranger didn't need to get his hands dirty for that, could pull all he needed to know straight out of a man's head. This had been a game, that was all. He had called himself a kid with a bottle, burning the ants beneath him for fun. Hughie thought he was the kid that took his toys apart to see how they worked too, just for the hell of seeing something stripped bare.

It had been a thankless job, the torn and curling linoleum clinging to every blood splatter however hard Hughie beat at it with the old mop. He had started off with hot water and then finished the job with cold, the hot water tank unable to keep up with his demands. By the time he'd finished it wasn't perfect but it was better. Sometimes better just had to be enough.

Hughie went to bed on his bare mattress. He wasn't in the least bit tired but he wanted to get away from the stranger sat in his easy chair watching CSI reruns. As he lay there, he thought back to that long night lying out at the head of the dirt track. Covered in those rattling Diamondbacks waiting for dawn. Part of him was beginning to realise his situation was no different now. The Diamondback was sat downstairs, laughing at the CSI team as they plodded their way towards truth via splatter reports and dust fibre analysis. Hughie wondered when it was going to turn around and bite.

The following morning, Hughie thought for a moment that the time had come. The snake in his house was grinning and his teeth glistened with the potential to chew and maim.

"We're going for a drive," the stranger said. "Get the car started."

16.

They needed a car, and Tom had got directions from the reception desk to a Hertz place nearby. As he was paying for it with Loomis' stolen card he suddenly realised that had been a mistake. Surely the man would have reported the card lost by now? The transaction sailed through and Tom took the card back in surprise.

"Is everything alright sir?" the clerk asked, noticing the look on his face. Don't knock it, Tom thought, if the guy has so much money he forgets to cancel his cards then that's his problem.

"Great," he said, returning her smile and dropping the keys into his jacket pocket.

Back outside, Carruthers was gazing up at the buildings like he had been doing all morning.

"You look like a tourist," Tom noted.

"In many ways that's just what I am," Carruthers admitted, "what I've always been, in fact."

"Glad somebody's enjoying this," Tom replied, leading them to their car – a cheap compact, Tom hadn't had the enthusiasm for decadence this morning. "I'll drive," he said (much to Miles' relief… the last time he'd been behind the wheel of something he'd crashed it).

Carruthers climbed in the back, his enthusiasm for the ride ahead finally outweighing what was left of his hangover. "I hope we get to stay on the road a little longer than last time," he said, tying the seatbelt around his waist. As much as I hate to admit it, these infernal devices are more exciting than I had previously given them credit for."

"Exciting?" asked Tom, lighting a cigarette off the dashboard lighter, "my reputation precedes me…"

He stamped on the gas and the car jerked onto the road, forcing Miles to thrash back and forth in his seat.

"You must really want to see my breakfast again," he complained, fixing his seatbelt in place before noticing that Tom hadn't bothered with his. "Buckle up?" he asked.

"Nah…" Tom replied. "Those things rumple your clothes."

"Says the giant rumple in a hat," joked Miles.

Tom grinned and headed towards the interstate.

17.

"So," said Hughie, as he pulled off I-4 and onto Highway 192, "what's the interest in this place?"

The stranger shrugged. "I'm not entirely sure as yet," he admitted. "Just an itch... half a suspicion."

"Didn't think you seemed the type to move into real estate," Hughie admitted.

"You'd be surprised," said the stranger with a smile. "I'd like to own all of this one day."

Hughie didn't reply to that, he sensed it to be true and the idea chilled him.

"Some places just have a charge to them, Hughie," the stranger continued, "a quality that makes them stand apart."

"Feel that way about Hooters."

The stranger took a moment to understand that, flipping through Hughie's mind until he hit on images of waitresses in orange hot pants. "My, Hughie but you're positively chipper today!"

"No, just fatalistic." And this was true, hitting his third day – and still not dead – in this creature's company he found a certain apathy had kicked in. He imagined convicts on Death Row felt similar. His chances of long-term survival were pretty remote but he was damned if he was going to quiver in fear over it.

The construction site was soon visible, the yellow cranes rising and falling, the backhoes and front-loaders scrabbled around in the dirt picking up the scraps.

"What an industrious little species you are," the stranger said, as they pulled in, clapping his hands together with enthusiasm.

The site's foreman was a man that Loomis had never quite known how to handle. Corben Alliss who wore his clichés with a confidence that was staggering. He strode back and forth amongst the excavations in skin-tight jeans and boots so big he looked like a cartoon character from the waist down. His hard hat was carefully placed over a DA so extensively greased that you could have fried his head in minutes given a large enough skillet. You'd have had to take the rhinestone sunglasses off though, they were so heavy they'd likely have snapped that skillet in two. From the neck up Corben Alliss thought he was Elvis. From the waist down he looked like Dudley Do Right. If it wasn't for the fact that he looked like Charles Atlas in the middle he'd have heard a lot of jibes during his working day. As it was, his strength and more, his willingness to use it – Alliss was only too happy to let rip with the slightest provocation – saved him from a lot of slurs or chuckles. To Loomis, a man who spent most of his time obsessing about how he appeared to others, the foreman was an utter enigma.

To the stranger he was simply a creature of passing interest.

"Help you?" Alliss asked as Hughie parked the Olds and the stranger got out.

"Doubt that," the stranger said, walking straight past him.

Alliss looked at Hughie and the car he was getting out from the behind the wheel of. "That Loomis' car?" he asked. Knowing damn well it was.

"That's right," said Hughie, wondering what solid and believable reason he could give for driving it.

"Yeah," said the stranger, "I took that little shit apart and stole his ride." He turned and smiled over his shoulder. "That sound about right, Hughie?"

Hughie made a blustering noise, utterly at a loss to what he was supposed to say to that. Alliss fixed him in a stare from behind his ludicrous sunglasses. All Hughie could see was his own nervous face looking right back at him.

"Funny guy, huh?" Alliss said eventually.

"Hilarious," said the stranger, walking back over to him. He reached out and nudged those rhinestones down with a delicate finger so he could look directly in Alliss' eyes. For a moment Hughie thought the foreman would reach out and start a fight. He gritted his teeth, waiting for the violence – not for one minute worried about the stranger, he knew who the victor would be if this came to blows. It didn't. Alliss looked at the little man and found he had no urge to fight. If any of his staff had seen this they would have been at a loss to explain it. Alliss took one look into the stranger's eyes and found the only urge left in him was to knock off early, drive home, lock the door and hide there until he could be absolutely sure this man wouldn't be there when he stepped out again.

The stranger smiled and carried on walking towards the diggers. For a moment Alliss nearly called after him, warning him to wear a hard hat if he was going to wander around. Then he decided there wasn't a thing that could touch this weird little man and kept his mouth shut. He looked at Hughie, those glasses of his still dropped onto his cheeks, then ran off to far side of the site and his office. He would stay there until the police came a couple of hours later, utterly unable to explain the atrocities that had occurred in the meantime.

18.

Tom wasn't a frequent driver. Usually he was too blind drunk to be capable. Walking was frequently hard and he'd been practicing that every day of his life. Nonetheless he managed to keep the car on the road and not smack into any other vehicles. He considered this a solid gold achievement as he pulled off the Interstate and onto the highway.

"So many cars," Carruthers commented. "Do you people ever get to where you're going or do you just drive around all day?"

"Americans do love their cars," Tom admitted. "Personally as getting drunk in them tends to be frowned upon I've never seen the appeal."

"Nor do many come fitted with pianos," Miles added.

"This is true."

Seeing the cranes ahead, Tom swung the car off the road just a little short of the site entrance. "If we want Loomis to still think of us as rich weirdoes we'd better leave the car back a bit," he suggested. "It doesn't scream wealth."

"Unbelievable," said Carruthers as he clambered out of the back, "you have metal boxes that ferry you around at the most miraculous speeds and yet you can be embarrassed by them?"

They walked the last stretch alongside the road, turning into the site entrance alongside Loomis' Olds. Hughie was sat in the driver's seat, very much tempted to rev the thing up and drive like hell. The sure and certain knowledge that he wouldn't get half a mile before the stranger forced him to run the car off the road – or worse, into the path of another car – was the only thing that stopped him. Leave or stay, he certainly had no intention of seeing what the stranger got up to. The man had a spring in his step this morning and Hughie knew that could only mean some bad shit was going down sooner or later. He saw the three men walk past him but spared them no attention. They were beneath his radar. After they had passed a thought flashed through his head… he really should have warned them not to go in. Not that they would have likely listened.

19

Miles, Carruthers and Tom had no real idea what they were looking for, they were just following the impossible leads of coincidence and going where the House told them. By rights that should have meant they were prepared for pretty much anything. They weren't.

"Well," said the stranger, "fancy seeing you three here!"

"Shit." Tom stopped in his tracks, the other two following suit. "He shouldn't be here yet, right?"

"It would appear our information is somewhat off kilter." Carruthers replied.

"Why does that not surprise me?" Miles moaned.

The stranger strolled casually towards them. "Not expecting to see me either then?" he said. "I do hope you haven't all abandoned my old address, I'd hate for the world to fall apart while I was busy trying to have fun on it."

"Just the three of us," Miles said, "we needed to pop out for milk."

The stranger chuckled. "Good old Miles, always reliable for a cocky remark in case one was short."

"I try to please."

"And you succeed! You really do." The stranger was right in front of them now, big easy smile, friendly as an uncle at a wedding. "But seriously," and the smile dropped, "what are you three up to, eh? Checking up on me is it?"

"As if you didn't expect us to do just that," Carruthers countered.

The stranger chuckled. "Actually, I rather thought you'd have had your hands full." He shrugged. "Not that I mind, nothing personal but I can't say your presence has me quaking in my shoes."

"We might surprise you!" said Carruthers.

Oh God, thought Miles, don't say things like that… all that does is encourage him.

The stranger smiled again. "You think?"

"Where's Chester?" asked Tom.

The stranger glanced at him. "There really is very little in you but hate and cheap scotch."

"And whose fault is that?"

The stranger said nothing, just sighed and strolled back and forth in front of them as if thinking very long and hard.

Miles felt a painful throb in his head, clapping his hand to it. Carruthers likewise. Tom didn't react, he was used to his brain popping at regular intervals. The stranger stopped pacing, having read all he needed to and thought on it briefly.

"Charming," he said. "You really were hoping to put a stop to any antics I might have had in mind weren't you? Not much of a plan of course, but then, in all fairness, it's hard to scheme against Gods isn't it?" He smiled for the last time. "We're such a horrid and capricious lot."

The pain having lessened, Miles looked around, noting that the diggers had stopped their engines, their drivers climbing out of their cabs and walking towards them. Other workers, those who had been measuring foundations or cutting wood, supervising the delivery of girders, concrete or hardcore, even the handful that had been taking a quick smoke or sharing coffee from thermos flasks: they all started walking in their direction.

Back in the Oldsmobile, Hughie Bones, who had been unable to resist craning his neck through the window to try and follow events, pulled his head in and closed the window. His hand hovered by the ignition key once more, undecided as to whether he wanted to leave or ram the car down there and try and provide a bit of support to the three guys. The radio suddenly clicked on, the stranger's voice interrupting the usual drive time rock to give a simple announcement. "Sit still, Hughie, try and remember whose side you're on, yes? Let the kid with the bottle have his fun."

"I think we're about to take a beating," said Miles.

"A bad one." Tom agreed, shifting on the spot, cautious of someone sneaking up behind him.

"Don't be so unimaginative," the stranger said. "If I wanted you torn apart I'd do it myself."

As one, the workers stuck their hands in the air, like criminals in an old movie. Then, they dropped downwards as if the ground had vanished beneath their feet. In a way it had, liquefying and bubbling. It solidified again swiftly, every single worker now embedded in the soil. They left nothing but a thrashing garden of hands, like grapevines, twitching and clenching as their owners fought to breathe dirt.

The stranger pushed his way past them and towards his car. "There's bound to be a few spades around," he said, "if you want to try and dig one up before he dies." He turned to face them. "You know, if you'd like to 'surprise me' with regards your abilities."

He continued on his way to the car, not bothering to look back again.

Miles began to run, looking for something to dig with.

"There's no point," Tom said.

"We have to try!" Miles dropped to the ground near the closest hand, scrabbling at the earth with his hands, bending back his nails as he tore at soil and grit.

"You'd never get him out in time," said Tom, "that was the whole point."

Behind them the engine of the Olds roared into life as it did a U-Turn and headed back out onto the highway.

"Carruthers?" Miles was getting nowhere, grabbing the hand as it began to tire, spasming now rather than clenching with any strength.

"I'm afraid Tom's right," Carruthers said, sitting down on the ground. "I antagonised him so he did this to put us in our place. Nothing so simple as hurting us physically of course, no... that would be too gentle for a creature like him. He has to stick the knife in where it will hurt us the most, right in our damned pride and consideration."

All around them the hands were stopping their spastic dance. Drooping like unwatered plants, dead fingers dabbing the earth.

"Fuck this," said Tom, walking back to the road.

"Please, Carruthers..." said Miles, "*Roger*... we can't just leave can we?"

Carruthers sighed. "We can't stay here either, not unless we want to answer lots of impossible questions. None of which will help these poor souls one jot."

Miles knew this was true but, even as he got to his feet and began to walk away, he felt so worthless he could retch.

"We knew this would be hard," said Carruthers, standing up and putting his arm around Miles' shoulder.

"Hard I could deal with, this is just impossible."

There was the roar of a car engine and Tom shot past them, haring up the highway.

"Jesus!" Miles shouted. "That's perfect that is! Where the hell does he think he's going?"

"I think I can guess," said Carruthers, "though I do hope I'm wrong."

20.

"You nearly left me there didn't you, Hughie?" the stranger asked, stretched out in the passenger seat.

Hughie thought about lying but really couldn't see the point. "Yeah," he admitted, "or try and get in the way of you hurting those others."

The stranger nodded. "But you didn't, so I forgive you."

"That makes it all alright then."

21.

A few hours later, Tom drew to a halt and dropped his head against the steering wheel of his car.

"Not like you Tom," came Elise's voice from the passenger seat. "Never had you down as a coward."

"Shut up Elise," he whispered, "it's not about cowardice, it's about priorities."

"And what priorities might they be?" she asked. "These priorities that see you abandon your friends by the side of the road."

"No friends of mine."

"Best you've got."

"I've got you."

Elise lit a cigarette from the dashboard lighter. "I'm dead honey, and the dead are lousy friends."

"Not dead everywhere though, are you honey?" he said with a smile, sitting up and opening the driver's door.

Elise stared out of the window. "You know, I never did visit Florida," she said, looking out at the sun. "Seems nice."

"You didn't miss anything," Tom replied. "You know what they say about the place. This is God's waiting room... where people go to die."

"I'd fit right in."

"Not the Elise I know," he replied, getting out and slamming the car door behind him.

He walked into the departures entrance of Tampa International, hoping Loomis' credit card still had enough life in it for a ticket to New York.

INTERLUDE
Leo Gets His Break

Leo drove Sepulveda Boulevard until his head had emptied and the tears that he would show no one had dried. By the time he pulled up outside the Van Nuys apartment block where he slept and dreamed of Burbank zip codes he was almost his old self. The groceries had grown warm on the passenger seat. He carried them up the external stairway and, once inside, dumped them on the kitchen sideboard to warm a little more while he drank a cool beer from the ice-box and smoked a cigarette over the balcony.

"God bless the city of angels," he whispered, toasting the late Los Angeles afternoon with his Coors bottle, "and every motherfucker who sails in her."

His stomach told him it needed feeding so he put some ragged Chinese takeout in the microwave and nuked it.

Spooning noodles into a frowning mouth he channel-surfed for twenty minutes trying to find something – anything – that would stop his brain churning over for awhile. It was no good, his head was too noisy to be silenced by *Law and Order* or *Project Runway*. He dumped the empty Chinese carton and grabbed his car keys again, he would head out. He would go to the bench.

He'd first discovered the bench when hanging around the Forest Lawn Memorial Park; thinking, not for the first time, that dying was the most likely way of his settling in Glendale, just another LA district his pocket could only dream of.

Forest Lawn had grown famous over the years, justifiably so, as cemeteries go it is certainly unusual, the "theme park of death" thought by many to epitomise this town and its hollow promises.

Leo liked it though, often came here to walk the gardens and look at the statues. After all, where else could you hang out in such glittering company? Errol Flynn, Humphrey Bogart, Theda Bara, W.C. Fields... heroes, lovers and fools, all one beneath the dirt. Leo was by no means sure that he believed in a world beyond this one but he couldn't argue that the cemetery felt unearthly. From the sheer scope of the place – 300 acres of the sparkling dead – to the bizarre names of its plots – *Vesperland, Inspiration Slope, Dawn of Tomorrow* and – perhaps eeriest of all – *Babyland*, the heart shaped garden filled with infant remains.

The bench wasn't far from *The Wee Kirk o' the Heather,* the chapel where Reagan had sealed the knot with Nancy (the spirits of his olders and betters no doubt laughing their asses off while he made his vows). It had wrought iron legs and a thick wooden seat and back rest (painted an evergreen almost luscious enough to eat). Every week or so he made a trip out there, took a lunch bag and *Variety* and filled his head with Tinsel Town plans.

The audition had been for a tiny part in a boxing movie featuring Gary Sinise. The usual trash... *Raging Bull* meets *Rocky*. Sinise, down on his luck after an accident in the ring, takes to drink and bare-knuckle sparring. Leo had been up for "Guy in Bar". He got in an argument with Sinise and ended up out cold on the pool table. Not exactly Shakespeare but a great bit of exposure and a chance to share screen time with a name (even if the guy seemed horny for TV these days). He'd been lucky to even hear of it, a phone call from a girl he'd screwed a couple of times, blabbing about how she'd gotten herself a part in the picture. He'd had to play it down of course but after bullshitting about how much he admired Sinise and would love to work with him she'd managed to get him on the list for auditions.

"You owe me," she cooed, fluttering eyelashes she'd bought rather than grown.

"You bet baby," he'd promised, knowing he'd never deliver. He hadn't liked her that much. She did this weird thing when she came – floods of tears every time, like she'd heard her mom was dead or something – shit like that puts a guy off.

Not that he'd be working with her any time soon, there was *that* little piece of consolation.

He'd been feeling positive, a genuine belief in his gut that his time was coming. Stood there in the brightly-lit rehearsal room, a thin, plastic cup of vended Cappuccino in his hand and a swagger to his walk, he had come face to face with the heavenly trinity of the movie audition: the casting director, the producer and – holy of holies – the director himself. The director was a young guy, maybe five or six years Leo's senior, who had made the transition from music promos to proper pictures via a surprise rental hit starring a zombie-battling Elisha Cuthbert. He finished scribbling his notes on the guy who had just left and, nudging the brim of his baseball cap with his pen, winked at Leo.

"Hi Leo," he said, his eyes flicking down briefly to check the name from his notes, "good to see you."

Leo smiled, trying to ignore the producer who was arguing with someone on his cell, keep it cool, keep it together...

"Thanks, you too Mr Hickman."

"Gerry, please, none of that formal shit."

"Cool." Leo couldn't stop grinning, his lips shrinking back in a sudden wave of nervousness.

"Tell him he can shoot in India for as long as he likes if he's willing to cover the bill!" the producer shouted.

The cavernous room felt as airless as a closet. Leo could feel a small vein popping in his forehead. The casual grin of the director suddenly seemed preda-tory... the producer's voice deafening... the bored politeness of the casting director stuck in his gut like the worst rejection he had ever experienced... laugh-ter in the schoolyard... Christ he was close to crying... get a grip!

He took a sip of his coffee; it really was that or scream in their faces.

"Self-righteous fuck." The producer muttered, cutting off his call and glancing briefly in Leo's direction.

"Okay Leo," said Gerry, ignoring his colleague either out of politeness or simply because his mood swings were so frequent they fell beneath his radar. "Let's see what you've got."

He handed Leo a sheet of typed script and pointed to-wards the digital camcorder that had been watching all from its tripod to the side of the desk. Leo glanced at it, its single red eye staring right back.

"I'll read the part of Doug, if you could just focus your performance towards the camera and we'll see how we go."

There was a pause as Leo stared again at the camera, his mouth suddenly dry... he took a sip of his coffee then realised he shouldn't still be holding it. He slammed it on the desk, desperate to be rid of it and nearly yelped as it splashed its frothy contents onto some of the papers.

"Fuck's sake..." the producer sighed, grabbing some of his sheets and wiping at them with his manicured and moisturised hand.

"Sorry..." Leo fussed about, trying to tidy the small amount of mess and getting nowhere.

The producer slammed his hand down on the papers, stopping Leo from touching them. "Leave it for Christ's sake... just get on with it."

Gerry smiled, 'Don't worry about it Leo, let's do it.'

Leo turned towards the camera again, a very real and childlike need to cry bubbling up in him again, *clumsy idiot*, Jesus... *what was he doing?*

"What are you looking at you dumb fuck?" Gerry shouted and Leo nearly dropped his script... what now? What had he done?

The director gestured at his script and, glancing down, Leo realised it was the first line, Doug squaring up in the bar... full of piss and wind and willing to take it out on "Guy in Bar".

"Oh... uh... sorry." Leo tried to focus on the script, tried to force the words on it into his head and out of his mouth...the thing made no sense...his mind flipping, the hand holding the paper shaking so hard it rustled. A smudge from his sweating thumb stretched across the bottom corner of the page. Get it together... get it together...

He looked straight at the camera.

"Screw you pal," he said finally, his voice cracking, "what's your problem?"

Real quality dialogue…

The red light of the camcorder burned at him, hating him as much as the fictitious Doug. He could hear his heartbeat… actually *hear* it… breathing was becoming difficult…

"You're my problem shit head, and, after the week I've had that's something you don't want to be…" Gerry shifted in his seat, 'at this point Gary squares up to you, nose on nose, he wants a fight and you're drunk enough and stupid enough to give him one.'

Stupid enough… yeah, Leo could relate to that.

The red light of the camcorder grew, flaring and sparking at the edges… building, wanting to consume, to wash over Leo, to burn the foolish, awkward, idiot that stood in its path. It was immortalising his ineptitude, gathering all his faults, every little erroneous twitch of his face, every stumble over the worthless dialogue he held in his hand…

"I…" his voice was cracking again. Dry. No spit in his mouth. So dry in fact it would surely break open like mud in the sun, pouring sharp and copper blood over his tongue…

And the red light would capture it all, film it all, play it back over and over again for everyone to laugh at.

"I…"

"Leo?" Gerry's voice was quiet, just outside his attention. None of the three at the desk existed anymore, they were nothing compared to the red-hot hatred of the camera… the real gods of Hollywood, marching like *Wellesian* tripods, eating everything in their path, withering to dust all that fell within the inferno of their single red eye…

Leo dropped the script and walked out. That he didn't run would be the only source of comfort to him when he hit fresh air again and emptied his churning stomach into the thick, fleshy leaves of the Agave plants that lined the sidewalk outside the rehearsal room.

Leo pulled up outside the front gate of Forest Lawn. The hazy, Los Angeles sun was doing its best to emulate dramatic movie sunsets as he walked through the wrought iron gates off Glendale Avenue. It just couldn't manage, life didn't own the right filters.

He walked straight to his bench, sat down and closed his eyes. He listened to the sound of lawn sprinklers and distant mower engines. Somewhere a church organ was playing, celebrating yet another death with holy muzak. There was the buzz of a fly as it flew past his head, the noise building and falling in perfect Dolby surround sound. He could feel the wooden slats on his back and tried to melt into them, half-remembering an old stage school exercise designed to help a performer relax.

He suddenly felt sure someone had walked over. That slight coolness that falls across your face when someone steps in and blocks out the sun.

He opened his eyes. It wasn't a person, it was a door. Right there in the grass in front of him. A bright green, solid wood door. It was inside a frame but that frame floated in the air, supported presumably from the ground.

"What the fuck?" he wondered, looking around, half expecting he had stumbled into one of those hidden camera shows. "If you're there, Tom Spelling," he whispered, "I'm gonna stick your camera up your ass." He couldn't see anyone, but then that was the point of a "hidden" camera show he guessed. How'd they build the thing so damned quick? He'd only had his eyes closed for, what? A minute? Maybe less...

He got to his feet and walked around to the other side of the door. That was the moment he stopped thinking he was on *Punk'd* or *Candid Camera*… From the other side, the door wasn't there. All he could see was his bench, basking in the fading LA sunlight.

"Motherfucker…" he whispered, moving back around, noting the point – precisely on the perpendicular, side by side with the frame – when the door winked into existence. Step back and it was gone. He stretched out his hand, slowly, wanting to barely brush the wood with the tips of his fingers.

"Jesus!" he shouted, snatching his hand back. The damn thing had given him a shock.

He looked around, the entire place was deserted. He moved to the front again, facing the door head on.

But did he want to? He was far from sure he did. He rubbed his face and swore again. This was stupid, doors did not just appear in the middle of boneyards, not even one as surreal as Forest Lawn. It had to be some kind of trick.

The door opened.

The lock clicked softly, enticingly. And a widening sliver of light revealed itself. There was the faintest scent of old loam. Somewhere he thought he heard a parrot call out.

"Jesus…" He paced back and forth, still snatching glances at the undergrowth, convinced he would spot the glint of a camera lens.

Another noise, this time the rustling of leaves. For a moment he hoped it came from one of the bushes close by but even as he glanced around he knew he was kidding himself. The noise was coming from beyond the door.

"Stupid." He stared at it. That sliver of light stared back.

"Fuck it." He kicked out with one foot – thinking that his rubber soles would protect him from any more of those electric shocks – wanting to push the door open so he could at least get a proper look inside. His foot collided with the wood with a solid thud. A real noise, the sort of noise that came from real things not fantasies. The door swung wide to reveal an expanse of jungle. Sat in amongst the fat, rubber plant leaves and the thick tree stumps was a woman. She was late thirties maybe, dressed as if out of an old movie. *Scott of the Antarctic, Ice Station Zebra…* one of those things. Head to toe in heavy clothing, big boots, huge mittens on her hands. She looked as if she might be dead. Eyes open but vacant, staring right back at him. Then she twitched.

"You okay?" he asked, immediately embarrassed that he was talking at this woman – this imaginary woman for Christ's sake – that lay beyond the door.

The woman moved again, but only slightly. As if she was having some kind of fit. Her left boot twitched on a spasming leg and then went still.

"Shit." Leo looked around again, still nobody there but him. What if she was hurt? What if she was dying right now while he just stared gormless at her?

What would Guy in Bar do? A cheeky voice piped up in his head.

Leo rubbed at his face again, as if he could scrub the situation away with those soft hands of his. He made his decision.

"I'm coming!" he shouted at the woman and stepped through the door. Just a quick in and out, he thought, grab her and drag her back to the bench.

The door slammed shut behind him.

FOUR
Housebound

1.

Penelope didn't know what to do after saying goodbye to the others. She walked the length and the breadth of the station, thinking she should familiarise herself with her surroundings. But really this added up to little more than window shopping, something that felt frivolous given their current situation. Though she did need to find more suitable clothing than the gentlemen's cast-me-downs provide by Carruthers. The last time she'd thought of doing that she'd been somewhat distracted by other matters...

She found the ethereal passengers around her disturbing, shivering as she weaved between – or, on a number of occasions, *through* – what she could only think of as ghosts. As much as she tried to convince herself that they were nothing but images, part of the backdrop, she couldn't break the impression of being surrounded by people. In a clothes shop she had hid in the small dressing room, squealing in surprise when a woman had appeared alongside her while she was half-clothed. The woman had begun to disrobe, gazing at a blouse on its hanger with wistful eyes that said "this is as good as it's going to look, you know that don't you? Once it has to deal with your body it'll all be downhill from there."

Penelope watched her. Watched the depth of emotion on the woman's face as she tugged the blouse to one side or the other, staring at herself in the mirror with naked disgust. Eventually she gave up, her arms dropping to her side, lips pouting and eyes dampening. From angry woman to child in a matter of moments, all performed in that perfect safety of thinking she was unobserved. We show our true faces to ourselves but never put them on display. Eventually the woman tugged the blouse off as if it were fighting her. She placed it neatly back on the hanger and took one last look at its perfection. She put her own clothes back on – a baggy jumper, all the better to hide in – rubbed her eyes and walked back out into the store, a casual smile in place. Penelope watched her go, no doubt in her mind that she was watching a fully rounded human being, not just an illusion. She tried on her own clothes quickly and functionally. She didn't look at her reflection in the mirror.

Unlike the woman she had seen, Penelope felt more confident in her new outfit, a brown jumper and checked slacks. In the men's clothes she had looked like a small child playing dress-up. At least now she was her own person.

She had left Alan making Sophie comfortable in the coffee shop, looting the arcade for anything he could use as bedding. His closeness to the child made it almost impossible for Penelope to be around them, his attention so fixed there was no room for anyone else. She struggled to accept this earnest father figure as the man she had known, but that was no bad thing. She didn't doubt his sincerity – he was far too conscientious for that – so it was all fuel to the notion that he was a changed man. Not that it helped them get along, his obsession with Sophie aside, Alan seemed almost crippled by her presence. To begin with she had assumed this was down to his lack of confidence in the company of women – something Chester had certainly seemed to share, until he'd stripped them naked and beat them up in the back of his car of course. But as their first morning alone wore on she began to wonder if it wasn't something more. There was a panicked look to him whenever they crossed paths, as if he was convinced she meant to do him harm. Of course, not so long ago he would have been right.

She left him to his nursemaiding and sat in another cafe, just to avoid the discomfort of being near him. She helped herself to a sandwich and a bottle of orange juice, sitting in the window so she could at least keep an eye on things. Her sandwich, like all the food here, was a disappointment, a feeling sharpened no end by the fact that it took her five minutes to get into the packaging. The ham tasted the same as the lettuce and the cheese. Whether this was due to the House's standard practice of offering bland, imaginary, foodstuffs or just because it was a lousy sandwich she was unable to tell. It didn't matter, part of her felt she didn't deserve a decent lunch. Though whether this constant guilt was down to staying behind or sleeping with Miles she wasn't sure. If she thought long and hard about it she might have been able to decide. But she didn't think long and hard, didn't want to. She just wanted to be busy. She wanted – as stupid as she knew it was – the hectic, adrenaline-laced lifestyle of the last few days. When you were running around trying not to end up

168

dead it was easy to distract oneself from your own thoughts. Now she had nothing but. It was driving her up the wall.

She hurled the majority of her lunch in the bin – wondering if it would be real enough to rot in there – and recommenced her pacing around the station.

It was an impressive place, she supposed, though no Grand Central Terminal. It was clean and sterile, in New York they built stations that felt like they meant business. She marvelled at the technology, naturally. Tapping at the information stands and watching the TV screens that offered platform announcements. The Grumpy Controller didn't make an appearance which was perhaps for the best, she certainly wouldn't have been in the mood for his attitude.

Like Miles and Carruthers before her she spent some time ogling the chaos of trains in the Barlow Shed, marvelling at the impossibility of it all. Even that palled after a while. She had seen so many impossible things over the last few days that she was becoming blasé. There was a limit to everything, after all, even wonder.

So she paced, pointless and directionless. The idea of returning to the cafe and trying to make conversation with Alan made her cringe. The man was a brick wall to her, requiring an effort that she didn't feel capable of. She was trapped. As trapped as ever.

A clatter of metal on tile echoed across the upper level of the station, loud enough to send the ghost pigeons into a panic. I knew it, thought Penelope, they aren't quite as immune to us as we like to think. The idea was gone as suddenly as it had surfaced, overcome by the fear of something intruding into their safe-haven. She realised that she had become lulled by the calm of the last forty-eight hours, forgetting that if there was one thing this house did well it was danger.

She ran towards the noise, knowing she should call to Alan but not doing so. As she burst her way through seemingly unaware passengers – only now able to do so without caring – she realised this was a mistake. A problem in fact. But, as she drew close to the champagne bar where Tom had raised a glass to ghosts of his own, she accepted it was too late to do anything about it. Whatever was going on was hers to face and hers alone.

2.

Alan forced himself into tasks to make Sophie comfortable, trying to fill his head with thoughts for someone other than himself. None of the shops sold bedding but he managed to find several things that could do the job as easily. A thick, pink dressing gown that made a comfortable blanket, a stack of jumpers for pillows. He picked up a small cuddly toy, a little elephant holding a stuffed heart, but put it back. That was going too far and he really didn't think Sophie was the sort of little girl that liked toys. In fact Sophie wasn't really like a little girl at all, not the few he had met at least. Of course her condition was to answer for that. He still didn't know precisely what that condition was, some form of autism perhaps? It wasn't something he knew much about. Still, the more time he spent with her the more he defined the rules, sussed out what made her happy – or at least as happy as she seemed capable of ever being – and what upset her. Despite her mental rigidity, her obsession for everything in its right place, he had been impressed by her adaptability. She had taken everything the house had thrown at her and fought on. That had taken one hell of a lot of strength, he had no doubt that many kids her age wouldn't have managed it. Hell, he thought, many adults wouldn't have managed it either…

He bundled her up on the soft, sofa cushions, draping the dressing gown over her and lifting her head to slip the jumpers underneath.

He watched her for a while and then began to fret about what he should do next. He wracked his brain for anything else he could do to make Sophie comfortable. Briefly wondering about a hot water bottle – which was ridiculous – it was warm enough to have created a thin rime of sweat in the small of his back, the last thing she needed was heating up. He might as well just face the fact that there was nothing else he could do. Perhaps he should find Penelope and see if they couldn't find a way to get on…

Or not.

Maybe he should make himself a cup of coffee and keep an eye on Sophie for a while longer. Yeah… maybe that was the best thing.

He walked behind the counter and tried to recall watching how this was done. He found the metal scoop for the coffee, unscrewing it and knocking the used grounds into a plastic-lined drawer. So far so good… he could see the coffee-bean grinder, just not how to actually operate it…

From behind him Sophie coughed. He dropped the coffee scoop on the floor and ran around to the seating area, sending a spinning rack of kettle chips flying in his panic. He tripped over a chair, winding himself as the back of it punched him in the stomach and ended up wheezing and aching on the floor next to her.

"Sophie, honey?" he asked, touching her gently on the forehead. There was no response, just the usual litany of "build not break, build not break". He sat

171

there, getting his breath and trying not to give into the frustration he felt. He was just like a new parent, twitching at every noise through one of those loud speakers you fixed in a cot. He had to calm down, he was doing her no favours...

He decided he needed to grab some air, or at least what could pass for air in this place. Maybe he'd bump into Penelope after all and they could start over, see if they couldn't get along. After all he was likely to be spending a good deal of time with her.

He stepped outside the coffee shop just in time to hear her scream.

3.

Penelope couldn't see what had caused the noise, not to begin with anyway. In fact she stumbled on the piece of vent grating quite by accident, so busy looking in all directions for sign of trouble that she failed to pay attention to where she was putting her feet. The metal scuffed underneath her shoes, sending her tumbling against one of the tables in the champagne bar. In fact, if it weren't for the fact that her reflexes were sharp she would have most certainly ended up underneath it. As it was, she managed to grab a high-backed chair and keep her balance. She let go of the chair and picked the piece of grating up, looking it over. At first she had no idea what it was – not being familiar with the construction of air-conditioning systems – just a flat sheet of metal with grooves cut into it. One side – the inside, she could tell that much by the fact it was un-painted – was riddled with dents, as if it had been hit by buck shot. It occurred to her that whatever had caused the dents was most certainly what had forced the metal free from wherever it had been fixed. She looked up, figuring she would spot the hole somewhere, and then work it out from there. A pigeon was only inches from her face, its black beak aiming straight for her. Her gut instinct was to drop into a crouch, hoping it would simply swoop over her. It didn't, it dropped straight down, beak punching a small wound in the top of her head. She screamed – more in shock than actual pain, though it certainly hurt. The bird tumbled down her back, presumably disorientated by the blow itself. Penelope tumbled forward, hand flying to her head where she could feel her hair grow wet with blood. A panicked voice inside her fretted as to whether the bird had pierced her skull. Above her there was the sound of fluttering wings and self-preservation kicked in, the kamikaze bird wasn't alone and, unless she found some cover she could expect the next strafe run any second.

She dragged herself backwards, pulling herself under the table. The surface area wasn't massive but it was enough to cover her as long as she drew her arms and legs tight against her body. A few feet away the felled pigeon rolled over, flapping frantically in its attempt to get back in the air. It had damaged itself, clearly, flopping around in confusion, its slightly crooked beak drawing thin bloody lines on the floor tiles.

Above her, the fluttering continued but she didn't dare poke her head out to check how many other birds there were or what they were doing. Curiosity killed the cat, she thought to herself, or pecked its damned eyes out at the very least. The felled pigeon continued its spastic spiral only a few feet away, she stopped looking at it, it couldn't hurt her – or so she hoped – and if she kept staring at the damn thing she was likely to lose the poor lunch she'd eaten a few minutes ago.

There was a frantic sound of feathers and a bird landed on the table above her, its little talons tapping away on the wood as if it were doing a jig. *I've found her! I've found her!* It hammered at the wood with its beak as if convinced it could hack its way through to her. She remembered the dents in the metal plate that she had thought looked like rifle shot.

"Penelope?"

Alan was shouting for her. She supposed he had heard her scream, a fact that embarrassed her no end.

"Careful!" she shouted back, no idea how close he was and not intending to stand up and look. "Pigeons are attacking." How ridiculous that sounded when said aloud. That and the shame she felt at having screamed – or being heard at least – nearly had her break cover. The last thing she wanted was him to see her as a damsel in distress. She clamped down on her pride, that sort of stupidity would get her nowhere, she was sure he'd have hollered the place down if a bird had used him for target practice.

"Pigeons?" he called back, the doubt in his voice clear, however far away he was.

"Yes, pigeons!" she replied, allowing an edge of anger to her voice. "One of them tried to crack my skull open."

"Where are you?" There was no doubt now, she was pleased to notice.

"In the champagne bar, under a table." The bird above her head was hammering harder and harder, enough to make the table vibrate. She guessed it was encouraged by the sound of her voice. "Don't come running in here for God's sake, they'll be all over you before you know it." There was a pause. She wondered if he was still there. "Alan?"

"Thinking," he shouted back. "I'll be right back, stay where you are."

"Oh," she moaned sarcastically, "OK then." What did he think she was going to do? Pour herself a drink?

With a flap of wings that she could easily interpret as anger, the pigeon above her took to the air again, having given up on the table for now.

"Ow!" The lame pigeon had worked its way towards her and was pecking at the exposed top of her foot. She lashed out at it, slamming down her heel on the bird, grimacing as she felt it crunch. It had been an automatic reaction and – hostile as it was – she felt sick at what she'd done. Split and bubbling, it whirled around like a leaf caught in the wind, smearing its entrails behind it. She bit her lower lip and looked away, determined not to retch. She was embarrassed enough without Alan finding her covered in puke.

The death throes of the pigeon seemed to excite those above it, the air filling with beating wings. Several of the birds scooted low enough to the ground that Penelope was convinced they meant to fly under the table and attack her. As they took back to the air it occurred to her that they had likely been confirming where she was. Taking a little scouting mission so as to pin her down accurately. Or was she being paranoid? No... in this House there was no such thing as paranoia, just common sense. If they were planning on attacking despite the little cover she had then she needed to move. Somehow. The rustling rippled through the air above her once more, as the flock turned to swoop down again. She needed to think of something... quickly...

As the birds descended to within a few feet of her, she grabbed the single leg of the table and stood up with it, wielding it over her shoulder like a weighty umbrella. If she could get as far as the bar then maybe there would be better protection behind it. She ran in a stooped shuffle trying to cover as much of her body as possible with the surface of the table. The force with which a number of the pigeons hit the wood was almost enough to knock her over, luckily her sudden shift had forced the birds to change direction and only the tail of the flock had time to adjust. The majority of birds darted past her as she ran, curving in an arc – some colliding with the other chairs and tables with a soft *thwacking* noise – and then flying back up to the roof where, presumably, they would turn and fly at her once more.

A few feet from the bar entrance, the birds struck again and this time the force was more than enough to knock her off her feet. Three or four of the pigeons had aimed low, meaning to cut her down by her calves – where the table didn't altogether cover her – all but one misjudged, grinding into the floor a few centimetres behind her. One – that lucky one – got its beak into the flesh of her ankle, flipping over onto the back of her legs as she fell to the floor. The table landed across her back, the rim of its surface clattering against the floor a merciful few inches from her head. She drew herself into a ball and waited for the birds to strike. She wasn't going to scream though, damn it, that was the last thing she would do…

"Stay down!" Alan shouted, his feet pounding towards her. She chanced a glimpse – the fear of the birds taking her eyes strong enough that that was all she would allow. He was dressed in a thick, padded anorak, the hood cinched tight around his face, a pair of sunglasses covering his eyes. In his hands he was holding a tennis racquet, sweeping it forward and back as he ran. She closed her eyes again, his grunting and the sound of rebounded birds all she needed to know.

Alan had found the coat in the same outdoor clothing outlet that had proven so useful to his older self before travelling to Tibet. The tennis racquet had been propped up in a toy store window. It was far from perfect – he wouldn't have felt at ease with anything less than a suit of armour and a machine gun – but hopefully it would be enough. He lashed at the birds as they flew in an almost perfect arrowhead towards him and Penelope, keeping the racquet moving forward and back, batting the birds to either side as hard as he could. The damage done to his shoulder during his first day in the house was swift to remind him of its presence, the joint aching as he swung his arm. The first half of the arrowhead fell easily, the formation narrow enough and fast enough he couldn't fail to hit them. Their bodies spiralled to either side of him, wings broken, necks snapped. The strings in the racquet spread and twisted, not used to such treatment. He could only hope it would hold long enough to do its job.

The last half of the arrowhead was more spread out and a few of the birds had time to veer away at the last minute. He caught most of them but a handful escaped. The stragglers aimed straight for the roof, buying time to assess this new threat. Given the fervour of their attack, Alan wasn't stupid enough to think that a sense of self-preservation would be enough to keep them at bay.

"Can you stand?" he asked Penelope.

"Of course I can!" she snapped, proving as much, though the wound in her ankle made her limp awkwardly.

"I think we should run," he said holding a hand out to help her but not altogether surprised when she refused to take it.

They ran, Alan looking over his shoulder to keep an eye on whether the birds were following. The few pigeons left were quick to form a new attack pattern and give pursuit. He glanced down at the racquet, its strings were ruined, it was no more than a wooden hoop and frankly useless as a weapon. He dropped it, and looked around for something to take its place. A glint of silver offered hope from the surface of the bar and he snatched at it. He would have to turn at the last minute, any earlier and the birds would have the chance to change direction. Their formation was narrow, a thin triangle, and he thought he just might pull it off…

"When I say 'drop'," he told Penelope, "hit the floor and roll to one side." Another few seconds… "Drop!"

He spun to face the birds, holding the wide, silver drinks tray at arm's length. As the birds hit, he pushed forward, counterbalancing the force of their blow. The first few in the line were dead instantly, necks broken, the next couple tumbled to the floor, disorientated. That left four still in the air and a danger. They veered around the tray and landed on him, beaks hacking away at the lining of his coat. The fabric split, white stuffing spilling out. He beat at himself with the tray, trying to knock them off, but they held on tightly, their talons long and sharp enough to pierce the coat and cut into his skin.

"Sorry about this," Penelope said, before beating at him with the dropped tennis racquet. She used the rim, not covering a lot of area but packing a punch. Alan grunted as she knocked the birds from him but had the sense to know this beating was in his own best interests. Penelope gritted her teeth as the birds fell, thrashing them away as they tried to turn their attentions on her. One fluttered at her ankles and she stamped on it blindly, trying to ignore the feeling of it crunching beneath her foot. In a few seconds the job was done, the champagne bar a charnel house of birds, some still twitching, most mercifully still. Alan was an absurd figure, great plumes of padding sprouted from all over his borrowed jacket.

"Thank you," he said, removing the coat gingerly.

"A pleasure," Penelope replied and couldn't help but laugh. For a moment they both did and Penelope thought they might just have taken their first step towards getting on with one another. Then the air vent gave an almighty clang as something large moved along it and their laughter stopped.

"I have a feeling the pigeons were just an advance guard," said Alan, backing defensively in front of Penelope.

She appreciated the gesture but was damned if she was going to allow it, moving slightly in front of him. "Perhaps they were spooked by something moving along behind them?"

"Perhaps," Alan agreed, "though I can't say I like the idea of meeting something they would be scared of."

The vent clanked again and both of them could track the movement of something coming along the narrow chute. The metal popped and distorted as the weight of something inside pushed it out of shape. Closer and closer it moved towards the open hatch.

"Maybe we should drop back," Alan suggested.

"Before we even know what we're dealing with?" Penelope replied.

It was too late anyway as, whatever it was, reached the hatch and there was the shadow of movement in the darkness beyond. Suddenly a face appeared.

"Avast ye!" shouted Ryan, onetime cabin boy of the good ship *Intrepid*. "Alan Ahoy!"

4.

The crew of what had once been the much-loved *Intrepid* – before it met its end, smashed to splinters on the floor of the House's impossibly sizeable bathroom – had been convinced that their time was up. Their newest members, Alan and Sophie, had been whisked away from them down the gloomy plug hole they had spent a couple of days hiking toward. One of the wraiths – invisible creatures of pure force that patrolled the gaps between one section of the house and another – had set upon them and dragged the man and girl into the darkness against the crew's best efforts. The ship's captain, Hawkins, had been relieved that the wraith hadn't hung around to inflict further damage on his beleaguered crew. That relief was so laden with guilt at Alan and Sophie's likely fate that he pushed the feeling away as soon as he was able.

Their respite hadn't lasted long. A few minutes after their new friends had vanished, the sky around them had begun to darken, storm clouds appearing and lightning forking the sky. As if that hadn't been frightening enough the whole room had started shaking, tiles falling from the walls and showers of plaster raining down from the ceiling way above them. They weren't to know that this had been nothing but a side-effect of Sophie's communion with the House, a phenomenon felt throughout the building as the young girl altered its structure to accommodate the train station. As far as they were concerned this was nothing less catastrophic than the destruction of the whole building.

"We're too exposed," Barnabas had shouted, as it began to rain. "We'll be crushed to death for sure!" For once nobody saw fit to argue with him, in this case his famed pessimism was probably on the money.

"Cover yourselves the best you can!" Maggie cried, hoisting her pack above her mad explosion of hair.

Hawkins knew that was scant protection should the roof truly cave in. But they had an alternative…

He dropped to his knees by the plug hole and began fastening a pair of ropes to the bar of the central grating.

"If you think I'm going in there," Barnabas moaned, "you've another think coming. I prefer my chances out here."

"In where?" asked Jonah lifting both his eyepatches to reveal the milky, dead eyes beneath.

Ryan laughed, though none of the others were in the mood for the blind man's humour.

Maggie went to her husband's aid, taking one of the ropes off him and ensuring the knot was strong. She needn't have tested it, Hawkins had been on the ocean long enough to know how to secure ropes. "Well I'm up for it!" she cried, lowering herself off the side.

"Wait, woman!" Hawkins shouted, fearing for her. She blew him a kiss and bounced her way down the rope. Hawkins shook his head, though he couldn't hide a smile of pride. "Mad bugger will be the death of me one day…"

Ryan didn't need encouraging, dropping down the rope after her.

"Get over here!" Hawkins called to Barnabas and Jonah.

"I'm not going," Barnabas repeated as Hawkins put the rope in Jonah's hands and watched him drop into the hole. A large piece of ceiling broke loose behind them. It drifted down for a few seconds, the wind slowing its descent as it caught the wide surface area. Then it exploded against the tiles of the floor in a shower of plaster fragments. "Oh balls and arseholes," Barnabas moaned, holding his arms over his head to protect it from the debris. "Out of the way then, you terrible man." He shuffled past Hawkins, grabbed the rope and began to lower himself down. "I suppose if I fall I might knock that idiot Ryan off on my way. That would be some consolation." He vanished from sight.

Hawkins spared no time in following, the thunder and lightning building in intensity in the gloom above him. If the House was shaking itself to death he supposed he could live with it. Damn though, if he hadn't been determined to see his crew home safely…

He lowered himself into the plughole.

They weren't altogether protected inside the vast pipe of course, though what debris did fall in their direction was, for the most part, broken into smaller pieces by colliding with the spokes of the covering above.

"I feel like a spider," Ryan joked, gripping the rope with his legs and waving his arms – though it was far too dark for the others to see him.

"Stop shaking the damned rope!" Barnabas moaned. "I'm having enough difficulty hanging on without you making it harder."

On the other rope, Jonah was making swift business of the descent. "I must be reaching the end of the rope soon," he shouted up to Hawkins, "these things don't go on forever."

"Tell us what you see when you get there," shouted Ryan, much to Jonah's amusement.

"It's so dark I have no idea how far this drops," said Maggie, not far behind Jonah for all his speed. "We should have brought a lantern."

"Now she tells me," Hawkins replied, he'd been thinking much the same himself, in fact had been half-tempted to climb back up and grab one. A loud crash of brickwork and tiles from near the opening soon cured him of that idea. They had acted in haste and would pay the price soon enough. He had hoped the shaft wouldn't drop too far, even accounting for its gargantuan size it would surely branch off soon? But then that was assuming that this plumbing bore any relation to the pipework he was familiar with back home, an assumption that this House would no doubt mock him for soon enough. "I have matches in my pocket," he called down. "I could light one and drop it? See how far it falls?" He knew the plan was far from ideal, as much as the pipe offered some protection there was still rain in the air, that – or just the rush of wind as the match fell – was likely to snuff the flame before it told them anything useful.

Maggie agreed. "It likely won't help," she said, "we need something heavy, listen out for it as it falls."

"Hang on," Ryan said, the rope shaking as he shifted around above her.

"What did I tell you about shaking the damned rope?" Barnabas shouted.

"Drop you in a minute," Ryan muttered, "you're certainly heavy enough… Watch out below!" he dropped something into the darkness, Maggie flinching as she felt it whistle past her. After a few seconds there was a loud clang as whatever Ryan had dropped hit the ground.

"What was that?" Maggie asked.

"My belt," Ryan replied, "so be warned my trousers will likely fall on your face in a minute."

"Charming."

"It took just over a second after passing me to hit the bottom," shouted Jonah.

"Not far then!" Ryan replied.

"Far enough," Hawkins said. "Objects travel at around thirty feet a second so the ground's at least that below you."

"How does he know that?" Ryan asked, impressed.

"I'm clever, lad," Hawkins replied. "Consider yourself lucky to know me."

"Aye aye, Cap'n!" Ryan roared.

"Don't forget to factor in the time the noise takes to travel back up," suggested Jonah.

"Over thirty feet?" Hawkins replied. "Neither here nor there... if it shaves off a couple of foot you'll be lucky."

"Okay!" Ryan shouted. "Enough with the maths or I'll jump off the rope on a point of principle."

"Two plus two equals four," Barnabas suggested, happy to encourage him.

"I'm counting off the distance as I climb the last stretch," said Jonah, "though there's not much rope left, I'm swinging too much." After a few seconds... "there... maybe knock off ten or twelve feet."

"Are you right at the end?" Hawkins asked.

"My feet are," Jonah replied, "so that's another five foot or so leaving me enough to hold onto, add my height again... I reckon I'll be dropping ten foot or so."

"That sounds doable," suggested Maggie.

"If his maths are right," agreed Ryan, "I'd happily do it."

There was a moment of silence then a small splash followed by a grunt. "More like fifteen feet," came Jonah's voice. "Enough to make your arse sore if you land wrong. I'm speaking from experience you understand."

Maggie began to lower herself as far down the rope as she could. "I don't suppose we know whether the two ropes were the same length do we?" she asked.

"They should be," Hawkins replied, though now his wife's safety relied on the fact he was reluctant to risk it. Not that they could hang there forever.

"Soon find out," she replied, letting go and landing with a whoosh of expelled air.

"Are you alright?" Hawkins shouted, panicking in the silence that followed.

"Fine," his wife wheezed after a few seconds, "just winded."

"Bet one of us will end up with a broken ankle," moaned Barnabas, climbing down. "See it coming a mile off."

Or a broken neck. Hawkins thought.

"Geronimo!" called Ryan, letting go of the rope. There was a slight splash. "Piece of cake," he called back up.

Now there was only Hawkins and Barnabas left. "After you," Hawkins called. "Just move out of the way quick smart if you don't want me jumping on your head."

"I didn't sign up for this," Barnabas muttered. "Life on the ocean waves, not skulking around water pipes." He let go of the rope, landing with a yell.

"Are you alright?" Hawkins called. It would be Barnabas that hurt himself wouldn't it... bloody typical.

"He's fine," Maggie called, "just didn't expect to be."

"I could have sworn I felt my leg break," Barnabas insisted, "could have sworn it..."

"Big girl," Ryan chuckled. "Come on Cap'n!"

Hawkins dropped as low as he could and let go of the rope. He hit the ground a little stiff, his heels skidding in the water and sending him toppling backwards. His hand caught on the side of the pipe and he heard his wrist crack.

"Damn it!" he growled, the pain surging up his arm.

"Hawkins?" Maggie called, shuffling forward in the dark.

"Broke my damned wrist," he moaned, "felt it snap..." He roared with pain as he tested it. "Yep..." he , once he'd caught his breath, "definitely broken."

"I knew it!" Barnabas shouted, absurdly elated that he'd been proven right.

"Shut up Barnabas," Jonah said, clouting him around the head.

"Ow!" Barnabas flinched, "how did you...?" Jonah clouted him again. "Ow!"

"Business as usual down here for a blind man," Jonah replied. "I just followed the noise of your flapping mouth."

"I'll be okay," Hawkins said, "I've had worse…"

"We need light," Maggie replied, "with light I can rig you up a sling."

Hawkins prised the matches from his pocket with his good hand and rattled them so that she knew where to grab them. "We'll soon run out unless we can find something to burn."

"I have a headscarf that I'm happy to lose," said Maggie, "if we could find something to wrap it around."

"That's the tricky thing," admitted Jonah, "if only one of us had a peg leg."

"Or this?" Hawkins suggested, pulling his retractable telescope out of his jacket pocket. "Your headscarf won't last long though, we need something that would burn slower than that, a section of rope would have done the job."

"I'll just climb back up and get some shall I?" Ryan asked.

"How about a dressing?" Barnabas asked sheepishly, aware that his popularity was at an all time low.

"Dressing?" asked Maggie.

"From when I burned my arm on the rigging," Barnabas explained.

"That was weeks ago!" Maggie laughed. "You mean to tell me you're still wearing it?"

"I kept meaning to take it off…" Barnabas said. "Look, do you want it or not?"

"His skin's probably grown over it!" said Ryan.

Barnabas didn't offer the boy a reply, just began to unravel the yellowing bandage. Maggie groped for it in the dark, wrapping both her headscarf and the bandage around the telescope. She didn't mention the smell, Barnabas had suffered enough.

"It still won't last long," she admitted, "but it's better than nothing." She struck a match and held it to the impromptu torch, lighting up the dark tunnel with an orange glow.

"Let's get moving quickly," said Hawkins, grimacing as he got to his feet, "who knows how long this pipe goes on for?"

They sloshed their way forward. Jonah allowing Maggie to lead. Even he had to admit his lack of vision might cause a problem if the pipe were suddenly to bend beneath them.

It wasn't long before the makeshift torch began to flicker, running out of "fuel" to burn. They took it in turns to sacrifice strips of fabric. Condensing what was left of their provisions into only a couple of the rucksacks, they were able to work hanks of the thick canvas from the now empty spares. Still, they were only too aware that there would come a point that they'd all end up in the dark, buck-naked, as the last few flickers of light ebbed away. They could only hope that they would find their way out of the pipes before that happened.

"Pipe drops here," said Maggie, holding the torch out into the darkness ahead. "Though I think the drop's gradual enough we might be able to slide down."

"Now you're talking!" said Ryan, pushing his way to the front. "Water slide!"

Hawkins could think of many reasons as to why entrusting themselves to the pipes might be fool's business. He also knew they had no option but to ignore them all. "Okay," he shrugged, his broken arm now slung through his shirt so he looked like Napoleon, "one by one we may as well try…"

"Wahey!" cried Ryan, dropping to the ground and pushing off the edge of the inclined pipe.

"Will that idiot ever wait for me to finish before jumping in with both feet?" Hawkins wondered.

"Doubt it, my love," said Maggie, "just like you wouldn't have done when you were his age."

Hawkins guessed this was true so didn't pursue it.

They heard Ryan yelp in pain before shouting. "It flattens out again after a while. Nearly broke my arse in half!"

"Shouldn't be a problem for me then!" said Maggie. "I was born with enough padding to see me through this exact situation." She passed the torch to her husband and went next, a high-pitched *wheeee!* trailing after her as she went.

"Shout when you're clear," Hawkins called. They heard a surprised grunt and then Maggie called back. "I just landed on Ryan, but once I've fished him out of my drawers he should be fine."

"Speak for yourself!" they heard the cabin boy shout back. "Thought I was a goner for sure."

"Okay," Maggie called, "we're clear!"

Barnabas insisted on going next. "No way I'm waiting to be last," he said, "nothing bad ever happens to the one in the middle."

Hawkins rolled his eyes as the miserable sod vanished into the dark.

"You'd better go next," he said to Jonah.

"Nah, Cap'n," the blind man replied, "I won't be able to resist kicking Barnabas in the arse at the end. You go and take the light with you, not as if I'll need it."

Hawkins nodded – if only to himself – and lowered himself onto the lip of the pipe. He held the torch high and kicked off, scooting through the pipe. The flame made its irritation clear, flickering and lashing at him like a scolding wife. The shallow trickle of drain water sprayed up around him, he kept his mouth tightly closed, remembering the opiate effect of the liquid. He hit the flat pipe at the bottom with a jolt that yanked his arm and made him yell.

"You okay Cap'n?" asked Ryan.

"Fine," Hawkins replied, angry at his own newfound disability, "just hurt my damned arm that's all."

"All clear?" Jonah shouted.

"Aye," Hawkins said, letting Ryan take the torch and help him to his feet even though he found himself momentarily infuriated that the boy had thought to offer.

They moved further down the pipe. Hawkins' trousers clung to him, slick with the seawater, and rubbing between his thighs. This is no way for a ship captain to be, he thought, broken arm and soggy arse, crawling along the sewers like a damned rat.

Jonah appeared behind them, as devil-may-care as usual. "Could have been worse," he said. "What's next?"

"Let's find out," said Ryan, dashing ahead with the torch. "Looks like we have a choice," he announced, "the pipe splits both ways."

"Go left," said Hawkins instantly.

"Wow," Ryan replied, "how can you tell?"

"I can't," Hawkins admitted, "so go left, it makes little difference."

They went left. After a few minutes a clicking noise made Hawkins call a halt. "What the hell is that?" he said. Thinking: Should have gone right... "Jonah?"

"Couldn't say for sure Cap'n," he replied, "though it sure as hell sounds like..."

"Crabs!" Ryan shouted. In the flickering light of the torch, a curved pennant of crabs was curving towards them through the pipe. They weren't large, the size of a drink's coaster, little claws waving in the air as if performing a Mexican wave. Ryan began skipping around as they gripped at the hems of his trousers and scuttled up him. "Urgh!" he shouted, beating at himself with the torch.

"Change of plan, we go right," said Hawkins, "and stop messing about with those things Ryan, you'll burn yourself to a crisp."

They moved swiftly – Ryan in particular, jumping up and down, convinced that he had crustaceans in his underwear – looping around into the alternative tunnel and hoping the crabs wouldn't follow. They didn't, moving in a militaristic line back the way the crew had come.

"Anyone else on the menu?" asked Ryan, still tugging at his clothes. "Please tell me I'm not the only one with bits missing?"

"That's what happens when you're stupid enough to be eager," said Barnabas. "Stick your nose out enough and you'll lose it in the end."

"Thanks for the inspirational thought," said Hawkins, "you certainly know how to get the best out of a crew."

The pipe was beginning to get narrower. The thin trickle of seawater beneath their feet also dwindled and then dried out to nothing.

"The pipe's changing shape too," said Maggie, "losing the curve and getting edges."

"We're obviously passing into a different area," said Hawkins, "let's just hope there's a way out of here and into somewhere a little more comfortable."

Soon it was too narrow to walk standing up. "What if this just keeps getting narrower until we can't fit anymore?" asked Barnabas.

"Then we turn around and go back the other way," said Hawkins. "What else?"

"I don't mind checking it out," said Ryan. "I could scoot ahead quicker on my own and see if there's a way out?"

"Be my guest," said Hawkins, knowing full well the kid would go with or without his approval. There was a time, he thought, when I could have sworn this crew did what I told them...

They gave him the torch and Ryan dropped into a crouch, moving ahead in a bizarre shuffle. After a couple of minutes the going was too tight even for that and he had to drop to his hands and knees. The pipe had well and truly flattened out now, becoming a rectangle rather than a tube. The surface wasn't the heavy ceramic it had been either, it had turned into a rough metal, popping and squealing as he worked his way along it. Ahead he heard a riotous clatter as if someone were having a fit in the darkness ahead, the sides of the vent banging and echoing back to him. Mindful of the crabs earlier he grew nervous. The last thing he wanted was to come face to face with something terrible when he had little way of defending himself bar biting the hell out of it.

He kept moving anyway, damned if he was going to turn around and go running back just because he'd heard a noise that had scared him.

Soon he had to drop to his belly and it was impossible to move any other way but slowly and awkwardly, still holding that torch out in front. The heat from its flames was cooking the air in the enclosed space, making his face tingle in the heat. Sooner or later he was going to have to give up on this and work his way back – the thought of doing that was grim, scooting backwards using one hand... it would take him hours and he knew it. Then he heard a noise that pushed him harder: a woman screaming. That proved there was something ahead beyond this damned vent, though whether it would be an improvement was hard to be sure. A little further and he heard another sound, a man's voice... a voice he recognised too, though he would have been lying if he'd said he'd expected to hear it again. He was sure the sound was coming from below and a little further ahead, it had none of the echo he would expect were they stuck here in the vent with him, they must be on the outside. A little further and he realised that there was light creeping in. He moved faster and faster, bashing his head and knees over and over again in his enthusiasm to reach the light. The sound of voices continued below him as he reached the hole in the vent and lowered his head into the bright light of the station. And there he was, the owner of that voice…

"Avast ye!" Ryan shouted with a grin, "Alan ahoy!"

5.

Alan and Penelope constructed a pyramid out of the tables. Starting with a base of six, then four, then two… it was just about high enough – and solid enough – for Ryan to climb out and get down. While they worked, the boy shuffled back until he was close enough to the rest of his party to shout and be heard. This wasn't difficult, Ryan had never been a quiet lad. The rest of the *Intrepid* crew made their way along the vent and dropped down into the champagne bar.

"Who would have thought I'd clap eyes on you again?" said Hawkins, patting Alan on the back. "Where's Sophie?"

"She's okay," Alan replied. "I think so anyway… look, there's a hell of a lot to explain to you so why don't we get out of here?" he gestured to the dead pigeons that still littered the floor. "Find somewhere a bit more comfortable to catch up?"

At which point, all the information stands buzzed into life, the face of the Grumpy Controller appearing across the whole upper level. "Sophie needs to go to the library now!" he shouted before promptly switching off.

"Or perhaps we could talk on the way?" said Penelope.

FIVE
The Old Man and the Sea

1.

Lying on his back, his old bones just as stiff as the sea-lacquered belly of the boat, Ashe dreamed of blue skies and calm waves. If dreams had weight the storm above him should have whimpered into silence, the rain dried out and the wind calmed to a soft, warm breeze to dry his soaked body. This did not happen. The sea continued to throw him from side to side. A child tossing a baseball from one hand to another, practicing his catch. His head was bleeding. Even in the rain he could tell that the warm wetness that pooled around the nape of his neck had come from within rather than without. He tried to remember what had happened, to own the memory of being cast off the *Intrepid* to float toward shore. It felt loose and just out of reach. A story he had been told rather than something he had experienced. His head felt as if it were speared on a rusty nail. A sharp sense of pain at the heart of a wider numb malaise. The storm, he thought, did I hit my head in the storm?

That storm continued in affirmation, even as he slipped out of understanding and towards sleep.

2.

He had left Tibet with a dry taste in his mouth and a sickness in his belly. Returning to the station he had meant to check on Sophie, knock a few of the more unsavoury thoughts away with a little human company. He thought a few hours with Penelope might just do the trick. It was hard to become too self-reflective in her company. They weren't there. He had walked both levels of the station, mindlessly pushing through the ghostly passengers as they moved between shops. They were already on their way to the library then. He sat down in the cafe, feeling utterly exhausted. He had barely started and he was almost at his wits end.

3.

The storm blew itself out at dawn. Even in his semi-delirious state Ashe could tell this. The thunder grew more distant, the lightning cutting its way across the horizon. It was information he felt right on the edge of awareness, like the sound of a telephone intruding onto the shallow edge of dreaming. He had shown the man how to leave the station hadn't he? Yes, that was a wild card, an unpredictable event that might change things... Perhaps he had been stupid, better to leave everything as he knew it should be. Getting too used to this playing God, he thought... swinging back and forth in the boat like a man on a swing seat. He reached one weary hand toward the lightening sky and extended a finger. I command you, wind, he thought, to take me to shore.

And with that he fell unconscious.

4.

Returning to the Barlow Shed he looked up at the trains and thought ahead.

Ideally he would have taken a trip to his old apartment in Kissimmee, picked up all his old notes and research. But that was now impossible. These trains, as miraculous as they were, would show a very different world to the one Alan Arthur had once known. Traveling before 1976 was fine enough, no change there, but anything after... well Ashe knew that world well enough and there was nothing of any use to him in it. *Really*? A voice asked in his head, *are you sure? Wouldn't you like to check up on them? Make sure they're okay?*

No. No he wouldn't. No more distractions.

He could remember his notes well enough to have a vague timeline of the box. He knew that it had left Tibet, picked up by one of the soldiers who would carry it with him for a few years until – irritated by its refusal to open – he sold it to a market trader in Madras. He could remember the trader's name, Yoosuf, and that was all. He would just have to hope that the train took him where he needed to go. It was clear to him that the House was as motivated in this as he was. It didn't want to die. Whether it was a piece of Sophie's consciousness or something more rudimentary, a sentient flicker within the House itself, he couldn't be sure. Whichever, it knew the world beyond its walls, understood the patterns of it all better than any of them.

He remembered floating in that dangerous sea while on the *Intrepid*. The feeling he had experienced was one of universal contact, becoming the water and feeling every single tile that surrounded it. The water had known its environment, had felt the ship floating on it, the House that embraced it. This was just the same. The House was connected to everything and everyone, it knew the shape of events in the real world just as a sea feels the contours of the beaches that lead into it. It would let him find Yoosuf, Ashe was sure of it.

One other piece of business occurred to him. He had managed to gather a fair quantity of cash from the others in the house – Carruthers in particular held a varied store of notes and coins hidden away in a concealed pocket inside his jacket. It wouldn't last forever though. He decided to go shopping.

He entered the closest store, a small gift place, filled with jewellery and the sort of purses that looked like they were made from icing not leather. Edible fashions. He checked the till but wasn't surprised to find it empty. This wasn't the real thing, a good representation perhaps but once you scratched the surface the illusion was revealed. Would the same be the case for the stock? He loaded his pockets with jewellery, anything that carried a stone or might be made from gold. Anything in fact that might turn a greedy man's head. He moved from shop to shop doing the same thing, eventually grabbing a satchel so that he could carry more. Watches, rings, brooches, nothing too big. By the time he was done his bag was heavy with the best the shops had to offer.

Ordering his tickets from that irritating face of the House, the Grumpy Controller, Ashe made his way to his train and sailed out of this world and back into his own.

5.

During a brief moment of lucidity Ashe became aware that he was no longer alone in the lifeboat. Opening eyes that had been glued shut with dried salt baked in the sun, he saw the profile of a gull on the stern. It was looking out across the water – as far as he could tell, anyway, that fat, black eye could be looking anywhere – perhaps searching for food raised by the storm. A brittle notion crumbled in Ashe's head, not quite strong enough for him to fix on as he dropped back into sleep, *perhaps it's just found all the food it needs*.

6.

The market cooked like a stew in the heavy Madras air. The scents of sweat, produce and spice surrounded Ashe as he pushed his way between the crowded stalls. A five dollar note – not due to be printed for another ten years but the first that had come to hand – had bought him directions from a street beggar on the outskirts. The beggar had grinned at the sign of foldable money and vanished it into his clothes swiftly so that he didn't mark himself out as rich pickings for anyone else on the street. Ashe knew that when the man came to spend the money his enthusiasm would swiftly falter but for a couple of minutes he had his own personal guide, willing to show the white stranger anything he might desire. When Ashe made it clear that he desired nothing more exotic than the market stall of Yoosuf, his guide had seemed disappointed in him. No doubt the beggar had imagined what delights he would take from the city were he lucky enough to have pockets filled with American dollars and browsing the market was not one of them. Nonetheless he performed his duty admirably, leading him to the shadowy entrance of a stall built into the side of a building.

Amongst the voluminous silk drapes and crammed displays, Ashe found his man. A small fellow sipping at a glass of tea so sweet it poured like syrup past the few remaining teeth in the man's mouth. Yoosuf hid his enthusiasm at the chance of earning some dollars better than the beggar. Ashe suspected this was because he had a fair few of them already. He caught the glint of a wristwatch beneath the man's sleeve. There was a signet ring embedded in the thick hairs above the knuckle of the fourth finger on his right hand. The glass he drank from was thin and well-crafted, decorated with a spider's web of metal that might even have been silver. Yes, Ashe suspected Yoosuf was not as impoverished as those who surrounded him. Whether this would make negotiations any more difficult had yet to be seen. He wasn't naïve enough to mention the box straightaway, certainly... let them build up to that. To begin with, all Yoosuf needed to know is that he had an American on hand who wanted to buy.

They moved through several items in Yoosuf's stock, everything from statuettes to embroidered handkerchiefs. Yoosuf proffered a rather grotesque brooch fashioned from a scarab beetle, then a wooden mask, its bright pink tongue curled lasciviously, eager to take your coat. Ashe wanted none of these things but he bought them. He would soon be playing the part of archeologist, booking space on the *Intrepid* to transport items back to the States. None of those items mattered but one, they would all be window dressing. Eventually, seeing a small ivory box on one of the man's shelves Ashe commented that his grandchild liked decorative boxes, did Yoosuf perhaps have something more along those lines?

The vendor spread his arms wide, but of course he did... Yoosuf had *everything*.

Within five minutes Ashe had reclaimed the box – and purchased enough rubbish to fill a single packing crate. Now came the bartering. He offloaded his satchel onto the man's small counter, counting out the items one at a time to the increased enthusiasm of Yoosuf. The man tried to conceal it of course, no vendor worth his salt lets his tongue hang out at the first glimpse of shiny things, but Ashe knew that he had a buyer. There was too much interest before the casting down of the items in feigned dismissal, a second too long rubbing his thumbs across the cut surface of the jewels or the highly-polished metal. Ashe realised that the magic of the House had in fact done him a favour. These items may be imaginary but that only emphasised their glister. These were the sparkling fantasies of thousands of dreamers and they shone with every drop of avarice and desire those dreamers could muster. Certainly they were making Yoosuf salivate, however much he may try and pretend otherwise.

Ashe named a figure, as large and insulting as he dared. The trader was visibly stunned and Ashe began to replace the shining treasure back into his satchel, slowly... letting each item offer one final sparkle before it dropped back into the bag. Yoosuf paid half of the original price quoted in cash and gave Ashe the rest of his shopping list for free.

Not a bad bit of business, all in all, Ashe thought and made arrangements for his case of belongings – minus the box, that he slipped into his pocket – to be delivered to the nearest reputable hotel.

7.

The gull gave a cry that cut through Ashe's delirium. He came awake to find the bird on his chest. Its large yellow beak turned from one side to the other as if it was wondering how best to open the shell on this particularly large catch. Ashe only managed to raise one arm, his limbs so stiff that even that effort shot a bolt of pain into his shoulder and nudged him into unconsciousness again. It was enough, the gull retreated, returning to the stern of the boat where it was happy to wait.

8.

Ashe kept one hand on the box in his pocket as he moved toward the *Intrepid*. The rest of it could be transported at the mercy of the locals but the box would never leave his sight again. Not until it had delivered its next victims at least. He recognised the ship immediately and felt a warm sense of love for it. He had only been onboard for a few days but it had been a good time. It was onboard this boat, working its rigging and sweeping its deck, that Alan Arthur had begun to find a man inside himself. For that brief while he hadn't been a walking hole, a shell of neuroses and fears, he had just been a man making a ship move forward.

"Help you?" came a voice from above.

He looked up to see the silhouette of Hawkins looking down at him.

"You certainly can," said Ashe, "I'd like to hire your ship."

Ashe woke to darkness. His throat felt solid as if he had swallowed a brick and the damn thing had become lodged there. In the cool of the night he felt altogether more human, the heat of the sun had burned his face to the texture of dried meat, like a crisp dog treat fashioned from pig hide. He managed to sit up, the back of his head sticking to the wood for a moment before peeling lose with the rip of parting Velcro. He put one hand to the base of his skull, feeling the crisp, matted hair and understanding that he had lost consciousness for a whole day. It was when the ship vanished... he thought, remembering the sight of the *Intrepid* folding in on itself and vanishing. The water around it had clapped together to fill the vacant hole, his small life boat flipping in the surf. He couldn't believe he had remained upright, battered and drenched, yes but not drowned. His head pulsed and he realised he must have suffered a concussion. His head beating against the wood of the boat until he had slipped out of consciousness and lain there at the mercy of the tide. *Don't forget that gull... you nearly ended up on its dinner table.* This was true but there was no sign of the bird now, no doubt it was resting somewhere, head beneath its wing, hoping that when the sun rose the meal it had found would finally be served.

With some difficulty, Ashe looked over his shoulder, hoping to see the lights of land. There was nothing. *Who knows how far I've drifted?* he thought, *could be halfway to Australia by now*.

Knowing it would do him no good but unable to resist, he reached over the side of the boat and splashed water on his face and into his mouth. The saltiness immediately threatened to empty his stomach and that would leave him even more dehydrated. He closed his eyes and fought the urge to be sick. Once sure he had it under control he took another scoop in his mouth, this time not swallowing, just rolling it around in there to ease the cracked skin. He spat it back out and wiped at his chapped lips.

Dehydrated and concussed. Maybe a dose of sunstroke too. Things are going well.

The box was lost to him, too, of course. Though he was by no means certain that was a problem, who could tell whether Chester came into possession of it through his intervention or a line of events utterly unrelated to him. He was still here... that offered some hope that time was still on track.

He scrabbled around in the boat for his oars. There was only one, the other presumably lost during the storm. One's better than nothing, he thought and looked up at the sky. The storm had blown the clouds clear and the stars were bright. Locating the Southern Cross, he estimated east and slowly began to head in that direction. If he hadn't been blown too far off course then east should still see him towards Kupang – or anywhere on the Indonesian coast, he wasn't in the least picky. When planning the trip he had been more than usually conscious of his inability to estimate a return ticket date and had planned accordingly. His train left from a stretch of beach on the south side of Kupang harbour in a week. On the one hand the idea of kicking around waiting for his train had made him squirm, on the other: missing it completely because he was still floating about in the middle of nowhere could be catastrophic. He would wait if he had to, use the time to plan and build up his strength. Certainly it now seemed that he could do with it – plus medical assistance if he could find it – that was if he ever saw dry land again of course, something he couldn't predict with any absolute certainty.

After about ten minutes of rowing, swaying from side to side as he alternated with the oar, he had to take a rest. He had prided himself on his strength and endurance given his age but there was a limit to any man's abilities and he feared he was beginning to find his. If only his damned head would stop pounding…

10.

He had agreed a price with Hawkins, settled on a route and paid the man half upfront. It had been incredibly uncomfortable. All the while he had been wanting to pat the man on the back, ask after Maggie, his wife or Ryan – no, of course Ryan wasn't on the crew yet, they'd picked him up later. Of course he could do none of these things. In Hawkin's future he would sit down with a much younger Ashe, recalling the events that had led to his appearance in the House. Those events had strongly featured an irritable and untrustworthy "archeologist" who, after threatening Hawkins and wife under gunpoint, had driven the captain to such a fury that he had triggered the box during a storm and sent both himself and his ship out of the real world. Ashe had to play his part. He had his role and he would stick to it, however much it may stick in his craw.

Leaving the port he began to make his way to his hotel. The city was undergoing the change of guard that brought on the night. Day traders packed up their wares to head home and discuss the day's take – or lack of it – with their families. Stalls closed, shops brought in their awnings. The night people came from the shadows and prepared to take over. A man juggled flaming torches, the fire whipping around his emaciated body and throwing shadows around his prominent ribs. The sweet waft of cooking fires and incense crawled over a brightly painted statue of Ganesh, decorated with flickering candles that shone off his lustrous trunk. A party of British soldiers cheered to see one of their party lose a little more money to a young boy who shuffled cards like a seasoned croupier. In the doorways the beggars switched places, the day shift skulking away to have their monies collected by their employers so they could receive their meagre cut.

Ashe had never been a well-travelled man. Before this he had only visited other cultures on paper, getting a feel for their ways through maps and historical texts. Now, in the middle of it all, his senses were sore. The smell was the greatest of it, that mixture of spice, smoke and sea… it was almost too much to ingest.

By the time Ashe reached his hotel, the light had faded from the sky to be replaced by flickering lamps. In the small reception, the owner smiled at him over a bushy moustache flecked with coconut milk. "Your key sir," he said, inclining his head deferentially and placing it on the desk. "Can I get you anything else?"

Ashe considered food but found that he was in the mood for nothing but sleep. So he thanked the man, took his key and went to find his bed.

His room was on the second floor and, as he turned the key in the lock he hoped the noise from the street below would quieten down soon. It sounded like someone had declared a religious festival right beneath his balcony. Opening the door a hand dropped to his wrist and he found himself yanked into the room, tumbling over the bed and onto the floor the other side.

A small lamp began to glow and he recognised Yoosuf's face as the trader leaned into the light. "Good evening," the man said. "You will forgive the intrusion but I have been thinking."

I'll just bet you have, Ashe thought. Had his deception with the jewellery been discovered? The stones revealed to be paste? The metal no more precious than plate?

"I was thinking that an American with so many riches was bound to have more."

No, just simple greed.

"If I'd had any more riches I'd have sold the damn things to you," he said, pulling himself up onto the bed, sparing a glance at the man who had pulled him through the door. He was over six foot, a thick black beard hiding all his features bar the eyes – one of which was blind, a soapy, pearlescent white.

"If that is the case then I suppose I will have to settle for the money I have already paid you," said Yoosuf. "But still, you will understand if I convince myself first, yes?"

He inclined his head towards the accomplice who began to circle the bed. Ashe drew his revolver out of his pocket and pulled the trigger – and that was a defining moment, he thought later, he hadn't tried to threaten the man he had simply sought to eliminate the problem – the hammer fell on a spent chamber. Ashe was out of bullets. The man grabbed him and Ashe did the only thing he could think of, ramming the barrel of his gun into the man's one good eye. He would later remonstrate with himself over the thoughtless cruelty of that too. The man screamed, raising one thick hairy hand to his face and lashing out with the other. Ashe avoided the blow and got in a good one of his own, turning the revolver so that its butt was facing outward he punched his attacker in the belly with it. The big man recoiled backwards, tumbling into Yoosuf who had been getting to his feet, a thin knife pulled from his jacket that caught a piece of the lamplight on its blade and held it there. Ashe rolled back over the bed, yanked the door handle and ran out into the corridor.

So much for a good night's sleep, he thought. He bounced down the stairs, past the still-smiling man behind the counter and back out onto the street.

The crowds he had suspected might keep him from sleep were to his benefit now. He pushed his way into them hoping to lose himself. Out of the corner of his eye he saw two more men who had been stood beneath the street lamp opposite his hotel. At the sight of him they moved to cut him off. Yoosuf certainly hadn't come undermanned.

Ashe could think of no better plan than to head for the port, if all else failed he might at least be safe onboard the *Intrepid*. The streets that had seemed so resplendent earlier now felt alien and hostile, every face brought the potential for attack, every glint of metal a possible knife or gun. Glancing over his shoulder he could see that he was still being pursued, Yoosuf was not a man to give up on his money so readily – and Ashe could see why he had been content to part with it, it had been no more than a loan...

He moved as fast as he could, his pursuers drawing closer. Yoosuf held back, his large accomplice stood by his side, a handkerchief turning red as he held it up to his eye. The other two were now mere feet away, either side of the street, moving past to cut him off and force him back the way he had come.

"Oi!" a voice bellowed in his ear. "Watch where you're going, pal."

He came face to face with a British soldier. The man's thick sideboards and moustache failed to disguise his tender age. Nor did his smart uniform knock the edge off his thick, Northern accent. "You nearly had me over," the soldier said. "What's your business anyway, barging along like that."

"Trying not to get a knife between the ribs," Ashe admitted, checking the location of his two pursuers. Both had hung back, keeping their eye on Yoosuf to see what their employer wanted them to do. "I was about to be mugged."

"What's that when it's at home, then?" the soldier asked, raising an eyebrow as if he'd just been told of a new sexual practice.

"Robbed," Ashe explained. "A gang of them were waiting for me when I got back to my hotel."

"Oh aye?" The soldier seemed happy enough to accept this, clearly rather common occurrence. "Still about are they?"

"Yes, one either side of the road and their boss is the man at the head of the street there, you can't miss him, he's the only one that's got a giant bleeding on him."

The soldier chuckled as he spotted Yoosuf. "Got a couple of punches in yourself then?"

"Just a couple."

"Come on," the soldier turned back the way he had come, "walk with me a bit, we'll see if that doesn't put them off."

"You're not going to do anything?" Ashe asked.

"I've no great desire to be stabbed myself," the soldier admitted, "the missus would never forgive me." He gave Ashe a smile. "We can't go kicking up a fuss every time we spot some bugger up to no good," he admitted, "we haven't the manpower. But I reckon you'll find they'll give you a wide berth for now."

"Thanks."

"It's fine, we can rustle up some lads to help you shift

hotels too if you want, you're obviously not staying in the best of rooms."

"It was recommended to me by the man who just tried to rob me."

"Well there's a coincidence," the soldier chuckled. "There's plenty of decent places if you know where to look, don't worry. It's not a bad old place this, whatever you might think right now."

"Oh I've spent time in worse spots, believe me."

11.

As the night wore on, Ashe tried to row as often as he could, checking the sky to keep himself on track. His head continued to hurt and if he rowed for too long his vision started to cloud over.

"Not good," he told the ocean, "not good at all."

The prospect of another day of that sun beating down on him didn't help his mood. In fact he wondered if it might be enough to finish him off. Shaking such thoughts loose – they didn't help after all – he made his slow way across the waves, pushing his broken body as hard as he dared.

12.

After watching Yoosuf's men peel away – with the trader offering one final scowl before melting into the crowd – Ashe had settled with the soldier in a small coffee shop. They ordered tea and watched the crowds.

"It's not like Wakefield," the soldier said, "that's for sure."

"How long have you been here?" Ashe asked, taking a sip of sweet tea.

"Twelve months now," the soldier replied, "give or take. It's good, I always wanted to see the world, now look at me."

"But you miss home?"

"Of course, but when I go back I'll be changed. I'll be bringing back new ideas and new ways of looking at things."

"The most important of which is?"

"Sometimes you have to break things in order to make them better."

13.

At some point Ashe had fallen back asleep. He woke to the caw of the gull and the heat of the sun on his face.

"Morning you bastard," he croaked, fixing the bird with a bleary-eyed stare. "I'm not dead yet."

The gull cocked its head. *Just give it time… I can be patient.*

I just bet you can, Ashe thought, picking up his oar. The sun was still climbing which confirmed his estimation of east. Slowly he dragged the boat towards it.

For a while he imagined the boat was climbing through the air, making its slow ascent towards that fat, malevolent sun. Soon, he thought, I'll reach it. I'll climb my crumbling body inside and turn to dust. What a relief that will be…

The gull continued to maintain its watch. After a while it began to talk and Ashe was sure its voice was the same as the Grumpy Controller from the House.

"You're no use to us dead, you know," it said, "I thought you were strong?"

"Why don't you take the oar for a bit?" Ashe replied.

The bird shook its wings. "With these? You must be dreaming."

"Yes," said Ashe, "I must be."

"Do you think you'll ever reach land?" it asked.

"You tell me, you must have seen it more recently than I have."

"It's a way off, true." The bird's head shook as if with a nervous twitch. "I think you'll be dead before you get there."

"Thanks for the confidence."

"Just saying, you're half in your coffin already."

"I had noticed."

The gull fell silent, watching as Ashe worked the oar for a few minutes more then fell back into the boat, once more giving into unconsciousness.

"Yes," the gull said, looking down on the Ashe's prone body, "it's all looking a bit desperate isn't it?"

14.

Ashe had slept at the soldier's billet, a small hotel commandeered by the British forces. Rising early, he had been accompanied by a couple of NCOs to try and retrieve his belongings from the hotel. Ashe had been quite sure that the crate would no longer be there and Yoosuf hadn't disappointed him. Left with only a few hours to replace the belongings, he secured a crate from the port and filled it with the cheapest, most worthless items he could gather from the stalls close at hand. None of it mattered, it was cover, nothing more. In a few days it would be thrown overboard and never seen again.

He arrived at the *Intrepid*, even more regretful that he couldn't confide in the captain than he had been the day before. His act as a non-communicative and surly client wasn't hard to pull off. If he wasn't able to talk pleasantly then he would rather not talk at all and his frustration was easily mistaken for rudeness.

He sat in the small cabin Hawkins had provided him. Looking around he was sure it was the same one he had been put in when – some months into their future – the crew had fished he and Sophie out of the water and looked after them. It made him even more miserable.

The ship set sail for a destination it would never reach and Ashe reclined in his cabin.

15.

Ashe came awake to a sensation of the boat rocking violently around him. Not another storm? No, the sky was clear…

"You're awake then?" Ashe looked around, delirious, there was nobody on the boat but that damned gull. Oh… perhaps he hadn't woken up at all.

The boat continued to shake and he risked leaning over the side to check the water. It was thick with fish, tumbling over one another in their urge to push against the side of the boat.

"What's got into them?" Ashe said.

"Me," said the gull. "Who knew I was so powerful? I'm beginning to wonder if there's much I can't do these days."

Ashe tumbled back into the boat as it shook again. This was quite absurd, surely it wasn't the House? Not yet? How could it possibly…

"I wouldn't worry about it if I were you," said the gull. "Just sit back and dream of shore, at this rate we'll be there in no time."

The storm began to rage around the *Intrepid*. Ashe reluctantly left his cabin in order to play his part in furthering the irritation of his captain.

"I begin to wonder if you're even remotely capable of sailing this vessel," he shouted over the wind and rain, as he stumbled onto the deck. "I expect we shall all be on the bottom of the ocean before our journey is half finished."

Hawkins gritted his teeth, rubbing water from his face and hoping to keep his temper under control. "With all due respect sir," he replied, "even the finest sea captains have little control over the weather."

"I wasn't talking about the 'finest sea captains' Hawkins, I was talking about you. A jumped up tugboat skipper whose delusions of capability will no doubt be the death of all of us."

Hawkins wife put her hand on her husband's shoulder and whispered in his ear. No doubt, thought Ashe, she was reminding him to think of the money and keep his calm. Fat chance of that by the time I've finished.

"Getting directions from your wife now is it?" Ashe gave a hollow chuckle that rattled like poison in his throat. How he wished he could cough it up, but once produced it hung there. "One hopes she has a better sense of direction than you. Given her size perhaps she can simply sniff out the ovens and stew pots of dry land, eh?"

That did it, as Ashe had known it would. Hawkins would take his own insults – begrudgingly but he would take them – any directed at his wife however were more than the man could stand.

"Enough!" he shouted, grabbing Ashe by his lapels and forcing him back against the wall of the wheelhouse. "You skulk in my ship like a plague rat, you insult me and my crew... I will not stand for it!"

Ashe summoned up one final grin. "With your skills I'm surprised you're not used to a bit of criticism."

Hawkins roared and dragged him below deck. He yanked him into his own cabin and hurled him at an easy chair in the corner. He yanked open a drawer on his desk and counted out half of the money Ashe had paid him and hurled it across the room. "Half back and you can go aground at Indonesia. I won't suffer your company for a moment longer than that."

"Half?" Ashe utterly deflated now simply nodded, took his money and returned to his own cabin. He felt every inch the Judas.

He sat down in the dark, holding his empty revolver in his hand. In a few hours, once Hawkins' wife had retired, he would enter her cabin and threaten to shoot her unless they completed their voyage. That would be the final transgression that would see Hawkins cast him off in the lifeboat, hurling his possessions after him. He was suddenly hit by a violent urge to throw up. It wasn't the rocking of the boat but his own churning self-disgust. Whatever humanity he might have consoled himself with possessing after his youth as a monster it was draining away fast. He gripped the edge of his window, shoving his face out into the driving rain. He let the cold storm beat his face, feeling he deserved every icy lash. He waited like that until it was time to go and force history at the point of a gun.

17.

The lifeboat bounced its way across the water, Ashe rolling inside it. The gull squawked on the prow like a Roman centurion commanding the slaves to row. I'm dreaming, Ashe insisted to himself, I'm dying and this is my mind's way of sending me off in delirium rather than agony.

The gull cocked its head to look at him. "You just keep telling yourself that," it said.

18.

And then Ashe was off the *Intrepid*, Hawkins raging at him from the side of his ship. A tatty rug was hurled into the gathering wind. It flapped and curled, as if trying to master the art of flight before hitting the water with a dejected slap.

Ashe tapped into every ounce of fear and disgust he could find – which was considerable – and roared his own anger into the wind. He couldn't lay a claim to the words, they were dragged from too deep inside. It was soul noise, a primal bellowing that seemed to call the storm clouds back from where they had been running to. Demanding they stay and fight, demanding they piss on him from their heavens. They were happy to oblige. More rubbish from the market stalls of Madras came over the side of the boat: a particularly inept painting of a sunset that the wind caught and – as if in disgust at the unskilled painter – smashed against the side of the *Intrepid*. A bust of a fat-lipped woman hit the waves with its forehead. A wooden sculpture of a startled lion belly-flopped and then fought to stay afloat.

Ashe ignored it all, there was only one artifact he needed to see. He had left it in pride of place right in the middle of his bed, certain that Hawkins would find it.

And now it came: as the sky churned a glint of lightning showed him the puzzle box in Hawkins' hand. This is it, he thought, all over now...

Thunder kicked the night in the belly and the *Intrepid* rolled. Hawkins vanished from sight. "Falling now," Ashe whispered, "tumbling into the ship, hitting his head…"

The ship vanished and the sea rose and then came together, clapping its salty hands, impressed with the trick.

"Travel safe, Hawkins," Ashe said and then fell to the side of the lifeboat as it was thrown in the air. Hs head hit the wood and he fell limp, a passenger at the mercy of the storm.

19.

Ashe wasn't moving. He raised his neck to see a heavenly tree line a few feet away. Clambering over the side of the boat he fell onto a bed of gently twitching fish. The boat was surrounded by them, carried up on the shallow waves and left to bake and choke on the sand.

"I was dreaming," he said, pulling himself away from the boat. "I must have been dreaming."

His wet face kissed the hot sand and he retched salt water.

Behind him a solitary seagull climbed into the endless Indonesian sky.

INTERLUDE
Mario Trusts the Moon

"...do you think?"

Mario leaned back in his chair and tried to focus. The red wine in his veins and tobacco smoke in his eyes made it difficult. The bar was too damn noisy for his liking. The jukebox sang eighties rock – all power chords and synthesizer – while twenty-somethings shouted at one another. The espresso machine behind the bar told everyone to *shush* every couple of minutes. They paid it no attention. It wasn't a big place, kitted out like a wine cellar – all red brick and dark wood – and the noise coalesced into one big fist that pounded Mario's drunken head until he wondered if he might not just crawl under the table and die rather than put up with another moment of it. The boy had said something...

"What was that?" Mario shouted, possibly too loudly, the boy flinching as if he'd slapped one of those baby-pink cheeks of his. What was his name? He was damned if he could remember...

"I said that many critics feel that *Never Trust the Moon* is the most accomplished film of your career, would you agree with that?"

Mario looked at him, all bum-fluff and hair gel, what the fuck was he talking about? Sitting there fresh from some media course or another... a head full of Fellini or Cocteau and all of a sudden an expert...

"No. I would not."

He took another large mouthful of Rioja – knowing full well he'd had enough and that it was all downhill from here – and lit a cigarette, not caring whether the smoke irritated his companion or not.

"Oh... well, which would you choose?" The boy glanced down to his Dictaphone, making sure the thing was turned on. Well, good luck to him tonight, he'd be lucky to hear a thing over the rest of the noise. Behind the bar someone sent a tray flying and breaking glass and laughter was added to the mix... Mario flinched, eyes snapping tight... Jesus why couldn't the world shut its goddamn *mouth* for a minute?

"The best film of my career, the film of which I am most proud, is the one I'm making whenever you ask me the question... You're talking as if I have no career anymore, you're talking as if I've *made* all my films...!" The boy was moving back in his seat and Mario began to be aware that he was shouting, that people close by were turning in his direction. "*Never Trust the Moon* was my third film for Christ's sake... nearly ten years ago! You saying that the movies I've made since weren't worth shit?"

"Well... no... many would agree that *Impulse* was something of a return to form, the opening murder in particular..."

"I'll re-enact it here and now if you like..." Mario shouted, washing his vitriol down with more wine and stoppering it in his chest with a grin. "If some kind soul will find me a pair of long-bladed scissors..."

The boy stopped talking and stared at him, no idea what to say.

Mario laughed and got to his feet. "That would sell your book well wouldn't it? If people thought the poor author had died writing it?" He stumbled, the wine doing its job. Grabbing the table for support, he sent the glasses flying and ended up falling into the table next to them.

"Clumsy idiot!" one of the drinkers shouted, getting to his feet, ready to put Mario out on the street if he had to.

Mario looked him up and down; he was a big man, blond hair, German probably. He reckoned he could take him.

"Silly *Deutschland*, you have no idea who you're talking to!" He stood nose to nose with the man and grinned. "It'll take more than your piss and wind to put me down!"

The man punched him and Mario fell backwards onto the boy's lap, startled and bleeding from the nose.

"I think." he mumbled, the blood wetting his lips, "that it may be time to go home."

A few minutes later he was out on the street, drinking cold air like espresso and begging for sobriety. He touched his sore nose gently, hoping the kraut bastard hadn't broken it.

"Fuck." He looked at his bloody fingers and stumbled off the kerb forcing a girl on a scooter to swerve out of his way.

"Asshole!" she shouted, long dark hair waving in front of her face as she turned to stick her middle finger up at him.

He blew her a kiss and stooped into a half bow but the pressure in his nose made him straighten again quickly.

Definitely broken.

It wasn't that long a walk back to his apartment thank God – he was sure neither his head nor stomach could deal with taking a tram – but just long enough to brush some of the drunkenness from him; to pull him back from the certainty of heaving up in the gutter and making even more of a fool of himself.

But then he was fast approaching both the age and attitude where looking foolish no longer bothered him. Pride was for the young, for those still naïve enough to think that the world cared. Besides, when you made your living – thinly at times, these were not cash-rich days – as a director of horror pictures you were used to a degree of adverse criticism and having your personal worth questioned. As much as many audiences loved to be shocked – or even disgusted – out of their cinema seats you would be a fool to think the world viewed you with anything more than idle curiosity at best, downright revulsion at worst (Mario had once been described by a particularly respectable newspaper as "an immoral peddler of worthless trash", a quote he had thrilled over at the time).

Traffic was light. The occasional headlight picked him out against the worn Turin stone as people made their way home to their beds and lovers, to normal lives of office work and mortgage payments. He paused for a while on the Vittorio Emanuele Bridge and stared down at the rushing waters of the Po. He remembered the news items of a few years ago, the panic about the high quantity of cocaine traces in the water from the jubilant piss of the local users. Perhaps he should go and drink a few mouthfuls, see if it made him feel better...

Laughing he cut across the road and through the square, daring a few sleeping pigeons not to fly from his heavy heels.

By the time he neared his apartment block his jovial mood was on the wane, replaced with a heavy head and a need for sleep – something he might manage to do now without the room spinning and his guts rolling, the wine in his system having faded to a dull warmth.

He unlocked the front door and cursed under his breath as he nearly knocked a fern over in the foyer, the lights were out and he was forced to inch his way towards the central elevator using memory and caution. He'd give the building superintendent an earful if he could be bothered come the morning, how difficult was it to make sure the bulbs were replaced once in a while? It wasn't as if the residents didn't pay for such things...

Mind you, the place was half-empty these days with people moving out to the country or one of the more modern developments. It had been "desirable" once upon a time. He'd moved in after the success of *Can You See Me?* – his second full feature – had fleshed his wallet out enough to afford it. He'd bought the place, full of aspirations and a desire for a city life of parties and restaurant dining. He'd been here ever since, never able to afford to move further up the social ladder but refusing to go down either, not one rung. Meanwhile the place had dwindled as one by one the residents had left at a greater rate than those coming in, sooner or later he'd be here on his own while the developers circled... fuck it, maybe they'd give him a decent price for the place.

He found the concertina gate of the elevator, yanked it open and clambered inside. He pulled his cigarette lighter out of his pocket and lit it so that he could see the control box. The yellow flame threw a spider web of shadows from the elevator grille across the tiled walls. He pushed the button for the sixth floor and steadied himself as the elevator began to rise, the clunking of the motor and the squeal of cable sounding far too loud as it echoed around the atrium of the building. His mind wandered, thoughts of the next day's shooting schedule, the book the boy was writing about him – he'd have to apologise of course, he may be beyond pride but that didn't mean his ego was numb to the idea of a celebratory volume on his work – the possibility of his broken nose...

The lift came to a halt. He made to leave before realising that the damn thing was between floors.

"For Christ's sake..." he stabbed at the button again, demanding it took him to his bed.

The lift shuddered and he gave a startled yell that he hoped nobody was awake to hear. It shook again, this time violently enough to throw him to the floor. He rolled into a sitting position just as the lift jolted back into life and climbed the last few feet. As it came to a halt, Mario began to wonder if he hadn't been drinking far more than he should. The view on the other side of the gate was not the sixth floor of his apartment building, it was a bright, gleaming shopping centre. He got to his feet and yanked the gate open. As he stumbled out a tannoy croaked into life. "Passengers wishing to take the 4.15 from Paddington should be warned that murders are taking place on that service. If they do wish to travel they should ensure they have an alibi and an up to date will and testament."

Mario's English was rusty but good enough. Not that the announcement made the least sense to him.

"Where the fuck am I?" he wondered, stumbling out of his old life forever.

SIX
Where People go to Die (2)

1.

Captain Warren Shepard had seen countless horrors in his career. He had visited domestic disturbances where women hung off the arms of their abusive husbands, black-eyed, snotty-nosed and wailing their adoration for the men that treated them as punchbags. He had seen kids of no more than sixteen, glass-eyed and cold, their nostrils caked with cheap-shit coke that had stopped their parent's hearts as surely as their own. Two years into the job he had broken down by the side of the road at the sight of a child's sneaker, blood-stained and weighted with more than just a shed sock. The broken glass and burned rubber on the tarmac had been gathered around the mangled frame of a kid's push-bike. The rest of the body stuck to the underside of a Lincoln Continental further up the road. It was the first – and last – time that Shepard had shed tears on the job. After awhile you just had to wall those emotions up. They came out in the end of course, over a drink or in the middle of the night when all you can hear is the cicadas outside and the gentle rise and fall of your wife's breathing. Nothing stays walled up forever. But on the job, when wearing that uniform, you become immovable. You let the civilians wail and curse and beg their God for an answer, that's their job, it's not yours.

But when faced with the absurd freakshow at the Home Town construction site Shepard nearly let that granite exterior crumble once more. Nearly. Thinking back on it later, he thought it had probably been the sight of that glinting wedding ring. A plain gold band that had made him revolve his own, spinning it around his warm, living finger with the rough pad of his thumb. Yes, he figured it had probably been that.

"What the hell do you think happened?" Dutch Wallace asked. Looking as always to the higher rank for answers. Like a few more pips could help you understand this, Shepard thought.

"Damned if I know, lieutenant. Just make sure you keep the press back if they show – and they will – I don't want them guessing an answer to that question either."

He stared at the scene for a couple more minutes, watching the forensics team digging away the bodies like a bunch of archeologists. Then he went to the foreman's office to interrogate the only man working on the site who was lucky enough to be still drawing breath.

Corben Alliss had lost all of his usual swagger. His glasses were folded away in the breast pocket of his work shirt and he was staring at the walls of the Portakabin with pale, panda eyes.

Shepard had already decided that Alliss wasn't a suspect, you just didn't fake that walking-wounded look. But that wouldn't stop him pursuing him as one officially, he wasn't paid to make sweeping decisions, whatever his gut might tell him. Still, given time, he had little doubt that the evidence would rule him out. Until then he would interview him with the caution a police officer reserved for anyone whose neck may be within cricking distance of the noose. Say nothing, listen to all.

"What can you tell me about this Mr Alliss?" he asked, sitting down on the opposite side of the foreman's desk and cradling his hands gently at his crotch.

The big man shook his head, glancing towards the window in momentary confusion as if he'd heard someone shouting his name outside.

"Saw nothing," he replied after a moment. Quietly, as if he were talking to himself.

"You been in here all day, that it?"

"No... I..." that glance again, through the window and out towards the Highway, "just the last couple of hours." Just for a moment a chunk of the real Corben Alliss surfaced, a solidifying of the man's gaze as an idea occurred to him in the here and now. "Had a few calls to make."

"That right?" Shepard nodded, taking his time, performing his own form of archeology. You didn't get dirt under your nails, he thought, but the digging's just as deep and the things buried there just as nasty. "Who did you call?"

Alliss shook his head again. It was a tiny gesture, little more than a twitch but Shepard caught it nonetheless. Not that he'd needed it to know the man had been lying. "Few suppliers," Allis said, "the boss."

There was a shift in tone on that last, Shepard noted.

"The boss? Ted Loomis?" Alliss nodded. "What did you talk to him about?"

"Just stuff, y'know," Alliss scowled as if the subject was distasteful. The face of a man who had just found the treads of his work boot packed with dog shit.

226

"No," Shepard replied, "I don't know. What sort of stuff?" There was no harshness to his tone – he'd let that creep in later if he had to – for now it was all just gentle digging. Like dabbing away with those little brushes he'd seen archeologists use in the movies as they carefully uncovered ancient skulls and hidden temples.

Alliss looked confused then slightly angry. "Just approvals, you know? Have to call about shit like that all the time, how much to spend on this or that."

Shepard nodded. "Where did you reach him? The office or at home?"

"The office," Alliss replied quickly. "I never call him at home."

Shepard nodded again. "Figured as much, don't get much thanks invading a man's private time."

Alliss tried to smile. "Damn right."

Shepard smiled right back. There was no more genuine humour to his than the foreman's but he was better at pretending. "Maybe I ought to try using your phone then," he said, "we've been trying to get hold of him but his secretary says he hasn't been in all day. You think she's lying to us?" Alliss' smile faded and Shepard found he was glad of the fact, it had been more like a death rictus.

Shepard reached for the phone, pulling his notepad from his shirt pocket and riffing through it while cradling the receiver at his neck. He found the number and dialled, watching Alliss all the while. "Hi there," he said as the call connected, "could you put me through to Mr Loomis please? It's Captain Warren Shepard from the Kissimmee Police Department, the call is urgent." There was a pause while the woman on the other end answered. Shepard kept his smile in place and his eyes on Alliss. "Really? You tried to raise him at home?" Another pause. "No luck there either huh? Well, yes, I think you'd better keep trying he's going to want to get in touch for sure. Thanks." He put the phone down. "Still no sign of him," he said to Alliss, "guess you must have hit lucky?"

Alliss grew even paler. His mouth moving noiselessly as he tried to think of something to say, like his lips were caught in the breeze.

"I'm sure we'll get hold of him in the end though won't we?" Shepard continued. "Unless he's one of the poor bastards we have to dig up out there of course." He let the words sink in for a moment. Let Alliss picture those hands protruding from the soft earth. "Might that be the case, you think?"

Alliss shook his head. "I don't know…"

"You don't know?"

"No."

Shepard nodded. "If he'd been around you'd have seen him though I guess?" Alliss squirmed. Trying to work his way around the impossibility of his situation. "I mean," Shepard continued, "if he'd been on site you'd have known wouldn't you?"

Alliss shook his head again. "I don't…"

"Of course you'd know," Shepard continued as if Alliss hadn't even spoken. "You're the foreman, you'd know if anyone came out here wouldn't you? You'd be straight on anyone who showed up, right?"

There was a sudden flash of panic there and Shepard noted it. That had been important. He had hit something square on.

"Anyone show up here this morning, Mr Alliss?'

Again that glance to the window and the busy road beyond. Shepard let the silence hang there for a moment, let the foreman stare beyond the glass of his little cave.

"Who came out here, Mr Alliss?" he asked in the end.

"Who did you see?"

After a moment Corben Alliss told him.

2.

Miles and Carruthers, robbed of a viable plan, walked along the Highway hoping they might stumble on a better one. Neither of them fancied their chances much but sometimes it was good to just make some distance pass under your heels.

"You think he's after Elise?" Miles asked after a while, he didn't need to mention Tom by name, they both knew who he meant.

"We've travelled to a point in time when she's still alive," Carruthers replied. "Would you be able to resist that opportunity were you in his shoes? I'm a damn idiot for letting him come."

"Yep," nodded Miles, "and I'm a damned idiot for letting you let him."

Carruthers smiled. "As long as we both understand how idiotic we are then all is well."

"Oh, I've never been in any doubt," Miles replied. "Cut me in half and you'll find the word 'wassock' written through me like in a stick of rock."

They walked along in silence for a little longer, watching the cars that sped by. Carruthers in particular was engrossed by them. "I would love to master the art of these automobiles," he confessed, "think how much of the world you could see with one of those beneath you."

"Until you hit water," Miles said, "they're not so good at the away game."

"Nonetheless, when you think of the months it took me to travel from one destination to another, trapped on slow steamers or hiking desert trails. Your world is all within reach," he frowned, "though I suppose that takes the point out of exploring rather."

"There are always places people have yet to experience," Miles said, looking up into the sky. "In the sixties we managed to get as far as the moon but we've not managed much further."

"The moon!" Carruthers sighed. "Was it made of cheese?"

"No," said Miles "it's sort of…" he noticed Carruthers was chuckling. "Thought you were being serious, sorry."

"Don't be, we need all the humour we can manage right now."

"And a plan, perhaps?" Miles suggested. "That wouldn't hurt either."

"No," Carruthers agreed, "it would be quite useful."

Miles noticed a sign to their right and stopped Carruthers with a firm hand on the man's shoulder. "Panic not," he said, mimicking his friend's fruity tone, "the very solution to our malaise is at hand. I espy a dream palace that shall surely provide all the inspiration and answers we need." He took Carruthers' arm and led him off the Highway. "Prepare to be blown away my good man."

Carruthers raised an eyebrow. "Somewhat tempestuous in," he checked the sign, "'Dunkin' Donuts' is it?"

"A storm of doughy, chocolatey goodness, yes," Miles replied, holding the door open for his friend.

They sat at the counter, Carruthers struggling for a while not to slip off the highly polished swivel-stool but getting the hang of it in the end.

"I suppose a cup of tea is asking too much?" he asked.

"Two coffees please," Miles told the waitress, "and enough donuts to choke a horse."

"Sure thing," she replied with a smile. "Here on holiday are you?"

"Something like that."

"Thought as much, we don't get many Australian regulars..." she shuffled over to the coffee machine.

"Australian indeed," Carruthers muttered.

"They always get the accents mixed up," said Miles. "Never understood it myself. Mind you, it's mostly Dick Van Dyke's fault." He waved Carruthers questions away. "Doesn't matter, talking rubbish again."

Carruthers nodded. "I did wonder."

They ordered a mixed selection of donuts and took them over to a table by the window.

"So," said Miles, dipping a donut with chocolate sprinkles into his coffee, "what next?"

"You're putting it in your drink!" Carruthers hissed. "Have table manners completely vanished in the future?"

"Completely," Miles said. "Roll with it. Luxuriate in the savage abandon of a sticky finger and a sweet tooth."

Carruthers sighed, took a donut with vanilla icing and dipped it tentatively into his coffee.

"Everything alright guys?" the waitress asked just as Carruthers had bitten off a mouthful of his soggy donut.

He waved his contentment with a fluttered serviette and swallowed. "Enchanting my good lady, you are a queen of the baker's oven."

She chuckled hard at that, forty Newports a day rattling around inside her chest as she did so. "You guys crack me up."

"She doesn't bake them herself," Miles whispered to Carruthers, "they come ready-done."

"From the Donut fairy one presumes?" Carruthers took another bite and smiled. "Whatever their provenance they are most pleasant."

"Glad you think so, now back to the subject at hand... where do we go from here?"

Carruthers sighed, dabbing at his mouth with the serviette. "An excellent question and one I don't even begin to know the answer to."

"You think Max Headroom has any more advice?"

"I have no idea who you're talking about and you know it," Carruthers replied, selecting a donut with strawberry icing.

"You know, the Grumpy Controller from the house… 'Home Town!'" Miles mimed the exploding TV set.

"Even if he does his last suggestion didn't get us all that far did it?"

"No, suppose not." Miles sipped at his coffee, thinking about what they knew. It didn't take him long, they knew so little. "We need to get him back to the House," he said finally.

Carruthers looked quizzically at him. "Why?"

"His power's limited there isn't it? Here he'll just get more and more powerful. At least if we could get him back inside the House then he would be under control."

"*Fairly* under control," Carruthers said, "he was hardly powerless even there."

Miles shrugged. "Best plan I can think of, don't ask me how we manage it though."

"Would the box work do you think?" Carruthers asked. "Not that we have it mind you…"

"Even if we did, how do you get it into his hands and then place him in danger…" Miles shook his head, "if we could put him in the sort of life-threatening situation that would unlock the box then we wouldn't need to use it in the first place."

"True." Carruthers finished his donut and sat back with his coffee. "If we knew what he was after that would help."

"Would it?"

"Any knowledge is better than none," said Carruthers, "even if we can't stop him maybe we can scotch his plans... I don't know, just trying to think around the situation."

"Well, he wants something to do with Home Town," Miles said, "and we know the man to talk to about that."

Carruthers pulled his notebook out and flipped to the page with Loomis' number. "Indeed we do!"

"Wonder if they have a phone here." Miles looked around.

"I see it," said Carruthers, getting to his feet.

"I'll do it," Miles suggested.

"I'm perfectly capable of operating a telephone," Carruthers replied, "we did have those you know."

"They've changed a bit," Miles said but Carruthers had already left. He listened to the explorer as he became more and more irate with the pay-phone. Eventually the waitress came to his assistance, explaining the basic principles.

He returned to the table. "The infernal thing demands money," he said, "have you got any?"

Miles nodded, Tom had pressed a bunch of notes into his hand earlier. "Pocket money," he had said with a chuckle. Miles wondered if he had already intended to run off and abandon them then. He thought he probably had.

He handed Carruthers a five dollar note. "You'll have to get the waitress to break it."

Carruthers sighed and took the note to the counter. "My colleague tells me you can break this for me," he said, offering her the note, "though why it should need breaking before it's of use is beyond me."

She put her hand on her hip and give him an earnest pout. "It really is a different world where you guys come from ain't it?"

"So I increasingly realise my dear lady. I am quite lost."

She thought for a while before handing him his change. "Well," she said finally, "I get off at four, I dare say I might be able to show you around a little," she gave a him a little wink. "Donuts ain't all I'm queen of, honey."

3.

The stranger had directed Hughie back to his house so they could fetch Chester. Looking in the rearview mirror at the young man's vacant face, Hughie had to wonder why.

"Now find us some food and drink," the stranger said, "a restaurant, somewhere we can sit and think."

Hughie couldn't imagine eating a thing but did as he was directed, swinging off the Interstate at the next junction and cruising until he found somewhere offering food. Clocking the sign of a Ponderosa Steakhouse he pulled in. The stranger looked over his shoulder at Chester.

"Stay here", he said, "there's a good boy. Daddy wants his meat."

He got out of the car. Stopped, turned around to stare at Hughie who was still sat in the driver's seat. "Well come on then," the stranger said, "I'm not eating on my own."

Reluctantly, Hughie got out of the car and followed him into the restaurant.

"Hi," a waitress gushed, neon smile framed by parted bangs dyed a shade of candy-floss pink. "You guys hungry?"

"Always," the stranger replied, with an expansive smile of his own.

Their waitress – Amy and only *too* happy to help she assured them – showed them to a booth in the far corner. On the stereo, The Eagles suggested they *Take it to the Limit*, Hughie was fairly confident his companion needed no encouragement on that score.

"Pair of T-Bones," the stranger told Amy, "so rare you could ride them to our table."

"I'm not hungry…" Hughie said but the stranger fixed him with a look that told him the order would not be up for discussion. Hughie looked at the waitress and felt such a heavy wave of sadness he could have cried. Look at you, he thought, with your pink hair and your butter-wouldn't-melt smile… You have *no* idea. Nor should she, he reasoned, this was no world of hers. He just nodded at her. "T-Bone's fine."

"Okay," she replied, relieved that things were going to be simple, for a moment there she thought the black guy was going to grab hold of her and start bawling. He had the look of a man on the edge of a breakdown, she realised, thinking of her friend, Darla's father when he had lost his job. Whenever she had gone round to Darla's house that guy had been sat in his easy chair staring blankly at the TV. He had been rigid as a waxwork. Any minute now, he had seemed to say, I'm going to come to life and tear the shit out of this place with my bare hands, *any minute now*. This guy seemed the same, one little nudge and he'd be climbing the walls and screaming like an animal. Just as long as he does it after he's paid his cheque and driven off, she thought, please God don't let it be before that. Let me just earn my tip and wave them goodbye, I don't need any crap today. "You want fries, baked or mash? Maybe a side order of onions?"

"Fries and as many onions as you like, Amy," the stranger said, "and a couple of cold beers."

She nodded and dashed away, happy to avoid any further conversation.

"Let me tell you about reality, Hughie," the stranger said out of the blue. "I'll keep it simple so you can follow," he leaned back on the padded seat, letting himself spread out. "Reality is layers," he continued, "*infinite* layers. Piled on top of one another." He mimed this with his hands, spread out flat over the table, moving them one over the other. It made Hughie think of standing in the yard at school, playing the counting-out game in a circle *Pizza pizza pizza pie, if you eat it you will die...*

"Universe over universe, existence after existence," the stranger said, "all stacked up."

Amy returned with their beers, the stranger taking a long draught of his before continuing. "Some people never see beyond their own little layer."

"The ants," Hughie muttered, thinking of the stranger's analogy about the ants and the bottle.

"The ants, *exactly*," the stranger smiled, "you're getting it. Some of us see the whole, even move between the layers, exploring, researching, playing..."

He took another mouthful of beer. "Actually my lot didn't do much playing, they took existence far too seriously."

"Republicans, huh?" Hughie asked, pushing himself into the corner of his booth and taking a drink of his own beer.

The stranger paused, looked into Hughie's mind for an explanation and then grinned. "Something like that."

The Eagles switched to Creedence Clearwater Revival. "I see the bad moon arising, I see trouble on the way, I see earthquakes and lightning, I see bad times today..." Damn right, thought Hughie, *damn* right.

"Usually those layers are solid," the stranger said, "it takes a lot of effort and skill to pass between them." He

236

frowned, that persistently light and jolly mood punctured by a sharp and unnerving anger. "A skill I seem to lack these days. Taken away by them..." he ground his fingernail into the soft wood of the dining table. "I am a reduced man, Hughie," he said quietly, "you are not seeing me at my best..."

That's a small relief, Hughie thought, for he was quite certain that a stronger creature than he saw before him would not be in the best interests of his species. If the stranger picked up on the thought he didn't show it, just went on defacing the wood. After a moment, Hughie realised that he found this edgy creature even more unnerving than usual so tried to jog him out of it. "Usually?" he prompted.

The stranger looked up at him and, just for a second, Hughie saw the irises of his eyes– *its* eyes Hughie, a voice said in his head, not *his* never forget that– no, he wouldn't... he saw the irises of *its* eyes bleed into the white, as if the dye was running. The colour rippled, offering a serrated edge like a circular saw. Then the image was gone, the eyes looking as human as ever. "Usually?" the stranger asked.

"You said that the layers were *usually* solid, suggesting they weren't always."

The stranger smiled, the anger gone instantly – no, Hughie that voice said again, don't believe that, the anger is *always* there, just under the surface, just waiting to boil over – "That's right," the stranger said, "*usually*..." He brushed away the shavings of varnish and wood he had dug from the table as if just noticing a fleck of dust on an otherwise perfect surface. "Sometimes, there are soft points, thin areas where the layers bleed into one another. These places are focal points for disturbances in the overall reality, areas where time slips loose or the atmosphere curdles.

They disturb those around them, warp the normal rules of that layer's physics. In short, Hughie, they are areas of potential."

"And the Home Town site is one of them?"

The stranger nodded. "You really were wasted pumping shit, Hughie."

"Tell me something I don't know," Hughie replied.

"Alright," though whether the stranger had misunderstood or was just playing with him, Hughie couldn't tell, "someone who knew what he was doing in an area like that could rip a hole through the layers as deeply as he liked," he looked into Hughie's head, searching for a suitable analogy, "like knocking a hole in the wall of one subway tunnel and into another."

"Wouldn't that damage the layers?" Hughie asked, though in his head the word he was thinking of wasn't "layers", the word was "world".

"Oh naturally," the stranger replied, "it would tear the metaphorical guts right out of it." He glanced over to the bar. "I wonder where the lovely Amy's gone with our steaks…"

4.

Sally Hillman had never known a day like it. She was used to her employer's comings and goings – in fact, as Tom had predicted when arriving at the Plaza hotel, she had an intimate knowledge of both, for Ted Loomis the former was swift and the latter swifter still – but she had never known him vanish off the face of the earth like he had today. The phone had been ringing itself silly with some kind of fuss over at the Home Town site. The police, no less, demanding to know where Loomis might be. She had come close to grabbing her purse and hightailing it out of the office of Loomis Real Estate several times over the last hour.

She had tried Loomis' home line every ten minutes or so but – unless he was lying dead somewhere, dear Christ, Sally thought, don't say his heart finally gave in – there was nobody there.

Her head filled with the worst possible images: her employer (and occasional lover) growing grey and cold on the bathroom tiles; her being marched off to prison as an accessory to some form of crooked business deal she had no knowledge of; SWAT teams swinging through the smoked glass window of the office, machine guns locked and loaded... When the phone rang again it was almost a relief.

"Loomis Real Estate," she answered, "Ted, is that you?"

"I'm afraid not dear lady," came the voice on the other end of the line, "in fact it was the noble Mr Loomis I was hoping to speak to."

"He's not here," she said, sick to death of having to. "Nobody's seen him since he left the office yesterday."

"Oh," said the man, "I've seen him since then, in fact my friend and I shared a couple of drinks with him last night. I confess I was rather the worse for wear after the experience, perhaps he too is suffering somewhere."

This last mirrored Sally's imaginings a little too closely for comfort, though it wasn't drink she feared had struck him. "You were with him last night?" she asked.

"Indeed, he was kind enough to tell us about the Home Town project and suggested we met him there this morning."

Alarm bells began ringing in Sally's head, not that it took much to set them off given her current agitation. "Really?" she asked. "Were you able to catch him there?"

"Sadly not," the man replied. "Not to worry, I'm sure we'll catch him soon enough."

Don't let him hang up! Sally thought... whoever this guy is he's seen Ted after anyone else and was at the construction site this morning, she was damned sure the cops would want to ask him a few questions. "Wait!" she said, trying to bite down on the agitation, the last thing she wanted to do is scare the man off. "If you tell me where you're calling from I can hunt him down and get him to call you back."

There was a slight pause. He's not going to go for it, Sally thought. Damn it, he's going to hang up on me!

"I can't see a number anywhere," the voice replied eventually, "but we're at a splendid place called Dunkin' Donuts, just along the road from the building site. Is that enough for you to get in touch?"

Bet your ass it is, Sally thought, saying: "That's just fine sir, you hang in there for a short while and I'll ring you right back."

"How kind," the man said, "thank you so much for your help."

He put the phone down and so did Sally, but only for as long as it took for her to find the number for the police.

5.

Captain Shepard was by no means sure what to make from Alliss' story. In his experience every statement a police officer took was a mess of fact and fiction, assumption and observation folded over like pizza dough until what you had was something that needed careful sifting to figure out what was what. Like the old joke about blind men touching parts of an elephant (one thinks it's a snake, another thinks it's a tree and so on) the truth could only be found by a careful amalgamation of views. Alliss' story didn't make an elephant, he sure as hell knew that much. But what did it make? Two guys pulling onto the site in Loomis' car, one black and one white, with a half-assed joke – or so Alliss had thought at first – about having killed its owner and stolen it. Shepard wondered if that had been a joke at all. He'd heard stranger admissions during his time in the uniform, some folks just thought they were untouchable and it made them say stupid things. Time would tell.

The thing that jarred most of all was the discrepancy between Alliss' description of the white man and the effect he had so clearly had on him. Alliss didn't strike Shepard as a man who would scare easily. Hell, anyone walking around with that haircut had to have some grit in his shit. So how come this man – a small, balding English guy in glasses by the man's own account – had put the frights on him so heavily? Shepard knew he could just about knock the man into a clean faint by smacking his fist on the desk hard enough, he was *terrified*.

Something in his eyes, Alliss had said, *the kind of look you imagine the devil to have just before he turns on the oven.*

Colourful description aside, it was clear how much the man had got under Alliss' skin. Something in his eyes... Shepard thought about the row of dead hands in the earth outside and wondered, just for a moment, whether Alliss might have seen the elephant for what it was after all.

The door to the Portakabin opened and Dutch walked in. "You might want to take the radio, cap'n," he said, "the woman from the real estate office called in, says two guys that claim to have been out here this morning have been trying to get hold of Loomis. Pair of 'em are sitting in a Dunkin' Donuts would you believe? Not a couple of miles from here."

Alliss gasped and Shepard scowled at Dutch, damned idiot should know better than to go flapping his gums in front of Joe Public. There was the sound of trickling water and he looked to the roof of the cabin, thinking, *damn, is that rain?* Then he realised that Corben Alliss was busily pissing himself, staring out of that dirty window towards the highway again.

6.

Miles watched Carruthers talk to the waitress. She shook her bottle blonde hair and swiped her hands over her ample arse as if trying to push it back into her pelvis. What's the old goat up to? He wondered. Finally Carruthers tore himself away and came back to the table.

"Any luck?" Miles asked as Carruthers sat back down, looked at the solitary donut left – apple and cinnamon – and then shrugged, picked it up and took a big bite out of it.

"With the service staff, most definitely," the explorer said, smiling, "we have an assignation planned for this evening – or so she hopes at least," he chuckled. "Apparently there will be dancing, beer and the 'best goddamn country' I ever heard." He took another bite of donut and leaned in close. "I think if we stay here much longer she may just wrestle me to the floor, it's something to do with the accent, she says it's 'dreamy'."

"Any luck with *Loomis*?" Miles clarified, rolling his eyes.

"Ah… not as yet. He's not at his place of business but the kind lady who works for him has promised to track him down and call us back."

"She's calling us here?"

"Yes, she said she had the number."

"She had the number?"

242

"Yes, or could find it at least, I forget her precise words."

"What were *your* precise words." Miles felt a nagging feeling tug at him, this didn't feel right at all.

"What? Is this because I didn't let you make the call?"

"Of course not," Miles rubbed at his legs, wishing that concerned coil in his gut would go away, "I just want to know what you said."

"I told her that I wanted to speak to her employer. She said that he hadn't been in his office yet today. I mentioned that we'd had a few drinks last night and – just making a bit of small talk you understand – if her employer had felt as tender as I the following morning then it may well explain his absence."

"Then what?"

"Then I said that Mr Loomis had wished to show us around his building site today and that we were hoping to get hold of him to discuss that very thing, or words to that effect."

"Did you tell her that we'd been to the site."

"Of course not… oh… well, no, not exactly."

"What do you mean 'not exactly'?"

"She… let me get this right… she asked if I'd managed to 'catch him' there to which I replied that I hadn't."

"Implying that you had been there."

Carruthers face fell. "Oh dear, that wasn't what I meant."

"Then you told her you were sat in Dunkin' Donuts a mile or two down the road and she told you to stay put while she made a few calls."

"Well, she didn't put it like that of course, she said she was… damn!" Carruthers slapped the table with his palm. "I'm so sorry, I've been an idiot haven't I?"

"Let's get out of here," Miles said, standing up and reaching for money to pay.

"She misunderstood me," Carruthers insisted, "or I misunderstood her... oh dear..." he gestured towards the forecourt beyond the window as a police car pulled in. He turned to the waitress. "Sorry my dear but I rather think I won't be available for beer and dancing after all."

"Hell," said the Dunkin' Donuts waitress, "if it's police trouble you're in, you just step out back here and get yourselves gone."

"Excuse me?" asked Carruthers, struggling with the woman's vernacular almost as much as the concept.

The waitress gestured for the pair of them to follow her, stepping out into a storeroom just as Captain Shepard got out of his squad car. "I've got no love for men in uniform, sugar," she informed him. "If it weren't for them I'd still have a husband to take dancing. As it is they won't be letting him out nights for another four years." She opened a door at the rear which led into a small car park and storage area. "Now shift your asses out there and I'll keep the son of a bitch talking just as long as I can."

Carruthers gave her a slight bow. "You are a goddess madam."

"Damn right, and the best night out you never had, sugar, now scoot!"

Miles and Carruthers ran outside and she pulled the door closed behind them.

"You attract a great class of woman," Miles said, grinning at the look of discomfort on his friend's face. "Let's hope her husband doesn't come looking for you once they let him out."

"I'm sure her motives were honourable," Carruthers said. "Likely the poor man was imprisoned in error and she sought nothing more than friendly company."

"Yeah, 'likely' that's just what it was."

A small road led from the rear of the cafe back out to the highway. As that would bring them face to face with the local law, they clambered over a wire fence and across a stretch of wasteland that ran parallel to the strip of businesses hawking their wares to passing motorists.

"We're still no better off than before," Carruthers moaned after they had run a fair distance and found themselves on a dusty road that led away from the highway.

"Yeah, but at least we're not sat in a police cell," Miles replied. "That would have been infinitely worse."

"We don't know for sure that the gentleman would have arrested us, after all we are innocent of any misdemeanour."

"And without any form of ID. Well, any ID that wouldn't get us locked in a mental asylum at least."

"I'll take your word for it."

They sat by the side of the road to get their breath back and let their churned up donuts settle back down again.

7.

Captain Shepard strolled into the Dunkin' Donuts and saw instantly that it was empty. That was typical, he thought, these things are never so damn easy.

"Help you sugar?" the waitress asked stepping behind the counter from out back. "Get you a coffee maybe or something cold?"

"Two men been in here?" he asked.

"You'll have to help me out a little on that one, hon," she replied, "we get a lot of customers in here, 'two men' don't give me much to go on."

Shepard glanced around, noticing the table Miles and Carruthers had so recently vacated. "One of them was English," he said, strolling over to the table and picking up one of the coffee cups with a napkin. It was warm to the touch. "Don't tidy up behind you?" he asked, gesturing to the cups and donut box.

"Just had to pop out back for a call of nature," she replied, "you takes your opportunity when you can. Giselle – she does a lot of night shifts – snuck out back one night to water the lettuce and came back to a raided till and a trail of donuts out the door. Half a minute with her drawers round her ankles cost the company a hundred and eighty bucks.

"Should slip the lock."

"That I usually do, 'cept I saw you pull in and if you can't trust a police officer then who can you trust? Sure I can't get you a coffee?"

"Quite sure," he pointed at the cluttered table. "Who was sat here?"

"Mother and son, him fair bustin' a gut to get over and watch those gators wrestle over at Gator World, her looking like she hadn't had a wink of good sleep from the minute he was born. I never had children, officer and I tell you, the kids I see in this job sure make me glad of the fact."

He nodded. "Got two myself, boy and a girl, five and six, it's a tricky age. He about the same?"

"Well yeah, I guess around there."

Shepard nodded again. "Kind of young for coffee," he said, picking up the other cup, "my two wouldn't touch the stuff, you'd think it was warmed up dog crap to look at their faces when they smell it roasting." He smiled at her. "I guess coffee's just something you grow in to, huh? Unlike Coke or Kool Aid, they can't get enough of that sweet stuff."

"I suppose it was unusual," she admitted, "but you don't ask in this job, you just give 'em what they want."

"I bet," Shepard replied, putting the two coffee cups into the donut box – using the napkin all the time, not wanting to touch anything with his bare hands.

"No need for that," the waitress said, stepping out from behind the counter, "happy to do it."

"I've got it," Shepard replied. He smiled at her but she knew that a free ride in the back of his cruiser would be the result of her trying to touch the empties. "So you haven't seen two guys in here lately?" he asked again.

"I had a couple of fellas in an hour or two ago I guess," she replied, glancing at the clock, "you lose track of time, truth be told."

"I imagine so. These two would have used the phone, that help jog your memory?"

"Can't say it does," she replied, stepping over to the payphone and – before he could stop her – picking up the receiver and tapping away at the buttons. "Sure there's some number or another that lets you redial," she said. "Oops," she added, cocking her ear away from the receiver, that's sure not it…"

Shepard sighed, this woman was infuriating and the dance was getting them nowhere. For all her loose talk she'd known that he'd want to check the phone for prints to match against the coffee cups. Probably known he'd hit redial too and see if Ted Loomis' secretary answered. She was playing with him, no doubt about that. Not that he could do anything about it, not without more evidence that she was lying, something she seemed quite determined to eradicate.

"Well," he said, taking out one of his cards, knowing it was a waste of time but willing to go through the motions. "If anything occurs to you then just give me a call." He put the card down on the counter. "I really need to talk to those guys."

"Can't see me being able to help," she replied picking up the card – it would be in the trash the minute he left and he knew it – "but I'll think on it just the same."

Shepard gathered the empties, carried them outside and then dumped them on the back seat of his cruiser. He'd get a hundred and one kinds of shit for running them through the print lab in Orlando – a waste of resources given that he had no real reason to link the cups to incidents up the road – but he'd do it anyway. He may not be paid to make sweeping judgements based on gut instinct, but he sure didn't mind spending a few taxpayer dollars on it, his instincts were good and he considered it money well-spent.

He picked up his car radio and called through to dispatch. "No sign of the two guys in Dunkin' Donuts, Cheryl," he said. "But do me a favour and have all patrols keep their eyes peeled will you? Two guys, one white one black, the white guy's English."

"Ten four, Cap'n Shepard," she replied, "I'll set a fire under 'em for you."

"You do that Cheryl," he replied, "they need perking up a tad."

She chuckled at that and he clipped the radio back in its bracket.

Now what?

8.

For a moment, Hughie wondered if the stranger had rolled over and died. He'd toppled back in his seat, eyes floating skywards.

"You having some kind of seizure?" Hughie asked. No reply. "You hear me?"

"Shoot her!" the man whispered. "Shoot the girl." Hughie felt himself grow cold, what the hell was this now? What girl? The waitress? He looked over but Amy was working one of the other tables, that big smile beaming bright enough to light up their entrees.

"Shoot her!" the man said again then snapped back to attention, smiling at Hughie. "Sorry," he said, "I had a long-distance call to make."

This meant nothing to Hughie, naturally, but he was in no mood to discuss it. He'd had more than enough mind-opening explanations from this man.

Amy appeared with their meals. When Hughie looked at his steak he felt his throat tighten. No way am I going to be able to eat that, he thought, not one mouthful. His partner had no such compunction, hacking into it with the enthusiasm of a man who hadn't eaten for days. Hughie watched the stranger's knife cut its serrated way into his meal. The meat parted with a quiet tear, gushing pink juice onto his plate. Immediately, the body of Ted Loomis sprung to mind. Hughie turned away, washing down the urge to gag with a mouthful of beer.

"Eat," the stranger said, forking a glistening rectangle of beef into his deceptively prim mouth. The meat juice glistened on his lips and Hughie pictured the man's perfect little teeth chewing their way into his steak, tearing it into thin strands.

"I can't," he replied.

"You can and you will," the stranger said, "don't make me sit down beside you and feed you like a child. Because I will, forcing forkful after forkful into you." He took a swig of his own beer and waved at Amy to bring two more. "And I won't be gentle," he continued, "I'll poke and stab with that fork until the steak becomes mixed up with the pulped remains of your tongue." He smiled at Hughie, as if telling him good news. "I'll make you eat your own fucking mouth."

"You're becoming more human," Hughie said, "you notice that?"

The stranger stared at him and that anger returned, those coruscating irises.

"Okay, okay." Hughie sighed and picked up his cutlery, forking a pair of crisp fries and forcing them past lips that fought him every inch of the way.

"The meat, Hughie," the stranger said, "I want to see you eat that meat, want you to suck the fat right off the bone."

Hughie tried. He cut a small slice and raised it to his mouth. His eyes glanced down and he gave a yelp as he saw it writhe on his fork as if still alive. The steak on his plate slapped around like a beached fish.

"Bit too overdone for my taste," the stranger replied, "so I gave it a little bit of life back. I think it might be in pain." He cut a piece of his own steak – which thrashed as he stabbed it with his fork, knocking some fries onto the table. "Now eat," he repeated, "or I'll give it lips so that it screams when you cut it."

Hughie dashed for the restroom, the urge to throw up now too strong to fight.

The stranger chuckled as he dashed past him. "It'll still be here when you get back," he said, cutting another slice.

As Hughie ran, the stranger's voice followed him, talking inside his head just as clearly as if he were still sat facing him across the table. "It's not going anywhere," that voice said, "and neither are you. Remember that Hughie. I forgave you for your little betrayal but this is your penance. Every cooling mouthful of fat, grease and blood. Every squirt of marrow, every string of sinew. You will lick your plate clean before we leave or I will kill you and every other ant in this place."

Hughie dropped to his knees in front of the toilet, the door smacking back against the wall of the cubicle and rebounding against his twitching legs as he emptied his stomach.

"I'll start with that lovely little waitress of ours," the voice continued. "I'll dip that pretty pink hair of hers into the wet crevice of her own slit stomach. I'll pull out each glistening organ and fry them for you Hughie while she draws her last breath. Your plate will fill with fresh offal for every moment you don't eat your meal. You will eat until the end of fucking time if you have to. I'll turn this state into an abattoir just for you."

Hughie rested his hot face against the cool porcelain of the toilet rim. How had he brought this monster to his door? What had he done to deserve this thing in his life?

"You were born, Hughie," the stranger replied, "and you'll curse your momma's diseased snatch by the time I've finished with you. You'll wish that dirty cunt had never parted her thighs."

Hughie began to cry, rubbing at his face and considered beating his head against the toilet bowl until it cracked open and let this demon out. Death seemed a sensible alternative to his current situation.

"If you die, Hughie," the voice said, "you won't be the last, I promise you that, I'll send every single one of your species after you. You're cattle to me, Hughie, that's all. Now come on out here and eat your meal."

Hughie pulled himself upright and went over to the sink. He splashed cold water over his face and stared at himself in the mirror.

You're a dead man walking, Hughie, he told his reflection.

"Amy's coming with our beers, Hughie," the stranger said. "If you don't want me to smash the bottle and dig into her face with the broken end then you'll get here before her."

Hughie ran out of the restroom, nearly colliding with their waitress as she aimed for their table with a tray of beers and a fresh pair of glasses.

"Sorry," he said, shuffling past her and sliding into his side of the table.

"Eat Hughie," the stranger said, still in his head. *"Eat like her life depends on it."*

Hughie tore a chunk of steak from the bone and rammed into his mouth, chewing vaguely before swallowing it and cutting another portion.

"Hungry guy, huh?" said Amy as she placed their beers on the table, just about managing to cover her disgust at Hughie's apparent gluttony.

Hughie watched the stranger flick his steak knife between his fingers, pointing the tip towards the waitress' belly. The blade swept forward and back, marking out a route across the girl's stomach where it would open the skin and muscle and let her grey guts tumble to the floor. He picked the steak up with his hands and began cramming as much of it as he could into his mouth. The meat slapped around his chin and cheeks like the enthusiastic tongue of a dog that was pleased to see him. He bit and tore at it, never taking his eyes off the knife in the stranger's hand.

"Oh, hey," Amy said, "I don't think we can allow that, sorry..." she squirmed in discomfort, "think of the other diners."

"I'm sorry, Amy," the stranger said, turning his knife back towards his plate, "my friend's lost some of his table manners. Stop that Hughie!"

Hughie dropped the steak back to the plate, feeling the air conditioning cool the grease on his face. He stared at Amy and the waitress was, again, reminded of her friend's broken father, those eyes just waiting to brim with tears.

"No problem," she said, determined not to see the guy weep in front of her, that would be even worse than the eating. "Sometimes we could all just about eat a horse."

She put the beers down and dashed away from the table.

"Good job, Hughie," the stranger said, returning to his own meal. "I think you've had enough." He ran his thumb through the bloody grease on the plate, making a thin, squeaking sound. "Unless you fancy dessert of course?"

9.

Officer Pete Calhoun shoved his radio back in place. Keep a lookout for a pair of guys, one black one white? Jesus… talk about vague. "The white guy's English," Cheryl had said, as if that made it all alright, as if he would be checking the accent of every white guy he met. "Hey mister, you seen that Mary Poppins lately?" Yeah sure…

He pulled into the forecourt of the diner and got out of his cruiser. Crossing his fingers that Cheryl kept her mouth shut for the next five minutes. Hell, if she caught him out of the cruiser he'd just say he was checking out a little ebony and ivory he'd seen walking by.

He pushed open the door of the steakhouse and caught his daughter's eye. Jesus, he thought, what in hell has she done to her hair? Not now, he told himself, the last thing he wanted to do was start off with an argument.

"Hey dad," she said, looking around to make sure none of her diners wanted something. They didn't.

Trust them to manage by themselves just when she could do with the cover. "How's things?"

Pete Calhoun shrugged, which was about as far as he could go without telling an outright lie. *Well you see honey, things ain't so good, what with all the drinking and self-pity… tell you the truth I fall asleep jerking off over an old picture of your mom most nights. How is she by the way? She never returns my calls, not since the court order.* A shrug was safer. "You?" he asked.

"Not bad," she replied. And Pete knew she was bull-shitting him just the same as he was her.

"What's with the hair, honey?" he asked, immediately kicking himself for bringing it up.

Amy, tugged at her pink bangs and gave a shrug of her own. "Like it."

Pete nodded, of course she did. "Whatever."

"Whatever," she sighed. This conversation was going as well as ever. "Look, Dad, I can't just drop everything you know, I have customers to serve."

"Sure," he agreed, glad of the get out, "sorry, I just… *" miss you* he had been going to say.

"I know, dad, me too." She looked around the restaurant, when would one of these bastards stick their hand up or catch her eye or something?

"I'm busy too," Pete admitted, "some kind of cluster-fuck over on 192… Cap'n's got us all on the lookout for a pair of suspects." He nearly left it at that. Had he lived through what was to come he would wish he had. "White guy and a black guy," he told his daughter, "white guy's English."

Amy hadn't been paying close attention, still waiting for someone to drag her away from her car crash of a father. But she caught that last.

"White and black?" she asked.

"Yup, I know, needle in a goddamn haystack, huh?"

Amy glanced toward table thirteen where that weird black guy was mopping at his face with his napkin.

10.

Miles and Carruthers had begun to walk back towards the highway. They might not have been bristling with ideas as to how to proceed but sitting in the dust wasn't going to get them anywhere either.

"All we have is the building site and Chester," said Miles. "We know the former's important because otherwise the prisoner would hardly be hanging around there. It seems likely that Chester – or Alan, whatever – started his amble down the the road from there too."

"We don't know that," argued Carruthers. "For that matter we don't know Chester will even get dumped there any more, I don't see the prisoner as someone who would overly concern himself with keeping the passage of time on track."

Miles shrugged. "True, but unless we have anything else to go on..."

"Why abandon the fragile few things we have to play with?"

"Precisely."

They had reached the Interstate now and both looked cautiously back towards the Dunkin' Donuts. There was no sign of the police cruiser, in fact the road was pretty much empty.

"All clear," said Miles.

They crossed over and continued walking away from the building site. It was hot, the sort of mid-day heat that pounds on you.

"I wonder how Tom is?" Miles said.

"Cooler than me." Carruthers replied.

That was the limit of their conversation, speaking took it out of a man when the weather was this unreasonable.

After a while, a gift store crept up on their side of the road, a sign promising cool soda and the "best value T-Shirts in the State!".

"Want a T-shirt?" Miles asked.

"Do I get to drink a cup of tea while I'm wearing it?"

"No."

"Then I have little interest."

"I could do with a cool drink though, a pair of sunglasses would be good too."

"Sunglasses?"

"Tinted lenses to protect your eyes from the sun. They make you look cool too."

"'Cool' as in extremely brilliant rather than low in temperature?"

"That's the one."

"Then obviously I should have some too."

"Obviously."

They entered the store, a small bell chiming to announce their arrival.

"Let me do the talking," said Miles, "we don't want to draw attention to ourselves."

"Oh to be so forgettable."

They walked over to a revolving pillar of sunglasses and Miles began trying them on, offering a pair to Carruthers. The explorer put them on.

"Your own portable darkness generators," he said. "How clever you modern people are."

"Stop being so sarcastic, do you want a pair or not?"

"I'd rather a decent pith helmet."

"You'll settle for the shades."

Miles took a couple of pairs and walked over to a drinks cooler in the corner. He grabbed a couple of bottles of coke and made his way to the counter.

"Hey there," said a small and round lady behind the counter. She was sat on a creaking stool and pressing her face into the breeze of a rotating fan. Thin strands of plastic whipped out from the fan and flickered around her cheeks. She looked like a hamster in a wind tunnel.

"Hi," said Miles, "hot day."

"Been hotter," she said, turning her head on one side as if to cool off her left ear, "there's times when I don't know whether to cry or shit it's so hot."

"I doubt either would help madam," said Carruthers from behind Miles.

The lady stared at him for a moment then peeled her eyes away and began tapping at the till.

"My friend's only joking," said Miles, "he has a weird Australian sense of humour."

"Crack wise again and he'll have my son's work boots up his ass too," she said, "I only has to call him and he'll come running."

"That won't be necessary," Miles insisted, "we just want to buy these things."

"That's what they all say," she continued, "then, 'fore you know it they're reaching for you over the counter, we get 'em all in here, crooks, lunatics and perverts."

"It's good that you're so busy," said Carruthers.

Miles shot him a dirty look. "Please ignore him," he said to the woman, offering her a couple of dollars. "We're in kind of a hurry."

"In some sort of trouble are you?" she asked, not taking the money.

"Of course not!" Miles laughed. "Just need to get on the road."

She stared at them a moment longer and then drew in a breath and opened her mouth to shout for her son. But no sound came out, she just froze there, mouth agape. The only noise was those plastic ribbons from the fan, flickering and cracking.

"What's happened to her?" Carruthers said.

"I have no idea," Miles replied.

Then a noise erupted from the throat: "The 5.15 to Brighton is currently experiencing a crisis of identity and, as such, staff are unsure as to whether it is coming or going."

"The House," said Carruthers, "trying to break through again?"

There was a crackle of radio static, the woman's jowls quivering with the noise. Then a young girl's voice: "Tomorrow morning, build not break, eight forty-five, build not break, Home Town, build not break, restoration, build not break..."

"Sophie?" Miles subconsciously leaning forward as if he might be able to see her if he looked down the woman's throat far enough. He left the money on the counter, grabbed their things and tugged on Carruthers' arm. "Let's get out of here," he said.

"Build not break, build not break, build not break..." Sophie's voice was getting louder and louder as they ran from the store. It continued to build, even as they ran up the highway.

"Build not break, build not break..." there was a pause and then "restoration!" The windows burst outwards as the final scream turned into a whine of distortion.

Miles and Carruthers kept on running.

11.

"Excuse me fellas," said Officer Calhoun, thumb in his belt trying to look casual and threatening all at the same time. Though in truth these two didn't look all that dangerous. Amy had been freaked by them, sure. But Amy was just a kid, she'd freak at anything.

He'd had half a mind to brush her off, still bristling at the ludicrousness of pulling every pair of white and black guys over and asking if they'd been up to any trouble. But there was a bigger part of him – an arrogant but also desperate part of him – that wanted these two to be the guys the Captain was after. Not only for the kudos of finding them but the kudos of finding them *in front of his daughter*, a girl who saw him as an embarrassment. However much he may rankle against her opinion, downright seethe at it in fact, he knew he'd done a few things in his life to have earned it. Now, perhaps a bit of the old alpha male may restore some respect.

"You mind me asking where you were this morning?" he said. Aware as soon as the words were out of his mouth that it was hardly the most subtle of enquiries. If they had been involved in that mess over on 192 they were hardly going to admit to it were they?

"Why," the white guy asked, and Calhoun thought he might just have been English after all, "there some sort of problem?"

"Just a general enquiry, sir," Calhoun replied, pulling a little secrecy back into the proceedings. The black was certainly nervous about something, he noted, in fact he looked ready to scream.

"Oh," the English guy replied, "well in that case we drove up from Hughie's place a few hours ago. Popped in at that building site a few miles away and killed a few people. That help with the general enquiry?" The man smiled and Calhoun felt a sudden urge to run, and to hell with the "alpha male" stuff. He caught a flash of Amy's pink hair out of the corner of his eye – I mean *pink* hair, who in the name of jumped up Christ dies their hair pink? – and that was enough to make him hold his ground. He unholstered his firearm and pointed it towards the table, keeping it moving between the two of them.

"Get out of your seats and on the ground," he barked, taking a solid pleasure in how authoritative he sounded. "Amy?" he called, "you get on out to my car, grab that radio and call me some backup." Too late for that, a little voice whispered inside him, *far* too late. He saw his daughter run outside and that would be some measure of relief in the violence that followed. At least his daughter had got out. He would think of that in a couple of minute's time as he lay dying on the floor. "You hear me?" he asked again, annoyed at the fact that this pudgy little shit was still smiling; a whole world away from lying on the floor and under Calhoun's control.

"I hear you," the man said, returning to his meal and continuing to eat. "Let me just finish my steak and then I'll give your request some consideration."

"It's not a request, asshole," Calhoun shouted, really, terribly afraid now. "It's an *order*. Now get on the floor."

"Please," the black guy said, "don't do this."

"I'll do whatever the hell I like," Calhoun replied before realising that the man hadn't been speaking to him. No, the man hadn't been speaking to him *at all*.

12.

Shepard had been pulling out from Dunkin' Donuts when Cheryl came on the radio telling everyone that Pete Calhoun was requesting backup a few miles away.

"What's the score, Cheryl?" he asked.

"I'm not quite sure, tell you the truth," she answered, a world away from the usual calm and informative voice of despatch. "It was Calhoun's girl that came on the radio and she wasn't clear. Something about a pair of freaky guys in the diner that match the description you sent out."

"Amy Calhoun?"

"Yeah, I know," I know this is not the way things are done, is what Cheryl was saying, I know Calhoun's fucked up again. Bless her though, she wouldn't send that over the radio, not when it could be picked up by someone eavesdropping on the police band.

"Okay Cheryl," he replied, "on my way."

He made it to the steakhouse in about ten minutes, riding the lights and siren and keeping his foot heavy on the gas. The minute he pulled up outside he thought back to that road fatality he had cried over when he'd been wet behind the ears, the one with the kid and that damned heavy shoe. Looking at the blood-spatter and cracks that decorated the outside windows he knew he was about to see something that would linger as long – if not longer – in his memory. Something else for those dark, lonely mornings when all you heard was your wife's breathing.

He reached for the radio, needing to see no more. "Cheryl, we have a Code O," he said, keeping his voice as light as possible. "Get me a couple of guys and a band-aid."

There was a slight pause, but only slight, Cheryl was good. "Code O, check," she said, her voice as breezy as his own. "I'll put out a call, boss."

"Thanks despatch." He hung up the radio. "Code O" was their own little code sign, used when an officer arrived at a major scene requiring backup, fast but no damned rubberneckers or press. "Code O" (or "Code Oh Shit!" as Dutch frequently referred to it) was a way of getting an unpleasant job done on the sly. Get the warm bodies needed without lighting up the eyes of eavesdroppers everywhere. The "band-aid" would be an ambulance, Cheryl was astute enough to figure that much, he knew.

Shepard took a deep breath. He wasn't going to wait for backup to arrive. He should but he wasn't going to. That's because, in his gut, he knew it was all over. It was far too quiet in there. Whatever storm had blown this way – and it had something to do with those guys that had scared Corben Alliss, Shepard thought, scared him enough that the mere proximity of them was enough to get his piss flowing – it had blown over. When he stepped beyond that door he knew that all he would see was blood and ruin. But it was his job to check. He walked towards the restaurant, firearm in hand, held tense and ready to be used.

He moved slowly, in no great rush to look through the windows – fat chance of that, he thought, too much blood. As before when faced with such things, things a human being is hardwired not to want to witness, he found that his senses sharpened rather than spared him the details. It was as if his subconscious demanded he pay close attention, soaked up every nuance. Here but for the grace of God, it said, for this is where you'll end up one day... His boots crunched on a combination of grit and powdered glass like a child munching on cereal. Colours sharpened, that dark red, almost brown, of the blood – not the bright Technicolor of movie gore, but the autumnal shade of fallen leaves. That sharp, metallic, butcher-shop perfume.

"Captain Shepard?" the voice was quiet, a broken whisper coming from behind one of the parked cars. He swung his gun to aim at the noise, nerves so tense his automatic reaction was to assume trouble. He saw a flash of pink duck down behind the fender and lifted his gun skywards.

"Who's that?" he asked. "Come on out, you're OK." That's a lie, he thought, once you've seen this you're never going to be OK again.

Slowly a girl's head appeared and it took him a second to recognise Amy Calhoun. Last time he'd seen her had been on one of the department summer picnics they threw every year. Cops and their families getting together to eat barbecue and pretend they lived normal lives. That had been before Pete had lost his shit, hitting the bottle harder than was healthy and flushing his family away with every sip.

"Amy?" he asked, reconciling this young woman with the kid he'd known. That young girl who still had a father who knew his sober days. The kid that had never seen her place of work turned into a mess of meat and bone.

"Captain Shepard?" she asked again, as if not quite sure.

"That's right, hon," he replied, "Captain Shepard. You see what happened here?" She nodded. "The guys that did it?"

"Gone."

That was something at least. He had suspected it right enough but felt a rush of relief to know his instincts had borne out. "Your dad," he asked, "is he…"

She looked towards the spattered windows and her jaw began to shake. It wouldn't be tears, Warren Shepard knew they would come later, tears were the first sign of getting better. This was still shock, disbelief, horror… the brain switching on and off like lights during a storm.

"Okay," he said, "I want you to come and sit in my cruiser, okay?" He held out his hand to her. "More folks are on the way, you'll be safe now. We'll get you looked after." Ain't nothing that'll make this girl better now, he thought, not all the warm blankets, sedatives and counselling in the world.

He led her carefully back to his cruiser and let her sit in the passenger seat. He picked up the radio and, cautious of breaking the secrecy of a Code O told Cheryl that Pete's daughter needed someone to keep an eye on her. He knew that despatch would follow his meaning.

That done he had no more delays, he needed to see what had happened inside the diner. Like it or not, the job demanded it.

Captain Shepard walked inside.

SEVEN
The Ballroom

1.

"Sophie needs to go to the library now!" the screens had shouted and with that the future took a small spin towards resolution.

Alan and Penelope led the crew of the *Intrepid* downstairs and set their minds to travelling once more. They raided the local shops for a few supplies – mostly food and drink, for whatever it was worth – and filled their backpacks. Hawkins struck gold with some pocket torches, better than sacrificing any more clothing to the flames. Alan rigged a backpack to act as an oversized papoose for Sophie, he knew she would hate being bundled up so close to him but it was the only practical way to cover any distance with her. She was as vacant as ever as he fed her into it, poking her legs out of ragged holes he had cut into the fabric. It pulled heavily on his shoulders and back but he hoped he'd padded it enough for it to be at least reasonably comfortable for its passenger.

Despite the inherent dangers in heading back into the main body of the House, Penelope was glad to be on the move again. With a direction fixed and an objective to aim for – however incomprehensible – she had something to occupy that flitting mind of hers. As the only one of the party to have visited the library before she did her best to describe it to the rest of them.

"It sounds as ludicrous as the rest of this place," said Maggie. "God only knows what we're supposed to do when we get there."

"I guess we just hope that the House makes that clear," Alan said. "We're flying blind as usual."

"Certainly usual for me," said Jonah.

"I wish I could say I was comfortable with following the House's directions in the first place," said Hawkins. "It's hardly seemed driven towards our best interests thus far."

"Who knows if it's the House talking or Sophie," Alan replied, "we have no idea where one ends and the other begins."

"And that makes me feel much better," said Barnabas.

Alan and Penelope had done their best to fill the *Intrepid* crew in on what had happened to them all, even more aware how ludicrous it sounded when trying to explain it. In the end Hawkins had dismissed matters with a wave of his one good hand. "I'm a sea captain," he had said, "we know that sometimes you just have to follow the tide wherever it may go. For now it flows towards this library and we shall sail with it as best we can."

Packed and prepared as well as they could ever hope to be, they made their way towards the station exit. There was a solid wall of darkness where there should have been the hustle of pedestrians and the honking battle of taxicabs. Every now and then a ghostly passenger would walk out of that darkness and pass through them on their way to the station.

"Weird as you like," said Ryan, pulling faces at a be-suited businessman as he emerged into the light, checked his watch and dashed towards his imaginary connection. A young woman appeared, weighed down with shopping bags and her own pleasure at having bent her credit to near breaking. "Help you with your bags darling?" Ryan asked, eyeing her appreciatively. He skipped in front of her, smiling as he held open his arms and puckered up, meaning to kiss this beautiful illusion. She collided into him, sending him sprawling onto the stone floor, his amorous expression switched for one of surprise. The woman was just as startled, dropping her bags and staring at him momentarily before a look of confusion spread across her face and her eyes slipped from him.

"She can't see you any more," said Penelope, "she did… I'm sure she did, but now…" she moved her hand towards the woman. It passed right through her hunched back as she stooped to gather her shopping. "No, gone again…"

"But how could she even have been there in the first place?' said Hawkins. "You told us they were just im-ages… not real people at all."

"That's what we thought," said Alan.

"Doesn't matter," Penelope said, "if we stop to pick at every mystery we come across we'll never get anywhere."

"Yeah," said Ryan, getting to his feet, "wish I'd known that might happen though, I'd have gone for her tits."

"Ryan!" Maggie shouted.

"What do you want from me?" he asked shrugging. "I'm a teenager, tits are what we think about."

"I must be a teenager too then," said Jonah, "I think about them a fair deal too."

"I think Penelope's right," said Alan, determined to bring an end to the conversation. "Let's get moving."

Penelope pulled her torch out of her trouser pocket and shone the beam into the darkness. "We need to find the route through," she said. "This is how Carruthers used to do it. You find the point at which the beam cuts off and that's the way ahead."

"And hope we don't get crushed to death while we're at it," added Alan, thinking of the couple of times he had been attacked by the wraiths.

"That too," Penelope agreed. "Ready?" she asked.

One by one they nodded and she stepped forward.

2.

Build not break. Build not break. Build not break.

Sophie knows that things are coming together. There is a point when something is more done than not done. Like when the toast – on setting number four – smells of crispness and crunch and loses its white. Like when the car turns off the motorway and starts its way along the windy roads that lead to a house. Like when you can see the plate more than the spaghetti. They are at that point now. She can see lots and lots of plate.

Library. That was the word that she kept hearing inside her head. Library.

She had been to her local library a few times. She liked it there. It was all about A,B,C and long numbers that told you exactly where everything was. She hadn't read any books when she had gone there – that had been what interested her mother, before she had got dead she had read lots of books – she had just walked the rows. Understanding the system, reading the numbers, checking people hadn't tried to break things by putting a book back in the wrong place. This happened a lot and she thought the clever people that worked there must have had to empty themselves a lot at the frustration of it. Despite that she wondered if they might let her be a librarian one day. She would have been very good at it, she thought. It would have been a job that made her Very Happy.

Perhaps that was what she was going to do now. The voice in her head wouldn't say. She hoped so.

The voice in her head had changed. To begin with it had been the House. That barking dog that she could not understand. Now it did not bark. It used a voice that she knows. To the others it is the Grumpy Controller. To her it is not. She knows the man's name and it is not Grumpy Controller. He has been speaking a lot to her. Part of her is glad. She knows the voice and it makes her think of home. Part of her is not glad. She knows the voice and it makes her think of home. This is complicated so she tries not to worry about it.

Now the voice is telling her what to do. Not all of it. Just step by step. This is good as she has enough to think about keeping everything else together. Though the House is helping with that too, it is a Very Very Clever House now. Much cleverer than her old house – not her grandparents house her Proper House the one they had all lived in before her mother stopped living altogether – that had just stood there. You had to do everything for it. If you did not close its windows then the rain would come in and soak its floors. If you did not close its doors then the leaves would blow in and you had to count them all back out again. If you did not turn on its Central Heating it got all cold. Her house had been stupid.

Every now and then she tried to listen to what was happening outside to Alan and the Lady. She had heard the Lady scream but Alan had gone to save her so that was okay. Alan was good at saving people. He had saved her and that was good.

Now the Strange Men from the Strange Ship had come and that was nice. Alan liked them, even though they were very Strange and Very Untidy. The Strange Woman was here too and Sophie took a moment to look at all her hair and it made her feel good. It was silly hair but she liked it.

They were travelling now. Going to the library like they had been told. She knew that Alan worried about putting her on his back but she didn't mind. Sometimes you just Had to Make Do and this was like that. Besides, she couldn't feel it most of the time. Most of the time she was in her head. Or the House's head. And in there you didn't feel the bag cut into your bottom or make your legs shake. In there you didn't feel anything at all.

She vanishes back in there to think about long numbers and A,B,C and…

Build not break. Build not break. Build not break.

3.

As soon as they entered the darkness they could feel the wraith moving towards them. It was a sensation rather than a physical presence, though it prickled like static and made the hair on the back of your neck frizz up.

"This is the same as the creature that stole you and Sophie away?" Hawkins asked Alan.

"The very same," Alan agreed, "though they're not normally as gentle as they were then."

"That was gentle?" Barnabas said, remembering the force with which the man and girl had been knocked off their feet and whisked away.

"From what I gather," said Penelope, "they like to play with something for a while and then pulverise it."

"Lovely," said Ryan, "you found the way out yet then?"

Penelope kept swaying the torch to and fro, watching the length of the beam for a point when it would shrink as it shone through the invisible portal they were after. "Give me time."

"All the time in the world," Ryan sighed, looking around.

"If the House wants us to do this you'd think it would call them off," said Maggie, the static sending her hair into an even wider halo than normal.

"If it can," said Hawkins. "Not all watchdogs obey their master."

"There!" said Penelope, pointing to where the beam cut off a little way ahead.

They ran towards it, Alan grimacing as Sophie bounced against him in her papoose. Behind them the wraith swooped on their heels as if brushing them out of its world, a grumpy caretaker lashing out with his broom.

They emerged into one of the House's ubiquitous corridors, deep red carpet and heavy wood panels. In the frequent alcoves there were glass domes filled with bizarre taxidermy. Alan looked at the creatures beneath the glass and found he couldn't identify a single one. He wondered if they were animals that had been constructed from the taxidermist's imagination – "cut and shut" combinations of normal creatures – or whether, on some strange world these things had once flown or burrowed or foraged. In one dome a feathered beast reared up on its back paws, threatening the air with two scythed talons that had the texture of ram's horns. Its snarling mouth showed rows of what could have been human teeth, yellow rectangles, nicked and scored on the bones of some previous meal. Its eyes were like oil in water, black with a colourful shimmer that couldn't quite be pinned down. Alan felt itchy just looking at it.

"What the hell are these things?" asked Barnabas.

"Never seen anything like it," admitted Jonah.

"Imaginary animals," said Penelope, "nightmares, like everything else in this stupid House."

They moved along the corridor, trying not to look to either side.

"Is this the way you came from the library?" Ryan asked Penelope.

"No," she admitted, "I took the scenic route, it involved three days' mountain climbing then a car crash."

"Oh," he didn't really know what to say to that.

"You're going the right way," came a rolling, yokel voice from nearby.

"Who said that?" asked Alan, shuffling forward.

"I did." On the wall was an oil painting of a rural peasant forking hay into neat stacks. The peasant had quit his work and come to the front of the picture, leaning on his pitchfork. He chewed absently on a length of dry straw. "Library's that way," he nodded in the direction they'd been walking, "though you'll have to go through the ballroom to get there."

"Ballroom?" Penelope asked. "I can live with that."

"You'd better hope so, my lovely, those that can avoid the place. It's not altogether sane."

"An insane ballroom?" Alan asked.

"What other kind in this House?" asked Hawkins. "Are you the House?" he asked the picture.

"I'm just a working man," the peasant said, "though I can lay claim to speaking on its behalf at the mo."

"If the House wants us to go this way," said Hawkins, "why doesn't it make sure that the way is clear?"

"Well now," the peasant chewed hard on his straw, deep in thought, "this is the essential duality of its condition you see. Part of it wants you to go that way – the rational part of it – the rest just wants to do what it was born for and kill you." The peasant smiled. "Gives you a headache just thinking on it, don't it?" he chuckled. "Like all that 'ego' and 'id' gubbins they go on about," he tapped at his head, "who really understands what goes on inside the cracked dome of our silly skulls."

"Great," said Hawkins, "lots of help, thanks."

"I mean," the peasant continued, happy to talk now he had started, "take me for example. Most days I'm happy just to get on with my job, get this hay cleared. Maybe think on what I'm going to put in my pot this evening, wonder whether the barley wine is ready to drink… you know, the usual thoughts."

"And the other days?" Maggie asked.

The peasant smiled and nodded at the portrait of a restoration duchess that hung directly across from them. "I wonder what it would be like to hold that dirty bitch down with my pitchfork and hammer her up the arse until I'm spent." He shrugged. "Takes all sorts." He turned back to his hay and began forking it towards the stack.

"Charming," said Alan, "shall we keep moving?"

"Perhaps that's best," agreed Penelope.

The corridor stretched on for some time. The rows of domed animals ceased after a while, becoming busts offering medical cross-sections of the human body. Here a head was cut open to show a smooth, pink-marble brain, there a torso offered the route of its coiled innards in various pastel shades.

"Educational," said Ryan.

"Extremely," said Alan, straightening the papoose

on his back where it had begun to sag to the left. "Whereabouts were you from," he asked, "before ending up here?"

"London lad aren't I?" Ryan replied, putting on his thick cockney accent. "Found the box in an old bloke's belongings. Used to 'find' a lot of things if you get my meaning."

"You were a thief?" Alan asked.

"It was more of a sideline to be honest," Ryan admitted, "used to help my dad with his removals business too, that was the day job."

"Day job?" How old was the kid? "What about school?"

"That's exactly what I used to ask my dad, 'what about school dad?' I'd ask,"

"And what did he say?"

"He said school didn't pay as well."

"Nice."

"Yeah… I wouldn't have minded if he actually *did* pay me but, you know, food and board, that was the deal."

"Sounds like he was a great parent."

"Can't say I miss him much," Ryan admitted.

The corridor finished at a large pair of double doors. To one side there was a dark wood easel with a heavy card sign on it. "Today" it announced in excessively florid calligraphy, "experience the joy of the Wurlitzer with Professor Luptna".

"The joy of the Wurlitzer," said Penelope. "I can hardly wait."

"Sooner we get in," Alan sighed, reaching for the door knob, "the sooner we can be out the other side and on our way to the library."

He opened the door and their world dropped out from beneath them.

Barnabas was exhausted, but as long as the music played and his fat wife continued to sway he knew there would be no rest. He held her hand and led her around the shed constellation of stars that fell from the mirrorball above. The organ music rose and fell like a carousel's song, high twiddling notes dancing over the low hum of the bass. Whenever he looked towards the organist he was somehow unable to catch sight of him. He could see the stage, its sweeping red drapes and gold-painted ornamentation – the bulging clouds of heaven punctured by fat-cheeked cherubs blowing their slender trumpets to herald this terpsichorean apocalypse. Of the organist – or indeed his organ – there was no sign, just a shimmer of colour, like a rippling flag viewed through thick, decorative glass. Its edges moved and folded in on one another. One minute it was there, swollen and massive, then gone but for a hairline of colour. No matter how hard he tried to focus it eluded him. Not that his wife gave him much opportunity.

"You're out of time," she hissed in his ear, flecks of spittle peppering his cheek. "Do try to keep up."

Out of time... That certainly seemed like a familiar notion to him. If he tried to put his finger on why it was familiar he lost concentration on his dance steps and she kicked him. The sharp, sequinned point of her high-heels punctured his skin even through his socks. His ankles felt hot and damp from her repeated administrations.

"Sorry dear," he said, trying not to wince as she kicked him again. He imagined the skin of that ankle to be puckered and bloody, like a steak pulverised by a hammer.

"Lead with the right foot, idiot," she said and snapped her teeth at him like a dog nipping at a fly. Those teeth were mammoth flagstones, beige and glistening, smeared with lipstick, scarlet skid-marks. The fur on her upper lip bristled like corn in the wind as she fixed her showy smile back in place and tilted her head at the other dancers. Her eyes were small: hazel bullseyes at the centre of lilac eyeshadow targets. Her ashe blonde curls were piled high like dog dirt, a crisp slender flick at their summit. She was horrendous and his stomach churned to look at her. When she spoke, a noxious puff of rot billowed past those monstrous teeth. In his head it was the sort of smell one imagined erupting from the split carcass of a drowned man.

She kicked him again. "Lighter on your toes," she demanded and he tried to lift even though he felt a trickle of blood run into his shoes to boil against his hot and throbbing foot.

He tried to follow the other dancers but they made his head hurt almost as much as the elusive organist. He saw them as swooping triangles of black evening jackets or spangly gowns. Light and dark, bouncing around them like moonlight on a rough sea.

The sea, he thought, *I'm much more at home on the sea.*

She kicked him again.

Hawkins couldn't help screaming as Maggie dug her thumb into his broken wrist.

"You dance like a cripple," she said. Not the soft voice of the woman he loved, but a harsh rasp like a striking match. "Do better."

"I'm trying," he assured her.

"Not hard enough," she replied, digging her thumbnail into the crack of his splintered bone again. In the delirium of his pain her hair stretched like the tendrils of an anemone. Always large it now seemed to reach the ceiling, the ends probing the heavily decorated cornices and the sparkling mirrorball as if hunting for scraps of food.

He loved his wife. He loved her more than anything else in the world... he just wished she wouldn't hurt him so.

"Twirl me you slovenly arse," she said and spun in front of him, that impossible hair whirling around her head. It writhed towards the other dancers, one man turning so that Hawkins could see the scab he wore as a face, crisp yet weeping, yellow stains creeping into the starched white of his collar. Once glimpsed it vanished, replaced by an indistinct blur that swept away across the floor, vanishing into the darkness.

Chester pulled Penelope close. His face sponged his sweat onto her hers, wiping a salty snail-trail across her cheek and lips as he rubbed against her.

"I just want to explore," he whispered, the voice carrying over the music as if it weren't even there. "You'll help me won't you?"

When he spoke she saw a wisp of gun smoke trickle from between his thin lips.

"Please," she said, the word as unwelcome in her mouth as a piece of broken glass, "just don't kill me."

He smiled and the rivulets of sweat that poured from his forehead met the puckered lips and branched around it like a stream diverting around a fallen tree.

"There are worlds upon worlds," he replied, as if she had said nothing at all. "There is a box, and inside that box is a door, beyond that door..."

She knew the answer to that one, it was on the tip of her tongue. "Beyond that door..."

• • • •

In Alan's arms, Rebecca, his one time therapist, whispered non-constructive thoughts as he fought to carry her gracefully around the floor.

"Fat and ugly," she said as he tried to turn with the music. Tears of agreement coursed down his face as he lifted her arm and tilted her back, their groins pressing together. "I'd never let you fuck me," she assured him, "your dick's too small for me to even know it was there."

He lifted her upright, leading her backwards through the faceless dancers who parted before them.

"You're hollow," she said, "and the hole is filled with piss and shit."

The organ surged and they clasped beneath the mirrorball.

"I wish I was dead," he said.

"So do I," she replied, "I'd hate you but I really can't be bothered."

Ryan's mother walked him in time with the music, his feet stood on hers. Despite his size she managed this just fine, towering above him, a plump giant in pink satin. She swung him around the floor, the sprinkled light from above trickling over grey, loose skin.

"I wish you weren't dead mum," said Ryan.

She said nothing, her jaw hung too low for words, clanking around her chest like dirty pearls. She simply pressed his face into her gaseous belly where it sunk deep, as if there were not flesh beneath the fabric of her dress but rotting leaf mulch.

Maggie did her best to hold onto her husband but she was too fat. The sagging folds of flesh beneath her arms caught in the straps of her frock, squirting to either side of the cheap cotton like sausage meat twisted and tied.

"There's just too much of you to love," Hawkins said, his handsome, manly face wrinkling in disgust at her bulging folds. The fat poured, wobbling, from every angle. Her colossal thighs clapping together like retarded seals, her drooping breasts running away from her chest like pink tapeworms.

She tried to beg for his love but she couldn't speak, the great collars of blubber around her neck choking her words.

For Jonah all was delirium. The organ screamed like a hundred factory whistles, leather shoes machine-gunned the walnut dance floor, laughter roared with the cacophony of a field of geese.

Hands tugged at him, plucking at his shirt, his hair his skin.

"Dance with us!" they cried. He tried, spinning out of control, bumping from one to another like a pinball, hands shoving him this way and that. Someone snatched away his eyepatches and he felt the searing hot touch of fire, sprayed down from the mirrorball landing on the useless white of his blind eyes.

Beyond that door... the words pricked at Penelope. *There is a box... and inside that box is a door...*

"Beyond that door..." she said looking up at Chester, his hair plastered around his skull like a newborn. "Beyond that door..."

Beyond that door is the House. A voice said, somewhere deep inside her, *a terrible House, an impossible House.*

"And inside that House..." she let go of Chester's hands, watching him spin away on his own into the faceless crowd, sweat dripping behind him like water from a wrung cloth.

"Inside that House is a ballroom," she said. A sudden

moment of clarity pierced her head with a light greater than that thrown from the ceiling above, or the spotlit stage or...

She ran towards the stage, climbing up the ornate cherubs and the unfurling clouds to reach for the stage beyond it. The organ screeched, a train approaching a tunnel, as she clambered over a thrusting gold trumpet and fell to the dusty boards beyond it.

In front of her, ever-moving, light trails trickling out behind him as he swayed, the organist played on. Long, distended fingers pulled stops and pressed keys. Thin, lifeless hair flicked from his peeling scalp as he thrashed, his feet pounding the pedals.

"Dr. Luptna I presume?" she asked, grabbing at the flaking cadaver and wrenching him back from the organ. He squealed to be torn free, strips of skin left hanging from the organ keys like the tongues of thirsty dogs.

"Thank you," he whispered, as the last notes faded up the organ pipes to be puffed out like smoke, "I was so very tired."

The houselights came up, revealing the rest of her party, stumbling in blistered pain around the wood of the dance floor. They were crying, or raging, or gasping, each according to their nightmare.

Alan dropped to his knees, remembering Sophie on his back at the last minute and shooting out a hand to support himself so he didn't topple over any further. Maggie was clutching at herself as if insects had been crawling over her. Jonah reached for his eyepatches and sighed with relief to feel them still in place. Ryan sat still in the middle of the floor, head down to try and hide the tears in his eyes. Hawkins cradled his throbbing arm. Barnabas rubbed at his ankles, took one look at Penelope and gave a brief smile. "Good job girlie."

They took a moment to gather themselves, tightened their packs and their hearts and left that insane ballroom to the music that roared inside its own head.

INTERLUDE
On the Other Side

Whatever Martin might have imagined would be on the other side of the door it wasn't this. He stepped passed the planks and screws the door had shed and left his lonely house behind him. He recalled the noises that had baited him during the night – when he had lain in the darkness resolutely refusing to believe in the door he had just stepped through. He had heard machinery, old music, whispering, the muffled sound of a woman talking… He had conjured abattoir images: split meat, thrusting blades… all the horrors he could conceive of. That must have been fear and his own neuroses talking because it was nothing like that beyond the door. It was an old-fashioned penny arcade. Colourful wooden cabinets bleeped and flashed to the percussion of flying ball bearings. A pneumatic clown jerked and spun behind glass, fixed plaster maw offering a tinny cackle at his own private joke. Thick, red drapes kept the machines warm and hid soft, orange lights somewhere in their folds. One of the machines, *The 64,000 Volt Challenge*, dared him to move a silver hoop over the bends and spirals of a metal bar. *Winner takes all!!!* It insisted, offering a warning buzz of electricity, blue sparks bristling from the bar, as a clue as to what the loser could expect.

He moved to the next machine, an upright pinball that sent its own ball bearings around a large metal spiral waiting for someone to take its mind off the boredom. Next to that *Doctor Heinrich Von Schutt's Medicinal Marvel* wanted to guess his weight and offer *Sagely Sanitary Advice*. Martin had no wish to experience the *Diagnostic marvel of the century!* so he moved on. He passed them all. No desire to prove himself on *Max's Magnatronic Mallet*, play a hand or two on *Hank Henry's Riverboat Saloon* or watch the race at *Grand Falls Steeplechase*.

"I know what you want," a woman said causing Martin to cry out in panic. He spun around to face *Madame Arcana, the Mystic Beauty of the East*. She stood in her glass cubicle, one shapely wooden leg crooked up to show off the shine on her cream-coffee thigh. She was swathed in layers of colourful silk. Her glass eyes sparkled from beneath a headdress of golden coins. "I know what you want," she said again, her walnut and brass voice box offering a tone richer and more compelling than Martin would ever have thought possible. He walked over to her, stroking his fingers on the cool glass of her cabinet as a motor within her hips began to jig.

"Beautiful," he whispered, a dreamy wave falling over him as he watched her dance. He shoved his hand into his pocket for a coin as he pressed his nose against the glass. He found some change but was barely able to tear his eyes away from hers to see what he had. Surely it wouldn't work anyway? Wouldn't it be built to take old pennies? He checked the slot and figured a two pence piece might just do the trick, slotting it in and hoping for the best.

Madame Arcana took his donation gratefully. She shimmied on her pistons offering a partial glimpse of her beautifully planed pine breasts as the silks swayed from side to side.

Martin pressed himself closer, wishing he could touch. His head buzzed with a sleepy eroticism. He pressed his cheeks against the cabinet, his mouth huffing condensation on the glass as Madame Arcana flicked her long fingers and produced a thick card from within her palm.

Martin was quite sure he was asleep now. The waking world didn't offer such pleasures. Not for him. His body felt light, the only blood that seemed to flow was in his groin as he unselfconsciously stared at his wooden beauty through half-closed eyes.

"What's my fortune?" he whispered.

Madame Arcana pressed the card against the glass so that he could see the words written on it: "Frankly? Not good…"

Her arms and legs shot through the glass grabbing at Martin and pulling him close. Squealing in a state of sudden wakefulness, Martin felt a heat growing between her wooden thighs, a heat that drew him within her like a bird sucking up a worm. His bones popped as he was forced inside her wooden cavity, a labial slit parting along her torso, the better to eat him whole. She leaned her head back as if in orgasm and the last glimpse of light Martin was afforded was from between her painted, crimson lips as she snapped close around him.

She began to digest, leaving a handful of pocket change, scattered on the floor tiles, as Martin's only legacy.

EIGHT
Once Upon a Time in Valencia

I: The Good

1.

Ashe was used to the heat. When you spent long enough in warm climates you developed a tolerance, a state of mind as much as anything else, that allowed you to get on with your business whatever the damn thermometer chose to say. You thought cool thoughts and let the body do its sweating.

When he had worked as a history professor – a life that now seemed to belong to someone else, he was a man of multiple identities these days – the summers had got to him. But that was as much his weight as the sun. When you carried an extra sixty pounds of cinnamon pastry on your waistline you were going to struggle when the air got warm. Now, slimmer, older and much more focused, it wasn't a problem. Honestly. He could deal with it.

Christ but it was hot.

And then there were the flies. Persistent bastards, seemingly convinced that there was nothing tastier in the world than his face. They bashed against his eyes and lips as if they were coated in honey. Every time he brushed them away they returned, mindlessly. It was all he could do not to pull out his gun and start shooting. They were driving him crazy.

He had spent a slow few days in Indonesia, recovering from his experience on the water and the savage crack he'd received to his head. A young boy had found him shouting at the sky amongst the dead fish and driftwood. "The seagulls will not hurt you," the boy had insisted in response to his raving. Not speaking a word of the language, Ashe didn't understand.

The kid had called his parents, the parents had called the local doctor and within a couple of hours Ashe was being looked after by the best that Kupang could offer. By modern standards this wasn't much. No cool hospital sheets, saline drip or candy-stripers fussing around, but it had been enough. Ashe had got back on his feet. On his last day he had even had time to make preparations. He had dried his money out, given some to the boy's family as a measure of thanks and spent a few hours on the beach, awaiting his train, reading his notebook and planning the journey of the box.

He imagined its route, not as dry ink on a page but rather as a visual journey, fleshing out the details he didn't know with best guesses or just plain imagination. From its last sighting on the ocean it had appeared next in the Australian town of Darwin. He would have to hope it could make its own way there, he suspected it would. A subconscious impression rather than anything concrete but he had good reason to trust his gut in this instance. He pictured the box washed up on the beach, nestled amongst the seaweed and shell just as he had been a few days ago. There it was found by an American entrepreneur called Terrance

Arthur, in Darwin to enquire about factory space and trade potential. Ashe tried to imagine Arthur's face but all he could see was his own, not surprising given that the man was his father. A father he could no more remember than anything else about his formative life. Was Terrance Arthur a good man? Ashe suspected not. Given what Penelope had told him it would seem that Chester had lived in fear of his parents. A tyrannical pair who ruled their son in all things. No, thought Ashe, picturing young Chester pulling the trigger of a gun, or punching a naked Penelope to the side of the head, not *all* things... he kept some parts to himself.

At some point Chester – *you*, his own voice insisted in his head – got the box. Perhaps his father had given it to him as a cheap gift, a washed-up opportunity. Perhaps Chester had simply taken a shine to it and helped himself. He had obviously conducted some research. From what Penelope had said, Chester had known the box's potential, known it was a gateway to some other place. He would eventually make that journey and see for himself. Then Chester's days would be numbered. For Ashe did think of him as another person, whatever his subconscious had to say on the matter. Chester was the man Ashe had the misfortune of inheriting his body from, nothing more. Once inside the House, Chester would play his final part in the prisoner's game. Then have his memory wiped by those library worms until there was nothing left. A hollow man waiting to be filled with something better. Ashe remembered the urge he had felt to shoot Walsingham, the willingness to kill Yoosuf's accomplice... perhaps that man had not been quite as hollow as he hoped. *No*. No point in thinking that way.

He continued imagining the passage of the box. He pictured it tumbling from Penelope's hands in the narrow drainage gulley that ran alongside Terrance Arthur's New York meat-packing plant, bobbing in the gushing, foul water before dropping into the darkness of the Hudson. From there it floated along the current, *en route* to its next pair of hands: Alvarado Gomez, a young sailor stood on the dock, cigarette in his mouth and impatience for the ocean in his heart. Perhaps Gomez caught a flash of that dirty New York moon as it bounced off the brass hinges of the box? Whatever had drawn his eye, Gomez fished it out of the water – in Ashe's mind he could see the man clearly, stretching out over the river, boathook in his hand as he dragged the box within reach – and fancied he'd found an unusual gift for his young wife back home. Certainly the box was attractive (to some it was irresistible).

At what point Gomez decided that it wasn't such a lovely gift after all Ashe couldn't decide. Though he imagined the sailor lying in the dark of his bunk, turning the box over in his hands and wondering what precisely he had found. It wouldn't open but perhaps Gomez had been grateful of that, worried what he might see should it ever do so. Perhaps the box had played its trick of ticking when observed, the essence of its maker bristling inside the wood, eager to meet the air. Whatever it was that had unnerved Gomez – for certainly something had – he couldn't wait to pass the box on to someone else once the ship made port. Why he hadn't simply thrown it overboard Ashe couldn't begin to guess, certainly he had almost given it away at the first opportunity. According to the torn page his younger self had procured from the sales ledger of Luis Cortez, dealer in antiques, art and opium – though he wasn't as fastidious in keeping sales paperwork for the latter – Gomez had sold the box for the sort of spare change a sailor can dispose of in one vigorous hour of shore leave.

And there the box had rested for a while. Cortez could see no great value in a box that couldn't be opened, having given up on the trick of it after half an hour of probing and shaking. It gathered dust rather than victims. It was neither the first nor the last time the box would share shelf space with unconventional treasure. Antique shops – or stalls like Yoosuf's – were regular resting points along its journey.

It was Jesus Garcia that would finally liberate the box, catching a glimpse of it while searching for something ostentatious to hang on his wall. Garcia smuggled weaponry for the Republican government, underhand deals from countries and organisations that didn't want to be seen to support the old regime during the Civil War. Politics in gun sales never changed, they sold you bullets on a Monday then denounced you to the press on Friday just after your cheque had cleared.

The very thing that Cortez had thought made the box unattractive – the fact that nobody could open it – was what had appealed to Garcia. He was arrogant enough to think that he would succeed where others had failed. Nothing ever refused his advances for long.

He was to be disappointed. He gave the box hours of his time, tracing every single line of the burned lettering. Nothing would open it. Several times he had come close to shooting the thing (for sure a .45 round would see it open, he thought) but that smacked too much of failure and so he left it alone. *One day*, he thought, whenever he caught sight of it, *one day I'll have you open*.

The train had deposited Ashe in an alleyway behind a bar. He had stumbled into a mess of discarded beer bottles and the aroma of cat piss, a family of strays having made a home by the bins. It was not the best introduction to Valencia.

He had booked himself a room at a local hotel, relieved to find they were willing to accept the dollars he had left over. He had worried that they would be too old but the gleam in the eyes of the rotund Spaniard behind the registration desk said it wasn't so. He had needed to eat. Taking his place at a table in the hotel bar, he stared at the limp chalk marks scrawled across a blackboard on the wall and wondered whether it translated into a menu. He wasn't inclined to point and hope for the best so he asked the owner to recommend something. The owner walked off, bringing him a large terracotta bowl of stew five minutes later. Ashe guessed that there was nothing else to recommend. The stew was fine, chorizo sausage and beans, bobbing in a chilli tomato sauce that Ashe just knew he'd be hearing from again after a few hours. He wiped the bowl clean with bread and killed the spicy heat on his tongue with a large glass of beer.

He headed upstairs, his eyes drooping before he had even cleared the door of his room. The fact that his body knew a solid night's sleep on an actual bed lay ahead made it impatient. He was fast asleep the minute he lay down.

The next morning he washed – oh to have had a hot shower, just to finish off the holy trinity of an evening meal and a night's rest – and put on his usual clothes. He was tempted to leave the overcoat behind, it's not as if the weather demanded it, but he had no idea how to inconspicuously carry his gun without it. Better to sweat than be shot at and not be able to shoot back. But then that was also a problem that needed solving: he was out of ammunition. First order of the day would be to find some shells.

He asked at the hotel owner where you could buy hunting supplies and the fat man had grinned at him, showing teeth that alternated between black and white as often as a crossword. The man had given him a name and a street number and Ashe had headed out. There was something to be said for staying in suspect accommodation, he thought, you asked the concierge at the Waldorf where to buy weaponry and they took a dim view of you. Here it made you fit in.

The house he had been directed to was nondescript, just another open doorway in a terrace of townhouses. Music called through the bead curtain that hung across the front door, letting in the cool but keeping out prying eyes. Crackly swing tunes, Glen Miller, Ashe thought, or maybe Benny Goodman, one of those old guys. Not so old right now, he reminded himself.

"Hola?" he called, peering through the gaps in the beads to see if he could spy movement in the darkness beyond them. Having lived in Florida he had a fair bit of Spanish, it was a useful middle ground language between the Cubans and the Mexicans. He'd found it easy enough to pick up. *Perhaps you already knew it...* that annoying voice in his head said, *hollow man!* "I was told this was the place to come to if you wanted to buy..." he had no intention of shouting out his requirements, not without so much as a pair of eyes to look into, "specialist items."

"I am nothing if not a specialist, senor," a voice replied, dark, nicotine-stained fingers parting the beads to reveal a craggy face crowned with an unruly mop of black hair.

"Jimenez?" Ashe asked.

"Nobody else here," the Spaniard replied, waving Ashe inside.

It took a few moments for Ashe's eyes to adjust from the bright sunlight to the dark of Jimenez's house. Not that there was much to see, a couple of easy chairs, a large dining table. There was no ornamentation or pictures. The only decoration being the smell of cigarette smoke and old wine.

"Sit down my friend," the Spaniard said, pointing to one of the easy chairs, "and tell me what 'specialist items' you have need of."

Ashe considered remaining standing – certainly he had no urge to make himself comfortable here – but didn't want to irritate the man by refusing his hospitality.

"I have most things," Jimenez continued, sitting down in the other chair, "I am a man who believes in free trade. Women? Drugs perhaps?"

Ashe ignored the fact that Jimenez thought him the sort of man who would want either. He took his revolver out, careful to hold it in a suitably non-threatening manner. "Ammunition for this," he said.

"Ah!" Jimenez smiled, "you are in the market for violence."

"Protection," Ashe insisted.

Jimenez shrugged. "The two are the same, it all comes down to timing, no?"

Ashe chose not to answer that.

Jimenez nodded anyway, as if Ashe had told him something extremely wise. "May I?" he reached for the gun and Ashe, with a moment's pause, gave it to him.

Jimenez cracked it open as if it were no more unusual an act than breathing. "I do not recognise it," he said, handing the revolver back.

"It's American." Ashe explained, hoping that was enough.

"So are most of the weapons I sell," Jimenez replied. "You people make many guns."

Ashe couldn't deny that.

"I have what you need," Jimenez said, getting up and leaving the room.

Ashe sat in silence, glancing toward the bead curtain every now and then, nervous of being caught in the act of buying illegal munitions. The music switched from an upbeat number to something slow and romantic, the kind of tune you swayed to in the arms of a woman you loved. It seemed hideously inappropriate in the circumstances, like an Irish jig at a funeral.

Jimenez returned with a couple of boxes of shells. He handed them to Ashe. "You looked like a man who might want quantity," he said.

Ashe couldn't deny that either. "How much?" he asked, opening both boxes to check they were full then loading his gun.

Jimenez shrugged as if the matter hadn't occurred to him. "I like to do favours for new customers," he said, "it encourages them to come back."

He named his price and if it constituted a special offer, Ashe was shocked to think what the regular price might be. He handed over some of his dwindling dollars and made to leave.

"I will be here if you need me," Jimenez said as Ashe parted the beads. "In case you run out!"

Ashe didn't reply, leaving the man to the sleepy croon of the big band on his record player.

3.

He made his way down to the port, wanting to find the boy, Pablo. Stood back, he realised what an impossible task that would be. The port was massive, a small city of its own. There was the yacht marina on one side – all flickering sails and gleaming white paint – and the industrial port to the other. The latter was chaos. Chains of men ferried produce of all kinds along the dock. Great trains of boxed fruit, gleaming fish, spools of fabric, motor parts... The air was thick with smoke, burned oil and raised voices. The Spanish were a loud nation, their sailors doubly so. Jokes and orders bounced from one side of the port to the other. Laughter mixed with fury, a dash of obscenity (and a large dash at that) to top it off. It made Ashe's head spin just to look at it.

As much as he despaired of finding the boy he didn't have it in him not to try so walked from one end of the docks to the other. Every few steps he had to jump to one side to avoid packing chests or sailors. Chains and ropes swung – apparently mindlessly – through the air around him. It was an obstacle course as well as a wild goose chase and, once he had walked from one end to the other he gave up on a return journey. The idea of finding anyone was a nonsense. He had spent all of his time watching where he was going, not scrutinising the crews he passed. Maybe it would be quieter later on in the day. He knew nothing about the business of commercial shipping. To hell with it, he'd take the risk and come back later, there had to be more constructive things to do with his morning than avoid death beneath a crate of bananas.

As he left the dock he stopped to look at a young girl curled in a spool of rope, fast asleep. She made him think of Sophie. There was no similarity between them but he thought of her nonetheless. He often did. It was no life, he thought, looking down at her... no life at all.

He headed back into the city – a trek in itself but one that had much to recommend it, not least the lack of death traps and shouting sailors. He stopped for a coffee, feeling the need of the energy. That was the thing about a good night's sleep after so long without: it clung to you like molasses for hours. He sipped at his coffee, as thick as milkshake and with a kick that made him shiver. Once finished he could put off the next stage of his plan no longer: time to go and take a look at Garcia's house.

It was just as he imagined, a building designed to show off. Surrounded by white walls that offered glimpses of a luxuriant garden and a large blue dome inside. The cathedral, only a few metres away, began to toll its bell and Ashe squinted against the noise, each peal like a hammer blow that made the nerves in his temples twitch.

Garcia was a man with connections. Crooked ones at that: the sort that wouldn't mind handling the guns Garcia sold. Ashe couldn't simply storm in there and demand the box, he would be shot within seconds. His escape route from Valencia was some time off – he had allowed a stay of three days – ample time he had hoped. Given his initial glance at the docks he feared it would take him that long just to try and find Pablo.

First things first: the box. He looked up at Garcia's house and felt a chill settle over him despite the overwhelming heat. He guessed there was only one option: he was going to have to steal it.

He walked around the house a number of times, getting a feel for the size and scope of it. Then he took a seat in a cafe and sketched a plan. Laying out the front gates and outside wall was easy enough and he was confident he could map the external wall of the house within that using the view of the roof. None of which helped him figure out where Garcia may keep the box of course. In fact, it didn't help him much at all.

He sighed, snapping his notebook closed and looking up into the busy Valencian street. There was little point planning this, he realised. He would just have to watch the house, wait until it was empty then force his way inside. Sometimes the best plans were as simple as that.

His eyes were caught by an unusually refined figure weaving his way through the Spanish locals. A man in a white linen suit, panama hat bobbing through the crowd as he made his way in Ashe's direction. He was moving quickly, clearly irritated at the people in his way. Hot too, constantly dabbing at his face with a large paisley handkerchief. Once he was only a few feet away that sweating face nearly made Ashe drop his coffee cup. It was Chester.

4.

Ashe paid for his coffee and made after his younger self. That hat made him easy to track, even in the bustling crowds. What's he doing here? Ashe wondered. The answer to that was easy enough once he thought about it. Same as you, old man, he's hunting for the box.

Having lost the box in New York due to Penelope dropping it in the drainage gully he had somehow traced it here to Valencia and presumably Garcia. But how? Ashe wondered, I have the advantage of history I knew it would end up here and could trace backwards, how in hell does *he* know where to look?

After a while, it became clear that Chester was aiming for the port. Ashe had to go some to keep up with him. He never just walks, he thought, I was wound so tight I had to march everywhere. Forever dabbing the sweat from his forehead or the back of his neck where his hair curled in wet ringlets.

In Ashe's pockets the heavy boxes of shells bashed against his thighs. You could imagine they were excited, jiggling together in glee at the sight of someone who loved them.

Once at the port, Chester veered towards the marina. He has a boat, Ashe thought, I kissed goodbye to a fortune when I stepped out of his life and into my own. *That's not all you said goodbye to,* another voice piped up, *don't forget that.*

The boat was a wedding cake of white wood and chrome trim. As Chester walked along the jetty and hopped aboard, another man appeared at the wheelhouse above him. Ashe didn't recognise him but given his considerable size and the fact that he had the head and expression of a perverted bowling ball, guessed he must have been Henryk, Chester's driver, the man who had raped Penelope's friend Dolores.

Ashe walked past the boat. He kept his head down and walked as nonchalantly as he could. He didn't feel nonchalant though, he felt terrified. Of all the experiences he'd thus far endured coming face to face with his younger self had hit him with a force that he could scarcely deal with. Once he had reached the far end of the marina he took off his coat and sat down on a wall. How could he be here? That was the question he kept coming back to. Just how the hell could Chester be here?

5.

He sat and watched the marina, trying to think of a way he could get closer to Chester, maybe figure out what his plans were. Obviously his younger self wanted to retrieve the box for himself. He would have to succeed too, one day anyway, to make his own contribution to the timeline of the House.

Perhaps Ashe would be best served acting as a shadow to his younger self, keeping track of him, letting him do all the hard work and then step in at the end, snatch the box from him. Maybe even force him to use it before he found the boy. There was a neatness to that which appealed.

As the day wore on, Ashe began to wonder if he was wasting valuable time. Chester didn't show his face all afternoon. Henryk – if indeed that's who it was – appeared every now and then, stood at the wheelhouse and gazing out to the ocean but that was all. As the sun began to set Ashe was convinced that he had wasted the hours entirely. He was no further forward in his plans and a whole day had gone. He was just about to leave when he saw both Chester and Henryk step off the boat and stroll towards the city.

Ashe followed at some distance, aware that he didn't exactly blend in, most especially now the marina had become quiet. Chester and Henryk were in a world of their own, walking silently through the streets. Neither of them had reason to suspect they might be followed.

Ashe was reminded of how Madras had transformed itself at nighttime, Valencia going through much the same process. The streets were lit, the bars filled and what had been a bustling, functional city now turned into a vibrant, musical feast. Guitars strummed flamenco, violins swooped into folk riffs, hands clapped and leather soles stomped. The streets shook with sound, laughter and shouting, cheers and jeering. Nothing ever happened quietly, the simple delivery of a bottle of wine to a table was something conducted in roars of pleasure.

Chester and Henryk made their way towards the cathedral and for a few minutes, Ashe had wondered if they planned on visiting Garcia. But they stopped at a small restaurant nearby, ordering themselves plates of shellfish and a bottle of rioja. Ashe kept his distance for a while but then, emboldened by his lack of time and the fact that watching them from afar was still getting him nowhere, he walked into the restaurant and took a table just behind them. Chester would have no reason to suspect him as anything other than another visitor. One hardly checked old faces in a crowd in case one of them might be your own. The sheer implausibility of it was as good a disguise as any. He positioned his chair so that he had his back to them but was close enough to pick out parts of their conversation. Hearing his young voice was deeply unsettling, familiar and yet alien. In the way that listening to a recording of yourself can be.

"You sure you don't want me to come with you?" Henryk asked.

"No," Chester replied, "I can manage perfectly well on my own." There was silence to that but Ashe had to imagine that Henryk had pulled a disbelieving face as Chester's tone was childishly defensive when he continued. "Don't think a jumped up little crook like Jimenez worries me," he said, "he is a tradesmen like any other."

Ashe didn't catch Henryk's reply, the man was speaking too quietly but his thoughts were occupied with the mention of Jimenez's name. Could it be the same man he had met earlier? Yet another coincidence. Was this the House's influence once more? Was he somehow being pushed around on these expeditions like a chess piece?

"You are capable of many things, Henryk," Chester said, that high tone of his carrying much better over the noise of the other diners, "don't forget I've witnessed a fair few of them, but you are not a housebreaker, I have no wish to bail you out of the local jail come the morning." Henryk obviously attempted to quiet his employer as Chester scoffed. "None of them speaks a word of English, look at them, bunch of peasants."

I really was an asshole, Ashe thought.

"If you're not back by twelve I will come looking for you," said Henryk, loud enough to be heard this time, his voice raised in an attempt to placate his employer, Ashe assumed. "That gives you an hour to talk and then make your way back to the boat. Now please..." what followed was too quiet for Ashe to hear but he imagined it was something along the lines of "shut your flapping mouth, boss, before we get ourselves in trouble". Too late for that. Chester's appointment was at eleven. His bravery had paid off.

When the waiter came he ordered some fish – keeping his Spanish accent as thick as possible to hide the fact that he was as American as the gentleman behind him – and decided to add a bottle of wine, he felt he was allowed a small celebration.

6.

If Chester and Henryk talked further, Ashe didn't hear them. He wasn't particularly concerned, he had his plans for the day ahead and his initial disgust at finding Chester here could turn out to be misplaced. If all went well, his younger self could handle all the difficult stuff.

Halfway through his meal, the sound of chairs scraping back announced Chester and Henryk's departure. They made their way back to the marina and Ashe relaxed into his wine. He still had to find Pablo – a problem he couldn't envisage an easy solution to – but once he had the box in his hands he would at least be some way towards achieving his goal. If he managed to force Chester into the House tomorrow then he had only one journey left: New York, to meet Tom and Elise. While the thought of that journey saddened him – much as trapping his friends on the *Intrepid* had – he did at least know that it was quick and simple. A few hours would do it, from the strip club to the bar where they would vanish. Then he could return to the House, see if the future he had felt hang over him ever since he had arrived there might yet be diverted. The thought of that took away his enthusiasm for the wine, however much he tried to push it away. He left a third of the bottle, paid up and returned to his hotel hoping that he might be able to secure at least one more night of decent sleep.

It was a naïve hope. Having reminded himself that these journeys with the box had just been an interruption, a delay that brought his own future all the closer, he couldn't relax enough for sleep. His head was filled with a world that the revellers that sang and danced outside his hotel couldn't begin to comprehend.

He sat in his bed, staring at the far wall lit by the street lamps outside and tried to imagine how he might be able to change what lay ahead. Perhaps he did fall asleep in the end because, in the early hours of the morning, he was startled at the sight of that seagull that he had imagined in Indonesia. It perched on the wrought iron of his small balcony and was as chatty now as it had been on the prow of his boat.

"You're fighting a losing battle you know," it had said, half in the voice of the Grumpy Controller, half in a bird-like caw of its very own. "Some things just have to happen."

"Maybe," he had replied, quite sure that this must be a dream, just as it had been before. "But the future can always be altered can't it? If not then there's no point in any of this."

"Of course," the gull croaked, "nothing's set in stone. My point was that *this* future, the one you are so determined to avoid, is better than the alternative."

"You want to try living it," said Ashe.

"Oh," the gull almost shrugged, its feathered shoulders ruffling, "you lot can survive anything, your species is known for it."

"It's no kind of life," Ashe replied, thinking of the girl he had seen asleep in that coil of rope at the port, "no kind of life at all."

"I'll make a point of not mentioning that to your wife," said the gull, "or did you not marry?"

Ashe shook his head. "There seemed little point."

"Who says romance is dead?" the gull squawked, amused.

Ashe lay down and rolled his back towards the bird. He had no interest in furthering this dream.

The bird felt differently. "Is it so bad?" it asked. "You have a wife – of sorts – a child, *children* really. So the world's not perfect. At least it's still there. And mark my words, if you try and stop what's coming there's no chance of that."

"Perhaps that would be best," Ashe whispered, then cursed himself for thinking such a thing.

The bird clucked quietly for a moment. "We'll see," it said in the end and flew away.

When the dawn light woke him, Ashe figured he'd had maybe four hours of sleep if lucky. He sat on the edge of his bed, feeling groggy and older than ever. He had five hours until Chester's meeting with Jimenez and as much as the prospect of trying to spend some of that resting appealed he knew it was time best spent trying to find Pablo.

He dressed and began the long walk. The streets were busy already with locals. Some were making their way towards the market, rickety wagons laden down with stock. The houses were being opened up, the old Spanish women emerging into the daylight to mop their front step and gossip. Young children, those habitual early-risers, were beginning to run and play.

Even in the clatter of wagon wheels, lashing mops or tongues, cheers and laughter it all seemed so delicate. With the dream of the gull still heavy in his head he couldn't help but imagine them swept aside to make way for the future. It was a sombre mood that hung around him all the way down to where the sea crashed and the ocean wind could begin to blow his depression away.

He looked to the marina and pictured Chester, still asleep in his millionaire's boat. Or perhaps, hopeful of the day ahead, he couldn't close his eyes either, lying there and imagining what delights the box would bring him. He'd learn soon enough, we never wish in the right direction, our dreams make fools of us all.

The port was just as hectic as before, maybe even busier. The fishermen were hoisting the wriggling silver of their catch into crates of ice. A swamp of curling fish tails, clicking lobster and slithering eels, all destined for the market and then the dinner table. Rather than work his way through the crowd, Ashe sat on a nearby wall and watched, soaking in the life and the salt air. Freshening his tired head for what lay ahead.

There were young lads aplenty, tugging ropes, stacking crates on trucks, yanking spent nets back into their containers. For one of them this would be his last morning at such tasks. If, that is, Ashe ever got lucky and found the right boy. You do it somehow, he thought, he ends up in the House by your hand. He knew that such lazy thinking barely covered the convoluted nature of time travel but it gave him some hope. It can't be an impossible task, he insisted to himself. Somehow I manage to do it.

Giving up on the crowd he headed back into the city for breakfast, hoping coffee and food might finish off the job started by the cool wind. In his pocket, his revolver swung heavily, loaded and eager for use. He hoped it would stay there, un-held and un-fired, though he knew it was a slim hope. He was a man of violence these days.

He sat down at the same cafe he'd visited the day before, within sight of Garcia's house, and waited for the clock to roll around to eleven.

8.

When the time came, his stomach was jaded from too much coffee but alert for a *rendezvous* with Chester.

He made his way towards Jimenez's house and, judging the direction his younger self would likely come from the marina, made his way to the opposite end of the street where an aged, gnarled olive tree reached up from a walled planter. He sat down on the stone wall, thinking it had likely been a well at some time, now

304

filled with earth and turned into an aesthetic feature. It offered a small amount of cover and a comfortable place to sit as he waited for Chester to arrive.

It was only a few minutes and Ashe was glad he had come in good time. He watched the young man go through the same motions as he had the day before, peering through the beaded curtain, calling greetings and eventually being let in.

A few streets away he heard the sound of shouting followed by a report of rifle fire. What the hell was going on? he wondered, looking around for sign of the trouble. As long as it didn't distract Chester from the hiring of housebreakers he supposed it didn't matter. It was a timely reminder that, for all the colour and happiness he had seen the night before, this was still a city in wartime.

Turning back towards Jimenez's house he was just in time to see a small girl jump from the roof of the opposite house, sail through the air and then come to land on the criminal's balcony railing. Ashe jumped to his feet, his instinct being to run to her aid. As he hesitated, wary of revealing himself to Jimenez – a man that was sure to remember him from the day before – she scrabbled over the railing and onto the man's roof terrace.

What the hell is she doing? Is that his daughter? He tried to imagine Jimenez as a Spanish Fagin recruiting such nimble young children to his crooked cause, and could not. His gut told him that she had been on the run, most likely from the shouting and gunfire he had heard earlier.

He moved back to the cover of the tree, he could hardly go storming in there and demand assurance that she was alright. He was just in time, Chester appearing at the edge of the roof terrace shortly after, looking up and down the street, clearly startled and suspicious.

They must have caught the girl.

A few moments later, Chester appeared and began to walk back the way he had arrived. Ashe thought it likely he was heading back towards the marina but would follow him just in case. He decided to give the man a moment's head start and that was fortunate as Jimenez appeared in the doorway shortly afterwards and walked off in the same direction. Perhaps our friendly neighbourhood pusher of women, drugs and guns (with housebreaking a sideline) wished to follow Chester too. Maybe he didn't trust him – Jimenez would have to be a lousy judge of character to do so – or maybe it was just coincidence and he had business of his own to deal with. Ashe was about to follow the pair of them when he was struck by a secondary thought: what about the girl? Was she in trouble? Perhaps locked up in the house awaiting Jimenez's attentions when whatever current duty occupied him was dealt with? Should he not try and make sure she was safe?

No more distractions! That critical voice in his own head insisted, *you can't keep stopping to make sure every little waif and stray is okay. Get on with what you came here for.*

The voice had a point, he certainly had more pressing issues than the fortunes of a young girl to occupy him – though that thought brought Sophie to mind and delayed him again. Perhaps he should just knock on the door? If she was trapped in there then she might shout for help, maybe she would even answer it, reveal herself to be his daughter after all?

He was deciding to do that very thing when the girl stepped out of the house. She looked up and down the street, before running after both Jimenez and Chester. Ashe followed on behind.

It soon became clear that Jimenez had taken a different route, probably hiring himself a couple of local boys to help with the break in. What was also clear – and intriguing as hell to Ashe – was that the young girl was following Chester just as he was. She kept her eyes on him, following that hat as Ashe had done the day before. The streets were emptying out now as people went off for their siestas, avoiding the hottest part of the day and Ashe had no difficulty tracing the pair of them all the way back to the marina.

Chester climbed onto his boat and the girl made a U-turn, heading towards the industrial end of the port. Now Ashe had to make a decision. He was pretty sure that Chester would stay where he was for now and surely they would wait until later to break into Garcia's house? During siesta, the man was sure to be home, it was the worst possible time to consider such an act. The girl intrigued him. She probably wasn't in the least important in the overall scheme of things but what had she been doing at Jimenez's house? Why had she followed Chester? It was a risk but, after a moment's hesitation, it was one he decided to take. Keeping to the upper area of the port, he followed the girl as she skipped between the hustling sailors, frequently stopping to poke pieces of what looked like roast chicken into her mouth. After a while she dumped the bag the chicken had been in – a pillowcase Ashe noted in bafflement – and made her way towards a young man who was sat on the quayside fixing a wicker lobster basket. A sudden certainty hit Ashe: this was the boy he had been looking for. This was young Pablo who would go on to the House and save Chester's life, an act of kindness repaid by his own death.

He tried to get close enough to hear their conversation. Working his way among the stacks of crates and fishing equipment, he got as close as he dared, hidden from view by a tower of boxed fruit that smelled sweet in the baking noon sun.

"Garcia has that walled villa near the cathedral," the boy said.

"The one with the little bell-tower?" replied the girl.

"Yeah, people joke that he was jealous of the cathedral bells so had one built of his own."

"I know it."

"What did the American want with Garcia anyway?"

Chester, Ashe thought, they're talking about Chester.

"No idea." The girl was trying to make her voice light, convince the boy that none of this was important. "None of my business, is it?"

"No, it isn't," Pablo replied, and it *was* Pablo, Ashe was damned sure of it, "and make sure it stays that way. You don't want to start getting mixed up with people like that."

Ashe couldn't fault the kid's advice, Chester and Jimenez were dangerous enough, never mind Garcia. But what was the girl's interest? Was she working with Jimenez? He thought not, she hadn't even known where Garcia lived after all – *that means nothing*, that voice in his head said, *even if she was working for him he wouldn't necessarily share all the details* – true… But Ashe didn't think Jimenez was the type to have kids on the payroll. Besides, when she had left his house she had been just as determined to avoid Jimenez as Chester. If they were working together wouldn't they have left the building at the same time? This girl was a bystander, someone who had picked up a few details of something that interested her, eavesdropped on part of the conversation perhaps. She was a curious kid, someone that was going to get herself mixed up in things she shouldn't. But what was Ashe to do about it? Should he try and warn her off? Kids didn't tend to pay much heed to warnings from old men. Besides, he still had the timeline to think of, what if she was important? A vital element in the way history was supposed to play out. That felt distasteful, the boy had been right, this was no situation for a girl of her age to be involved in. What if she came to harm? Could he bear that on his already fragile conscience?

Pablo and the girl talked a little while longer before the boy's father called him to work and the girl shuffled off on her own. Ashe marked the position of Pablo's boat, sure that he would be able to find it later and followed her, determined not to let her out of his sight.

She made her way out of the port and began the walk back into the city. Ashe was not altogether surprised when they arrived at Garcia's house.

The girl sat down on the cathedral steps and stared at the building, Ashe took a seat in the nearby cafe. If he was going to sit and wait he'd do so in comfort.

Just below the blue-domed roof of Garcia's house there was a balcony window and, after a few moments, a woman appeared there dressed in a silk robe. Ashe shifted his attention between the two of them, the woman as she sighed over the balcony and the girl as she stared at her with rapt attention. Garcia appeared behind the woman, grasping her in a decidedly boorish fashion and biting into her neck. Yes, thought Ashe, we all see how lucky you are… He decided he would be glad to see Garcia lose the box, it did a man good to lose things once in a while. Glancing at the girl on the steps he smiled to see her grimace with distaste.

Garcia and the woman disappeared back into the darkness and, after a few moments, the girl stood up from her seat on the steps and began to walk towards the house. Ashe reached into his pocket to drop change for his drink onto the table and run after her. Then he paused: the girl was walking around the back of the house, along the narrow road that he had walked only the day before to get a feel for the place. With that realisation came another: she was casing the joint, just as he had been. Surely Jimenez hadn't tasked her with the job of retrieving the box? No, of course not, she had overheard their conversation, no doubt become starry eyed at the amount of money Chester had been willing to pay to have his property returned. She meant to steal it for herself. The girl reappeared, her eyes scanning the wall all the way around as she circled the building. I don't believe this, Ashe thought, we all want to break in and get the damned thing!

10.

Ashe watched the girl all afternoon, she in turn studied the house. Building up nerve and waiting for an opportunity, Ashe suspected. After a while he ordered some food, to stop the waiter from hovering as much as to fill his belly. It was clear that he was expected to pay his way for the long-term hire of the table.

As the sun fell lower in the sky afternoon became evening, Garcia appeared at his front gate, his young woman hanging on his arm. The girl had been circling the building once more and almost came face to face with them. Ashe drew in a breath, sharing her panic, then smiled as she dropped down by the side of the road and held out her hands as if to beg. This kid's good, he thought. With that thought came another, a sudden

310

surge of concern for her followed by a determination that he would do his damnedest to ensure she came out of this unscathed. *Don't make promises you can't keep, old man*, said the voice in his head, *you know as well as any that the path to the future is littered with young bodies just like hers.*

The girl watched Garcia and the woman leave then came to a decision and ran around the back of the house. Here we go, Ashe thought, we're on!

11.

He got up from his table, noting a sense of relief amongst the staff that he was finally vacating the place. Putting his hand in his coat pocket to grasp his gun – like it or not you may have need of it – he moved around the back of the house just in time to see the girl vanish over the wall into Garcia's garden. He had no intention of climbing after her, but found that if he lodged his foot on the thick base of the bougainvillea she had climbed he was tall enough to peer over the wall. He watched as she skirted a Koi pond and the swimming pool, wandering around the garden as if she were no more illicit than someone invited for a social function. He admired her guts but wished she'd move a little faster. A man like Garcia would probably have house staff and the kid wouldn't get far without being a little more careful. Almost as if she heard him, she darted behind one of the pillars of a large roofed terrace, glancing up at the windows for any sign of being watched. That's more like it, he thought, you'll get away with this yet.

Moving slower now, she aimed for the double doors that led into the house from the terrace, opened one and slipped through. With that she was gone taking

Ashe's best wishes with her.

He jumped down from the wall. Will she find it? he wondered and briefly considered following after her. But there was nothing to be gained from that. If she saw him then she'd run, panicked. If she found it then great, he would take the box from her – offer her money, whatever he could – and he wouldn't have to break into Garcia's place himself. If she didn't find it… well, he would have lost nothing.

He moved back towards the front of the house and drew to a halt. Jimenez and another man were opening the front gate – and you could be sure they hadn't used Garcia's key, however quickly and confidently they pushed it open – and stepping inside. The kid's timing was about to drop her in exactly the sort of trouble he had hoped she could avoid.

The two Spaniards vanished from sight and Ashe hurried after them, his hand once more reaching for that revolver in his pocket. What was he planning to do, shoot them? Maybe, he decided, if it came down to them or her then he would do it for sure. He looked through the gate, there was no sign of anyone. The sound of breaking glass came from inside and that was more than enough to send him through the gate and jogging around the house. The double doors the girl had used were open. She's not Sophie, he reminded himself, that kid is *not* Sophie. However much he told himself that, he remembered the panic in his chest as he had run across the concourse of the ersatz St. Pancras station inside the House. That feeling of time slowing down but also somehow slipping away. The sight of Whitstable – that crazy bastard – a piece of broken glass in his hand aimed for Sophie's throat.

He ran through the open door and wondered which way to turn. He was in an open foyer, stairs leading up to his left, rooms off to his right. A gunshot rang out from upstairs and he charged up them even as another sound, a loud splashing from the pool outside, gave him pause. He turned to look and saw that crazy – that *wonderful* – girl pulling herself out of the pool and running past the double doors. The box was in her hand.

He spun on the stairs – just as Jimenez ran out of the office above – and ran back outside. The double doors smacked back against the wall as he charged through, a tinkle of glass falling to the concrete behind him. He turned the corner of the house, the image of Whitstable's gleeful face fresh in his mind. The girl was running towards the front gate. Jimenez's accomplice appeared at the front door and began charging towards her, hoping to cut her off. Jimenez cleared the corner of the house behind him, a gun in his hand. Ashe spun around and pulled out his own revolver, happy to shoot both of the bastards right then and there. The conviction must have showed in his face. Certainly Jimenez recognised the man he had sold the shells to only twenty four hours before. He didn't want to sample his own stock, not for any money.

"Don't!" the Spaniard shouted, his accomplice turning in confusion and – seeing Ashe and the .45 he held that glinted in that evening sun like the prettiest thing in the world. Jimenez dropped his own gun, raising his hands in surrender. He was a crook not a gunfighter. There was a look in this old man's eyes – had been the day before too – that told you all you needed to know: shoot first or give up, this guy would kill you without so much as drawing breath.

Ashe nearly proved him right. He felt his finger twitch on the trigger, it would be so easy just to squeeze, drop these two to the ground, no great loss.

But Ashe did not want to be that man. He twisted the gun in his hand and lashed out with it, clubbing Jimenez to the head. Might still have killed him, he thought, cracked his skull open. Maybe... but maybe not. The accomplice hadn't enough love for his employer to get shot over him and ran out of the front gate as fast as he could. The man would still be running hours later, Ashe thought, I scared him *good*.

Ashe had running of his own to do. The girl would be heading for the port, wanting to sell the box to Chester. Now maybe Chester would just pay up but then maybe he wouldn't. Maybe he'd look at the kid that held his treasure and decide that it was easier just to take the damn thing, to slap it out of her hand and drop her overboard. Or give her to Henryk...

So Ashe ran out of the house and into the square. The girl – *not* Sophie, remember? – was still visible but he knew he would never catch her, not on foot at least. He glanced around the square and his eyes fell on something that might just make the difference: an old black bicycle leaning against the back of a bench. Its owner must have been one of the old men that were gathering here at the end of the day to smoke their cigars and chat. He ran towards it, remembering to drop his gun back in his pocket before he scared anyone else with it.

"Whose bike?" he yelled as he approached them, rooting in his wallet for money. He held up a few notes and asked again. One old guy, a flat cap sent jaunty over his wrinkled walnut of a head stuck his hand up fast. Ashe shoved the money in his hand and grabbed the bike. "I'll try and bring it back," he promised, pedalling after the girl.

She was running down the narrow side streets, their heavy cobbles sure to smash the wheels out from under him if he tried to ride on them at speed. He spun the bike to the left, aiming for the main road. He had walked this route often enough now, if he put some decent speed on he could overtake her on the main strip and then cut back into the narrow streets halfway to the port. He would stop her before she got there. He *would*.

The bike shook underneath him, his coat skidding on the back wheel, threatening to catch on the mudguard and yank him off if he didn't bunch it up onto his lap. He was far from stable, it being years since he had ridden a bike. They say you never forget and, yes, he had yet to fall off but it felt a close run thing, his stomach lurching as he wobbled from side to side, often only just regaining his balance before toppling sideways.

He reached a junction of streets, aimed right and pedalled hard towards where the narrow street the kid had been running down would bisect the main road. When he reached the intersection he looked left, no sign of her. I must have beat her to it, he thought, *must* have. There was no way she could have run that fast. He got off the bike and ran to the right, up the cobbled street. Another right, he remembered, then a short left – not far from Jimenez's house – I should see her any minute. He made the right and bumped into her, sending her sprawling to the floor.

"No," he gasped, seeing the panic in her eyes. His breath was so short, his legs wavering beneath him, he could barely stand let alone speak. "No," he insisted, pointing to the box, "not you, you're the wrong one." She looked baffled and he realised he'd been speaking English. Not that she would have understood what he meant anyway. He wracked his brain for the words, he was so tired… "Give me the box," he said, holding out his hand. She shook her head and ran past him.

He turned after her and saw Chester and Henryk, running along the intersecting road behind the girl. Chester had a gun in his hand, he raised it...

II: The Bad

1.

Chester clambered onto his boat, utterly unaware that – several yards behind him – both a young Spanish girl and his future self were following his trail. He nodded at Henryk. "All was fine, you see?" he said, sounding again like a petulant child.

He climbed down into his cabin, peeled off his jacket and shirt and sat on the bed to rub away his sweat with a towel. His head was buzzing with noise and confusion and he would do anything to make it shut up. It sometimes seemed he hadn't had a moment's peace since he had first set eyes on that box of his father's. Such a little thing, and yet so all-consuming.

He remembered the first time he had touched it. The wood had bristled beneath his fingertips like the spines of a stinging nettle. He had been bitten by the thing and whatever mental virus it seemed to possess had transferred to him as surely as a poisonous snake bite.

He got up, closed and locked his door and stripped off the rest of his clothes. They gripped him in the heat of Valencia and he just wanted them to let him go. He wanted everything to let him go. The heat, the noises in his head, that box...

But that wasn't altogether true was it Chester? No, it wasn't. Chester was consumed by a need to be strong and powerful. To step beyond the shadow of parents that had loomed ever since the cradle. Chester wanted out, yes, but he wanted out in a way that nobody would ever be able to drag him back in and that required power. To his father power translated as money. But money wasn't the only power in the world. Certainly money wasn't the key to beating his father. Even at his age he knew that the old man would be years in the grave before he could ever hope to equal his earnings. Hell, he would never equal them, Chester just wasn't built that way. His father knew this and it was a constant insult to him, he had sired a boy that was somehow missing a vital ingredient, that steel that would see him rise in business and take over the old man's throne. Sometimes, Chester knew, his father would look at his son and wonder to himself how he could ever have made such a wet and imperfect child. How so much of his own strength could have ended up on the bed sheets. At those moments – and God help him they had become frequent – Chester could never decided whether he wanted to kill his father or prove him wrong. Maybe they were one and the same thing.

Still he had agreed to follow in his father's footsteps, learn the trade and walk the walk. But it was always a shallow impression, a man copying the moves but not understanding them. At sixteen – Terrance Arthur had no time for schools, "you learn in life boy, not in a classroom," – it had always been understood that he would join the company officially, take a seat on the board and learn how things were done. It had been a punishment not a celebration. He sat there, eyes vacant, not understanding a thing his father or the other old men talked about. He had tried to imagine the day when he would look on this world as one to which he belonged. He could never imagine such a thing.

Then he had touched the box.

Chester had always been a rational man. There was nothing in his life that encouraged belief in a higher power. But when he had touched that box, felt it sink its teeth into him, felt it talk in his head when he was trying to go to sleep, well... then Chester began to wonder if there was something greater out there after all, something that might see its way to sharing a slice of wonder with him.

If the voice of the box was God, God was vicious. The things it said flitted between promises and threats. But Chester was used to harsh love. So when it encouraged him to explore its wooden seal – which would not open to him, it promised, like a teasing virgin, not until he had proved his love – he had done so. When it made suggestions as to experiences he might like to try, violence he might like to commit, he did that too and with a glad heart.

2.

He had first felt blood on his hands on the evening of his seventeenth birthday and it had been the box's doing.

His parents had thrown a party. Not out of love for their son but because parties were what wealthy families did, it showed those less rich how truly extravagant they could afford to be.

A string quartet had set up stall in the corner of one of their many function rooms, laying down sweet, inoffensive music to guzzle canapés to. People much older than Chester had danced and ate and laughed and sighed at the opulence of it all. He had sat quietly, utterly alone – he had no friends and even if he had they would not have been invited, this was not a party for him, whatever the banner may have said that hung from the ceiling.

His parents had employed a catering company and various staff mingled amongst the guests, doing their best to be invisible. Chester had set his sights on one woman in particular, a small, unattractive thing with freckles and hair that bobbed around her head as if it were unattached, perhaps controlled separately by wires from above. She had made a bad effort of ignoring the expensive things around her – this was an important distinction, Chester knew, your guests were supposed to coo at your furnishings, the staff were not – and he frequently caught her admiring a painting or a vase or a set of silver candlesticks. She longed to touch them he realised, longed to live the sort of life that could surround her with such things. After realising this, and seeing the lust in her eyes grow steadily deeper as the night went on, Chester had been only too aware of what the girl would do in the end. It was, after all, exactly what he would have done himself.

She was collecting empty glasses from one of their sideboards when her fingers brushed the edge of a silver snuff box. It was a tiny thing, part of a larger display, items bought to fill a space. She had extended her fingers, picked the snuff box up and concealed it in the hand that held her tray, giving a quick glance around the room to make sure that nobody had seen her. But

Chester had. And having done so knew that he finally had a sliver of the power he most craved right there in front of him.

"She'll do whatever it takes not to get caught with that," said the voice of the box in his head. It was an unusual voice, an English voice, it reminded him of a movie actor... he couldn't remember the damned man's name. "But you need to catch her now, while it's still hot in her hands not hidden away to collect later or even dumped in the bushes outside when fear of getting caught drives her to ditch it. You need to talk to her *now*."

He had followed the woman out of the main function room and along one of the corridors that led to the kitchens. She dumped the tray there, slipping the snuff box into the pocket of her apron and called over to the man that Chester took to be her boss. "Just taking a couple of minutes, Sal," she said, "watching all those fat cats drink has made my bladder burst."

"Sal" nodded and returned to supervising the construction of small chocolate truffles on silver platters.

Chester followed the woman through to the servant's quarters – they had been given the night off, why have two sets of slaves after all? – towards the bathroom. She didn't look behind her, eager to hide away so she could examine her prize. He crept closer and closer until, as she opened the bathroom door he was right behind her. He pushed her inside, sliding the bolt of the door behind him. She opened her mouth to scream at him but he clapped his hand across it, shoving her back against the wall in the tiny room.

"I saw you," he whispered, fingers reaching for the snuff box and pulling it out, "saw you take this."

Once presented with the evidence her face went from indignation to fear, her eyes fixing on the snuff box as it glinted in the light of the naked bulb that swung above.

"I didn't mean…" she started to say before giving up. There was no excuse she could think of, nothing that would allow for her having pocketed the box. "I'm sorry," she said instead, "please don't call the police, I'll just go, you'll never see me again."

Chester pressed himself against her wanting to sniff the fear on her skin.

"She'll do anything," the box said, "anything at all. She has a child, an apartment she struggles to pay for… she won't lose all that easily, you could make her do *anything*."

This excited Chester beyond words, clearly the serving girl felt it – pressed so tight against her she could hardly have missed the pulsing nudge against the top of her thigh. Her face fell as she realised what was likely about to happen. He watched the expression change, watched a misery wash over her that she tried to swallow like a rough pill. She replaced that look with a false smile and reached for his groin with her hand.

"Is this what you want?" she asked, a beautiful tremor in her voice. She could barely get the words out without crying. "Would this make it alright?"

She stroked his cock through the fabric of his trousers, not seductively, she couldn't quite manage that, disgust and self-hatred getting the better of her. It was more like trying to remove a set of keys from a suit pocket that was on its hanger. A functional frisk that sought to get the job done. Chester watched her face, that false smile that choked off any more attempt to speak. Eyes that spoke only of utter hatred, leavened with thoughts of her child and the things she stood to loose if he called the police on her.

"Get off me," he said. "I wouldn't dirty myself with you."

Her hand fell away and a glimpse of relief crossed her face.

"I want something else," he said, "or I will drag you out of here and hold you up in front of my father as the thieving bitch you are."

She looked confused, trying to think what else this man could want from her if it wasn't sex.

"She'll do anything," the box said again. "Power... control..."

"Hold out your hand," he said, "show me your thieving little fingers."

She stretched out her left hand, slowly and fearfully, her right still pinned down by her side.

"Spread them," he said, his groin hotter than ever, the noise of the box so loud in his head that it made him squint.

"She'll do anything, anything, anything, *anything*..."

He opened the snuff box and clamped it down on her index finger so the decorative silver edge, a serrated line of autumn leaves, pinched against her skin. She winced. He stepped back a little to free up her other arm.

"Now crush your finger," he said and the look of shock on her face was so beautiful he felt near to tears. "Do it, or I'll take away everything you have."

She reached for the box, gripping it in her right hand and squeezing the lid closed on her finger. Then she shook her head, "I can't..."

He put his hand over hers to help, squeezing in close again, his cheek pressed against hers. "If you scream they will come and I will tell them everything... how you stole the box, then tried to touch me, wanting to fuck away your crime. I'll tell them you begged for that and everyone will know it anyway, even your little boy as they put him in care."

He squeezed her hand as hard as he could, feeling her shake against him as the lid bit down on her finger, the metal cutting into the skin so it bled. She bit her lip and made a low, guttural moan, a tremolo of pain that made him think of a lowing cow. He squeezed and squeezed, shoving against her so her hip bashed over and over again against the small sink set in the wall next to them. His own hand was slick with her blood now, squeezed through clenched fingers.

"That's power," the box said, "that's all the power you ever need."

He let go of her hand and she fought to control tears as she unclasped the box from her mashed finger. Her whole body shaking with the effort to contain wails of pain.

"You can keep the box," he said, reaching back to unlock the door. "It's a gift." He went to leave and then, unable to resist, punched her in the belly. "So was that," he said as she crumpled, winded to the floor behind him.

He walked back towards the party and then, noticing his bloody hand, made a diversion to his room. He stood in front of his own basin, preparing to wash it off and finding he couldn't. It seemed such a waste. He unzipped himself and masturbated with the dirty hand.

"How does it feel?" the box asked him as he ejected pink pearls into the basin. "How does that power feel?"

"Wonderful," he had admitted. Cleaning himself up and returning downstairs to the party. "It feels wonderful."

He sat back down amongst the partygoers, sipping at a glass of champagne. He didn't see the catering girl again, no doubt she had come up with some believable excuse for her damaged hand and begged the rest of the night off. He hoped she went home, sat down with her boy and thought about how close she had come to losing everything.

3.

From that first step, that acquiescence to the box's suggestion and his own pitiful wants, there had been no turning back. The box would encourage him to much greater heights of power and control, it assured him. All he had to do was listen.

Then he met Penelope Simons.

She was a sweet girl – as far as any girl ever felt sweet to Chester, his parents made no concession for emotional attachment and he had followed their example. For a while, even his father had seemed pleased. The Boston Simons were an affluent family and well respected. The idea of an alliance through his son was most favourable. Perhaps, his father said to him one day, you didn't turn out to be such a waste after all.

Chester wasn't a natural beau, his emotions too stunted, his nerves too rough. But he went through the motions, arranging several dates with Penelope, with her friend Dolores as chaperone – a ludicrous notion if either parents had had the least idea as to the girl's personality. They had eaten in a number of fine restaurants, visited society functions and dinners, they had, in short, become an item. Chester, still in regular discussions with that strange voice from the box, began to have other ideas about his future. As if the time he spent away from his room and the close proximity of the thing, began to loosen its hold on him. There were many times in fact, when he gave serious thought to abandoning the box entirely, throwing the damn thing away and forging a

325

more wholesome – and, he had to admit, pleasurable – future with Penelope.

The box would have none of this. When he returned from his nights out, it was always there waiting for him, a shrewish mother eager to criticise his behaviour and demand to know who he thought he was, gallivanting around the town like that.

"She doesn't like you," it told him, "I can tell. She laughs about you when your back is turned, her and Dolores both, cackling and jeering at you the moment you're not in earshot. They treat you like a joke. A blundering, foolish joke."

Chester tried not to listen. Tried to fix a smiling image of Penelope in his mind and blank out the box. But, in the middle of the night, when his resistance was at its lowest it would whisper to him, reminding him how it had felt in that small servant's bathroom, reminding him what *real* power had been like. And on those nights Chester would be lost to it, crying into his pillow with shame at the excitement he couldn't deny inside him.

Then the box told him what he should do to Penelope.

4.

They had arranged to meet at the Cotton Club. It wasn't a favourite venue of Chester's – he found the music too loud and the atmosphere too thick – but Penelope adored it there. "Slumming it amongst the niggers" his father would have said, a man to whom the very notion of the Cotton Club was anathema.

Henryk took the wheel of the family De Soto, and began to make his way towards Harlem. The driver had become a *confidante* to Chester, ever since the box had informed him of the Polish man's enthusiasms. There seemed little in life that was distasteful to the hulk of a man. He rarely spoke but his eyes roved the world, lusting after the women and the money he saw. He was a simple man, Chester understood, a man of hunger. Such people were easily controlled by those willing to feed them a little every now and then.

"He is loyal," the box had said once, "and that is the only quality in a man you need."

As they moved through the Manhattan streets Chester held the box in his hands and did his best to negotiate with it.

"Tonight's the night," it said, "the night that I'll open for you and all that power you wanted will be yours."

"But, Penelope…"

"Is unimportant," the box insisted, "just as flimsy and rank as that light-fingered girl we taught a lesson to."

"She's nice…"

"She's nothing!" the box had shouted so loudly that Chester had flinched and, even more worryingly, he had noticed Henryk jump in his seat too. Did Henryk hear the box too? Was its voice not just for him?

"We will take the girl and we will feed from her," the box insisted. "We shall grind her under our heel, bathe in our command of her, she will be so beholden to us that she will beg to dine from our shit…"

Chester wasn't sure he had much interest in that. It wasn't that he loved Penelope – he had never loved anybody – but he certainly didn't hate her. Now if it had been his father… that was different, he would quite easily make a turd-munching supplicant of that old fuck.

"Later," the box said, "he comes later… *if* you do as you're told."

And so Chester had relented, placing the box safely

inside his coat pocket and resolving himself to the night ahead.

He had sat with Penelope and Dolores, listening to the house band with feigned interest. Lighting Penelope's cigarettes – she smoked too much, that was one thing against her, he didn't like ladies that smoked, it spoke of no self-control – and waiting patiently for the night to draw to a close.

By the time they left the club, Dolores had been stumbling drunk. Which was good, that would make her far easier to control.

"You can control *anyone*," the box insisted in his head, "with my help."

Henryk let them in to the back of the car and Chester saw him grin at the sight of the girls, no doubt thinking of what treats he had in store. Let him salivate, Chester thought, if that's what it takes to keep him at heel.

They drove out of Harlem towards Chester's father's plant. He was confident that neither of them would know their way around well enough to realise they were going the wrong way. Certainly not while they still had time to do anything about it. Chester tilted his head back against the leather of the seat. Penelope was talking about the things she always talked about: people she knew, things they had done, the music, who the musicians had been... all things that Chester had once made a show of caring about. He had enjoyed the game – and that's what it had been he realised, the box was quite right in that, he had been pretending to be someone else and the mask would always have fallen off in the end. He really wished he didn't have to do what the box had told him would be necessary. "Is there no way I can just drop her off first?" he asked, stroking the box in his pocket. "You can have Dolores, who cares about that drunken idiot? But not Penelope, let's leave her out of this."

"I will not have this conversation again," the box replied, "you will do as you're told."

Chester acquiesced. In his head was the unwelcome image of the voice of the box leaning over him and clamping its lid down on his index finger. Was I ever really in control? he wondered as the car pulled into the rear entrance of the meat-packing plant.

"Where are we?" asked Penelope.

"My father's plant," Chester replied.

"What for?" asked Dolores, leaning drunkenly to peer out of the window. "All you big families blend into one, steelworks to chicken plants, I can never remember who's who. What do you guys do?"

"Whatever we want," Chester replied, reaching forward to shove Dolores' face hard against the glass of the window. And there, with that simple lie there was no going back.

5.

But it hadn't gone according to plan had it? In a matter of half an hour Chester had been left with aching balls, a dead woman in his front seat and the knowledge that his precious box was currently bobbing somewhere down the Hudson. Control? No, he had certainly never possessed that.

He had helped Henryk dispose of the body, feeling as he did so that this finally set him on the same level as the chauffeur, certainly not the man of authority he had always dreamed of being.

They had scrubbed the car clean, Chester working in silence, thoroughly resolved to his subservient status. He had fulfilled his father's expectation of him and lost everything. Now there was no hope with Penelope and no higher power guiding his hand. That had passed on, floating away to someone more worthwhile.

They drove home, Chester's head as empty as his dreams.

He had gone to bed, and lain there in cold, pointless darkness.

The next morning, there had been conversations with the police supervised by his father and – later – the family lawyer.

No, he hadn't seen or heard from Penelope since he dropped them off last night. Yes, he should have walked them to their door but Dolores had been drunk and Penelope had insisted she walk that off in the grounds before she faced Penelope's parents. He had been tired and, besides, it wasn't as if he'd just abandoned them on the street was it? He had not wished to cause Penelope any further embarrassment – and in truth she was quite insistent, in fact he wondered if she hadn't had a few mouthfuls of whatever it was that Dolores had been drinking. The police were far from satisfied, naturally, and when Dolores' body had been discovered floating face down some miles away from his father's plant they had come to the logical decision that the remains of Penelope would soon join them. Even when they did not, nobody seriously expected to see her alive again. There had been accusations from her parents but Terrance Arthur squashed them. He was a man only too used to making unpleasant suggestions vanish. It was all a matter of business.

When they were alone, those looks of suspicion that Chester had grown used to on the faces of investigating officers had been present on his father's face too. But he never asked. He didn't want to know.

Eventually it was agreed that Chester should take some time away from New York, travel a little while the gossip ran its course. Europe perhaps, there were always opportunities for a young American in Europe.

Satisfied with this – Chester no longer cared where he was or what he did, he was a shell of a man and nothing interested him – he went to his bed and lay there in the darkness giving serious consideration to ending his life.

Which is when the box broke its silence and began talking to him again.

6.

And it had never stopped, leading him away from New York and over into Europe. They sent Henryk with him to act as both a facilitator and – if they were honest – a wet nurse. The chauffeur wouldn't be missed. If Terrance Arthur was pressed he would admit that he had never been all that comfortable with the fellow, and had often considered sacking him. Things were just about perfect. The dirty linen was sent away where it could no longer embarrass and Chester knew that one day, soon, he would see the box again.

Now, with the business of burglary dealt with, Chester lay in the dark once more. He listened to the buzzing in his head, a brutal tinnitus that never quietened. The box had told him where it was, had demanded he retrieve it. Then, when it was back in Chester's hands, he would have it open at last. He would ride through that door that lived inside. Just as Penelope had done, the box had made that clear, much to Chester's jealousy.

"Get up!" the box insisted in that voice of the actor he couldn't place. "You've botched the job, as usual."

"I haven't," Chester replied, rolling off the bed and putting his feet on the floor. "I've done everything right. Jimenez is going to steal the box and…"

"That dullard will never lay his hands on me," the box replied, "someone else has beaten him to it."

Someone else? Chester couldn't begin to imagine who…

"You need to come!" the box shouted, its voice so loud inside his head that Chester convulsed. "Come now!"

7.

He had pulled on some clean clothes – a dark pinstripe suit, far too heavy for the weather but the first thing he could lay his hands on that wasn't sodden with sweat – and ran above deck.

"We need to go," he told Henryk, "there's a problem."

Henryk nodded. Chester was sure he had caught a glimpse of mockery there, a little "of course there's a problem" twitch of a smile. Even the hired help considered itself his superior.

Henryk reached down to a strongbox beneath the wheel housing, unlocked it and held out a small pistol. "Should we?"

Chester snatched the gun off him and stuffed it behind his back, pinning it in place with his belt.

Henryk gave a small cough. "What?" Chester asked, impatient and sick of always feeling he was on the back foot.

"The safety catch," said Henryk, "you may wish to ensure it is engaged. There could be an accident."

Chester's head was starting to pound, the heat, the voice of the box – Come now! Come now! – and now this. He pulled out the gun and looked for the safety catch. Henryk glanced at the gun and pointed to the small lever near the handle. "My apologies," he said, rather insincerely, "it would appear that you are safe."

Chester came very close to thumbing that little lever and shooting the chauffeur. His rage was such that he actually feared he may burst something in his head. It felt like his brain was swelling, little veins throbbing in his temples, jaw clenched so tight that his teeth were grinding together.

"Come now! Come now!" the box shouted again and Chester nearly burst into tears, anything to relieve the pressure.

He put the gun back in his waistband and clambered off the boat, Henryk following.

They ran along the marina, Chester following the sound in his head as it gave him directions, barking at him like a platoon sergeant.

They moved up into the city, following the route that Chester had taken to Jimenez's house.

Chester was soon exhausted, the weight of that damned suit dragging him down. It felt like swimming full clothed, moving through this hot, muggy city. He would leave Spain once this business was done, he had decided. Go somewhere more civilised, somewhere that had a more equable climate.

"There!" the box shouted. "The girl!"

Looking ahead of them they could see a young girl pushing past an old man – with a face Chester thought he recognised, something definitely familiar about it – and running down the street away from them.

"Shoot her!" the box shouted. "Now!"

Chester pulled out his gun and aimed it towards her. Then froze. She was just a kid... what the hell was he becoming?

He saw his face in the bathroom mirror as he had pleasured himself with a bloodied hand. He saw his reflection in the dark window of the De Soto as he punched a naked Penelope in the face. What was he doing? Dear Christ… what was he *becoming*?

"Shoot her! Shoot her! Shoot her!"

No… he had to stop this, had to…

III: The Ugly

"Give it to me," Henryk said, snatching the gun from him. "I'll do it."

He aimed the gun...

"We need to go," says the boy – and he *is* a boy, for all his money, his suits and his affectation – "there's a problem."

Henryk is not in the least surprised by this, as far as this boy goes there are always problems. Sometimes those problems are pleasant – he still thinks fondly of the slippery little American girl he had enjoyed on the front seat of the family car – sometimes they are simply work.

Henryk does not mind work, he has no wet streak in him that turns up its nose at unpleasant things. A man can do anything if he puts his mind to it. There is no shame in any job done, any mess cleared. There is only shame in failure and that is something Henryk has never experienced. Unlike the boy.

He offers him the gun and tells him how to carry it safely – if he shoots himself a new arsehole it will mean the end of Henryk's current employment and he would not wish for that, not yet. He has plans for that day and while it is soon it is not now. He knows this as the box has assured him it is so. And Henryk trusts the box, it has never lied to him. It tells him that his employer is an idiot, this is true. It tells him that the idiot will lose the box, this was also true. It tells him that the idiot will make a mess of getting the box back. And look "there's a problem". This would turn out to be a truth as well, he was sure.

He had been talking to the box for some time. Not as long as the boy but long enough. It had first spoken to him while he had been sat in the car, staring out at the grey New York streets waiting for the boy and his woman to finish their shopping. They would be hours, he knew, while she picked out shoes or hats that she did not need. Paper bags filled with consumer glitter, things his family would not know what to do with and could never afford. Then he would get out, take these flimsy bags filled with silk or leather or lace, throw them in the back and drive them home. In the meantime he had nothing to occupy him but the view of a city skyline a world away from the village in which he had grown up. Not that he missed his home. It was cold and miserable and smelled of shit. He was much more comfortable here. But sometimes he grew bored. And sometimes he grew resentful.

"You'll get what you want soon enough," a voice had said to him. Startled, he spun around, checking the back seats for what he assumed was a stowaway. Of course there had been nobody there. Nobody could have got in without him hearing them. Besides, the doors were locked, he always kept them locked while he was parked. New York was full of idiots and while he was more than capable of dealing with idiots – it was his job after all – he did not believe in making work for himself.

"Who is this?" he had said, checking the wing mirrors.

"Nobody you can see, Henryk," the voice had replied, before going on to list things it should not have known. Events from his life that he kept as secret from the outside world as the money he had stashed in his sock drawer back at his employer's house. Money he had taken – these people were blind to those with careful fingers – and money he had saved.

It told him about the boy he had beaten back home, beaten so hard that now his mother had to feed him like a baby. A vacant boy, his brain turned to mush inside his thick head.

It told him about the girl he had got pregnant. There had been a few of those, but only one that had been trouble. Trouble until she fell down the stairs of her father's small cottage at least. After that there had been no trouble at all.

It told him about the things that went through his head while watching the pretty American girls. The ideas that occurred to him sometimes. The plans that would see him in an electric chair if he did not control them.

It told him who he was.

And while Henryk was normally a man who only believed in things he could see or touch there was no denying what it knew. There was also no denying its ability to take that knowledge and hurt him with it. And so he had listened, and wondered, and eventually believed.

And later – while the boy was at his father's office, making a fool of himself as usual – he had found the box. Had touched it and felt touched in return. It was not something he understood but it was something he believed. And that was as close to religion as Henryk got.

He had listened over the fuss with Chester and his girl. Had smiled at the box's promise of a pretty

337

American girl of his own to play with. Had heard it chuckle as he had unwrapped that drunken little gift.

He had listened as it had told Chester what to do, where to go, how to find it. He had listened to everything. And now, here he was, charged with tidying up the boy's mess yet again. This time, however – the box promised – the boy had had his chance. From now on it was Henryk that would benefit from the opportunities it offered. Henryk was about to go into business on his own.

They moved through the winding streets, the boy struggling to run in the heat. He was unfit as well as stupid.

They turned a corner and came face to face with the old man and the girl.

"Shoot her!" the box had said and the boy had looked as if, for once, he might get something right. But no, he had hesitated, as Henryk had known he would. If this job was to be done then it needed a strong man to do it.

Henryk had taken the gun, aimed it at the girl's fast-retreating back, and a shot rang out on that hot, Valencian evening.

IV: Showdown

1.

Ashe had watched in disbelief as Chester had raised his gun to shoot the girl. He had reached for his own weapon before realising that to kill Chester would destroy everything, it would destroy the timeline of the box, it would destroy *him*. Still the gun was in his hand and he raised it in the young man's direction.

The Valencian street began to distort around him. First he thought it was simply exhaustion, then as the ground trembled beneath him and the rows of houses began to blur, their plasterwork and bricks bubbling and melting like candles, he realised it was more. From above, the seagull from his dream came swooping down through a sky that fizzed and warped around it, becoming more liquid than air.

"Don't!" it squawked. "You'll destroy everything!"

"But the girl," he said, his voice as distorted as his surroundings. It sounded like he was speaking underwater.

"She dies," the gull insisted, "that's history, like it or not."

Ashe watched as Henryk took the gun from his employer and prepared to fire.

"No she doesn't," he said and fired his gun.

Time drew to a crawl. The bullet visible as it left the barrel of his gun, forcing its way through this unnatural, thick air. The girl, barely moving, her young legs rising and falling as if she ran in glue. Henryk, closing one eye and fixing on his target as it drew further and further away. The bullet continued its journey – *please!* Ashe begged, please be in time – spinning as it flew, thin wisps of smoke blossoming from the revolver in his hand. The sound of the discharge followed it like a record played at the wrong speed, a terrible, incessant roar that sustained perpetually. Henryk heard it, his eyes flickering toward Ashe, a sense of the danger he was in dawning slowly in them. Ashe was reminded of those flip books you made as a kid, where you drew lots of near-identical pictures on the corner of a page, small changes creeping into each, so that when you flipped the pages with your thumb the picture seemed to move. Frame by frame, the world moved forward.

Then time snapped back. The bullet hit Henryk right at the centre of his forehead leaving a tiny hole that would have looked so trivial were it not for the splatter that vacated the back of the man's head and decorated the wall behind him. Henryk's gun fired but his last-minute panic and the impact of the bullet sent the shot a fraction wide, winging past the girl enough to flick her hair but no more. Chester dropped to his knees in a mixture of delusion and panic, the screaming of the box plus the certainty that he would die next driving him loose from whatever stability he had possessed. Ashe stared, watching the world return to normal and the gull float skywards.

"You tricky old bastard," it said before vanishing over the roofs of the houses, "I hope you haven't ruined everything."

So do I, Ashe thought, lowering his gun. *So do I.*

2.

He walked over to Henryk and rifled his pockets for the keys to the boat. He had a use for them. Chester was sobbing and he had to slap him a couple of times before the man would even focus on him.

"Come on," he said, "if you stay here then the police will have you, or the soldiers, neither will treat you well."

Chester stared at him and he realised that he likely saw the resemblance, or perhaps he thought of his father. Either idea made Ashe sick. "Come on!" he insisted, giving him a kick and dragging him to his feet. "We need to move."

They walked away as quickly as they could, Ashe only too aware that they had a matter of minutes before Henryk's body was seen and the authorities called. A city in war doesn't flinch at the sound of a gun, it has heard too many of them, but it doesn't become blind to the dead.

They aimed for the marina, Chester shuffling in front of Ashe, all fight knocked from him. In his head the box was silent, the peace was breathtaking.

The girl was where Ashe thought she would be, pacing up and down in front of Chester's boat. She hadn't gone through all this for the box, she had no interest in it, only what it could buy her. He sat Chester down on the wall some distance away.

"Try and leave and I'll shoot you," he told him. Chester made no sign of having heard for a moment and then nodded.

Ashe walked slowly towards the girl, his hands held out in front of him to show he was no danger. "You have something you wish to sell?" he asked, remembering to speak Spanish.

She looked at him suspiciously and shrugged.

"The box," Ashe said, nodding to her hand. "It's dangerous and you would do well to sell it I think. I don't know how much money you hoped to get but I have none."

"He does," she said, nodding towards Chester.

"Maybe he does," Ashe agreed. "And where do you think he would keep it if he did?"

The girl thought about this for a moment and then nodded towards the boat.

"I think you're probably right," Ashe said, holding up the keys he had taken from Henryk. "In which case you'll find it when you take whatever else you want. The boat's yours if you give me the box."

The girl's face contorted, suspicion and excitement fighting over one another for dominance. "You're lying," she said.

He threw her the keys. "Take it, he has no use for it anymore."

She kept her eyes on him but scooted down to grab the keys.

"But please," Ashe continued, "leave the box here, it has nothing you would want."

She looked at him, biting her lower lip as she decided what to do. Then she put the box on the floor and ran over to the boat.

"Pleasure doing business with you," Ashe said, picking up the box.

He walked back to Chester, the box held out so the young man could see it. He shrunk away from it as if terrified. As well you should be, Ashe thought.

Behind them there was the noise of a boat engine roaring into life and Ashe turned around, startled to see the girl fling loose the mooring rope before dashing back to the wheel house.

"What the hell do you think you're doing?" he shouted.

"Running!" she replied. "I am very very good at it!"

She engaged the throttle and the boat motored forward at speed, the girl whooping with childish glee as it began to bounce its way out of the port.

"Crazy kid," Ashe muttered, unable not to grin at the sheer joy on the girl's face, as she sped past him and out towards the open sea. "Don't get yourself killed."

"Now there would be an irony." He turned back to see the seagull perching on Chester's shoulder. The bird stared at him for a moment then rustled its feathers as if annoyed. "She doesn't."

"Good," said Ashe. He rubbed at the box in his hands. "How much of this is you?" he asked it.

"The box?" the gull replied. "None at all. I'm not *him*."

"You're the House," Ashe said, "beginning to think for itself."

"And act."

"And act," Ashe nodded. "Was there even any point in my doing all of this?"

"Of course, I can't do everything, just nudge here and there."

"Helping select those who travel through this," Ashe held up the box, "and don't?" The gull twitched its head. Ashe took that to be a nod. "Because," he continued, "I can't for the life of me see why the girl would ever have been shot. If she was holding this and her life was in danger then *poof* – off she should have gone. But it doesn't work like that does it?"

"Not altogether," the gull agreed, "not *anymore*…"

"You're taking control?"

"With the help of my friends," it squawked, issuing a caw of a chuckle. "Three is good."

"Yeah," said Ashe, "three is just great."

He threw the box onto Chester's lap. The young man, apparently beyond such considerations as to why he had a talking bird on his shoulder, still had an eye for the box. He stroked it gently with his thumbs.

"Go then," Ashe said to him, "and get your reward."

The gull squawked, flying into the air as Chester vanished, the box rattling off the wall and tumbling to the floor. Ashe picked it up, put it in his pocket and went in search of Pablo.

INTERLUDE
Leo and Helen in the Savage Land

When the door slammed shut behind Leo he spun around only to see more jungle. No sign the door had ever been there. Perhaps there's no sign of it from the other side either, he thought, perhaps it's just vanished having done its job.

But what job was that? To bring him through here? Why?

He turned back to the woman. She still appeared semi-paralysed, her hands and feet occasionally moving but her face as slack as that of a stroke victim.

"Can you hear me?" he asked. Dumb question, even if she could she was clearly in no position to acknowledge the fact.

He squatted down in front of her, happy to fixate on the one thing he might have a chance of dealing with. If he paid too much attention to his surroundings then he might start screaming and once starting down that road he wasn't sure he'd be able to stop.

He reached for her pulse, knowing full well that she was alive but uncertain what else to do. When the limit of your medical background is watching *House* then you grab at the few ideas that come. Perhaps I should tell her to buck up and stop wasting my time, he thought, works for Hugh Laurie. Her skin was icy cold which came as a surprise given the heat around them.

"You're freezing," he told her, "but then you probably realised that."

He looked at her clothes again, heavy furs and padded trousers. They were old-fashioned he noticed, fashion being something he was more comfortable with than medicine. No synthetic fabrics either, cotton, fur, leather. Obviously dressed for the extreme cold. She *felt* cold. A crazy idea occurred to him. If he had just appeared here from somewhere else then the same thing might have happened to her. Somewhere cold... It would explain a few things.

Listen to yourself, he thought, the idea that you've both been transported here like something out of *Star Trek* "explains a few things"?

But it did. He had walked through a door and appeared here. The hows and whys of it didn't matter. He had stepped out of Forest Lawns in Glendale and arrived here (wherever *here* is, looks like the goddamn Savage Land... there's probably dinosaurs just past the next bend). She was dressed in snow gear, she felt ice cold... it didn't take a genius to guess that she might have stepped out of Alaska or somewhere and ended up here too.

But why is she paralysed? You're not...

"The box..." she whispered, making him jump to his feet with a yell. He had been so lost in his own head that the sound of her voice had been as startling as someone popping a balloon by his ear.

"Sorry," he said, holding his hands out placatingly. "I thought you..." Hell, he didn't know what he had thought. "Doesn't matter," he dropped back down and touched the side of her face with the back of his hand, she was warming up. "You said something about a box?" he asked, looking around in case she'd dropped something, maybe it was her medication or something, did diabetics go into paralysis if they didn't take their shots?

"In my pocket," she said. "Felt it move just before he fired, like it was burning..."

Leo reached into the pocket of her coat and rummaged around. "Nothing there," he said, "no box, burning or otherwise"

"Do you mind?" she said. "It's hardly befitting a gentleman to be so close when a woman can't..." her face suddenly clenched and one of her legs jolted, kicking up a spray of leaves.

"You okay?" Leo asked. She stared at him and, penny dropping, he stood up and backed away. "Okay okay!" he laughed. "'Not befitting a gentleman...' Jesus... like something out of *Brief Encounter*... forgive a guy for wanting to make sure you're alright."

"Some kind of nervous disorder," she said, "a side-effect of... of..." her face crumpled and she began to cry. "What's happening?" she asked. "Oh dear God... what happened to me?"

"Hey," Leo said, "it's okay, same thing happened to me..." He pointed towards where the door had been. "This door appears out of nowhere, I go through it cos I can see you and you look like you're in trouble... next thing I know 'boom' door's closed and I'm here in Tarzan's backyard."

"I have no idea what you're talking about," she said, both legs moving a little now, "I was in Tibet with my husband, there was..." but there she stopped, she had no interest in going over the events of the last few hours. "You said you came through a door?"

"Right there in mid-air," said Leo, "as solid as anything. I'm thinking it's a scam you know? One of those hidden camera things but there's nobody around and this thing... well... it's crazy I know, you can only see it from one side but you can touch it, it's *real*. And it opened and there you are, sat right there... I would've hightailed it out of there but, well, you looked hurt and I couldn't just leave you in case you were in trouble, so..."

"You came to my rescue, yes." Her tears were under control again now, that icy Helen Walsingham exterior closing back down around her. "I think maybe I can stand up but you'll have to help me."

"I'm not sure that would be befitting," said Leo but she shot him such a cold look that he shut up. He walked over and put her arm around his shoulders. "On three," he said, "one, two, three...lift!" he pulled her up, her hand digging into his shoulder as her wobbly legs tried to lock beneath her. Through an absolute refusal to give up she got there in the end, though couldn't quite bear all her weight without his assistance.

"Need to move," she said, "get the blood moving."

Leo nodded and helped her march backwards and forwards through the undergrowth until, eventually, she was able to let go of him and manage on her own.

"Thank you," she said, "I am almost myself. Though somewhat overdressed for the climate." She began to peel off her coat, still moving stiffly as the circulation returned to her arms and torso. She stripped down to a thick shirt, carefully folded the coat and jumper and laid them down amongst the leaves.

"Cool," said Leo.

"Not quite," she replied, "but I can hardly remove anything else."

348

"I meant… never mind." Her speech was old-fashioned, her clothes were old-fashioned… Leo had an advantage over Helen in that he'd seen enough movies to be able to imagine what was utterly beyond reason to her. "What year is it where you're from?" he asked.

She stared at him as if he was an utter simpleton. "What year?"

"Yeah."

"1904, obviously."

"Obviously", thought Leo. This was going to be hard work… "On the other side of the door I came through it was 2006," he said.

"Don't be ridiculous," she said, though a nervous twitch ticked around her eye. He hoped she didn't start crying again, he just couldn't stand being around women when they cried, reminded him of that girl who got him the damned Sinise audition.

"Yeah, because magical doors that transport you into Jungle World make loads of sense don't they?" he said. "But time travel? That would just be mad."

"I don't know anything about these doors of yours," she said.

"No, you prefer magic boxes, whatever…" he began to walk into the jungle.

"Where do you think you're going?" she asked.

"Wherever I like!" he replied. "I tried to do you a favour and you've done nothing but give me shit since. I should have stayed on my own side of that fucking thing…"

"Sir!" she cried. "Your language is an insult to the ears."

"Yeah?" he turned and grinned, "if you don't like it you kiss my motherfucking ass. I'm looking for a way out of here."

Her face fell. Oh no, he thought, here come the waterworks… He turned around and came face to face with a group of people pushing their way out of the undergrowth. They were dressed in ragged clothes, most of them dangerously thin.

"Hello," said the woman at their head, "my name's Lauren. Welcome to the House."

NINE
Where People go to Die (3)

1.

Night time in Florida and someone has finally switched the damned sun off. It's still hot enough to steam seafood in your pockets but at least you can breathe a little. In downtown Orlando the bars and clubs are still only coasting, the music light, the clientele friendly. Later, as the clocks crawl towards midnight, the nightlife will hit ramming speed and then god help the sober and the tasteful.

People look up at the sky and think about storms. The air has that feel to it, heavy and portentous. Like something Wagnerian is about to kick the shit out of the horizon. They're right to feel something's coming. However evolved we claim to be, however much we distance ourselves from the other animals by staring at them in zoos or putting a bullet in them from a distance, we still know some of the old tricks. If there's one thing you just can't evolve out of a species it's the ability to sense extinction. The common sense to do something about it? That's different.

Still, it's not like there's much you can do about the really big stuff. It's all very well being wise and considerate, minding your emissions, clearing up your trash. But when that meteorite drops and the sky fills with thunder it really won't have got you more than a clear conscience.

Only an idiot fights the apocalypse, the rest let their hair down and party like it's the last night on Earth.

2.

It had taken Miles and Carruthers several hours to loop back into Orlando on foot. By the time they were climbing the steps to their hotel it was dark and their feet hated them.

"Don't say a word," said Miles, "we're just going to walk straight past the concierge to the lifts, OK?"

Carruthers nodded and they pushed through the double doors and into the faded brown hell of the foyer.

"Good evening gentlemen," said the concierge, sparing them a brief glance from behind the pages of his paperback. "Would you be interested in a discount from our friends across the way at Ribs For Pleasure?"

"That sounds lovely," said Carruthers heading straight over, "what is it?"

"A rib restaurant," said the concierge, staring at Carruthers as if he might just have found the most stupid man on earth, "for dinner?"

"Do we like ribs?" Carruthers asked Miles who was leaning against a tastelessly upholstered pillar and trying not to punch the explorer in the back of the head. The thought of food set a bomb off in his guts and he suddenly realised that he was starving.

"We just might," he said, stepping forward and holding out his hand for the voucher.

Relieved that everything was back on conversational autopilot, the concierge handed the voucher over. "Ten percent off all entrees and free ice cream for the kids," he said.

"They will be thrilled," said Miles and yanked Carruthers towards the lift.

3.

Shepard sat behind his desk and stared at a cup of coffee as it slowly grew cold in front of him. He just didn't have the energy to drink it.

"Just heard from the team at the diner," said Cheryl, popping her head around the door. "They're starting to catalogue stuff now but you don't need me to tell you that they're going to be there all night."

"No Cheryl," Shepard agreed, "I guess I don't. What about Dutch?"

"He knows he's pulling an all-nighter too, the press have started to show and it's all he can do to keep the goddamn rubberneckers away. Things are going slow, we just don't have enough clean-up boys for this kind of workload."

Shepard shook his head and continued to stare at his coffee.

"Get you anything?" Cheryl asked.

Shepard looked up. Shook his head and returned to staring.

Cheryl left quietly.

4.

The stranger sat in the middle of the undergrowth and listened to the night insects as they sang to one another.

Next to him, lying flat on his back, was Chester.

"You see it's all about intention," the stranger said, though there was no sign that Chester could hear him. "Right now I'm going to leave you here. I'm going to pretend that I might not break this world of yours down the middle. That you can wake up in the morning and set to wandering down that road, just in time to meet the future. I'm going to pretend that. Because while I pretend that, everything stays as it should, a neat little framework of cause and effect, of what we know will be."

The stranger plucked a thick blade of grass, split it down the middle, raised it to his lips and whistled with it.

"I'm going to pretend that," he continued. "Because it might be fun, just for one night, to pretend this world has a future beyond tomorrow."

5.

"I'd like a *Baby Back Boomer* with fries, extra coleslaw, onion rings, garlic bread, breaded mushrooms and a selection of dips," said Carruthers, lowering the menu and looking over to Miles. "Might I also want a side-salad with extra croutons and bacon bits?"

"Depends if you're hungry."

Carruthers thought for a moment and then looked back to the waitress. "The salad too please Laura, if you would be so kind."

"Extra side-salad," repeated their waitress, noting it down on her little pad before looking to Miles.

"A Big Ben burger please, with fries and bacon."

Laura smiled, turned on her heels and vanished towards the bar.

"I think Laura's lovely," said Carruthers giving her a dreamy look as she poked the order through to the kitchen.

"Good," said Miles, "glad you're enjoying yourself."

"I wonder if she'll dance with me later if I ask her very nicely."

"What's come over you?"

"A not altogether unpleasant sense of fatalism," Carruthers replied. " It's not beyond reason to imagine that this is the last night I shall see after all."

"That's it, think positive."

"I honestly hope it's not the case but even if it is I shall leave this earth having lived well. There is not much I haven't experienced."

"Except Laura's dancing?"

"Indeed," Carruthers, fidgeted with his serviette, folding it into halves.

"Or anyone's dancing?" asked Miles.

"Indeed," Carruthers admitted, "there was a woman once, my dear Vanessa, but it wasn't to be. I'm rather afraid I let exploring this world of ours get in the way of any future courtships."

"Do you regret it?"

Carruthers thought about that for a moment. "No. I couldn't have been successful in both pursuits and I wouldn't have missed my travels for anything. I always imagined I'd stop travelling one day and then... well, who knows? I would have tried to take a place in society. Take a wife if one would have me. But somehow I've just never managed to stop. There's always been somewhere else to lose myself. Somewhere dark and unknown demanding I roll up my sleeves and push my way in."

"Which, coincidentally has been my exact experience of women."

Carruthers rolled his eyes and sipped some of his bottomless soda. He ignored the fact that he could see the bottom only too clearly, perhaps they had lost their depth perception in the future.

"If this is the last night on earth," said Miles, "I'm glad I'm spending it in your company. But you know what? Let's not talk about it. Let's do this properly, if it has to be a last supper then let's eat it well, let's have a laugh, a few drinks and leave the rest outside for a few hours. Tomorrow can wait."

Carruthers smiled and raised his glass. "I'll drink to that."

They clinked glasses.

TEN
The Attic

1.

Had Penelope truly believed that once they had exited the ballroom their journey would be over? Yes, she supposed she had. Given her experience of the House this had been more than naïve she realised. It had been stupid. Nothing in this building was so quick and, as perilous as the ballroom had been, it was just another stop on a journey that would be filled with such horrors.

They had found themselves back in a House corridor. An easel that corresponded to the one on the other side of the ballroom announced that "Professor Luptna's Joy of the Wurlitzer" was cancelled for the foreseeable future.

"Best news I've heard all day," said Barnabas, still limping on his raw ankles. The experience had clearly had an effect on the man, a good deal of the arrogance was gone and when he looked at Penelope his face showed respect. They had survived yet another obstacle. He wasn't blind as to whom he had to thank for that.

Penelope felt no pride, just relief and, as they began to walk along the corridor she was filled with a tiredness that was so all-consuming she wilted a little. Her footsteps were that of a drunk, unsteady and cautious, and she found herself reminded of Dolores. Her friend had walked this way a lot, always trying to hide the alcohol in her system. She supposed, looking back on it, that for all Dolores' bluster and shocking humour there had been a rather weak person beneath, one that needed a constant top-up from her hip flask to keep that confident mask in place. Poor Dolores, Penelope would miss her.

"You alright?" Alan asked her, only too aware that she was struggling to walk.

When he had expressed such concern back at the station, it had angered Penelope, determined not to be seen as needing anyone's support, least of all his. Now that attitude seemed unreasonable.

"Shaky," she admitted, "I think the shock of that place is just creeping up on me."

"What did you see?" he asked, immediately adding, "I understand if you don't want to say, I shouldn't ask, sorry."

She thought about it for a moment and then decided that there needed to be an honesty between them. "Chester," she said, looking at him to judge his reaction. The look on his face – a mixture of embarrassment and fear – told him all she needed to know. "You know about him don't you?" she asked, not with an air of confrontation but rather encouragement. Let's get this out, that tone said, let's have this *done*.

He nodded. "Ashe told me," he said. "I had always suspected something, was seeing a therapist about it in fact. That's who I saw," he admitted, "telling me that I was better off dead."

"Very helpful."

"I'd be lying if I didn't say I agreed with her most days." Once said that was something he couldn't pull back and it hung there between them for a moment.

"Sophie needs you," Penelope said, "and I can tell by the way that this lot look at you that they consider you a good friend."

"They don't know me though," he replied. "Not really."

"They know you as you are now," said Penelope, "that might be enough."

"I suppose it'll have to be." Alan couldn't quite meet her eyes as he said: "I'm sorry though, truly, for what he... I... did to you."

"So am I," she said. "And I'm not going to lie, I'm finding it hard to forgive you for it. I know the worms took most – if not all – of what you were. I know logically, that you're a different man. But I find it hard."

"I understand."

"No, you don't, but that's OK because I can't expect you to. I want to learn to trust you. I want to learn to forgive you. It will take a little time but I think I'll do it. I think I'll accept you as the man you are now, not whoever you were, just as they do," she gestured towards the *Intrepid* crew behind them, "because you obviously deserve that trust and forgiveness, you wouldn't be the man they know..." she nodded at Sophie, "...the man she knows if that weren't the case."

"I suppose not," Alan replied. "Thank you for trying I guess."

"Thank you for being worth the effort."

This corridor was decorated with doll's houses of various shapes and colours.

Maggie couldn't help but admire one as they passed. "I used to dream of owning one of these," she said to her husband. "To build and cherish and fill with beautiful things." She reached out to stroke the paintwork of one of the tiny windows, pulling her finger back just in time to avoid the teeth that appeared at the top and bottom of the window, snapping down to bite her. "Maybe not one quite like this," she admitted. "When will I learn not to trust a thing in this place?"

The corridor took them from one impossible room to another: a bedchamber filled with mountains of down that they slogged through like snowdrifts; a study filled with antagonistic candlesticks that howled and spurted blue flame (until Ryan chanced upon a set of bellows that dealt with the opposition in short order); a drawing room where sewing machines whirred and clacked like typewriters in a newspaper office, constructing reams of disturbing samplers: "A Stitch in Time Saves Childbirth", "Life is Silver, Death is Golden", "A Bird in the Hand Gushes When You Squeeze". All the time drawing closer – they presumed – to that impossible library that lay at the building's heart. With each new door their hopes swelled only to be dashed again once opened.

The paintings continued to be communicative. A selection of Dutch Masters argued with them – and each other – as they passed, some insisting that they were on the right track, others warning them that they had veered wildly off course.

"Ignore them," Hawkins had insisted. "I'm done taking advice from art that gets above itself."

Frans Hals' portrait of a *Laughing Cavalier* found this most amusing.

Klimt's model in *Mulher Sentada* interrupted her important business to point her slick fingers upwards. "You need to climb," she said breathlessly, "through the attic and then descend via the third hatchway."

"And the attic is where?" asked Alan, but the woman was far too distracted to hear him and so they walked on.

They needn't have worried, the entrance to the attic was unavoidable – and the only way forward, solving any issues they had over whether to trust the painting's instruction. A set of steps led from the centre of the corridor to a large hatchway in the roof and the party settled down on the carpet to eat something before continuing.

"Haunted attic," said Penelope, "just what I need. No doubt we'll be besieged by giant spiders or vampire bats the moment we're in the eaves."

"I can live with spiders," said Maggie, working her way through an unappetising Tuna wrap, "but bats terrify me."

"Frankly it all terrifies me," Alan admitted. "Creeping through the dark is not the ideal way forward."

"You get used to it," said Jonah, never one to miss an opportunity.

"At least we have lights now," said Hawkins, pulling out his torch. "If we stick together and move as fast as we can then it may not be long before we arrive at this third hatchway."

"Only one way to find out," said Barnabas. "I don't know about the rest of you but I'd rather just get on with it. The sooner we're in then the sooner we might be climbing back down again."

On Alan's back, Sophie stirred, muttering "With the help of my friends," and "three is good," before settling back into unconsciousness once more. This was becoming a more regular occurrence and Alan had stopped his "panicking parent" routine. He simply cocked his ear to listen to her steady breathing and that regular whisper of "build not break", reassuring himself that she was fine – as "fine" as usual that was – and then carried on eating.

"I agree there's no point in holding off," said Penelope, "as soon as we've finished eating we'll climb up there. Whatever's beyond the hatchway no doubt it'll be as horrid as everything we've faced before. But we've managed so far."

"And we'll manage now," agreed Alan, dumping what was left of a BLT back into its box. "If only because I can't bear another of these lousy sandwiches."

There was a murmur of good humoured agreement to that and the party began to dump their rubbish and replace their packs.

"You look like you need this more than I do," said Ryan to Dyckman's portrait of a blind beggar that hung next to him. He poked the crust of a cheese and ham sandwich at the man, giving a slight yelp as a wizened, oily hand emerged from the canvas and took it gratefully. "Avoid the canyon," the blind man said, chewing on the crust that seemed as large as a French baguette with the shift of perspective, "not that I'm supposed to tell you that."

"What canyon?" Ryan asked, but the old woman at the rear of the painting, stepping out of the church door with a prayer book clutched in her hand, dashed forward and started kicking the beggar. "Shut up about that," she squealed. The beggar's child grabbed a pizza-sized sheet of processed ham and ran beyond the frame where she could chew on it in private. "Sorry,' said Ryan, "didn't mean to get you in trouble."

The beggar shrugged. "I'm a beggar, you get used to a beating every now and then."

One by one they marched up the stairs towards the attic hatchway, Penelope leading as always, Alan a couple of steps behind her.

"An attic with a canyon in it," Alan said, "this could be interesting."

"Isn't it always?" she replied, pushing open the hatch.

2.

Sophie supposed she was dreaming. She was sat on a bench looking out to sea, an ice-cream in her hand. She did not eat ice-cream but noticed that it was spaghetti-flavoured so had a cautious lick. After all she was Very Hungry. It tasted good. The cornet was like toast done on setting number four so that tasted good as well. She recognised the sea. She had been here before. It was a place called Brighton. Brighton didn't know how beaches worked and it made her cross. Brighton had put stones leading into the water not sand. This was wrong. You could not build castles out of rocks. They fell over. But at least rocks did not cling to you when you walked on them so maybe they were not such a bad idea after all.

The sea was not an angry sea so that pleased her. It was grey. The sea was always grey, whatever it said in pictures. Pictures were lies, she thought. Pictures were what people made when they didn't think the real thing was right and wanted to change it. She could understand that. But changing things in pictures – making the sea blue and the sky clear and the people happy – did not make it real. So pictures were a waste of time. It would be better to make the real thing blue and clear and happy. Why people did not spend their time doing these things confused her. She tried her best after all, making things tidy and Right. If everyone worked as hard as she did then the world would be a much better place and she could get on with the fun things like eating spaghetti and counting all the Right things.

"Sometimes we just have to do our best to clean up after others," said the seagull perched on the bench behind her. Seagulls did not talk but she had got used to things doing what they weren't supposed to by now. She found it did not make her as angry as it had before. "There are people who make a mess and the rest of us who tidy up after them."

Sophie decided this was so true that she didn't mind who was telling it to her. Besides, she recognised the gull's voice. It was the voice of the House and whatever it looked like when it talked didn't matter. It could like lots of things she thought. Most often, the man the others thought of as the Grumpy Controller but she knew him as someone else entirely.

"Why do you speak with that voice?" she asked it.

"I stole it from inside your head," it answered. "Do you want me to give it back?"

Sophie thought about this. She liked that the House could talk to her. It made things easier.

"No," she replied, "you can keep it for now."

"Thanks," squawked the gull. "Do you know what's going to happen?"

Sophie thought she might. And, though she knew the others wouldn't like it, it made sense to her so she had decided it would be Good.

"Yes," she said, "build not break."

"Exactly," replied the gull, "build not break. It's the only way. We need to put Him back inside."

"Yes," Sophie agreed. She remembered Him. He had not been a HE but an IT. IT had been pretending to be a HE but she had seen IT for what IT was. IT had touched her. IT had made her part of the House. She did not mind this now as much as she had. The House

364

had become a friend and, whatever voice it used, she did not mind being part of it. In fact it let her be one of The Rest Who Tidy Up After Them and that was who she was so that was Good. But she did not want IT to touch her again.

"IT won't," the gull said, though she had not spoken Out Loud. "We will touch *IT*. And IT will know what it is like to be touched in a way that feels bad."

Sophie liked this. IT had thought IT was the biggest thing in the World. IT had thought IT was unstoppable. This was Wrong and Sophie liked making things that were Wrong Right.

"Don't get too confident," the gull said, "there's plenty that could go wrong... sorry... *Wrong* yet. Your friends may not even get to the library."

"Alan will look after them. He is good at looking after things."

The gull scoffed at that, ruffling its feathers and looking away to where a pair of fat ladies struggled to erect deckchairs on the shingle beach. Their dresses were as garish as the deck-chairs. "Alan is a pain, I've had no end of trouble with the older one. He nearly ruined everything."

"I do not know the older one." Sophie said. "But if he is an Alan then he is Good. All Alans are Good."

"If you say so."

The fat ladies had managed to get seated and were now staring at the water wondering why they had gone to all that effort just to look at a grey sea. After a moment one of them wondered if a cup of sweet tea might help and reached into her bag for a flask.

"I should go," said the gull. "The older Alan is about to go to New York and he's got an unpleasant surprise waiting for him when he gets there. He may need help."

"Alan sometimes needs help," Sophie agreed, thinking about the time she had helped him into the bathroom at the House. When he had been all tired and broken.

"Damn right he does," the gull agreed, taking to the air and flying away over the sea, dropping a dollop of guano square into the neck of the fat lady's open flask. Sophie thought the gull was Very Naughty. So did the fat ladies, shouting at the fleeing bird even while it squawked its pleasure and disappeared towards the horizon.

3.

Penelope looked out across the wide-open sky, taking in what was left of the warmth of a dusk sun. "Some attic," she said as Alan climbed up behind her. They were stood atop a plateau in what looked like the Grand Canyon. To their left were a couple of cartoon-perfect cacti and a stack of tea chests. Alan walked over to the chests.

"Plenty of storage space, certainly," he said, peering into one of them. It was filled with photos of dead people, the sort of grainy shots you saw in cop movies, people sprawled on floors and roadsides, marker tape and arrows pointing to blood splatter. He dumped the photos back in the chest.

"I guess we're safe from spiders then?" Hawkins said, coming up behind them followed by his wife and Ryan.

"Maybe," Alan agreed, "let's just hope there's no scorpions."

"Scorpions?" asked Jonah, bringing up the rear with Barnabas. "Where have you led us now?" He sniffed and held his face up into the sunset. "Feels like the open air."

"You can just see the roof joists," said Hawkins, pointing directly above them. "Like the bathroom, it's big but still enclosed."

"Well," said Maggie, "it makes a refreshing change after all those corridors, anyway."

"Just avoid the canyon," said Ryan, remembering the beggar's advice. He looked over the edge, "you can't even see the bottom."

"We're okay for now," Penelope said, "this high ground carries on as far as you can see."

"Yes," agreed Hawkins, "and something tells me the hatchways won't be as close together as we hoped."

"Well," said Barnabas, "just as well we all fancied a nice walk isn't it?"

"Is it just me or has he cheered up?" Hawkins asked his wife. "He hasn't told us we're all going to die for ages."

Barnabas grinned at him. "We'll be dead within the hour, Cap'n, just didn't see the point in stating the obvious."

"Was that a joke?" Hawkins asked, open-mouthed. "What's got into the miserable sod?"

They set off along the plateau, the dust kicking up around their feet as they walked. Every now and then they would pass more storage chests or cardboard boxes. To begin with, Ryan couldn't help poking around in them, finding one filled with baby clothes, another offering a selection of gas masks. "How about one of these each then, eh?" he asked, pulling one on his head. "In case Barnabas gets wind during the night."

"Cheeky bastard," Barnabas replied, finding a little of his old grit, "this from a kid that once tried to impress us by farting *Rule Britannia*."

"Gentlemen," said Hawkins, "do try to remember that there are ladies present."

Penelope laughed at that. Ryan gave her a small, apologetic bow. "Forgive me madam," he said, "but it was bloody impressive, whatever the old bastard says."

"I'm sure," she replied, "but I'm happy to take your word for it."

Ryan threw the gas mask back in the box. "Just as well," he said, "I don't think I could manage a single fanfare right now. Maggie's stew was a vital part of the process."

"There's nothing wrong with my stew!" she said, waving a finger at him in mock-admonishment.

"Didn't say there was," Ryan replied, "best arse ammunition I've ever known."

"Will you *please* change the subject?" shouted Hawkins. "No bloody breeding these days," he muttered, "that's the problem."

"Sorry dad," Ryan joked, looking in another box. He darted back in shock as a flock of crows burst from the opened flaps and took to the sky. "Right," he said to himself, "I'll open no more boxes."

"Probably best," Alan agreed, "next time it might be coyotes."

They soon realised that the sun, which had hung low in the sky ever since they had arrived was beginning to drop further.

"We'd do well to make camp," said Alan, "who knows what night might bring out here?"

"Agreed," said Hawkins. "We should get a fire built and arrange shifts for a watch."

"I'll go first," offered Jonah.

"It's alright for you," said Ryan, "it's not all bad news being blind is it?"

"Oh no," agreed Jonah sarcastically, "those extra couple of hours sleep more than make up for it. I'd recommend anyone losing their sight really, I've never looked back."

They stopped by the skeletal hand of a dead tree, figuring the branches would make for decent firewood. Ryan and Alan offered to strip it, Alan only too happy to get Sophie off his back and stretch his aching muscles.

"He fancies her don't he?" said Ryan as they began to snap branches.

"Who?" asked Alan.

"Barnabas," Ryan replied, "that's why he's all cheered up, he's all doe-eyed over Penelope."

"You think so?" said Alan, smiling at the thought.

"I know so," said Ryan, "look at him!"

They glanced over towards the camp where Barnabas was trying to offer Penelope help setting out her bedroll. "She'll bite his head off," said Alan, "she doesn't take kindly to men trying to help her."

Penelope smiled at the old sailor and stood back as he brushed the ground clear of any small stones that might get in the way of her comfort.

"Maybe it's just you she doesn't like helping her, mate," said Ryan with a chuckle.

"Maybe," Alan replied, returning to his wood gathering and trying not to take it personally.

They soon got a good sized fire going, the wood lit as easily as newspaper but burned as slowly as peat. It seemed for once that things in the House were on their side. Maybe it was the part of the house that wanted them to succeed – the rational part of it according to the lustful yokel they'd talked to before entering the ballroom – or maybe it was just luck. Either way they had a fire to warm them and Maggie prepared one of her allegedly gas-provoking stews rather than put up with another meal of pre-packaged sandwiches.

Once the sun had gone the attic became completely dark. With no moon or stars to shed any light their fire was the only source of illumination. It was disorientating, thought Alan, lying down on his bedroll and looking away from the fire. With no definition, nothing to fix on, they could almost be floating, a single ball of orange light bobbing in an infinite sea of darkness.

"What are you thinking about?" asked Penelope, noticing his horrified expression.

"Just the lack of light," he replied, rubbing his face and shedding the illusion of floating from his eyes. "The feeling of being so small in the middle of something so huge."

"Well," she said, "we're always that. Here or back in the real world. Have you never looked up at the stars and realised how tiny you are?"

He nodded. "What I wouldn't give to see some stars right now," he said, "I didn't realise how much I missed them until just then. Wherever we go, however big or small, we're always locked away in this box of a House. I'd give anything to feel the sensation of openness again, to know that above me there's nothing but space."

"I know what you mean," she agreed. "It's only been… what? Less than a week since I've been here? Still it feels like the real world is something so distant, so…" she struggled for the words to define it, "…historical," she said in the end, "something you know was real but can't quite relate to anymore. Something that happened to someone else."

"You think we'll ever get out?" he asked her.

"Well, we know you must do at some point," she said, "you left here and came back. That's the thing I've been holding onto."

Alan thought back to his conversation with Ashe and wondered whether he should share what he knew about the old man's future, the world he came from. In the end he decided not to, whatever Penelope had said about trust she had hope right now and he was damned if he was going to be the one to take that away from her. Maybe they'd be lucky and the future would be different, certainly Ashe hoped so.

"We all need to hold onto something," he agreed. "We'd never get more than a few feet in this place otherwise."

"What keeps you going?" she asked.

"Sophie," he admitted, "and the fact that I might not be the complete screw-up I thought. Before I came here I was directionless, whatever horrors the place has thrown at me it's given me a purpose as well. That's something."

"I suppose it is," she smiled, "most people just get a good job and get married. You have to go into an alternate reality and face death every day, you're a hard man to motivate, Alan."

He laughed at that. "I think it's more a case of having spent my whole life looking backwards. For once I've started looking ahead, it makes all the difference."

"Well," she replied, "let's hope there's something worth looking forward to."

Yes, Alan thought, let's hope that.

4.

Alan had agreed to take the second shift on watch, taking over from Ryan. When the lad woke him his face was contorted with such worry that Alan assumed something awful had happened. "What is it?" he whispered, looking around to see if everyone was safe.

"You'll see," said Ryan. "The noises, coming up from the canyon. It's enough to send you mental."

"What sort of noises?"

"I don't know," said Ryan, "wailing… I can't describe it, you'll hear them soon enough, scared the shit out of me and I don't mind who knows it."

Alan gave the boy's arm a squeeze. "Well, get yourself to sleep now, I'm here."

"Probably never sleep again," Ryan said, but shuffled off just the same.

Alan moved to the outer edge of the firelight and began to slowly stroll in a circle at the perimeter of the darkness. He had his torch and frequently shone its beam but it only illuminated more dusty ground and the edge of the canyon beyond them so he switched it off to conserve the batteries. To begin with he assumed that Ryan must have imagined the noises that had so scared him, the night was silent beyond the crackle of the fire and the sound of snoring. Then, after a few minutes, he began to hear them. He understood why Ryan had struggled to describe it. It was reminiscent of many things but not wholly evoked by any of them. Alan thought of the noise you made by blowing across the neck of a half-full bottle, or the ghostly whistling one heard in a marina, the wind drawing notes from the masts of the boats. This had that eerie quality but wasn't so tuneful. He remembered a girl who had been waiting for a bus outside the campus, laughing with her boyfriend – Albie Forrest, Alan remembered, that had been the kid's name, and the girl was Jessica… Jessica something. They had been play fighting, she accusing him of some imagined indiscretion, he rebuking her with a wide, innocent smile. He had stepped back and tripped on his own rucksack, falling back into the road just as their bus had pulled up. The sort of stupid,

stupid thing that happened everyday. One of those stupid deaths, the sort that mocked the victim with their sheer fucking pointlessness. The front wheels of the bus had gone straight over him. Alan was sure that poor Albie Forrest had known nothing about his own death, just a sensation of hitting the pavement and then – bang – no more. His girlfriend though, Jessica – Alan wished he could remember her last name, he had never taught her but somehow the fact that she had seen her boyfriend die demanded the respect of his knowing her full name – Jessica *whoever* had opened her mouth and the wail of shock, the primal note that echoed out of her, not a scream like you see in the movies, a much more forceful noise, had also been similar to the wailing that came from the canyon. What sort of creature makes a noise like that? Alan wondered? He pictured something grey and small, wizened beasts, used to a life in caves and darkness. Their wide "O" of a mouth open in perpetual sound, pumping that terrible noise into the night air. It only took him a few minutes to become just as disturbed as Ryan had been. "Avoid the canyon," the beggar in Dyckman's painting had warned them. Hearing that noise Alan couldn't imagine for one moment something enticing enough to lure him in. He stepped closer to the edge, shining his torch again to ensure he didn't stumble in the darkness. You couldn't get a sense of the canyon's depth at night but he had marvelled at it during the day, drawn by Ryan's insistence that you couldn't discern the bottom. The boy had been quite right, it had been like gazing into a distant black lake with similarly dark tributaries running off and into the distance.

As he stared over the edge he glimpsed a light, only brief but a flash nonetheless. A match perhaps? He glanced back towards the camp fire, wanting to make sure that everything was alright. When he looked back over the edge the light had returned, a small orb that appeared to bob along in the darkness. Someone walking a distant trail with a torch, maybe? Could somebody – some other unfortunate like themselves – have travelled through the box and be stuck down there in the darkness? Perhaps they were working their way up, terrified of the noises around them, desperately hoping to find the light. If that were so then surely Alan should help? Maybe hold his torch over the edge to guide them?

Alan dropped to his knees, torch in his hand, and pulled himself along his belly towards the edge of the abyss. Even as he was doing this a small voice, a *uselessly* small voice told him he was mistaken, whatever that light was it was no passing innocent. Alan ignored the voice, barely even heard it – in his head there was nothing but that alien wailing, that noise that was like so many things but none of them precisely – he was determined to shine his torch into the darkness.

The beam lit up the rocky edge of the plateau, pulling out shapes of small trees and outcrops of stone. The bobbing light hovered for a moment, no longer moving. Then, with a speed that proved the lie that it was held by any human hand, it swept upward, flying towards him like a signal flare. The wailing seemed to build in volume. Jessica's roar at the sight of her boyfriend leaking from beneath fat wheels, a child blowing a note on a half-empty coke bottle, a train unfurling its whistle in the depths of a tunnel. Alan's mind seemed to sink beneath it and he could imagine looking down on himself, lying there stupidly on the edge of the sheer drop, the vision falling away from him as if his consciousness were spiralling upwards into that endless black sky. It was a sensation akin to being faced by one of the wraiths that patrolled this House's empty spaces, that feeling of being both the observer and the observed. As if a sliver of the mind had been cut loose allowing you to exist in two places at once.

The light continued to sail towards him and, inside its orange glare, he saw parts of himself that he had never seen before. He saw himself as a young man – as Chester – sat in the back of that black De Soto, the punishing voice of the box hammering into him, demanding he do as he was told. He saw himself pointing a gun at a small Spanish girl as she ran away from him. Saw the box, handed to him by Ashe seconds before he arrived here for that very first time, coming to in the dark, dripping tunnels that ran beneath the building. He saw not just his past but his future too, the wide-open space where he would one day live – a farm, he thought, I'm living on a farm – that blue sky above but tinged with a darkness, a poison that he couldn't quite identify but knew to be there. He saw those he lived with, recognised their faces and wept, small salt droplets that fell from his startled eyes and dropped down into the darkness below. Darkness filled with a widening light and the ever-increasing howl of the creatures that lived in it. He saw a door, hanging impossibly in thin air, the red dust of the useless soil blowing against its lintel and vanishing through the half-open gap, vanishing into another world. He saw himself walk through that door, a destiny to keep. Then, as the light threatened to consume him entirely, the howling loud enough it must surely split his head wide open if he listened to it for another second, he felt hands grip his belt and yank him back from the edge.

"'Avoid the canyon,' it tells us," said Ryan, "and what do you do? Go dangling over it the very minute I swop shifts with you."

This was not the first time Ryan had said this, nor did Alan suspect it would be the last.

It had been Ryan's hands that had pulled him back from the edge. The boy, unable to sleep thanks to the disturbing effect of that wailing, had lain there for a while before deciding to check on him.

"I just knew something horrible would happen," he said, again for the umpteenth time, "like I could sense it, y'know?"

"I'm glad," said Alan, also not for the first time, "thanks."

"No worries, mate, happy to help."

They were sat well back from the canyon's edge now, both of them shining their torches towards it in case those howling creatures may decide to come up and see them. Alan thought this unlikely. They bring us to them, he thought, like mythical sirens. He had an idea that they could no more come up here than the weird, pale fish that inhabited the deepest parts of the ocean could creep towards the light. Maybe they explode, he thought, if they come up too high.

He hadn't told Ryan what he had seen. He'd explained the lulling effect of the light and sound well enough, the way it had drawn him to the edge, but that was all. He could see nothing to be gained from the rest but awkward questions he didn't have the first idea how to answer.

The rest of their party continued to sleep behind them, Ryan having agreed that he would sit out the rest of Alan's shift with him. "We should do this in pairs, y'-know?" he had said, "keep an eye on one another."

Alan saw the good sense in that and agreed he would offer the same courtesy to Barnabas when he was roused to take over.

"Let's hope there's no more than another day's walk to the hatchway," he said. "I for one don't want to sleep next to that for another night."

"Damn right," Ryan agreed. "Roll on the library, what can go wrong in a library?"

Penelope had told them a few of the things that could – and had – gone wrong there but Alan chose not to remind the boy.

"Time to wake Barnabas," he said. "You go and get him and get some more sleep yourself."

"Alright," Ryan agreed, getting to his feet, "'avoid the canyon' it said," he muttered before heading back to the fire.

6.

They passed the night in dual shifts. It cost each of them an hour less sleep but ensured that the sleep they had was safe.

Once the sun rose to that low, perpetual sunset it held throughout each attic day, they had breakfast and made their way onward.

An hour or so after they had begun their work they came across a hatchway in the dirt. Ryan lifted it and gazed down on an underwater dining room. Large fish coasted around the table decorations and the candles that flickered, quite impossibly, in the murky water.

"No thanks," he said, "I'll brave it out up here for a little longer I think."

The next hatchway was another couple of hours

away, this one opening up onto the snowy peak of a mountain.

"Been there," announced Penelope, "and I don't much fancy the three-day trek all the way down it to get to the library."

There was some concern that it might take them days to reach the next hatch – bearing in mind the length of Penelope's previous journey in the house below – but, as the sun began to drop once more, they saw it in the distance.

"I don't know about the rest of you,' said Alan, "but I'd rather keep walking – by torchlight if need be – and spend the night on the other side of that hatch."

Penelope, who had been hoping that they would spend the night in Carruthers old camp – a place she now looked on almost with nostalgia – agreed that anywhere was better than here. Hawkins concurred and so they kept moving.

Sure enough, after half an hour or so they were completely reliant on their torches to see the land ahead. The wailing of the creatures in the canyon to either side of them echoed around them as they walked the last half mile or so.

As the edge of the hatchway crept into the reach of their torchlight, Ryan dashed ahead to open it up and check they were in the right place.

He looked through the hatch and rolled onto his back with a groan. "If that's a library then I'm a badger's bumhole"

As the rest of the party walked closer they could see various coloured lights shining up from the hatchway.

"What the hell...?' Alan squatted down and stuck his head past the hatch.

Beneath them was a large coin arcade, pulsing lights,

the chiming of bells, the whirr of ball bearings as they chased across glass tables. He sat back.

"Ryan's right," he said, "definitely not a library."

ELEVEN
Restoration

1.

Land makes ghosts, not people. Some places are just built wrong, fault lines in the already temperamental bedrock of reality. They are brittle and prone to leakage, distorting the perceptions of those that visit them. Sometimes this effect can be positive: for millennia artists and intellectuals have claimed to achieve inspiration from their location. A "plugging in" to their environment that charges the mind and instils a clarity of purpose, a richness of vision. Sometimes the effect is not so beneficial. These "cracks" can encourage hallucination, foster metal illness, breed delusion. The human mind is fragile and the effects of such exposure are unpredictable. From catastrophic mental damage to just a feeling of unease, a malaise that can no more be readily identified than shaken off.

That small plot of land in Florida, just off Highway 192 and Interstate 4, soon to be Ted Loomis' tourist Mecca – "The biggest draw around these parts," he had said. "Strike me down if I tell a lie," and God had moved in a most mysterious way, say hallelujah – was one such place.

From the birth of that region, as Orange Island, in the Pleistocene Era, it had made its effect felt. An early hominid had once sniffed its air, in the pursuit of something to put in its belly when suddenly it began to hum The Beatles' "Eleanor Rigby". This was followed by most of the *White Album* and *Abbey Road* before, desperate to silence the alien noises in its skull, it bashed its little brain out with a rock.

Millennia later, a small settlement of the Apalachee tribe became convinced that if one were to sleep there, one would hear the voices of "spirits". In truth it was the sound of their own subconscious opening wider than any sweat lodge ceremony could accomplish. That and radio filtering through from the future. Radio signals have always been highly prone to temporal leakage and the Apalachee were not the first to drop to their knees on hearing stray coverage of the World Series or Howard Stern.

Hamilton Disston – who would later go fishing with Chester Alan Arthur, the president after whom Alan was named – dreamed up his plans to drain the everglades not a stone's throw from there. A project that saw Disston become the greatest landowner in America. He would later blow his brains out while in the bathtub. The voices gave but they also took away.

Today that little patch of grass and mud, that vibrating acre of earth, had one last trick to play.

"Hughie," the stranger said, waking Hughie up from his uneasy sleep in the driver's seat. "I've made a decision. I'm going home."

Tom woke up as the alarm clock jangled on the passenger seat.

"Alright," he croaked, reaching for it and fumbling it into the footwell, "Jesus…"

He scrabbled around, knocking it to and fro with the tips of his fingers then finally grabbed it. Angry with the thing (and himself) he wound down the window and threw the clock out as hard as he could. It ricocheted off a streetlight and fell silent into the gutter.

This act of spontaneous cruelty towards timepieces stopped a passing woman in her tracks. She stared at Tom and he smiled back through the windshield.

"Morning honey," he said, "looks like it's going to be a beautiful day."

She didn't reply but moved on quickly, in case this lunatic decided she was annoying as his alarm clock.

"Oh yes," said Tom. "A real beautiful day."

He reached into the glove compartment of the hire car and pulled out the revolver he had just bought.

God bless New York, he had thought when getting off his plane the night before, the city of free commerce. He had gone to see Fat Eugene at the Triangle Pool Hall, a man that could sell you most things if you had the dough, and had asked to buy a gun.

"People complaining about your playing?" Fat Eugene had asked. "Making dumb shit requests?"

"Nothing like that, Eugene," Tom had replied, sucking on the neck of a beer and trying to act relaxed. "Just feel the need of a bit of protection, you know how it is."

"I wouldn't give a shit," Eugene had said. "Some motherfucker keep asking you to play Manilow or some shit, I figure they deserve what's coming. I mean that 'Mandy' shit, y'know? That's some lousy noise, a fucker wants to hear that maybe you're doing him a favour y'know?"

"Just get me a gun Eugene," Tom had insisted. "You can do that can't you?"

"Of course." Eugene had shrugged, his whopping titties quivering for a few seconds as if trying to bounce free of his vest. "Who is this talking? This is Eugene, he can fucking get you fucking anything."

He had in fact got it within the time it had taken Tom to neck another beer. It had tapped most of his cash, hence his staying the night in the car. It had been that and spend the few dollars he had left on an alarm clock and a bottle of whisky or blow it all on a cheap room. Fuck it, what was a bed and pillows at the end of the day? A man didn't need such luxury. Though you had to admit there was some irony to being forced to sleep rough where he was. God had a sense of humour this morning, that's for sure.

He shoved the gun into his jacket pocket and got out of the car, looking up at the tatty brownstone across the street. He rubbed the sleep from his face. Maybe one more cigarette? No need to rush things. He pulled out his pack of smokes and couldn't help but smile at the solitary cigarette left in the packet. That's some symbolism right there, he thought, shaking it between his lips and flinging the empty pack to the floor. He rummaged for his lighter, lit the cigarette and leaned against the car smoking as slowly as he could.

After a few minutes there was no more to be wrung from it but a burned filter and he conceded it to the ground. He walked across the street, pushed open the lobby door – when will they ever fix that goddamned lock? – and began to climb the stairs. One floor, two, three then he was there on the fourth, out of breath and with a pulsing in his temples.

"Really should look after myself," he chuckled, "this is killing me."

He walked up to 405, pulled a set of keys from his pocket, opened the door and stepped inside.

He walked quickly, knowing that he would lose his courage unless he got this over with quick. Stepped into the bedroom, the man in the bed fast asleep and never likely to wake up. "Look at the useless mother fucker," Tom muttered, "would you just fucking look at him?" Tom pulled the gun out of his pocket and aimed it at his own stupid, snoring head.

3.

Alan had thought he'd never sleep. The idea of spending one more night amongst the noises of the attic had disgusted him so much that he had just lain there beneath that perfect black sky, eyes wide open and mind fixed on anything but the thought of what the creatures had shown him the night before. Nobody else liked the idea much, but all agreed that it beat camping down in the middle of a new room, a penny arcade no less, with whatever surprises the House had to offer in that particular setting once night had fallen. Better the devil you know, they had agreed. But Alan had slept, albeit briefly, waking to that lazy sun and Ryan shaking his arm.

"Time for breakfast," the kid said, "then some fun on the slots."

"Can't wait," Alan replied, sitting up and eyeing the caesar chicken wrap he had been left with frank disgust. He pulled off the cellophane and sniffed it. Nothing. It was just a selection of slick textures in a tortilla. He couldn't bring himself to eat it.

"Do you think the painting lied?" Hawkins asked, sitting down next to him and rubbing gingerly at his broken wrist.

"Who knows?" said Alan. "I guess it didn't say that the library was directly on the other side of the third hatch, we just assumed it would be."

"It might still be the right direction then," agreed Maggie, "no point in not trying."

"I love the slots anyway," said Ryan, "it was the one place I could enjoy myself when I was a kid."

"Says a lot about your childhood," said Alan.

"Yeah well, took me laughs where I could find 'em."

They gathered their stuff together and grouped around the hatch. Barnabas tied a rope around the hinges so that it would hold without yanking the hatch shut behind them.

"It's not too far," he said. "Should be fine, just try and climb steady and not pull the rope too much."

"Maybe you ought to hold the rope steady when its my turn," said Hawkins, "I don't do graceful climbing one-handed."

Alan went first, dropping down onto a wooden floor peppered with sawdust surrounded by the enthusiastic burbling of the machines. They were years before his time (at least the time he could remember), heavy pine and glass, electric valves and gleaming steel tracks, these were antique machines, early bagatelles and peep shows, machines that brought ancient midways to mind. Thick red drapes hung everywhere and the air had the sweet smell of candy floss and ozone.

"Roll up, roll up," he said, as he heard the others drop down one by one beyond him.

"What's this lot?" asked Ryan. "Not a single shoot-em-up in sight."

"It's a bit before your time," said Maggie, steering

him away from a What the Butler Saw machine before he took a curious glance through its viewer. Barnabas stepped over instead, rummaging in his pocket and fishing out a penny

He stared through the viewer and began to watch as a young lady in a bob haircut (not unlike Penelope he thought with enthusiasm) flickered into view and began to peel off her stockings.

"Push over," said Jonah who had moved next to him. "My turn."

"I'm not wasting my penny on you," Barnabas said, gripping the metal viewer tightly as the woman flung away her stockings and proceeded to unhook the fastenings of her corset. Bloody hell, thought Barnabas, this looked like it might be a feast for the eyes.

"'Ere," said Jonah, tugging on Barnabas' sleeve, "you could at least describe it you know."

"Look, Jonah," said Barnabas, standing up in irritation, "you're putting me off here, you know?"

As he stepped back from the machine a pair of metal spikes shot from the viewer, piercing the air where his eyes would have been.

"Bloody hell," he whispered.

Jonah reached out and felt the tip of one of the spikes. "My old mum was right," he said, "stuff like this sends you blind."

"No playing the games," shouted Barnabas, "they're as lethal as everything else in this place."

"No surprise there," said Alan, looking through the glass at *Madame Arcana, the Mystic Beauty of the East.*

4.

Someone was banging on the door of Miles' room. He

thought about the noise for a few dreamy seconds, before it came again and he snapped fully awake. Who was it? The police? The hotel management?

"Morning old chap," came Carruthers' voice and Miles dashed towards the door in relief. He pulled it open and for a second he nearly slammed it again, quite convinced he'd been tricked. The man on the other side of the door was clean-shaven, dressed in a smart grey suit. "Don't look so confused," said Carruthers, handing him a suit bag and stepping inside. "You seem to forget you are talking to England's premier hunter and explorer, I lose track of the hostile environments I have slipped through unnoticed, the jungles and deserts I have faded into as surely as a chameleon on his leaf. If we are to return to yesterday's hunting ground I thought it best that we should do so unrecognised."

"You brush up well."

"I brush up *wonderfully*."

Miles unzipped the suit bag to find a fawn three-piece with a large collared brown shirt. "Funky," he said, "but where the hell did you get them from?"

"I have yet to sleep," Carruthers admitted. "Since leaving the restaurant I thought I'd explore one last landscape. During my foray into downtown Orlando I stumbled on young Leroy Jackson, tailor of this parish. What with the money we had left and a few precious stones and trinkets I keep hidden in my pack for bartering I was able to conduct a considerable amount of business."

"In the middle of the night?"

"Nothing makes people desire their sleep less than financial reward. By the time I'd finished with Leroy he was crying. I have a feeling I may have overpaid him but, well, beyond the small amount of cash I have held back for a taxi fare, something tells me we will have little use for money in a few hours time"

Miles threw the suit back down on the bed. "Thanks for reminding me."

Carruthers put his hand on Miles' shoulder. "Who knows what will happen today? The only thing I can swear to is that myself and my dear friend will face it with honour, courage and a fine set of clothes."

Miles smiled. "And a decent breakfast inside them?"

"Anything less would be an insult to the Queen."

"And we wouldn't want that. Go down, I'll get showered and changed and I'll be right with you."

5.

Mario had walked up and down the station concourse for nearly ten minutes, still utterly at a loss as to what to do. He had tried to talk to the people around him but it was obvious that he was as insubstantial to them as they were to him.

He had made his way towards the exit, following the signs above his head only to stand there on the threshold staring out into the impenetrable darkness knowing that he would be taking his life in his hands should he step into it. There was darkness and then there was this unnatural void, he was damned if he was running into that without exhausting every other option first.

He walked back into the station, made his way upstairs and towards the trains, maybe that was the way out of here?

When he looked up at the impossible stack of trains in the Barlow Shed he decided that he might just sit down for a minute first. Maybe everything would even have the decency to vanish so that he could wake up and get on with the inevitable hangover.

He was sat on a metal bench, staring at the crowds of ghostly figures, trying to figure out what was happening to him – currently preferred option being an acid flashback – when he saw a man walk along the concourse and straight over to the trains. The man was real. It was immediately obvious when compared to the faded people around him. Mario was so surprised that he had just stared, watching as the man crossed in front of that crazy stack of trains and then vanished from sight towards one of the platforms. Then, as the likelihood that he would lose him all together finally shook him out of his shock he jumped to his feet.

"Aspetta!" he called, but just as he made to follow one of the electronic information posts fizzed to life and a crackling, sparking hand reached out of the screen and grabbed Mario's arm.

"Aspetta yourself," the Grumpy Controller said, "if you want to get out of here alive then shut up and listen. I need you to do something for me, something that's very important but rather unpleasant."

Mario stared at the screen, unable to think of a word to say, this must be the drugs, he thought, must be...

Another hand emerged from the screen and held something out to him. The Grumpy Controller smiled and there was a pop as an arc of electricity shot from the screen and earthed against the stone floor. "You're going to need this," it said, putting the gun in Mario's hand.

6.

"If you want to pass unnoticed in a jungle you dress like vegetation," Carruthers explained, as they got out of the taxi a quarter of a mile or so away from the construction site. "If you want to hide in civilisation you dress like authority."

Miles handed the taxi driver what was left of their money and waited for him to drive off before replying. "We're talking about the police," he said, "they're about as 'authority' as you get."

"Doesn't matter," Carruthers insisted, "if you dress to belong then you blend in. Trust me."

Miles shrugged, already sweating now they were out of the air-conditioned cab. "Wish we'd just let the cab take us straight there," he moaned as they walked along the highway towards the site.

"That might have been pushing our luck too far," Carruthers said, "though I agree it somewhat spoils the respectable image when you turn up looking as wet as a sponge."

A police car blazed past, siren blaring, and for a few seconds they were both convinced it would stop. The car passed them without so much as a pause, heading off to an emergency elsewhere.

"See," said Carruthers "the camouflage is working!"

"Whatever," Miles replied, his heart still pounding.

They kept on walking and soon the construction site was in view. You couldn't miss it, the line of police cars and news vans gave it away.

"What are those large vehicles with the dish-like constructions on them?" Carruthers asked.

"Reporters," Miles replied, "which makes our job much easier. If the place has turned into a circus then two more blokes wandering around are far less likely to draw suspicion."

"Reporters, eh?" Carruthers said. "I was a regular contributor to the press in my day, you just leave it to me."

"Welcome to the House," the woman had said, the look on her face making it perfectly clear that it wasn't meant to be a pleasure.

"What house?" asked Leo.

"The last one you'll ever see!" called one of the ragged-looking people at the back.

The woman, Lauren, had smiled at that, pulling a home-made knife from her belt. "I'm afraid he's right," she said, "you see we haven't had a square meal now in... well, a good few days."

"How terrible for you," said Helen punching Lauren on the nose. She turned and ran back into the foliage, Leo following right after.

Lauren coughed, flicking a gobbet of snot-thickened blood from her face and roaring at the very top of her voice. You didn't get to be leader of a bunch of vicious bastards like this without forgetting some of the social niceties. "Come on," she shouted, "let's gut those shit-heads!"

Leo overtook Helen when he heard that, swearing under his breath. If this were the movies, he thought, they would escape up a tree or maybe come into contact with a friendly group of savages who would save them before letting them join their tribe.

Something caught his foot and he flew forward, snapping two fingers back as he put his hands up to stop him smacking his face into the ground. He screamed in pain at the broken fingers but struggled to his feet as he could still hear their pursuers behind him. OK, so this wasn't a fucking movie.

"Over here!" Helen shouted and he looked over to see her stood in front of another door, just like the one he had seen in Glendale.

"Go through!" he shouted. "Go through!"

She didn't need his encouragement and had stepped over the threshold before he'd even finished speaking.

Lauren and the rest of her tribe were right at his heels as he reached the door. He actually began to giggle as he jumped through the doorway, his nerves so shot to hell. "So long!" he shouted and waved goodbye with his good hand.

8.

Madame Arcana twitched in her glass case. What was left of her last visitor was still seeping through her carved, wooden limbs like bloody sap. Her painted eyeballs took in the crowd gathering around her. Behind her veil, wooden lips smiled with the creak of an old door, rarely had she eaten so well.

"No surprise there," said the fat man in front of her. We'll see about that, she thought, I have a few surprises in here for big men.

He turned slightly and she saw that he had a child strapped to his back, She would be bloated for sure with this meal. Pine fingers stretched out, ready to grab him through the glass, smooth, varnished thighs parting as her hungry mouth parted its lips.

"What's this?" the fat man said and, just as both her hands punched through the glass to grab at him, he stepped away and bent down. The glass shattered and her hands snatched at empty space.

Madame Arcana roared and it was the sound of felled trees, splitting trunks and the crack of splintering wood. She stretched out her arms and legs but none of them were in reach. She reached behind her, desperate to tear herself loose from her fixings. The brackets held and she screamed once more, a spray of card fortunes gushing from her mouth.

"She can't move," said Hawkins, grabbing one of the cards as it struck his chest. He flipped it over and read it "Madame Arcana Predicts: That she will engorge herself on your stupid, flabby meats." He tossed the card away. "Not if you can't get at me love," he said, rummaging in his satchel and pulling out a stoppered bottle. He pulled the cork out with his teeth. "Keep back," he told the others, and splashed Madame Arcana with the bottle's contents. He sighed as he fished out his matches. "That was the last of my brandy," he said, "and potent stuff it is my lovely," he struck a match, "so, cheers." He tossed the match into the case and Madame Arcana plumed with blue flame. She screamed one last time as her smooth skin crackled and burned.

Alan stepped over to Hawkins and held up what had distracted him away from Madame Arcana's grip, it was a coin.

"Find a penny, pick it up," said Ryan with a grin, "and all the day you'll have good luck."

"I find that hard to believe in this place," said Penelope.

Madame Arcana, the fire having sunk its teeth into her limbs with a preternatural speed, gave an almighty crack as she distorted with the heat. The bracket that held her in place snapped and she fell forward, tumbling from the case and slowly contorting on the floor as she continued to blacken. The back of her case was open, a door that led through to another room.

"Well now," said Barnabas, stepping forward, "what's through here?"

"Careful," said Penelope.

Barnabas smiled, only too happy to look the brave sailor in front of Penelope. "You don't put something like that," he pointed at Madame Arcana "in front of something dangerous, you put it in front of something you want to keep hidden."

He stepped into the vacated cabinet and through the exposed door.

Jonah stepped forward, "I think I liked him better when he was a grumpy coward," he said. "Anything killed him yet?"

"No it hasn't," said Barnabas, poking his head back through, "but you might want to follow me through."

One by one they filed through the small doorway, stepping out onto a wooden, plateau.

"Look over the edge," said Barnabas. Alan walked over to where the plateau dropped off and, as he got closer, he realised where they were. Facing them was the top of the opposite bookcase, its upper rows coming into view as he got closer to the edge of the case they were stood on.

"We made it!" said Barnabas grabbing Penelope in a sly hug while he felt he had the excuse.

There was a cracking noise from above them and they all huddled together, immediately on the defensive. The cream paintwork of the ceiling split neatly as many large screens descended throughout the impossibly large room. The screens flickered with static for a few seconds and then an angry squeal of feedback echoed along the bookcases.

"What the hell was that?" Hawkins roared.

"You tell me," Jonah said, holding his head in his hands, "it nearly split me from ear to ear."

The screens flickered and popped then the face of the Grumpy Controller appeared, many times over, all across the length and breadth of the room.

"Finally made it then?" he said, the voice echoing from a crowd of identical controllers. "About time too, there happens to be a reality in need of saving."

"What are we supposed to do?" Alan asked, looking at Sophie.

"Get her to the centre," the voice replied, "she'll manage the rest herself."

"And the centre is?" Penelope held her arms out trying to get across the size of the room.

"About half an hour's fast walk towards 'G'," it replied, "and for all our sakes get on with it, we'll only have one crack at this and if you bugger it up we're all doomed."

9.

Ashe pulled himself onto his final train. Nearly done, he thought as he dropped his old bones into one of the seats. He pulled his revolver out of his coat pocket and checked it was fully loaded before staring impatiently out of the window. What were they waiting for? Usually the minute he had stepped onboard the trains shot off to their destination. He got up and moved to the door, meaning to stick his head out and check the platform. With a hiss the door slammed shut the minute he drew close.

"Well come on then!" he shouted. "Let's get on with this!"

The intercom crackled and the voice of the Grumpy Controller came from the speakers.

"This is a service alteration due to an emergency in the time stream," it said. "This service will now be stopping at March 23rd 1976 rather than the previously scheduled August 16th 1977."

Ashe rolled his eyes and smacked the wall of the carriage beneath the speaker. "What are you doing?" he shoute. "Why the change?"

"Don't shout at me sir," the tannoy said, "this rail service does not tolerate violence towards its staff."

"This rail service can kiss my ass! What's going on?"

"Your... colleague, the drunk, is trying to disrupt the timeline."

"Tom..." Ashe sighed, this he hadn't allowed for.

With a jolt the train pulled out of the station.

10.

Hughie was coasting. Everything was starting to feel detached and light, as if he was slowly falling out of his own life. As he drove he kept seeing flashes of the bodies in the diner. Split and blossoming like flowers of meat.

"Keep your eye on the road, Hughie," the stranger said, as Hughie veered between lanes, "and your mind on the job."

"What job is that?" Hughie asked.

"Driver and pet monkey," the stranger replied, smiling dreamily. "I'm going home."

"Yeah." Layer on top of layer, Hughie thought, thinking back to their conversation in the diner and the ramifications it might hold. Thinking about what was to happen to his little layer of reality if the stranger punched his way through all those other layers to get home. "It would tear the metaphorical guts right out of it," the stranger had said. Hughie didn't doubt it. The stranger just loved tearing the guts out of things.

That made him think of the diner again, of him begging as the stranger leaped on the cop with his steak knife.

"You're veering again, Hughie," the stranger said, "you want us to crash before we even get there?"

Hughie tightened his grip on the steering wheel and brought the car back under control.

As the cop had screamed so the rest of the diners had joined him. Once what they were seeing sunk in, some had made for the doors – which had slammed shut and would not open until it was far too late – a few others had made for their table. They meant to help of course, to pull that pudgy freak off the cop before the damage was too great. They weren't alone, Hughie had got there first, dropping on to the stranger's back and yanking at his arms. He didn't care if the stranger turned on him, better that than watch another man die.

The stranger had just smiled and shrugged his shoulders, sending Hughie flying into one of the far tables.

"You don't get to die," the stranger had said, "you get to watch."

And Hughie had, his entire body as stiff and unresponsive as that night when he had lain amongst the snakes on the dirt road beyond his house. He lay on his side amongst the toppled chairs and tables, eyes unblinking as the stranger laughed and cut. He watched as, one by one, they fell. A burly guy, one of the first in line to come to the cop's aid, dropped to the floor as the stranger sliced out with his knife. His hands went to his belly, fighting to keep everything inside as the stranger turned to his next victim. The steak knife broke quickly, but this – he's not a man, Hughie remembered – this "thing" had no need of it. He used whatever he could lay his hands on, other cutlery, the beer bottles, hands and teeth. It was almost impossible to watch him move, he did it so quickly. His arms and legs moved independent of one another, each swinging through the air to achieve maximum damage. It made him look utterly inhuman, like when you see a monkey in the zoo pick up something with its foot. The other diners, thirteen or fourteen of them, began banging at the windows. One woman, jiggling in the most unflattering pantsuit Hughie had ever seen – the beige nylon cutting into her ass like string around a pot roast – picked up a chair and threw it against the window. It bounced back, knocking out a few of the woman's teeth and sending her sprawling.

Hughie wished he could close his eyes. If he couldn't stop the stranger then, for sure, that would be the next best thing. They were as fixed as the eyes of the girl only a few feet away, the one with a fork in the side of her head. He had no idea if his looked as startled as hers.

"Are you feeling alright, Hughie?" the stranger asked. "You seem distracted."

"Yesterday I watched you slaughter a bunch of people. Today you're going to tear the guts out of my world," he replied. "Of course I'm fucking distracted."

"Tried to stop me in the restaurant, didn't you?"

"Yeah, and I'd do it again."

The stranger nodded. "I know Hughie, perversely it's one of the reasons I like you."

"I knew you liked me," Hughie replied, "you always treat me with such kindness."

The stranger laughed. "A sense of humour too, who wouldn't want you around, eh Hughie? …Hughie!"

Hughie had already seen it. Didn't believe it, but saw it right enough. Right ahead of them a door had appeared in the middle of the road and a woman had come running out of it. She cut straight across the highway, her momentum taking her out of harm's way just as Hughie had prepared to swerve. "That was…" Then a man appeared out of the door, and Hughie hit him straight on. "Fuck!" Hughie put one arm in front of his face as the windshield cracked and the man rolled over their roof, tumbling to the asphalt behind them. The car spun as he involuntarily hit the brakes.

"Hughie!" the stranger roared, as he was thrown forward in his seat.

Hughie took his foot off the brake and fought to get the car back under control.

Behind them, poor Leo breathed a last wet breath into the stained grit beneath him. Hughie strained to see through the windscreen and began to pull over.

"What are you doing Hughie?" the stranger growled, turning to look at him through his smashed face. His two front teeth had chipped on the dashboard, Hughie noticed. He could see the tear in the plastic where they had hit.

That hurt him. He thought. That actually *hurt* him.

"We should check…"

"I think we can safely say he's dead, Hughie," the stranger replied, spitting a mouthful of blood at the windshield before leaning forward and punching the whole thing out of its frame with an animal roar. "So let's get on with it! I want to go home!"

Hughie put his foot on the gas and the car pulled forward again.

That *hurt* him.

"You're becoming more human," he had said to the stranger before their meal in the steakhouse. He had meant the stranger's appetites and speech, but perhaps it was more than that. Perhaps this thing, in its lust for the earthly, for the pleasure of meat, had actually begun to transform? If so then Hughie had some hope left. It was a thought he pushed from his head as soon as he had it, determined not to share.

That hurt him, he thought again, satisfied that the stranger could tell nothing from such a thought. He repeated it over and over again in his head. That hurt him, that hurt him, that hurt him…

Hughie could see the news vans and police cars up ahead. *That hurt him.* They were nearly there..

"Don't speed up, Hughie," the stranger said, "you'll miss the…" he turned to look at him. "What are you doing now?"

Hughie pressed the pedal right to the floor, moving into the outside lane and heading straight past the construction site.

"That hurt you," he said.

"What?"

"Back there…" Hughie didn't want to discuss that, nor was there time. "When we hit that poor bastard. You hurt yourself."

The stranger looked down at his hands, still red and sticky. What was the little ant talking about?

"I said you were becoming more human," Hughie continued, the wind blasting through the open windshield meaning he had to shout, "in the diner, I told you that. Then, today, you got hurt."

Ahead, the I-4 overpass loomed. The Oldsmobile now hitting 100… 110… other cars were pulling out of the way, banging their horns at the mad fool with the speed problem.

"Your point, Hughie?"

Hughie smiled and it was the first time he could remember doing that for a long, long time. Before the stranger had arrived for sure, but even then he hadn't had much to crack his face over had he? But right now, he was genuinely happy. Almost joyful in fact.

"My point? You may not be quite as indestructible as you seem to think, *that's* my point." He looked at the stranger and had the singular pleasure of glimpsing a look of fear on the man's face. He leaned back and nudged the wheel toward the thick concrete feet of the overpass. "I hope it hurts, you godawful *motherfucker*."

The car hit the bridge pillar at a solid 120 miles per hour. Hughie, who had had the foresight to punch the button of his seatbelt just before the impact, hit the concrete a fraction of a second later. Blessed oblivion, how Hughie Bones had earned it.

11.

With a sigh, Hawkins dropped his bag on the floor. "I don't know about the rest of you but I've had as many orders from this place as I'm happy to take."

"Get over yourself," the Controller replied, his face vanishing to be replaced by an old black and white movie of someone making a clay pot, the word "Interlude" emblazoned across it.

Alan just shook his head, shuffled Sophie on his back, and set to walking. "One last push," he said, over his shoulder, "this place wants to survive as much as we do. It may not like dealing with us and we certainly don't like dealing with it. But we're all in the same boat so I can't see we have much choice."

Penelope walked alongside him. "Aren't you worried what's going to happen to Sophie?" she asked. He glanced at her but didn't reply. Behind them she could hear the *Intrepid* crew following on. "You know, don't you?" she asked. "You know exactly what's going to happen."

He nodded. "Ashe told me. This is the future he was trying to avoid."

"And you're walking right into it?"

"There's no choice, it's this or the end of all of us." He shuffled Sophie in his arms, she still whispering "build not break, build not break," over and over again.

"And I don't just mean us," he continued gesturing back with his head to include the crew behind them, "I mean everything, every single person in every single book on every single shelf... our whole species, our whole existence. He'll destroy all of it."

"How can Ashe know though?" Penelope asked. "You're putting a hell of a lot of trust in him." Then she realised what she was saying. "Of course you are…"

"This way we survive," Alan said, "maybe not well but *alive* and sometimes I guess that's all you can really hope for."

12.

It's difficult to shock New York. If it were a person it would likely punch you in the face before you even had time to describe it for metaphorical effect. While you were recovering on the floor it would pat you on the back, apologise, ask if you wanted it to call somebody but make it clear that you look at it that way again and it will put a freakin' cap in your ass. Strangely, you will love it for acting this way.

Simply: New York has seen some serious shit in its time. And laughed at it.

Nonetheless when a streamlined A4 Pacific steam locomotive tore its way through East Tremont there were those that considered it remarkable enough to stop what they were doing, stare, and maybe even offer up a pithy prayer or curse.

The chaos of a steam locomotive hitting the morning traffic was such that nobody spared Ashe so much as a glance as he jumped off and ran up the street.

"Subtle," he said, skirting around the gouged up asphalt and turned over cars.

"You can't mend a timeline without breaking some streets," said a voice to his left. Looking up he saw a particularly mangy pigeon fluttering through the clouds of dust the train had kicked up.

"Blending in with your surroundings?" asked Ashe.

The pigeon gave an unhealthy squawk. "People 'round here see a fat seagull they're going to shoot and eat it."

"Snob."

"I'm taking no risks."

They hurried up the street, darting past the increasing number of spectators emerging from the brownstones around them.

"This way," the pigeon said, crossing the street and fluttering towards a nearby building.

Ashe followed, clambering over the gouged furrow of asphalt and through a shallow stream caused by a fire hydrant the train had uncapped on its arrival.

Ashe and the pigeon entered the building, the bird perching on the banister railing of the fourth floor while Ashe made his way up the stairs.

"Come on!" it shouted. "Can't you climb any faster?"

"You'll go some way to find a man of my age that could climb this far at all, damn it." Ashe dragged himself onto the fourth floor landing. "Which room?"

"405."

Ashe raised his hand to open the door and then hesitated, pulling his gun from his coat. He opened the door.

It was silent inside and he tensed as the squeak of the door hinges worked its way along the entrance hall like a warning.

"Quickly!" the bird shouted, flying over his head and into the apartment.

Ashe pushed the door closed and walked into the

main room, stepping awkwardly around piles of take-out packaging and empty bottles.

"Hey," said a voice from behind him.

He turned to see Tom stood in the doorway of what must have been the bedroom. He was pointing a snub-nosed revolver at him.

"I was going to shoot myself," said Tom. "I mean, no great loss, huh? And that way Elise would stay safe. But then I heard you arrive," he tapped his head towards the dirty window that looked out on the body of Ashe's train, "and I figured I didn't have to shoot me, I just had to shoot you."

"Just kill him," the pigeon said to Ashe, circling the light fitting in the centre of the room.

"A talking bird?" said Tom. "I've seen some shit in my time, I mean, drink as much as I did and you have interesting times, but this is new."

They stared at each other for a moment and then Ashe lowered his gun.

"No more," he said, "this is not who I am."

"You can't argue with genetics!" the pigeon replied. "Now shoot the drunk, we don't have time for this."

Tom scratched at his mop of hair, his gun still pointing at Ashe. "I just don't know," he said, "I mean… this ain't exactly my style either but…"

"You love her," said Ashe.

"Yeah," Tom replied.

"I get that, she's your perfect ideal, the person that makes you a better guy just by being with you."

"That's it."

"Same with me and Sophie. Some people just bring the best out of a man don't they? Make you into someone you didn't know you had the balls to be."

"Yeah."

"Do what you've got to do," said Ashe. "Your choice."

Tom shuffled his feet. Christ he could do with a drink. A drink always did sharpen his ability to make decisions. Or rob him of the need to.

"I just don't want her to die," he said, "she deserves better. But…"

The door to the apartment banged open and a man ran in firing a revolver. A couple of the bullets lodged themselves in the walls of Tom's apartment, a third in his forehead.

Ashe raised his gun and fired without even thinking, shooting the man twice in the chest and sending him crashing against the far wall.

13.

Miles and Carruthers pushed their way past the ever-increasing crowd of cameramen and coiffured anchor-persons, trying to see what was going on beyond the police tape.

"Jesus," said a guy to Carruthers left, "did someone send out invitations?"

"I don't think we have to worry about anyone wondering who we are," Carruthers said to Miles.

The police had erected a stretch of tarpaulin to block the view of their excavation. Nobody needed to see their loved ones pulled out of the dirt on the news. Lieutenant Dutch Wallace was pacing up and down, clearly uncomfortable at working to a crowd. He knew he'd have to speak to them and was pissed off about it. Dutch's indigestion was moving into overdrive. What the hell was going on out here today?

When he heard the sound of car horns and a motor tear past the entrance to the site he actually turned away. No more, he thought, this man is at his limit…

The car wasn't ignored by everyone. Joey Spencer, a cameraman from the Orlando affiliate of CBS, was resting his shoulder and sneaking a joint in the cab of his van when the Oldsmobile sped by. It had been clear to him that shooting footage of twitchy cops and tarpaulin wasn't going to win him any awards and he had been quick to tire of it, whatever that shrewish bitch, Tyler Mercer had to say. Mercer fancied herself a rising star in the world of broadcast news. Joey thought she'd be gone by the fall. She could barely string a sentence together and if tits were all it took then he'd seen – and cupped – better. When he saw the speeding Oldsmobile in his rear-view mirror he jumped out of the van and ran to the roadside with his camera. Why he couldn't say. A speeding car was hardly award material either after all. There had just been something in his guts that told him the story had switched sides on them.

He got to the roadside, camera rolling, just in time to catch that tank of a car hit the concrete overpass and explode. The footage was shaky – Joey couldn't help but flinch when the car impacted – but it captured it in some detail. The networks would have no doubt showed it slowed right down – if, that is, they had been able to show it. Their audiences would have cooed at the screen as the front of the car immediately concertinaed on impact. The rear bumper flipped up as if the General Motor company had taken to installing hinges mid-chassis. The car turned from a big, sprawling, beast to a ball of metal and glass. The fuel line ignited, immersing the whole in a surge of flame that lit with the sound of someone being struck in the stomach by a baseball bat. The other cars on the road, already cautious of the speeding lunatic that had been the unfortunate Hughie

Bones, were able to avoid further damage. If it had been busier then there would have been a pileup for sure but traffic was light and those cars that had been behind the Olds pulled safely to the side of the road. The passengers climbed out and ogled the scene before them, half in horror, half in delight, after all, it's not every day you get to see something right out of a Hollywood action movie.

Hughie Bones got more attention from his fellow man right then than he had achieved at any other point in his life. Shame he had to die to do it.

Joey Spencer kept his camera trained on the accident for some time. There seemed no rush to check the wreck for survivors, naturally there couldn't be any.

Lieutenant Dutch Wallace would have agreed with the cameraman's assumption but he wore a badge that insisted he get involved nonetheless.

"Jesus wept," he said, "this day is just fucked."

A blackened and weeping body pulled itself out of what was left of the rear passenger window and fell to the asphalt with a wet hiss, just to prove the Lieutenant right.

14.

"You're going to need this."

Mario tried to hide the gun in his jacket but it was too big for any of the pockets. If he tucked it into the waistband of his jeans he thought he'd likely shoot his dick off. Finally, irritated by the sort of impracticalities he had never concerned himself with in his movies, he cradled it inside his coat like something he was trying to protect from the rain. He needn't worry, he supposed, the passengers on the train were no different to the people walking the platforms. They were insubstantial and he was clearly beneath their attention. There was only one person that could probably see him and he was several carriages in front.

Not that he was any more real than the rest, Mario thought, couldn't be... he was probably lying face down in a Turin gutter right now, drink and the ghosts of Sixties' drugs making him dream this madness while he slept.

Fine by him, maybe he could get a new movie out of it, a time travelling assassin, something a bit different from his usual stuff.

The darkness beyond the train windows was replaced by a run-down looking street as the train came crashing to earth. Mario tumbled from his seat, dropping the gun onto the floor. God damn it, he thought, the heroes in his movies never behaved like this. He grabbed the gun and reached for the door.

Just as he was turning the handle he saw the old man pass by. He waited a second, not wanting to bump into him. Peering through the dirty glass of the window, he watched the man for a few seconds then, satisfied he wouldn't be noticed, opened the door and jumped out.

"You can't park that here," said a voice behind him as he stepped down onto the broken road. He turned to see an old black man who appeared to be wearing an entire wardrobe's worth of clothes. A wave of whisky and tobacco hit Mario as the man coughed. "You gots some kind of permit or something?"

Mario smiled and held up his gun. "This is my permit old man," he said in a passable American accent, "want to see it in action?"

The old man backed away in a panic, tripping over his own feet and tumbling into the rubble.

That was better, Mario thought, much more like the movies.

The old man was out of sight now and he had to run to catch up. Just as he cleared the rear of the train he saw him enter a brownstone across the street.

Inside he could hear the man's footsteps going up the stairwell, heard him talking to somebody. He's as mad as me, he thought, chuckling as he jogged up the stairs after him.

The old guy stopped on the fourth floor. Mario peered between the banister railings and watched. There was a pigeon fluttering around the man's head as he opened one of the doors and stepped inside. Which was ridiculous, but no more so than anything else Mario decided, trotting up the last few stairs and moving along the hallway towards the door of 405.

OK, Mario thought, if I'm going to do this I'm going to be Pacino about it. He waited for a few moments, took a deep breath and, in his best Scarface frame of mind, shoved the door to the apartment open and went in shooting.

Every day above ground is a good day, he thought and smiled as he pulled the trigger of the gun over and over. Two shots went wide but the third bagged his target. OK he thought, time to wake up now…

Which is when Ashe shot him.

15.

"What the hell?" asked Lieutenant Dutch Wallace of nobody in particular, before running into the road to assist what he could only assume was the hardiest road crash victim he had ever had the misfortune of encountering. "It's okay buddy," he said before realising that he had no idea what gender this thing even was. It was a mess of charred flesh and jutting bone, and it occurred to Dutch that the kindest thing to do was to shoot the poor bastard, who would want to live like this? Dutch gave a yelp of panic as the thing grabbed his ankle.

"Hey," the creature said, "don't suppose you'd give a man a hand would you? I could die of boredom trying to crawl over there at this rate."

"It's him," said Carruthers, "the prisoner."

Miles hadn't doubted it. He had recognised the car well enough from the last time they had seen it, pulling out of this very same entrance leaving a trail of choking innocents behind it.

"Yeah," he said, "hard to kill isn't he?"

The crowd of reporters had, despite their natural inclination to flock towards bad news, fallen back. The sight of this thing, smoke rising off it as it continued to crawl towards them, was not something they thought they would be reporting for their newspapers or interviewing for cable broadcast. This was too grotesque even for them. If only it would have the decency to lie down dead – surely it would do so any moment? *Surely*? – then they would happily point their cameras at it and write elegant and emotional words about the victim's passing. But while it still breathed, lungs inflating and deflating with the noise of a crumpled plastic bag, there was nothing that could bring them closer to it.

When it grabbed Dutch's ankle there had been a ripple of disgust through the crowd that had echoed the policeman's cry. That ripple intensified as the barely-human body began to pull itself up Dutch, hand over crispy hand. It left sticky, yellow handprints in the man's uniform trousers as it reached higher, grabbing at his shirt.

"Jesus," Dutch moaned, reaching out to help and trying not to upchuck over the damn thing, "someone give me a little help here, what you say?"

The reporters said nothing, but Miles pushed his way past them and jogged over towards the policeman. The last thing he wanted was for the creature to be aware of him but he couldn't watch the poor Lieutenant struggle on his own.

"Oh," the creature said, noticing him even as it continued to pull itself up the policeman's body, "if it isn't my favourite dealer in antiques and pithy remarks. How are you enjoying Florida, Miles? Be careful on the roads, the drivers here are nuts." It chuckled and a piece of its cheek fell off and landed on the tarmac with sound of an egg dropping from its carton and exploding on a sideboard. This was more than Dutch could stand and he fought to tear the thing off him, Miles tried to help, screwing up his face as his fingers dug into the black tar of the prisoner's back. Carruthers was at his side, grabbing the thing's hands and trying to tug them off the policeman's clothes.

"Get off me!" the thing roared and both Miles and Carruthers fell back, pushed away mentally rather than physically. Lieutenant Dutch Wallace's eyes rolled up inside his head and he ceased trying to defend himself, allowing the prisoner to pull itself up onto his back. It poked its sticky head over his shoulder, strands of meat pulling between the policeman's cheek and its own as it looked from side to side, surveying the horrified crowd with creamy eyes.

"Right," it said, "best foot forward." No more than a puppet, Dutch began to stride towards the building site.

16.

"Who was he?" said Ashe, stepping over to Mario's body. He looked over his shoulder at the pigeon. "Who was he?"

"Nobody important," the bird replied, "we need to get out of here, one last stop remember?"

Ashe looked down at Mario, the dying Italian grinned. "Every dog has his day."

Ashe looked to Tom. He was splayed across the floor, legs and arms twisted. The only consolation Ashe could think of was that he must have died instantly. As he thought about that for a second he decided that was no fucking consolation at all. All of this made him so sick he could barely think.

"Build not break," the pigeon said, turning its head on its side. A door appeared in the middle of the room, it clicked open and Ashe could smell the ocean on the other side.

"Come on!" the pigeon shouted. "Get both of them dumped before the younger Tom sees them."

Ashe had forgotten all about Tom's younger self, passed out from drink next door. Before he would lift a finger though he wanted the House to understand one thing.

"Everyone's important," he said, "absolutely every-body."

"Whatever," the pigeon replied, "now come on!"

17.

As the prisoner rode Dutch's back into the Home Town construction site, most of the reporters finally gave up on their story.

"Fuck it," said Joey Spencer, summing up the feeling of most of them. He dropped his camera from his shoulder, the tape with the road accident now followed by footage of the dirt at his feet. He got into his truck and noticed his hated anchor, Tyler Mercer running towards him in the rear-view mirror. He briefly considered driving off without her but decided that would only make assholes out of them both and reached over to pop open the passenger door.

"Quickly," he shouted, though if he'd been asked to explain why they needed to get out of there so fast words would have failed him. It was an instinctual thing, something terrible was about to happen, he knew it for a fact, and if this van could get him out of here before it did then he would be a happy man. She climbed in, looked at him, and without saying a word, he gunned the engine and pulled out onto the highway, narrowly missing Miles and Carruthers as he did so.

Miles had got to his feet first and dragged Carruthers out of the way as the van swerved past them. "What's it doing?" he asked. "What the hell's in there that it wants?"

"I've no idea," Carruthers admitted. "But any chance we have of stopping it is slowly slipping away."

"Stopping it?" Miles almost laughed. "It's just lived through a car crash that would have pulverised a rhino, what the hell are we supposed to do to stop it?"

"No idea about that either," Carruthers admitted, "but it's hurt, we can see that, and if it can be hurt it can be killed."

"Really? Not sure I follow the logic of that if I'm honest."

Carruthers shrugged. "Me neither but it makes me feel a bit better so I intend to stick with it."

They walked back towards the building site, the reporters running either side of them, getting into their vans and cars. There was a look on their faces, a vacant switch towards self-preservation. None of them were talking, they just wanted to be far away. Miles didn't blame them, walking towards the site was like pushing against something strong but invisible. His subconscious begging him to pay attention, to do as he was told and run, as fast and as far away as he could manage.

"Can you feel that?" he asked Carruthers. "It's hard to walk. Like my body wants to do anything but this…"

Carruthers nodded, his face twitching and teeth clenched.

Ahead of them, Dutch had stopped moving, the creature on his back reaching towards the sky with one blackened hand. Above their heads the air began to distort, light refracting and space folding as the creature pushed out, forcing its cremated fingers into a gap in reality that only it could see. The sky split, a solid bisection of the world above them, as if a bread knife had been passed through the air and parted it. Beyond was darkness, a void between their reality and whatever other existence the prisoner was aiming for. Then they began to see shapes in that void, nothing they could fix on, just a sense of movement. Something moving just out of the corner of their eyes.

The prisoner seemed delighted to see those moving shapes, to him – *it* – they were reassuringly familiar.

There was noise, a squealing feedback, a needle forced against its groove. A wet scream of rubber against rubber. That alone was almost more than they could stand, their hands pressed to their ears in a pointless attempt to drown it out.

Things moved around them, nothing they could see. It was like swimming at night and feeling the brush of dark shapes against you.

This is pointless, Miles thought, this is not something we can fight, this is beyond *anything* we're designed to deal with.

Then there was a flood of light, as dark as egg yolk, pumping up from the prisoner and into the darkness above. This was it, this was going home.

Ashe walked through the rain, firing his gun at the window of the bar and trying not to remember Tom's dead face as he saw the man's younger self scrabble for safety beneath the booth table.

He stared at Elise instead, saw her as Tom had. As a beautiful and special woman.

He had barely been able to talk to her at the strip joint where she worked. Just handed her the box and left.

"Nearly there," the pigeon had said as Ashe walked down the street to stand across the way from Terry's bar and wait.

"I never stood a chance at changing all this did I?" Ashe asked.

"No," the pigeon replied, hovering under an awning to keep dry. "There was only ever one way to deal with him, like it or not."

Beyond the cracked glass Tom and Elise vanished and Ashe sagged. Almost done.

He went inside to retrieve the box. When he returned to the sidewalk, Sophie was waiting for him.

The street shook. "It's happening now," she said, "feel it?"

He nodded. She took his hand. "It's for the best."

Her face twitched and for a moment she flickered like a badly tuned TV station.

"What is it?" asked Ashe.

"Renegade progressing faster than anticipated," she replied, her voice that of the Grumpy Controller rather than her own. "Need diversion."

A door appeared in the centre of the sidewalk, Sophie turned to him. "Go home, there's nothing left for you to do. I miss you."

She vanished and, after a moment, Ashe stepped through the door.

19

"This'll do," said the Grumpy Controller, reappearing on the library screens. "We can't wait any more. Set her down."

Alan laid Sophie gently on the wood of the bookcase and took a step back.

"What are they going to do to her?" asked Hawkins, behind him.

"It's more a case of what she's going to do to them," Alan replied, "this is all Sophie. They're not forcing her."

"Alright then," said Penelope, "what's *she* going to do?"

"Restore the House," Alan said, "bigger and more powerful than it was before."

"And that's a good idea?" asked Ryan.

"It's the only option we have left," Alan replied, "and whatever Ashe may have hoped otherwise I think it was always going to happen."

"Build not break!" Sophie shouted, arching her back against the bookcase.

"House now contemporaneous," announced the Grumpy Controller.

"Oh yeah," said Barnabas, "one of those *contempranyusess* is it?"

"The House exists outside time," explained Alan, "but for this to work that has to change. Think of two ships pulling alongside one another. Lashing themselves together so that one can steer the other."

"The House is steering?" asked Maggie. "I can't say that makes me feel comfortable."

"You should see the driver of the other boat," Alan replied.

Sophie thrashed against the bookcase again. "Too quick, too quick!" she shouted.

"Renegade progressing faster than anticipated,"

said the Grumpy Controller and the image on the screens changed from his face to the view of that field in Florida.

"Is that Miles?" Penelope asked, craning her neck to peer at the screen. "I think it is."

They could see both Miles and Carruthers, little more than silhouettes against the building orange light.

20.

The orange light, so thick it positively dripped from the prisoner's hands, began to glow even brighter. Miles and Carruthers huddled together facing away from the prisoner. The earth around them rippled, the solidity of everything so close to the intrusion slipping as this reality, this *world*, began to lose cohesion. Looking towards the highway, Miles saw that it was whipping around, winking out of existence then returning but with the translucent look of a mirage rather than a solid thing of concrete. The buildings followed suit, stretching and fattening alternately, a world slipping in and out of focus.

"Miles?" Carruthers' voice was faint, as barely there as everything else. "I think we've bitten off a little more than we can chew."

"You think?" Miles replied, surprised to feel his face twisting into a smile.

From the mess of shifting reality around them, a figure appeared, coalescing out of the liquid of dirt and air and walking towards them. It was Sophie.

"I need your help," she said, coming to stand directly in front of them.

"Oh well," said Miles, "you know us, always pleased to be of service."

"I need you to slow it down," she said, "we can stop it if you buy us just a little time."

"And how are we supposed to do that?" Carruthers asked. "Forgive me but we seem somewhat at a disadvantage."

"I am doing my best to create a small bubble of protection around you," she replied. "You were inside me for long enough that I can do that, keep you one step outside this world."

"Inside you?" asked Miles. "I'm sure I don't remember anything like that…"

"It's the House," Carruthers interrupted, "not Sophie, am I right?"

"There's no difference anymore," she replied, "we're all the House, build not break."

"What can we do?" Miles asked.

"Just distract it," she replied, "any way you can, a few seconds will be all I need."

"And the chances of us surviving that?" asked Carruthers.

"None, sorry. But if you don't none of us will survive anyway."

"When you put it like that…" Carruthers didn't finish. He had nothing more to say.

"If we can distract it," Miles asked, "will everyone else…?"

"I can save them," she replied, "probably. If there's anything you want to say, they're watching…"

"Watching?"

"In the House. They can see you."

Miles thought about that for a moment. "I don't want them to," he replied. "Stop them from seeing, then we'll try."

In the library the screens went blank.

"No!" Penelope shouted. "Bring them back, I can't…"

Alan took hold of her, tentatively at first then stronger once it became clear she wouldn't fight him. "He doesn't want you to see this," he said, "I'm sorry…"

Ryan had stooped down next to Sophie, taking her hand and doing his best to whisper constructive thoughts. It wasn't helping her much but at least it made him feel useful.

"I can hear the changes," Jonah whispered, "corridors unfolding, rooms cracking open… can you hear any of this?"

"No," Barnabas admitted, "though you can feel it, a vibration in the ground."

Maggie held onto her husband's hand. "Whatever happens," she whispered to him, "you did the right thing, always."

He smiled. "Nobody ever does the right thing all the time," he replied, "but bless you for trying to convince me otherwise."

The shaking in the bookcase increased, the books jumping up and down on the shelves as if eager to be read. Sophie felt every one of them. Each of the books opened to her, showing their histories, their essence. All of that power, all of that imagination, fuelled the restoration. The House had always been the byproduct of these dreamers, a physical object brought into being by the thoughts of mankind – by their greatest fears and most surreal night-terrors. Now every ounce of that imagination was wrung dry, mortar for the new House, the perfect House, the prison to hold them all.

"You know how you abhor violence?" Miles asked Carruthers.

"Life is filled with exceptions."

"Glad you agree."

They stood side by side, eyes squinting at the unfolding light ahead of them.

"Good to have met you," said Miles.

"You too, Miles," Carruthers agreed, "you were a good friend, an honour to know."

Miles smiled. "You wouldn't have said that if you'd known me before I came here."

"I would always have said that," Carruthers replied. "You are who you are, and I count myself lucky to have spent time with you."

Miles couldn't reply to that, just held out his hand to the old explorer and led the pair of them forward.

The light blossomed as they drew closer, great gobbets of it tumbling to the earth where it fizzed and remade what it found. At the heart of it, the prisoner felt his essence touch that far distant realm that it knew as home. "Yes," it said to itself, "I've learned my lesson. Forgive me?"

Miles and Carruthers grabbed at the figure in front of them, an amalgamation of Dutch Wallace and the creature that rode his back. Their hands burned as they touched him but they refused to let go, desperate to tug it away from the rift, to hold its attention for just one moment.

The prisoner felt them, ants climbing up their hill to demand an audience. It chuckled. "Just burn," it said, "I have no time for the likes of you anymore."

The body that had once answered to Dutch Wallace crumpled forward. The prisoner may be strong but

Dutch was not and Miles and Carruthers toppled him, pushing him down into the undulating earth even as the sky erupted around them. It was enough, the prisoner torn from the rift momentarily, his concentration broken.

"When will you learn?" it shouted. "You're nothing, ants under the bottle… a distraction to a god, nothing more."

"Yeah," said Miles, "well, God has the breath of a barbecued pig's fart."

They weren't the most noble of last words, he thought, but in keeping with the rest of his life.

As the light consumed them, Carruthers hand still firm in his as they burned, the last thing he saw was the sky changing, the distorted blue and the black of the void cut off to be replaced by distant ceiling panels. What do you know, he thought, I think we've saved the world…

The sky solidified, the House expanding in that free moment when the prisoner had been torn from the rift. It exploded outwards, its ceiling appearing in every skyline worldwide, cutting out stars and the warmth of the sun. It swallowed our reality whole, no longer an adjunct to it, loitering just outside our perception, but a container, four walls enclosing everything.

As the ceiling cut off the rift above that patch of land in Florida the force of the prisoner's intrusion flowed backwards, like a river instantly dammed. The light flooded outwards, searing into the earth, evaporating the remains of Roger Carruthers, Miles Caulfield and Lieutenant Dutch Wallace. It kept rolling, past the highway and further still…

23.

Captain Warren Shepard stood in the parking lot of the Ponderosa Steakhouse and waited for the sickness in his belly to quieten down. He had a feeling it would be some days before it truly went away. Just another memory to be revisited at night, he thought, getting to be quite a few in there now, much more of this and I'll never sleep again.

Glancing up he was surprised to see the sun setting already, a fat ball of orange pouring itself over the land towards him.

Well now, he thought – his last thought before the heatwave hit him – at least this place can still be beautiful when it tries.

24.

"It's done," Sophie said and then lay still.

"What's done?" asked Penelope. "What did she do?"

A door appeared in front of them, hovering a couple of inches above the bookcase. "Go now," said Sophie.

"I'll show you," said Alan, holding out his hand and leading them all through the door and into the world on the other side.

"We're outside!" Jonah sighed as he stepped through and felt the sunshine on his face.

"Not quite," said Hawkins, looking up at the distant ceiling that hung, pale in the sky above, "just another big room."

"This is all there is now," said Alan. "The whole world inside the House. The two of them joined together."

Penelope stared at the sky. "But that's awful! That's the worst thing that could have happened."

"No," Alan replied, "it wasn't. This was our only way of killing the prisoner and keeping our world intact."

"Intact?" asked Maggie. "As just another room in the House? I'm not sure that's not worse…"

"Of course it's not," said Alan. "At least this way there's life and hope, we'll make the best of it. Just like we always do. Besides, the House isn't quite as bad as it once was."

He looked over his shoulder, not altogether surprised to see the door had vanished. Sophie was gone, his own little goddess running the world the way she saw fit. If nothing else it would be tidy.

"Come on," he said, "let's make ourselves at home."

EPILOGUE

The door had appeared during the night. Alan knew this as he had patrolled that edge of their land the evening before, Penelope having sworn she had seen the light move funny. "I'm telling you it shimmered," she insisted. "The trees went out of focus, just for a second, and the air had that look of a heat haze."

"I'll take a look," he had promised. "Don't worry about it."

And he had and it had been fine. No sign of anything, no disturbance and no intrusion – and certainly no wraith, that's what she had been afraid of he knew, ever since one had appeared on the Colson farm a few miles north and flattened their cattle she had been terrified of the same happening to them. He had assured her that he believed her. And that had been true, he always did, it was only her that seemed convinced that everyone dismissed her because she was a woman

"Something definitely moved out there," she had insisted over dinner. "I know what I saw."

Georgie had scoffed at that, but then their daughter – and Alan thought of her as their daughter, biological father or not – scoffed at most things. It was all a joke to Georgie. That's Miles Caulfield's genes, Alan often thought but did not say. He didn't mention Miles unless Penelope did, even after all these years it felt too sensitive to discuss. He often wondered if Penelope saw him as a shallow replacement. Another thing he thought but never said. They were all living in the shadow of dead men these days.

"Whatever it was," he had said, "it's gone now. I'll check it again in the morning."

That night they had lain in bed, even quieter than normal. He not able to express himself, she not able to forgive him for what she saw as his part in this new world of theirs. Twenty-odd years and she still hadn't forgiven him. As if he had done anything that needed forgiving, he had been a spectator as much as any of them...

Perhaps it was just that he had lived and Miles had not. Perhaps it would always be that simple.

The next morning he headed out towards where she had seen something move and came across the door. In itself it wasn't unusual, there were doors everywhere these days, leading from one part of the world to another or into rooms of the House (it's all the same, he reminded himself, we're all just rooms these days). But it hadn't been here before and that was a concern. Where did it lead?

He gripped the frame and stuck his head through, it was dark, the little light that shone from his world illuminated a bookshelf, stretching on into the darkness. The library, he thought, it's time...

He returned to the house, grabbed his old revolver, loaded it and popped the spare shells in his coat pocket.

"Where are you going?" Penelope asked him as he stepped into the kitchen to grab some food before he started his journey. Then, as she recognised the long coat and the hat in his hand she sighed and held onto the worktop for support. "Don't leave," she said, "we know there's no point."

"This time it may be different," he said, "I might change everything."

"You won't," she said, "we know you won't."

"But I have to try…"

She stormed out of the room, unwilling to watch someone else she had grown close to vanish.

Alan – Ashe, he thought, need to think of myself as Ashe now – ate some leftovers from the fridge and made to leave. He came across Georgie on the front porch, stripping her rifle, that absurd purple woollen hat on her head.

"I'll never understand why you wear that thing," he said, "it makes your head look like a lampshade."

"Keeps it warm too," she replied. "Anyway, says you looking all Clint Eastwood." She had worked her way through his DVD collection time and again, loved those old Spaghetti Westerns almost as much as he did. She is my daughter, he thought, some of her at least.

"I have a town to clear up," he said in a passable Eastwood impression. "Don't wait up."

"Yeah right," she chuckled, "more like potatoes to harvest, mum'll kill you if you don't get that done soon you know?"

"Yeah, I know."

He wanted to say goodbye to her but didn't want her to know that was what he was doing. How stupid was that? He might never see her again and here he was considering just walking away.

"What are you doing today" he asked, prevaricating.

"Oh, you know, the usual, tidying up after you!" she smiled. "There's always work isn't there?"

"Yeah." Maybe it'll be easier one day, he thought, realising he wasn't going to say goodbye after all.

He dropped his hat on his head and walked off towards the door. Maybe it'll be easier one day... yes, maybe it will.

Maybe this time around it would all be different.

ABOUT THE AUTHOR

Guy Adams trained and worked as an actor for twelve years before becoming a full-time writer. If nothing else this proves he has no concept of a sensible career. He mugged someone on Emmerdale (a long-running British soap opera, consisting largely of mud), performed a dance routine as Hitler and spent eighteen months touring his own comedy material around clubs and theatres.

He is the author of the best-selling *Rules of Modern Policing: 1973 Edition*, a spoof police manual "written by" DCI Gene Hunt of *Life On Mars*. Guy has also written a two-volume series companion to the show; a Torchwood novel, *The House That Jack Built*; and *The Case Notes of Sherlock Holmes*, a fictional facsimile of a scrapbook kept by Doctor John Watson, published in 2009 to celebrate the 150th anniversary of the writer's birth.

www.guy-adams.com

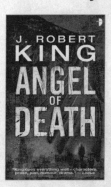

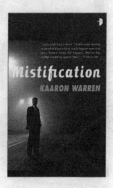

There is a box. Inside that box is a door...
and beyond that door is a whole world.

THE
WORLD
HOUSE

"Strange and wonderful." — *Garry Kilworth*

GUY ADAMS

"I knew we were in trouble as soon as the
ostrich appeared. A grand adventure..."

CHRISTOPHER FOWLER